CRIMSON FROST

Other Mythos Academy titles by Jennifer Estep

First Frost

Touch of Frost

Kiss of Frost

Dark Frost

CRIMSON FROST

A Mythos Academy Novel

Jennifer Estep

KENSINGTON PUBLISHING CORP.

www.kensingtonbooks.com

KTEEN BOOKS are published by

Kensington Publishing Corp.
119 West 40th Street
New York, NY 10018

ISBN-13: 978-0-7582-8146-3
ISBN-10: 0-7582-8146-3

First Kensington Trade Paperback Printing: January 2013

10 9 8 7 6 5 4 3 2 1

Printed in the United States of America

As always, to my mom, my grandma, and Andre,
for all their love, help, support, and patience
with my books and everything else in life

Acknowledgments

Any author will tell you that her book would not be possible without the hard work of many, many people. Here are some of the folks who helped bring Gwen Frost and the world of Mythos Academy to life:

Thanks to my agent, Annelise Robey, for all her helpful advice.

Thanks to my editor, Alicia Condon, for her sharp editorial eye and thoughtful suggestions. They always make the book so much better.

Thanks to everyone at Kensington who worked on the book, and thanks to Alexandra Nicolajsen and Vida Engstrand for all their promotional efforts.

And, finally, thanks to all the readers out there. Entertaining you is why I write books, and it's always an honor and a privilege. I hope you have as much fun reading about Gwen's adventures as I do writing them.

Happy reading!

Library of Antiquities

1 Balcony of Statues
2 Check Out Counter
3 Artifact Case
4 Raven's Coffee Cart
5 Entrance
6 Book Stacks
7 Study Area
8 Offices
9 Staircase

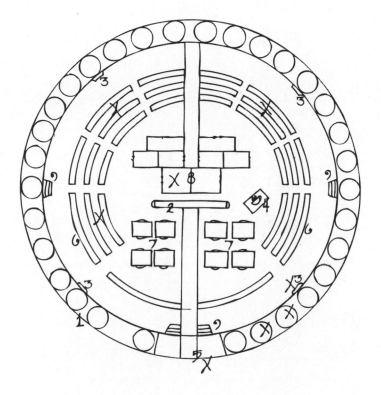

Chapter 1

"I have a confession to make."

Logan Quinn looked at me. "Really, Gypsy girl? What's that?"

I shifted on my feet. "I don't actually like coffee."

The Spartan stared at me a moment before his lips curved up into a teasing grin. "You probably should have mentioned that before now."

Yeah, I probably should have, since we were in a coffee shop. A large counter; lots of comfy leather chairs; wrought-iron tables; paintings of gods and goddesses on the walls; a display case full of blueberry scones, raspberry tarts, and decadent chocolate cheesecakes. Kaldi Coffee looked like your typical java joint, except that everything was first class and super-pricey all the way, from the fancy espresso machines that hissed and burped to the rich, dark aroma of the ridiculously expensive coffee that flavored the air.

Then again, such luxury was the norm in the upscale stores in Cypress Mountain, North Carolina. The Mythos

Academy kids accepted nothing less than the best, and Kaldi's was one of the most popular places to Hang Out and Be Seen when the students had free time, like we did today. Afternoon classes and activities had been cancelled so all the kids could attend some big assembly at the academy's amphitheater later on. I wasn't sure what the assembly was going to be about. Probably some more hearty reassurances from the professors and staff that all us warrior whiz kids were as safe as we could be at the academy, now that Loki was free.

For a moment, a face flashed before my eyes—the most hideous face I'd ever seen. One side so perfect, with its golden hair, piercing blue eye, and smooth features. The other side so completely ruined, with its limp strings of black hair, red eye, and melted skin.

Loki—the evil god that I'd helped set free against my will.

A shudder rippled through my body. Thanks to my psychometry magic, I never forgot anything I saw, but the image of Loki's double-face was burned into my memory. No matter what I was doing or whom I was with, no matter how hard I tried to forget what had happened, I saw the Norse trickster god's image everywhere I went. Gleaming in the windows of my classrooms, shining in the glossy surface of my dorm room desk, shimmering in the mirror, like a devil perched on my shoulder.

I shuddered again. It had taken all the strength I had not to scream when I'd brushed my hair this morning and had suddenly seen Loki grinning at me in my bathroom mirror, the perfect side of his face lifted up into a smile, and the ruined side turned down into a horrible, twisted sneer—

"Gypsy girl?" Logan asked in a soft voice. "Are you still here with me?"

I pushed all thoughts of Loki away and made myself smile at the Spartan even though I wanted nothing more than to wrap my arms around myself and huddle into a ball in the corner.

"I know, I know," I grumbled. "I should have told you that I don't actually drink coffee. I just didn't want anything to ruin our first date, and when you suggested coffee..."

"You went along with it," Logan finished.

I shrugged.

Maybe it was thinking of Loki and his split face, but as I looked at Logan, I was once again reminded of how different we were. Simply put, Logan Quinn was gorgeous, with his thick, ink-black hair and intense ice-blue eyes. His designer jeans, blue sweater, and expensive leather jacket only highlighted how strong and muscled his body was.

Next to him, I pretty much faded into the background. The most interesting thing about my wavy brown hair was how frizzy it was today. You might look twice at my eyes, which were an unusual shade of violet, but the only thing special about me was the necklace I wore. Six silver strands curved around my throat before their diamond-tipped points formed a snowflake in the middle of the design. A Christmas gift from Logan, one that I almost always wore, even though it didn't exactly go with my plain gray sweater, purple plaid jacket, and not-so-designer jeans and sneakers.

And it wasn't just our looks and clothes that were different. Logan was a fierce Spartan warrior who was the best fighter at the academy. I was still trying to figure out how to wield a sword, even though I was Nike's Champion, the girl picked by the Greek goddess of victory to help her fight Loki and his Reapers of Chaos here in the mortal realm. Something I had failed at pretty miserably so far, since Loki was now free and bent on plunging the world into a second Chaos War.

"You know what, Gypsy girl?" Logan said, once again interrupting my troubled thoughts. "Nothing could ruin this date. Ask me why."

"Why?"

He slung his arm around my shoulder and grinned. "Because I'm on it with you."

And suddenly, everything was okay, and I could breathe again.

That's why I was head over heels for the Spartan. Logan could be everything from fun and flirty to stubborn and infuriating, but then he went and said things like *that*. Was it any wonder I had such a massive crush on him?

Okay, okay, so maybe it had started out as a crush a few months ago, but given everything we'd been through, my feelings for him had quickly deepened into something more: love. At least, that's what I thought it was; that's what it felt like to me—this warm, soft, fizzy feeling that filled my heart whenever the Spartan grinned at me, whenever he teased me or tried to make me forget about my worries.

Like now.

I sighed and put my head on his shoulder. Logan hugged me to his chest. He didn't say anything, but he didn't need to. Just being close to him was enough for me, after all these months we'd spent dancing around each other.

"You guys ready to order?" the barista asked.

We stepped up to the counter. The Spartan ordered a triple espresso since he loved the caffeine rush, while I got a hot, honey-pomegranate tea. Logan started to pull his wallet out of his jeans, but I beat him to it and handed the barista a twenty-dollar bill.

"My treat," I said. "After all, I'm the one who suggested coffee in the first place way back when."

Logan nodded. "That you did. All right, Gypsy girl. Your treat. This time. The next round's on me."

We got our drinks and went over to a table in the corner of the shop next to a stone fireplace. Since the students had been given the afternoon off, we weren't the only Mythos kids who'd decided to come to Kaldi's and get something to eat and drink before the assembly started in another half hour or so. I spotted several students I knew, including Kenzie Tanaka, Logan's Spartan friend, who was on his own date with Talia Pizarro, a pretty Amazon in my gym class. I waved at them, and Kenzie winked at me before turning his attention back to Talia.

"What is *he* doing here with *her*?" A sneering voice drifted over to me.

I looked to my right to see Helena Paxton staring at me. Helena was a stunning Amazon with caramel-colored hair and eyes. Since Jasmine Ashton's death back in the fall, Helena had established herself as the new mean-girl queen of the second-year students at Mythos. She sat at a nearby table with two of her Amazon friends, all of them dressed in pricey jeans, stiletto boots, and tight, fitted sweaters; they had perfect hair, jewelry, purses, and makeup to match.

"I thought Logan's standards were a little higher than that. Guess I was wrong. Then again, guys will do anything—and anyone—to get some."

Helena's voice was low, but the cruel smile on her face told me that she meant for me to hear every word. I'd never done anything to Helena, except stand up for another girl she'd been teasing, but that had been enough to put me on the Amazon's hit list. Now, every time she saw me, Helena went out of her way to be snotty to me. Try as I might, I could never seem to get the best of the Amazon, not even dream up a quick comeback to get her to shut up.

Helena whispered something to her friends, and they all started snickering. My hand tightened around my mug of tea. Not for the first time, I wished that I had an Amazon's quickness so I could bean Helena in the head with it. But she would only catch the mug and throw it back at me before I could blink.

"Ignore them," Logan said. "They're just jealous that you're here with me."

I rolled my eyes. "Yeah. You and your ego."

His grin widened, and I couldn't help but laugh. No matter how bad things got, the Spartan could always make me laugh, if only for a moment. Something else that added to that warm, fizzy feeling in my chest.

We sat there in silence, listening to the murmurs from the other kids and the gurgles of the espresso machines. After all the battles we'd survived recently, it was nice to just hang out with Logan without worrying about what was going to happen next or what Reapers might be lurking around, masquerading as students, professors, or even the coffee shop staff.

But after a few minutes, the reality of the situation hit me. I was on a date with Logan freaking Quinn, one of the cutest guys at Mythos—and I had no idea what to say to him.

"So . . ." I said. "What do people talk about on dates?"

Logan looked up from his espresso. "What do you mean?"

I shifted in my seat. "I mean, you have a lot more experience at this than I do."

In fact, Logan had a reputation for being a total man-whore who went from one girl to the next. Me? I'd had exactly one boyfriend for a grand total of three weeks before I'd met Logan. So going on a date was still sort of a new experience for me. Besides, the Spartan had this natural, easy charm that made everyone like him—girls and guys alike. Me? I was about as charming as a wet sock.

"I know what we talk about at the academy. You know, weapons training, where Loki might be hiding, when he's going to come and kill us all, how we're supposed to stop him."

Actually, that last one was more like how *I* was supposed to kill the god. Yeah, me, kill an actual living, breathing, walking, talking *god*. And not just any god, but Loki, who was pretty much evil incarnate.

But that was the seemingly impossible mission that Nike had given me the last time I'd seen her a couple of weeks ago—something that I hadn't shared with Logan or any of my friends. Kill a god. I had no idea how the goddess expected me to do that. I had no idea how *anyone* could do that, especially me, Gwen Frost, that weird Gypsy girl who touched stuff and saw things.

Logan kept staring at me, and I found myself opening my mouth once more.

"I guess we could talk about how I'm actually getting a little better at using weapons, although I doubt that I'll ever be in your league. Or we could talk about Nyx, and how totally cute she is. Or Daphne and her healing magic. Or Carson and how obsessed he is with the winter concert the band is putting together . . ."

Babbling. I was finally out on a real date with Logan, and I was babbling like a wind-up doll someone had cranked into high gear.

Logan reached over and put his hand on top of mine, which was still wrapped around my mug. "Relax, Gypsy girl. Relax. You're doing fine. We don't have to talk about anything, if you don't want to. I'm just happy to be here with you. It's nice to just sit here and relax, with everything that's been going on these past few weeks. You know?"

His fingers felt warm against my own, but more than that, I felt the warmth in Logan's heart—and all his feelings. His strength, his bravery, his determination to fight Reapers and to protect me no matter what. All those images, all those feelings, flashed through my mind, driving away all my doubts about me, Logan, and everything else that was going on right now.

My Gypsy gift let me know, see, and feel the history of any object I touched. Given that, I had to be careful about touching things and, most especially, people. More than once, my hand had brushed against someone's, and I'd realized that what he said didn't match what he felt. That's what had happened with my first boyfriend. He'd kissed me, and I'd realized that he was really thinking about another girl instead.

But there was nothing to be afraid of with Logan. I knew all the Spartan's secrets, and he knew mine. Well, except for the whole *Gwen's-supposed-to-kill-Loki* thing. I still wasn't sure exactly how to bring that up, and I wasn't going to. Not today. There would be time enough to obsess and worry about that later. Right now, I just wanted to enjoy my date with Logan.

"How is it that you always know just what to do and say to make me feel better?" I said.

Logan grinned. "Just another part of that Spartan killer instinct. I can slay the ladies just as well as I can Reapers."

I rolled my eyes and leaned over to punch him in the shoulder—and managed to knock over my tea and his espresso. Liquid cascaded all over the table, most of it spilling off the far side and into Logan's lap. The Spartan jumped up, but he didn't have an Amazon's quickness, so he couldn't avoid getting soaked.

"Sorry!" I said, getting to my own feet. "I'm so sorry!"

I reached for the silver holder on the table, intending to rip some napkins out of it, but instead I ended up knocking it to the ground as well. The napkin holder *clang-cla-cla-clanged* across the floor.

By the time the holder skidded to a stop and the noise faded away, everyone in the shop had turned to stare at us. Embarrassment made my cheeks burn, while Logan looked like he'd had water dumped all over him.

"Sorry," I mumbled again.

"It's okay," Logan said, holding his hands out to his sides to keep from touching his now-sticky clothes. "I'll just go get cleaned up."

He headed off toward the bathroom. I sighed, picked up the holder, put it back on the table, grabbed some napkins out of it, and started mopping up the mess. After a few seconds, most people went back to their conversations—except for Helena and her friends. They were too busy laughing at me to talk.

I put my head down, ignored them, and cleaned up the liquid as fast as I could before wiping my hands off. I threw all the used napkins into a trash can, then sat down and slumped as low as I could in my chair. So far, this date hadn't exactly been a big success—or even just the fun time I'd wanted it to be. Once again, I'd messed up everything without even trying. Sometimes, I thought that was my specialty in life.

I was so busy brooding that I didn't pay any attention when the door to Kaldi's opened, and three men trooped inside. Once again, all conversation stopped, and I felt a collective emotion ripple off everyone in the shop: fear.

"The Protectorate," I heard Helena whisper.

The Protectorate? What was that? I'd never heard of them before, but apparently they knew me because the men walked in my direction, their eyes fixed on my face.

I tensed, then sat up in my seat, wondering who the men were and what they wanted. Could they be Reapers come to attack the students? I'd wanted to be alone with Logan, so I'd left Vic, my talking sword, in my dorm room. Stupid of me not to bring the weapon, even though we'd only been getting coffee. I should have known by now that nothing was simple at Mythos—not even my first date with Logan.

My eyes scanned the shop, looking for something I could use as a weapon, but the only things within arm's reach were the two mugs and the napkin holder on my table. I wrapped my hand around the napkin holder and put it in my lap under the table and out of sight of the men.

This wouldn't be the first time Reapers had attacked me. If these men decided to do the same, well, I'd think of something. Besides, one good scream, and Logan would come running out of the bathroom to help me.

One of the men stepped up and stared down at me. He was handsome enough, with blond hair and pale blue eyes, but his mouth was fixed in a firm frown, as if he constantly found fault with everyone around him. He looked at me, and I stared at him a moment before my gaze moved to the two men flanking him. One of the men was tall and slender, while the other was short, with a body that looked fat but was really all hard muscle.

The strangest thing was that the men all had on dark gray robes over their winter clothes. The robes reminded me of the black ones the Reapers always wore, although the men weren't sporting hideous, rubber Loki masks like Reapers did. Instead, a symbol was stitched into their robes in white thread on their left collars close to their throats—a hand holding a balanced set of scales.

I'd seen that symbol before. It was carved into the ceiling of the prison in the bottom of the math-science building on campus, and it had also been in the middle of the Garm gate that Vivian Holler had used to free Loki. My unease kicked up another notch. Nothing good was ever associated with that image, as far as I was concerned.

"So you're her," the first man said. "Nike's newest Champion. Not quite what I expected."

His voice was soft, smooth, and cultured, but there was obvious power in his words, as if he was used to being obeyed no matter what.

"Who are you?" I snapped, my fingers tightening around the flimsy napkin holder. "What do you want?"

"And you don't even have the good sense to know when you're in trouble," the man murmured, as though I hadn't said a word.

I snorted. Oh, I knew I was in trouble. I was almost *always* in trouble these days. The only question was how bad it would be this time—and if I could somehow manage to get out of it alive once again.

The man kept staring at me with his cold, judgmental eyes, and I lifted my chin in defiance. Whatever happened, whatever these men wanted, whatever they tried to do to me, I wasn't going to show him how confused and scared I was. Reapers thrived on that sort of thing. I didn't think these men were Reapers, since no one in the shop was screaming or trying to run away from them, but they weren't here for anything good. I could feel the hostility emanating from them in waves, especially from the leader.

The man tilted his head to the side. "I wonder what he sees in you." After a moment, he shrugged. "No matter. It won't change anything."

"Change what?" I asked. "Who are you? What are you doing here? What do you want with me? And why are you wearing those ridiculous robes?"

Anger made the leader's cheeks take on a faint, reddish tint, but the short, muscular man choked back a laugh. The leader turned to glare at him, and the other man pressed his lips together, although I could see his chest shaking, as though he was trying to swallow the rest of his amusement. The third man seemed bored, as if this was an errand he was eager to get over with.

Okay, this was getting weirder by the second. I looked past the men, wondering what was taking Logan so long, when the leader stepped even closer to me, his eyes glittering with anger.

"Gwendolyn Cassandra Frost," he said in a loud, booming voice. "You're under arrest."

Chapter 2

My mouth dropped open. "Me? Under arrest? For what?"

"Crimes against the Pantheon," the man said in a cold, cryptic tone.

"Crimes? What crimes? What are you talking about?"

He leaned down so that his face was level with mine. "Freeing Loki, for starters, you silly girl. Did you really think that you were just going to get away with it? That there wouldn't be any consequences?"

My mouth dropped open a little more. "But I didn't free him—"

"Get her up," the leader barked, cutting off my protests. "We've wasted enough time here already."

The other two men stepped around him and headed toward me. I leaped up out of my chair and scrambled back so that I was standing against the fireplace, just to the left of where the flames crackled in the grate. The stones felt warm against my back through my clothes. Normally, the sensation would have been a pleasant one, but right now it told me that I had nowhere to go—and no hope of escape.

I looked past the men at the other Mythos students, my eyes going from one face to another, hoping that at least one of them would come to my rescue—or just stand up and ask what was going on. But the other kids seemed just as stunned as I felt, and even Kenzie and Talia, whom I counted among my friends, remained frozen in their seats. Whoever the men were, the students seemed to know all about them—and they didn't dare interfere with them and whatever they were going to do to me.

Everyone except Helena, that is. The Amazon pulled her cell phone out of her purse, and I thought she might actually call for help. But instead, she held her phone up and snapped a few photos of me and the men. Then she bent down over the small screen, sending the pictures as fast as her fingers could text. The smirk on her pretty face told me that she was obviously enjoying this, whatever exactly *this* was.

Desperate, I raised the napkin holder, wondering if I could somehow distract the men with it long enough to shove my way past them and run out of the shop. Somehow, I didn't think that would work, especially since I kept getting glimpses of the swords strapped to their waists beneath the billowing folds of their robes.

"What are you going to do with that?" the short man asked, his words colored by a Russian accent. "It's not very practical, as far as weapons go. You should have brought your sword with you. I hear it's a fine weapon."

Vic? He knew about Vic? How?

"Come on, Sergei," the leader said in an impatient tone. "Let's get on with it."

"In a moment, Linus," Sergei, the short man, replied. "There's no use frightening and confusing the girl any more than you already have. We're supposed to be civilized about these things, remember?"

Sergei winked at me, his hazel eyes sly and almost merry in his tan face.

"Well, I agree with Linus," the third, thin man said. "We have a schedule to keep."

"Bah," Sergei said, waving his hand. "We should be able to make our own schedules, don't you think, Inari?"

Inari shrugged his slender shoulders. "We go where we're told, just like we always do."

"Sergei," Linus said, a clear warning in his voice.

He sighed. "Very well."

Sergei stepped forward and held out his hand, reaching for me. I tightened my grip on the napkin holder and edged away from him that much more, backing myself into the corner. I wasn't going anywhere with these men without a fight—

"Dad? What are you doing here?" a familiar voice called out.

Logan let the bathroom door close behind him and moved over to stand next to Linus, the leader.

"Sergei? Inari?" Logan asked, echoing the men's names. "What's going on?"

The Spartan looked surprised to see the three men, but unlike the other people in the shop, he didn't seem frightened by them. Then again, Logan wasn't scared of anything. Not Nemean prowlers, not murderous Reapers, not even my magic and the fact that I'd killed another guy with it. Nothing ever rattled the Spartan, not even the sudden appearance of three mystery men wearing creepy robes.

Logan obviously knew the men, knew exactly who they were, but that didn't ease my mind. Not at all. If anything, it only added to my tension, especially since he'd called one of them *Dad*.

And the men knew Logan too, enough to greet him. Sergei gave him a hearty slap on the back, while Inari respectfully nodded his head. Linus nodded his head as well, although his posture was still stiff, and his face remained cold. If anything, I could feel his dislike for me increase, as he looked back and forth between me and the Spartan.

"Logan?" I asked. "Who are these men?"

"Sergei Sokolov, Inari Sato, and my dad, Linus Quinn."

A sinking feeling filled my stomach. Why, oh why, couldn't Sergei have been Logan's dad instead? He at least seemed somewhat friendly. Linus, not so much. Not at all, in fact.

"And what do they want with me?" I asked. "Why are they here to arrest me?"

Logan frowned. "They're members of the Protectorate, which is basically the police force for the mythological world. But why would they want to arrest you? There must be some mistake."

"There's no mistake," Linus said. "Unless there's

some other girl I don't know about who helped Loki escape."

Shocked gasps rippled through the coffee shop, and everyone looked at me. After a few seconds, the surprised stares shifted to horrified looks that quickly melted into harsh, accusing, angry glares. Now, all the kids had pulled out their phones and were taking photos of me and texting them as fast as they could. The news would be all over the academy in minutes.

Sergei stepped to one side and gestured with his hand. I hadn't noticed him before, but a guy about my own age had followed the three men into the shop. He looked like a younger, taller, leaner version of Sergei, with the same hazel eyes, dark brown hair, and tan skin.

"Alexei, my boy, watch her," Sergei said.

Alexei moved over to stand next to me. He wasn't wearing a robe like the men were, but I could tell by the easy, confident way he moved that he was a fighter, a warrior whiz kid just like I was. Maybe a Roman, maybe a Viking, maybe something else. I had no way of knowing, and this wasn't exactly the right time to ask.

"Alexei Sokolov?" Logan asked, more confusion creeping into his voice.

Alexei tipped his head at the Spartan, but he never took his eyes off me. "Hello, Logan." He had the same Russian accent his dad did.

Logan looked at Alexei, then Sergei and Inari in their gray robes. Finally, he whirled around to Linus.

"What's going on, Dad? Why are you here? And why are you arresting Gwen?"

Linus put his arm around his son's shoulders. "Because it's my job as the head of the Protectorate. You know that."

Logan shook his head. "It's your job to protect the members of the Pantheon, to hunt down Reapers and put them in prison where they belong, not show up out of the blue and harass my friend for no reason."

Linus's face tightened until it looked as hard as the stone fireplace behind me. "This—this *girl* is no friend of yours." He spat out the words. "She's the reason that Loki is free, and she's going to stand trial and be punished for it—all of it."

Trial? Punished? Me? Every word he said made my fear and dread grow that much more. Despite the heat of the fire, I felt cold and numb. Oh yeah, I was in serious trouble, only this time it wasn't from Reapers who wanted to kill me—it was from the Protectorate, a group I'd never even heard of until five minutes ago.

"Get the handcuffs on her, and let's go," Linus said. "We'll continue this discussion later, Logan, and you can tell me exactly what you were doing here with this . . . girl."

Inari pushed back his robe, reached into his pants pocket, and came up with a pair of silver handcuffs. He held them out, but I kept my body plastered against the fireplace wall, wishing I could press myself through the stone and out the other side. I didn't always have to touch something to get a vibe off it, especially if an object had a lot of strong feelings and memories attached to it. Inari's handcuffs radiated with fear, rage, and desperation—all twisted and gnarled together like invisible strands of barbed wire stabbing into me.

I didn't want those handcuffs anywhere near me, much less touching my skin and forcing me to see, feel, and experience everything that all the people who'd worn the cuffs had. None of the memories, none of the feelings, would be good. Not with all those ugly emotions already emanating from the metal. I shivered and dropped my gaze. It made me sick to my stomach just to look at them.

"No," Logan said, noticing my reaction. He knew what would happen if they put the handcuffs on me. "No handcuffs. Gwen doesn't deserve them. She doesn't deserve any of this. You're making a huge mistake."

"There's no mistake," Linus said, his voice hardening. "Except that it seems you have the same foolish fondness for Frost women that your uncle did."

Anger stained Logan's cheeks. He'd told me once that his father didn't get along with his uncle, Nickamedes, the head librarian at the academy, but it looked like there was more bad blood between them than Logan had let on—and that it somehow involved my mom, Grace Frost.

"No handcuffs, Dad," Logan repeated.

His body tensed, his hands clenched into fists, and he eyed Inari like he was thinking about tackling the other man and yanking the cuffs away from him.

"It's okay, Logan," I said, not wanting him to get into trouble.

"No, it's not okay. Nothing about this is okay."

Linus opened his mouth, probably to order Inari to slap the handcuffs on me anyway, but the anger still burning in Logan's face made him reconsider. He stared at his son, then back at me.

"Fine," he snapped. "No handcuffs. I assume you won't be so stupid as to try to escape."

I shook my head. No, I wasn't that stupid. I knew there was no way I could get away from them. Maybe if I'd had a Valkyrie's strength or an Amazon's quickness, I might have had a chance, but not with just my psychometry magic.

"Good. Then let's go," Linus said.

And with those words, the three members of the Protectorate made me step away from the fireplace and forced me to march out of the coffee shop.

Linus and Logan walked ahead of me, while I was flanked on the other three sides by Sergei, Inari, and Alexei. Together, the six of us left Kaldi's.

As soon as the door shut behind Inari, I could hear the sharp *screech-screech-screech* of chairs being pushed back, along with the *thump-thump-thump* of footsteps. I looked over my shoulder. Everyone inside the shop had their faces and phones pressed up against the windows, trying to see what was going to happen next. I could have told them it wasn't going to be anything good.

I shivered again, but not entirely from dread this time. It was mid-January, and the air was bitterly cold. Hard pellets of snow gusted on the fierce winter wind, battering against our bodies, and the sky above was dark and gray, as though all the blue had bled out of it, even though it wasn't even four o'clock yet.

"Ah," Sergei said in a fond voice, turning his face to the howling wind. "It reminds me of Russia in the winter."

We set off down the sidewalk. Kaldi Coffee was located on the main street that ran through Cypress Mountain, and more and more people stuck their heads outside to stare at us as we passed. The ritzy suburb and all its high-end shops were here to see to the needs of everyone at Mythos Academy, so all the business owners and workers knew the score when it came to the mythological world. Most of them were former Mythos students themselves, who'd decided to settle down near the academy. The only folks who didn't realize what was going on were the few tourists who'd braved the cold to come shopping. They glanced out the windows at me for a moment before going back to their browsing.

"You're making a big mistake," Logan repeated. "Gwen didn't free Loki—she tried to stop it from happening. We all did."

"All? By that, I assume you mean you and your new group of friends," Linus said. "Something else we need to discuss. I thought you were finally calming down and learning how to be a real fighter, but it seems like you've gotten yourself into even more trouble than usual. Starting with this girl."

I didn't care if he was Logan's dad and apparently some big shot within the Pantheon. The way he kept saying *this girl* like I was the worst of the worst grated on my last nerve.

"I have a name," I snapped. "It's Gwen, Gwen Frost.

Obviously, you know it since you announced it to the whole coffee shop."

Linus looked over his shoulder at me. "Do not test me, girl."

My hands clenched into fists, but there was nothing I could do about his cold words—or the fact that he seemed to hate me on sight. Not exactly how I'd pictured things going if I ever met Logan's dad. Still, I drew in a breath, trying to push past my anger and fear and get to the bottom of things.

"Well, can you at least tell me where we're going?" I asked.

"You'll see," Linus said in a cryptic tone. "It's not far."

We reached the last shop at the end of the street. I'd thought the Protectorate might shove me into a black SUV, since that's how these things always seemed to go in the movies, but instead Linus crossed the street, and the other members of the Protectorate forced me to follow him. So they were taking me back to the academy. Good. At least I had friends there, folks like Professor Metis. She'd know what was going on and figure out how to make the Protectorate realize this was all just a big misunderstanding. That I hadn't freed Loki on purpose, that I'd done everything I could to keep the evil god locked away, even if I'd completely failed at it.

The main, black iron gate to the academy stood open, since the students had been given the afternoon off. No one looked up as we passed the two stone sphinxes perched on the twelve-foot-high walls on either side of the gate—except me.

Like all the statues at the academy, the sphinxes always seemed to be watching me with their open, lidless eyes, like they were just waiting for me to do something stupid so they could come to life, break free of their stone shells, leap down, and rip me to pieces. I wasn't quite as creeped out by the statues as I used to be, but their fierce expressions still made me pause and glance up at them whenever I walked through the gates.

But today, the sphinxes' heads were bowed, and their eyes were fixed on their feet, almost as if they were afraid to look up as the members of the Protectorate marched me past them. Weird. Even for Mythos. If there was one thing I could always count on, it was for the statues to be watching me. Now that they weren't, it almost felt like a pair of friends turning their backs to me in a deliberate snub.

"Keep moving," Inari said.

I dropped my gaze from the sphinxes and stepped forward.

As we walked, Logan kept arguing with his dad, while Sergei and Inari remained silent. Alexei was on my right, and he kept staring at me, curiosity shining in his hazel eyes. Once again, I wondered what kind of warrior he was. I didn't get the same *I-can-kill-you-with-a-stick-of-gum* vibe off him that I did from Logan, but I could tell that he was dangerous just like the Spartan was.

We wound our way along the ash-gray cobblestone paths that crisscrossed campus, eventually passing by my dorm, Styx Hall. I looked up at the turret where my room was. I wondered if the Protectorate knew about

Nyx, the Fenrir wolf pup that I was taking care of. Worry tightened my stomach. If they knew about Nyx, they would probably take her away from me. Most members of the Pantheon didn't trust creatures like Fenrir wolves because the Reapers enslaved, poisoned, and trained so many of them to kill warriors.

But I'd promised Nott, Nyx's mom, that I'd look after the wolf pup, and that's exactly what I was going to do. I wouldn't tell Linus and the others about Nyx, I vowed. No matter what they did to me. My mom had been a police detective, so I knew all about having your rights read to you, keeping your mouth shut, and asking for a lawyer. Sure, the Protectorate had said that I was under arrest, that I was going to be put on trial, but I had no illusions that meant the same thing at Mythos as it did in the regular mortal realm. In fact, I was willing to bet that it was going to be a lot, lot worse.

Normally, I would have enjoyed the walk across campus, but the rolling green hills that made up the lush grounds seemed to be deserted, adding to the doom-and-gloom atmosphere. I glanced at my silver watch. Almost four o'clock, which meant that it was time for the mysterious assembly. Most of the students were probably already gathered in the outdoor amphitheater. Well, at least no one was around to witness my walk of shame, even if Helena and the other students in the coffee shop would have texted the juicy details to all their friends by now.

I'd thought that we would start up the hill to the main quad so that the Protectorate could march me over to the math-science building and then down to the academy prison located there. But instead we veered left onto another path, heading toward the amphitheater that lay at the bottom of the hill next to the Library of Antiquities. I frowned. Why would we be going there? Surely, they weren't going to make me sit through some stupid assembly before they locked me away. Then again, maybe this was just another part of my impending punishment.

We stopped at the edge of the path, where it opened up into the amphitheater. Unlike the dark gray of the other buildings, the open-air theater was made out of bone-white stone that contained a rainbow of colors— sky blue, pearl pink, soft lilac. Those shades and more shimmered throughout the structure, as though a thousand Valkyries had given off sparks of magic that had somehow seeped into the stone.

The amphitheater was made out of a series of long, flat shallow steps that had been stacked on top of each other. The steps, which also served as seats, formed an enormous semicircle as they spiraled up the hill, and they all faced a stage that had been erected at the very bottom of the amphitheater. Four columns loomed over the stage, but my gaze flicked up to the tops of the columns, where stone chimeras crouched on round globes. Instead of glaring out at the crowd like usual, the chimeras' heads were lowered, and they were staring down at their curved claws, just like the sphinxes had. My unease cranked up another notch.

I dragged my gaze away from the chimeras and stared out into the amphitheater. Students, professors, and staff members had already gathered on the stone steps, all bundled up in heavy coats and gloves, their breath steaming in the sharp winter air until it looked like a thick fog had blanketed the whole area. No matter how cold it got, all the assemblies took place out here, instead of in the warmer, more comfortable gym. I wasn't sure why. The Powers That Were probably thought the amphitheater was more official or something.

Despite the fact that we were on the edge of the area, worried murmurs still drifted over to me, as the students wondered what was going on.

"What do you think the assembly is about?"

"Maybe the Pantheon's managed to imprison Loki again."

"Maybe not. Maybe Reapers are on their way here right now to kill us all."

And on and on the rumors went, leaping from one mouth and one phone to another. Mutters, whispers, chirps, and beeps floated through the air, creating a strange symphony of sound.

I spotted Daphne Cruz, my best friend, and Carson Callahan, her band geek boyfriend, sitting on the steps about halfway up the hill. They had their heads close together, looking at something on Daphne's phone—probably my arrest at the coffee shop, judging from the shocked expression on the Valkyrie's face and the pink sparks of magic that were streaking out of her fingertips like lightning. Daphne always gave off more magic whenever she was surprised, worried, or upset. I was willing to bet she was all those things right now—and so was I.

I'd thought that we would stay on the edge of the amphitheater until the assembly was over, but instead Linus jerked his head at Sergei and Inari, who stepped even closer to me. My dread ballooned up in my stomach and rose into my throat, threatening to choke me from the inside out.

Logan noticed the men's movements, and he quit arguing with his dad long enough to turn around. Alexei stepped in front of the Spartan, holding up his hands.

"I don't want to fight you, Logan," Alexei said. "But you know I will."

Logan looked at me, panic flaring in his blue eyes. Apparently, he knew what was about to happen—and that it wasn't anything good.

"Dad," he said. "Gwen hasn't done anything wrong. You have to believe me. Don't do this. Please."

Linus stared at his son, his face expressionless. Then, he turned away from Logan.

"Make sure that she stays still and quiet through this," Linus said. "I don't want any interruptions."

Inari and Sergei clamped their hands on my arms and dragged me forward, heading toward the steps that led up onto the stage. And I suddenly realized what the mysterious assembly was about—me and my supposed crimes against the Pantheon.

Chapter 3

Inari and Sergei marched me across the amphitheater, up the steps, and onto the stage, with Linus following along behind us. The three men's heavy boots slapped against the wooden boards, and the dull sounds almost seemed to chant to me. *Doom, doom, doom . . .*

We stopped in the middle of the stage, and I stared out at everyone who made up Mythos Academy—students, professors, staff members. I looked at Daphne, who had her hands up over her mouth in horror. Carson had a similar stunned expression on his face. Oliver Hector, Morgan McDougall, Savannah Warren. My gaze went from one familiar face to another. All the kids in my second-year class were here, along with the ones who'd apparently rushed back from the coffee shop for the assembly. Kenzie Tanaka, Talia Pizarro, Helena Paxton and her mean-girl friends. They must have raced up to the library, then hurried down the hill so they could get the last remaining seats at the very top of the amphitheater.

"Those guys have on Protectorate robes!"

"Hey, isn't that Gwen Frost? That weird Gypsy girl?"

"What's she doing on stage? What's going on? Why are they guarding her like that?"

More murmurs and questions rippled through the crowd, louder and sharper than before, but I shut them out of my mind and kept scanning the faces. Finally, I spotted Professor Aurora Metis standing off to the left side of the stage, along with Nickamedes, Coach Ajax, and Raven. The four of them made up the academy's security council and were responsible for keeping students safe at Mythos. I thought that had included me too, but it didn't look like that was the case—at least not anymore.

I stared at Metis, wondering if she'd known this was going to happen, if she'd tried to stop it. Worry filled her green eyes behind her silver glasses. Her face was tight with tension, and the tendons in her neck stood out against her bronze skin, like bowstrings about to snap. Beside her, Nickamedes was frowning, his black eyebrows furrowed together in thought. Ajax had his arms crossed over his big, burly chest. Only Raven seemed unconcerned, letting out a wide yawn and fiddling with her white hair, as though she was bored by the whole spectacle.

"Stay quiet through this, and it will go a lot easier on you," Linus murmured to me.

I glared at him, but he was already striding over to a podium topped with a microphone that had been set up in the middle of the stage. He stood there, waiting for the crowd to quiet down, before leaning forward and speaking into the microphone.

"Hello," he said, his voice rolling out like thunder from the bottom to the top of the amphitheater. "My name is Linus Quinn. Some of you may know me as the head of the Protectorate, the group charged with hunting down Reapers of Chaos. I'm also on the academy board of directors."

So Linus was one of the Powers That Were at Mythos. I knew there were folks who watched over the academy, some group of people responsible for running things, some board that came up with the rules, regulations, and even the froufrou lunch menus. I'd always jokingly referred to them as the Powers That Were. Now, I had a feeling I was going to find out just how appropriate my nickname for them was.

"I know you've all had a lot of questions and concerns ever since Loki escaped a few weeks ago," Linus continued. "Rest assured that the Protectorate has been investigating the incident and doing everything we can to track down Loki and his Reapers before anyone else gets hurt, like your fellow students who were recently killed at the Crius Coliseum."

Images flooded my mind at his words. Reapers storming into the coliseum, their curved swords flashing, their black robes billowing out like clouds of death. Kids fighting, running, and trying to get away. Kids screaming as the Reapers rammed their weapons into them. A Reaper plunging his sword into Carson's chest. Blood, so much blood splashing everywhere, like scarlet teardrops raining down on everything in sight—

Linus cleared his throat, snapping me out of my horrible memories. "Some serious accusations have come to light about what happened the night Loki was freed," he said. "That is why I and the other members of the Protectorate are here. To get to the bottom of these accusations, determine what really happened, and punish those involved accordingly."

Somehow, I knew what he was going to say next.

"It appears that a Mythos Academy student actually helped Loki escape from Helheim, the prison realm where the other gods trapped him centuries ago." Linus paused, then leaned forward even closer to the microphone. "That student is Gwendolyn Frost, the girl you see on stage before you."

Yeah, that was pretty much what I'd expected—and so was the crowd's reaction.

Shocked gasps rippled through the amphitheater, and just like at Kaldi's that emotion turned to horror, then anger. It seemed as if everyone drew in a breath, and then the surprised mutters exploded into a deafening roar. In seconds, everyone was on their feet screaming for my blood. A wave of collective rage and hate surged off the crowd, slamming into my stomach like a red-hot sword. Every angry shout, every enraged scream, every bitter word twisted the invisible blade in that much deeper, making me want to vomit from the phantom pain.

Practically everyone at Mythos had lost someone to the Reapers—a mother, a sister, a close friend—so the reaction was understandable. I wanted nothing more than to close my eyes, drop my head, and whimper at the feel of all the raging hate directed at me, but I forced myself to stand up tall and stare back at the people shouting curses at me.

"Quiet! Quiet!" Linus roared into the microphone.

It took several minutes for the crowd to finally calm down and for everyone to take their seats again. But they all kept staring at me, rage burning in their eyes. The phantom emotion kept stabbing me in the stomach again and again, until I had to grit my teeth to keep from screaming from the sensation.

"At this point, we have more questions than answers," Linus said. "To that end, we have arrested Miss Frost and will be conducting a trial and a full investigation into her actions. In the meantime, we will continue to search for Loki and his Reapers so we can deal with them accordingly. Rest assured, we will get to the bottom of this, and Loki will be imprisoned once more."

Linus's mouth twisted, and he looked at Metis, who lifted her chin in defiance. "In the meantime, in accordance with academy bylaws, Miss Frost will remain at Mythos until she is either acquitted or convicted of the many charges against her."

A series of harsh *boo-boo-boos* erupted at his words, and he had to stop speaking once more.

Linus looked at Metis again, as if this was all her fault, giving me a clue as to what had happened. The professor must have found out what was going down and had somehow managed to keep me here at the academy instead of being taken away and thrown in some Protectorate prison.

I could have told her not to bother. Everyone hated

me now because of what they thought I'd done—and maybe they weren't wrong to do so. After all, I was the one who'd found the Helheim Dagger, the last remaining seal on Loki's prison. But instead of keeping the dagger safe, I'd practically handed it over to Vivian Holler, the Reaper girl who was Loki's Champion, and she'd been all too happy to use the weapon and my blood to finally free the evil god. Sure, Vivian had tricked me, but the cold hard fact was that because of my actions Loki was out there somewhere, plotting with his Reapers about how to topple the Pantheon, about how to finally defeat Nike and plunge the world into eternal darkness.

Maybe everyone had a right to blame me.

Maybe everyone had a right to hate me.

Finally, after several minutes, the crowd quieted down again.

"Miss Frost has not been found guilty of anything yet, but in order for you to feel safe, I've arranged for her to be under close supervision while she is awaiting trial," Linus said. "Rest assured that a member of the Protectorate will accompany Miss Frost wherever she goes. In order to keep things as unobtrusive as possible, we've assigned a third-year student from the London academy to help watch over Miss Frost as she goes about her daily schedule."

Linus glanced at Alexei, who was standing at the bottom of the steps that led up to the stage, but he didn't point him out. So that's why Alexei was here—to watch me.

"This matter will be resolved in a few days," Linus

continued. "Until then, know that members of the Protectorate are here on campus keeping you safe. That is all."

A few polite claps sounded at his words, but everyone kept glaring at me, shock, pain, fear, and hate in their eyes—so much hate. Once more, their collective rage slammed into me, and I couldn't keep quiet any longer.

"I didn't do anything wrong!" I screamed. "It was Vivian! It was Vivian Holler! She's Loki's Champion! She freed him, not me! You have to believe me!"

"Get her out of here," Linus hissed. "Now!"

Inari and Sergei easily lifted me off my feet and carried me toward the edge of the stage, but I kept yelling the whole time.

"I didn't do anything wrong! I didn't do anything wrong!"

My screams echoed through the amphitheater and then rattled up into the sky and the heavens themselves, but no one cared, and no one came to my defense or rescue—not even the goddess who'd chosen me to be her Champion in the first place.

Inari and Sergei hustled me off stage, out of the amphitheater, and up the hill to the main quad. Students scrambled after us, everyone talking, yelling, and snapping photos with their phones. Eventually, my screams died down, and all I could do was just squint against the flashing lights. Inari and Sergei were still carrying me, so my feet weren't even touching the ground. I knew better than to try to struggle. I didn't know what kind of warriors the two men were, but they were easily stronger than I was.

Five buildings made up the main quad at Mythos— the Library of Antiquities, the gym, the dining hall, English-history, and math-science. Inari and Sergei headed for the math-science building. So they were taking me to the academy prison after all. The two men hurried inside the structure and then down, down, down we went, going through a series of locked doors and other security measures until we reached the bottom floor, deep underground.

The men finally put me back down on my feet, and I jerked away from them, rubbing my upper arms where they'd held them so tightly. We stood in a shadow-filled hallway in front of a door that was made out of the same dark gray stone as the rest of the building. Iron bars crisscrossed over the door, and two sphinxes had been carved into the surface. Once again, the sphinxes stared down at their feet instead of turning their heads and looking at me.

I'd never thought I'd miss the creepy stares from all the statues and carvings, but I was starting to. Somehow, they'd become part of my everyday routine, and I felt their absence, especially since it seemed like they couldn't even stand to look at me now. Maybe they hated me too, just like everyone else did. Bitterness filled me, burning like acid in my chest.

Sergei drew a skeleton key out from one of the pockets of his robe, while Inari kept his eyes on me. Please. As if I had the slightest chance of getting away from them. Sergei stepped forward, put the key in the lock, and turned it. Even though I knew it was coming, the loud *screech* still made me wince. Sergei pulled open the heavy door and gestured for me to step through. Like I had a choice.

I walked past him and stopped inside the doorway, staring out at the prison. The enormous circular room was shaped like a dome, just like the Library of Antiquities. Glass cells were stacked up three stories high to form the walls, while a hand holding a set of balanced scales was carved into the stone ceiling—the same symbol that was embroidered on the collars of the Protectorate's robes.

A stone table with a couple of chairs stood in the middle of the room, right under the hand-and-scales carving. That's where Preston Ashton had sat whenever I'd come down here to use to my psychometry to peer into his mind, to sort through his memories so I could tell Metis and the others what Preston's Reaper friends were planning. Something else I'd failed at, since I was the one in prison now.

A rustle sounded, and I looked over at a desk just inside the door. I wasn't sure how she'd managed it, but Raven had somehow beaten us here. She sat in her usual spot, flipping through one of the celebrity gossip magazines she always seemed to be reading. Raven was an old woman, even older than my Grandma Frost. Her hair was as white as it could be and matched the long, flowing gown she always wore, while wrinkles streaked her face, looking as deep and dark as the black greasepaint that football players swiped across their features. More wrinkles and brown liver spots covered her hands and arms, along with old, faded scars.

Raven leaned back in her chair and propped her black combat boots up on the desk. Her black eyes met mine for a moment before she went back to her magazine. Standing guard in the academy prison was one of the many odd jobs that Raven had at Mythos. Well, at least she had actually looked at me, if only for a few seconds. That made me feel slightly better, even if all the statues were ignoring me.

"Go on," Sergei said. "Go sit down."

I walked across the floor, with the warrior following along behind me. I started to drop into my usual seat, but Sergei touched my arm.

"Not on this side," he said. "You need to sit on the other side."

That's where Preston had sat, where I assumed all prisoners sat while they were being questioned. Some small part of me had still hoped that this was just a big misunderstanding, a giant mistake that could somehow be corrected. That hope immediately withered away and broke apart like a dead, brittle rose, although more cold worry, fear, and dread blossomed in its place.

I did as he asked, walking around and slipping into the seat on the far side of the table—the side with the chains. Thick metal chains lay on top of the table, along with a pair of handcuffs, and still more chains rested on the floor underneath, so that a prisoner's hands and legs could all be secured at the same time.

Sergei reached for the chains on top of the table, and I shrank back in the chair, the rough stone pressing into my spine. Preston had been the last person to wear those chains, and I knew what I'd see and feel if they were slipped onto my skin—the Reaper's unending hatred of me. I'd felt enough of that emotion already in the amphitheater. I didn't want to feel anymore.

"Don't put those on me," I whispered. "Please."

Sergei looked at me, surprised by my low, raspy *please*, but he put down the chains. I kept my hands away from the metal and made sure that no part of my bare skin was touching either the stone table or chair. It had been bad enough going into Preston's mind and sorting through his horrible memories of all the people he'd hurt, tortured, and killed. I didn't want to flash on the Reaper glaring at me across the table too. I just couldn't handle it—not right now.

Sergei moved over to stand by Inari, who was talking to Raven in a low voice. I wondered what was going to happen now. Would the trial start immediately? Would I be given a chance to defend myself? How was I going to get out of this mess? How was I going to convince the Protectorate that I hadn't freed Loki on purpose? That Vivian had fooled me just like she had everyone else? Those questions and a hundred more whirled around and around my mind, but I didn't have the answers to them—not a single one.

I didn't have long to wait, worry, and wonder. Five minutes later, the prison door screeched opened again, and Linus stepped inside, followed by Alexei, Professor Metis, Nickamedes, and Coach Ajax.

The coach turned, held out his hands, and stopped someone else from coming through the door behind him. "Sorry, Logan. This is as far as you and your friends can come. Don't worry. This won't take long."

Behind Ajax, I saw Logan standing out in the hallway. A few pink sparks of magic crackled in the air beside him, telling me that Daphne and probably Carson were out there as well.

The Spartan stood on his tiptoes and looked over Ajax's shoulder at me. "Gypsy girl!"

"I'm okay!" I called out in a shaky voice. "I'm okay!"

Logan, Daphne, and Carson all started talking at once, yelling at me that things were going to be all right, but Ajax ignored them and shut the door, cutting off their protests.

For a moment, everything was silent.

Then, Linus shook his head and turned to Nickamedes. "I hoped by sending him to school here that you could keep him out of trouble. But apparently, that hasn't happened."

Nickamedes stiffened at his words. The librarian was Logan's uncle on his mom's side of the family. In fact, Nickamedes looked like an older, more serious version of Logan with his black hair and blue eyes.

Linus kept staring at him. "Larenta would be so disappointed in you for not protecting Logan better than you have."

Anger blazed in the librarian's eyes, his hands clenched into fists, and he took a menacing step forward, like he wanted to punch Linus. I knew the feeling.

"Don't you dare bring Larenta into this," Nick-amedes snapped. "I still don't understand what my sister ever saw in you, you pompous, arrogant—"

"Enough." Metis stepped forward and put her hand on Nickamedes's shoulder. "That's enough. From both of you. Arguing amongst ourselves isn't going to solve anything."

"No, it won't," Linus agreed. "Glad to see you still have that level head on your shoulders, Aurora."

Metis grimaced, but she nodded, accepting his faint compliment. Still, unless I missed my guess, she didn't like Linus any more than Nickamedes did. I wondered why, what had happened between all of them, and if it had anything to do with my mom.

"But I still say that you're making an enormous error," Metis said. "Gwen is not working with the Reapers, and she certainly did not free Loki on purpose."

"Yes, it's the *on purpose* part that troubles me the most," Linus murmured. "That's what I'm here to get to the bottom of."

He started to walk over to me, but Metis planted herself in front of him.

"You march into my office this morning with no warning that you were coming to campus. Then, you tell me that you're here to arrest and put one of our students on trial for conspiring with the Reapers," she said, her hands on her hips. "You don't tell me who the student is, but leave me and the others to find out at the assembly along with everyone else."

"So?" he asked. "All of those things are within my right as head of the Protectorate. You know that, Aurora. As for why I didn't tell you who the student was, it's come to my attention that you've become quite . . . fond of Miss Frost. I didn't want you to do something foolish like warn her and give her a chance to escape justice."

Metis went completely tense and rigid, and it took her a moment to unclench her jaw. "So I want answers," she snapped. "Who made these accusations against Gwen? Why? What proof do they have?"

"You'll find all that out soon enough," Linus said. "Now, if you don't mind, I'd like to explain things to the girl so that she doesn't cause us any more trouble in the meantime."

Metis opened her mouth as though she was going to keep arguing, but after a moment she pressed her lips together and stepped aside. There was nothing she could do or say that would get him to change his mind. I knew it as well as she did.

Linus headed over to the table, followed by the others. Only Raven remained at her desk by the door, still reading. Every once in a while, she would glance in our direction, apparently wondering if the drama here would be as good as what was in her magazine.

Linus sat in the chair across from me. Sergei, Inari, and Alexei arranged themselves behind him, while Metis, Nickamedes, and Ajax trooped over and stood off to my right on my side of the table. Linus plucked a pair of reading glasses from a pocket on his shirt. He put them on, then reached into the folds of his gray robe. This time, he drew out a piece of white parchment, which he unrolled and spread out on the table between us.

"Gwendolyn Cassandra Frost," he said, reading from the parchment. "You are hereby charged with crimes against the Pantheon, including, but not limited to, conspiring with other Reapers of Chaos to kill your fellow students at the Crius Coliseum, stealing artifacts from the coliseum, absconding from the academy with the Helheim Dagger, and most serious of all, using the dagger to release Loki from Helheim. How do you plead to these charges?"

For a moment, I simply couldn't speak. It was like I'd been sucker punched in the stomach by a Valkyrie, and all the air had been driven out of my lungs. My mouth opened and closed, and opened and closed again, but no words came out. I couldn't utter so much as a freaking *syllable*. I hadn't done any of those terrible things—not a single one of them.

Sure, I'd been at the coliseum, but only because I'd been trying to complete an assignment for Metis's myth-history class. Everything else that had followed had been the doing of Vivian Holler, another second-year Mythos student. The Gypsy who was Loki's Champion. The girl who'd murdered my mom.

I didn't know where Vivian was right now, since she'd escaped with Loki the night she'd freed him, but I could almost hear her laughing. Somehow, someway, she had managed to convince the Protectorate that I was to blame for everything she'd done, all the lies she'd told, all the people she'd hurt, all the kids she'd killed. I knew Vivian was a good actress, but this was above and beyond even for her. *Bravo, Viv. Another masterful performance.*

I started to tell Linus all about Vivian, but Metis beat me to the punch.

"These charges are utter nonsense," she said. "Gwen is *not* a Reaper. The three of us know it, along with Raven, and you would too, if you'd spent any time with her. If you'd even bothered to ask us, before you decided to stage that ridiculous display in the amphitheater."

Nickamedes and Ajax nodded, backing up Metis. At her desk, Raven waved her hand, seeming to agree as well, although she kept right on reading her magazine.

"And the Protectorate will decide for itself what the girl is and isn't, and what she has and hasn't done," Linus said in his cold, calm voice, the one that infuriated me more and more with every word he spoke. "Obviously, the three of you cannot be objective where she's concerned. And neither can my son."

Nobody responded, although I could almost see the tension and anger hanging like a storm cloud over the table, making everything dark and ugly.

"I didn't do anything wrong," I said, finally finding my voice.

Nickamedes stepped forward and put a hand on my shoulder. "Don't say anything else to him, Gwendolyn. Not one more word. What Linus failed to mention is that anything you say now can be brought up at the trial.

And believe me when I tell you that he will use your own words against you. It's something he excels at."

Linus glowered at Nickamedes, but I decided to take the librarian's advice and keep my mouth shut. I didn't want to get into any more trouble than I already was.

Linus rolled the parchment back up, took off his glasses, and looked at me again. "Here's what will happen next. Anytime such serious charges are leveled against someone, the Protectorate is called in, and an investigation is conducted. We will be talking to everyone you know and everyone who might know anything about the charges against you. Your friends, your family, your classmates, your professors, everyone."

Everyone? He was going to talk to everyone who knew me? Well, it would be a pretty short list. Sure, I had a few friends, but most of the kids at Mythos knew me as Gwen Frost, that weird Gypsy girl who touched stuff, saw things, and could find lost items for the right price. I wouldn't exactly win any popularity contests, especially not now, after the assembly. Still, maybe this wouldn't be so bad.

"Evidence will be collected, and you will questioned about the findings, along with your actions. Then, a group of Protectorate members will make a final decision about your guilt or innocence," he continued. "You should know that the charges against you are some of the most serious I've ever seen, especially for a Mythos student. Despite your age, if you are found guilty, the punishment will be dealt out accordingly. At the very least, you will be expelled from the academy."

Okay, so maybe it *was* going to be that bad after all.

Still, I couldn't keep myself from asking the inevitable question. "And what about the very worst? What's the worst punishment if I'm found guilty?"

Linus looked at me, his eyes cold in his face. "Death."

Chapter 4

Death?

I could be put to *death* by the Protectorate, by the Pantheon, for something I didn't even do?

"If you are found guilty of all charges, you will be placed in solitary confinement in a Protectorate prison," Linus said. "And you will stay there until you are executed."

For a moment, the world went completely black, as though I was shrouded in darkness, as though I was already cold, dead, and buried in my grave. I blinked, and light blazed around me once more. Everything snapped back into focus, somehow seeming sharper than before. The hard, unyielding stone of the chair pressing against my back. The sinister gleam of the metal chains and handcuffs on top of the table. The faint musty odor that always filled the prison. All that and more assaulted my senses, slamming into my brain one after another, although they were all quickly drowned out by the rapid *thump-thump-thump* of my heart.

I wanted nothing more than to bolt from my chair,

race over to the prison door, yank it open, and run and run and run until my legs buckled and my lungs exploded from the strain. But I couldn't do that, not without making everything that much worse. So I forced myself to sit still and just breathe—in and out, in and out—just like my mom had taught me, just like she'd always told me to do whenever I was scared, upset, or worried. Right now, I was closer to panic—okay, sheer terror—than anything else, but I made myself keep breathing.

The panic slowly passed, although worry and fear still gnawed at my heart like rats chewing on a block of cheese. I finally looked at the others. Metis had a sick, stricken expression on her face, while anger made Nickamedes's cheeks burn. Ajax simply looked furious with his stiff shoulders and clenched fists, his onyx skin gleaming underneath the lights. Even Sergei, Inari, and Alexei were giving me sympathetic glances at this point. Only Linus remained calm and emotionless, his blank face giving nothing away of his true feelings.

"I didn't do anything wrong," I said again in a much fainter tone. "I didn't do anything wrong."

"That remains to be decided," Linus said. "Rest assured that we will conduct a thorough investigation and that you will receive a fair and balanced trial."

"Yeah," I said, sarcasm creeping back into my voice. "Because hauling me up there on stage at the amphitheater and announcing my supposed crimes to the whole freaking academy was such a fair and balanced thing to do."

Nickamedes's hand tightened on my shoulder, reminding me that I should keep my mouth shut, but the fear, shock, and panic were quickly simmering away, leaving nothing behind but anger. I embraced the anger, gathered up every single scrap of it and let the emotion sizzle around my heart until it had burned away everything else. As long as I was angry, I couldn't think about how serious the situation was or how close I was to losing everything that had become important to me these past few months at Mythos—including my life.

Linus's eyes narrowed at my words, but his face remained smooth. "Although I am personally against it, the academy bylaws state that you may remain at Mythos and continue with your classes and other school activities until the investigation and trial are complete and a decision is reached regarding your guilt or innocence."

Some of the tightness in my chest eased. At least I would still be at the academy with Logan, Daphne, and my other friends, not to mention Metis, Ajax, and Nickamedes. Together, we would find a way to get me out of this. I knew we would. We'd survived everything the Reapers had thrown at us so far. We'd survive this too.

"But your movements are restricted to campus, and you will be supervised and watched at all times," Linus continued. "In order to minimize the invasion and distraction to the other students, Alexei will be responsible for you during the day. He will accompany you everywhere you go on the academy grounds—your classes, the dining hall, the library, everywhere."

So not only was I to be investigated and put on trial, but I was going to have my own personal shadow too.

Actually, I imagined he'd be more like a spy, reporting my every move back to the Protectorate and getting me into even more trouble if I so much as chewed gum in class or cut across the grass on the quad instead of walking on the stone paths. Terrific. Just terrific.

"You will not interfere with Alexei in any way, and any attempts by you to slip away from him will result in your being kept here in the academy prison for the duration of the investigation and trial," Linus said. "Do you understand, Miss Frost?"

"Oh yeah. I understand perfectly," I muttered.

Alexei looked at me. He kept his face blank, but once again, I saw the curiosity in his eyes. I wondered why he'd been chosen for guard duty. Most likely it was because he was Sergei's son. I wondered if being in the Protectorate was a family thing, like being a cop, firefighter, or doctor was in some regular mortal families. I'd have to ask Logan. I'd have to ask the Spartan about a lot of things—and why his dad seemed to hate me when I'd never even met him before today.

"Inari and Sergei will take turns watching your dorm at night," Linus continued. "Just in case there is some truth to Metis's ridiculous idea that the Reapers are targeting you."

I glanced at the professor. We both knew why the Reapers were after me. Because I was Nike's Champion—and I was supposed to find some way to kill Loki. It looked like Metis hadn't told Linus that, though. I wondered what else she hadn't told him.

"We have already launched our investigation, and we will start the trial on Friday afternoon, two days from now," Linus said. "Metis will escort you here after your myth-history class. In the meantime, I suggest you reflect on your actions these past few months and prepare to account for everything you've done since coming to Mythos. That is all—for now."

Linus got to his feet, turned, and left the prison, his gray robe streaming out behind him. Sergei and Inari nodded at me and the others before they followed him. Alexei stayed behind, though. At first, I wondered why, but then I realized what was going on—guard duty was starting already. Marvelous.

I sat in the stone chair, wondering if my legs would actually work if I tried to get to my feet. A little more than an hour ago, I'd been having coffee with Logan, and my biggest worry had been how our first date was going. Now, my whole world had been turned upside down—again.

"Gwen?" Metis asked. "Are you okay?"

"Sure," I said. "Just fine and dandy for a girl who's about to be put on trial for her life."

"Don't worry, Gwen," Ajax said in his deep, rumbling voice. "We're going to get this sorted out. Nothing's going to happen to you."

I started to tell him it was too late for that, that everyone at Mythos hated me now, but I kept quiet. Instead, I focused on the one person who hadn't been in the prison with the others, the one person I needed to see.

"What about my grandma?" I asked. "Where is she? Does she know about this?"

Metis nodded. "She does. I called her as soon as the

assembly ended. She should be waiting for you in your dorm room by now."

I nodded. Grandma Frost would know what to do. She always knew what to do.

"Come on," Nickamedes said. "Let's get you out of here and back to your room."

I got to my feet, and we walked toward the prison door. Raven gave me another brief glance as we left, but she went right back to her magazine. I doubted she cared one way or the other what happened to me.

Ajax opened the door, and we stepped out into the hallway. Daphne and Carson were standing outside, but there was no sign of Logan, his dad, or the other members of the Protectorate. Metis, Nickamedes, and Ajax started talking in low voices, so I walked over to my friends.

"Gwen!" Daphne said. "Are you okay?"

The Valkyrie hugged me, her great strength making my back crack.

"I'm okay," I said. "For now. Where's Logan?"

Daphne shook her head, her blond ponytail swishing from side to side. "He went after his dad to try and talk to him about . . . things."

"Yeah. Things."

"Is it true?" Carson asked, his brown eyes big and wide behind his black glasses. "That they're going to put you on trial for what happened with Vivian and Loki?"

"It's true."

I told my friends everything Linus had said—except

that the punishment was death if I was found guilty. I didn't want to worry them any more than they already were. Besides, Metis and the others had said that they would straighten all this out. I had to believe them. I just had to. Otherwise, I'd go crazy on the spot, and Vivian, Loki, and the rest of the Reapers would have already won.

When I finished, Carson jerked his head. "Who's that?"

I turned and realized that Alexei was standing behind me. I hadn't even heard him move. "Oh, this is Alexei. My . . . guard."

"Alexei Sokolov," Daphne said in a cool voice. "I remember you. You gave me a run for my money last year at the spring archery championships at the New York academy."

For the first time, a hint of a smile lifted up his lips. "And you beat me in the final round."

"I did," Daphne said. "I know you have your orders from the Protectorate, but if you lay so much as one hand on Gwen or do anything to hurt her, I will break your fingers so badly that you will never be able to pick up a weapon again. Or anything else."

"Daphne!" I hissed, shocked at the threat of violence in her deceptively sweet voice.

"What?" she said. "I'm just telling him what's what."

Sparks of magic shot out of her fingertips, as if to punctuate her brutal promise. All Valkyries gave off flickers and flares of magic that were tied to their personalities and auras. I always thought it was ironic that

Daphne's aura apparently had a princess pink color, given how volatile and quick to anger she could be.

"Don't worry, Gwen," Alexei replied. "I know all about you and your friends, including the Valkyrie's temper."

"And how is that? Because I've never seen or even heard of you before today."

"I have my sources."

Something flashed in his eyes, something that looked a lot like longing, but a second later, his face was blank and expressionless once more. Weird. I had no idea how Alexei could know anything about me, but it looked like I was stuck with him, whether I liked it or not.

"Do you think Vivian is behind this?" Carson asked, running a hand through his brown hair.

I shrugged. "I don't know. The last time I saw Vivian, she was flying off on that Black roc with Loki strapped in behind her. But I wouldn't put it past her to try to make trouble for me, especially since Preston didn't succeed in killing me at the Garm gate."

I shivered once again, thinking about all the awful things that had happened that night. Vivian slicing open my palm with the Helheim Dagger and using my blood to free Loki. The evil god telling Preston to kill me, and the Reaper stabbing me in the chest with the dagger. Then me using my psychometry to touch Preston, to pull all the magic, all the life, out of his body and into mine so I could heal myself. Killing the older boy with my Gypsy gift, the magic Nike had given to me and my family.

"Gwen," Metis said, coming over to stand beside me, her phone in her hand. "Your grandmother just texted me. She's waiting for you."

I snapped out of my thoughts. "Thanks, professor. I'll go see her right now."

Metis nodded, then pulled me away from the others. "I don't want you to worry about any of this. Nickamedes, Ajax, and I will take care of everything. We'll make sure that Linus and the rest of the Protectorate follow the rules. We'll protect you. Okay?"

Emotion clogged my throat, making it hard to speak, so I just nodded instead. Metis and my mom had been best friends back when they'd been students at Mythos, so I knew that the professor meant every word she said. I just wondered what it would cost her to get me out of this mess—if she even could.

Chapter 5

I promised to call Daphne later, and she told me that she and Carson would be at weapons training in the gym in the morning just like usual. I said good-bye to my friends and followed Metis up the stairs and out of the math-science building. It was even colder now than it had been during the assembly, and the main quad was deserted. By now, the other students would have gathered in the dining hall, library, or their dorms to talk about what had happened.

The professor walked with me across campus, with Alexei trailing along behind. He didn't speak to us. In fact, he didn't make a sound. His clothes didn't rustle, his boots didn't thump on the cobblestones, his breath didn't even steam like mine did in the cold. Creepy.

We finally reached Styx Hall and stopped outside the dorm.

"Just try to just relax and put this out of your mind as best you can, okay, Gwen?" Metis said. "And know that Nickamedes, Ajax, and I are working as hard as we can to get the charges dropped."

I nodded. "I'll try. Thank you. And I want to say that I'm sorry for all this. I never thought—I never thought something like this would happen." My throat tightened once more, and that was all I could say.

"I know, and it's not your fault, none of it, no matter what the Protectorate thinks. Remember that."

Metis squeezed my arm, turned, and headed back up to the main quad. Alexei left too, following her, but I wasn't alone. Inari was outside the dorm, leaning against a tree right below my dorm room windows. He still wore his gray robe, and that, along with his black hair and dark eyes, made him seem like just another shadow that had been splashed across the landscape. Looked like the Protectorate wasn't joking when it came to keeping an eye on me twenty-four-seven.

I used my student ID card to get into the dorm and walked up the steps to the third floor where my room was, stuck in a separate turret from the rest of the building. To my surprise, an older woman was on her knees outside the door to my room, a rag in her hand and a bucket of soapy water on the floor next to her.

"Grandma?" I asked. "What are you doing?"

Geraldine Frost looked up at me with violet eyes that were the same color as mine. She must have come straight here from her afternoon readings because she was still wearing what she called her *Gypsy gear*—a white silk blouse, black pants, and soft black shoes with toes that curled up. Colorful scarves were wrapped around her body, and the silver coins on the fringed ends *jingle-jingle-jingled* together with every move she made. She usually wore a scarf as a sort of headband, but today her iron-gray hair was loose around her wrinkled face.

Grandma was a Gypsy just like I was, which meant that she had a gift just like I did. In Grandma's case, she could see the future. She made extra money telling people's fortunes out of her house in nearby Asheville, just like I used my psychometry to find things that had been lost, forgotten, or stolen.

Not anymore, I realized with a jolt. Given what had happened at the amphitheater, no one on campus would ever hire me to find missing items again. That shouldn't have mattered to me, but it did. Sure, tracking down lost cell phones and stolen bracelets wasn't the most exciting or glamorous job, but it was *mine*—it was part of my magic, it was part of me being, well, *me*. Now, it was just another thing the Protectorate had taken away by accusing me in front of the entire academy. I wondered what else I would have to sacrifice before this was all over with—and if it would really end up costing me my life.

I pushed those troubling thoughts away and stepped closer to her. "Grandma? What's going on? Why are you scrubbing at my door with that rag..." My voice trailed off as I realized why.

MURDERER. KILLER. REAPER BITCH.

Those words and other, even nastier ones had been spray painted across the door and the surrounding walls in bright paint—Reaper-red paint.

"I'm sorry, pumpkin," Grandma Frost said, throwing the rag into the bucket and getting to her feet. "I was hoping to get it cleaned up before you saw. Don't worry.

They just painted the walls. They didn't get into your room. I checked already."

I stared at the door and the walls. I could feel the anger radiating from the ugly, ugly words just as I'd felt it roll off the crowd at the amphitheater. I knew that if I leaned forward and ran my fingers over the paint, that the emotion would intensify, and I'd feel what the other kids had when they'd written those words—all their terrible hatred of me.

Suddenly, it was all just too much. My disastrous date with Logan. The Protectorate arresting me, then announcing the charges to everyone. Linus telling me the penalty for my supposed crimes was death. It was all just too *much*. Hot, scalding tears streamed down my cheeks even as I tried to hold back the wrenching sobs that shook my body from head to toe.

Grandma's arms closed around me, and she started rocking me back and forth. "Sshh. Sshh. It's okay, pumpkin. I'm here now. Everything's going to be all right."

I held on to her that much tighter and just cried and cried and cried. Letting it all out. My worries, my fears, my anger. Slowly, my body-shaking sobs died down to a steady stream of quiet tears, and then, even those dried up. I wiped the last of the tears off my flushed face, stepped back from Grandma, and stared at the ruined door, trying to ignore the empty, hollow ache in my chest.

"I guess Metis told you what happened," I mumbled.

Grandma nodded. "She did."

Sighing, I opened the door, and we stepped inside. A

bed, a desk, some bookcases, a TV, a small fridge. My dorm room looked like any other, but I'd added my own personal touches, like the posters of Wonder Woman, Karma Girl, and The Killers that hung on the wall, and the framed photos of my mom that stood on my desk, right next to a small replica statue of Nike.

I stared at the statue, wondering if the goddess would open her eyes and give me a sly wink like she sometimes did, letting me know that everything was going to be okay. But the figurine remained still and frozen in place. I sighed. It seemed that Nike wasn't too happy with me right now either. At least she wasn't bowing her head and looking away from me like all the statues had earlier.

But somebody was happy to see me—Nyx.

The Fenrir wolf pup had been snoozing in a wicker basket in the corner, but she scrambled to her feet at the sound of the door opening. Nyx had only been born a couple of weeks ago, so she was still tiny, only weighing a few pounds, but I thought she was the cutest thing with her dark gray fur and purplish eyes. She bounded out of her basket, pounced on my sneaker, and started growling and playing tug-of-war with one of my shoelaces.

I picked up the wolf pup and hugged her to my chest. Nyx playfully growled again, giving me a nose full of raunchy breath, but I didn't care. The wolf licked my cheek, and I felt her happiness that I was finally back so I could play with her.

On the wall next to my posters, a purplish eye snapped open to glare at me.

"Well, it's about time you got back," a voice said in a cool English accent. "Where have you been all afternoon, Gwen?"

I walked over and looked at the eye. Actually, it wasn't just an eye I was staring at, but half of a man's face, complete with a nose, a mouth, and even an ear. The face was inlaid into the hilt of a silver sword that was hanging in a black leather scabbard on the wall. Vic, my talking sword, the weapon given to me by Nike.

Vic had been around a long, long time, and he had plenty of attitude, especially when it came to telling people how exceptionally awesome he was. Sometimes, the mouthy sword got on my nerves, but right now, I just wanted to hug him close the way I was Nyx.

I held the wolf pup up, and she gave Vic a lick on his metal cheek just like she had me.

"Ugh! Disgusting. Someone needs a breath mint, fuzzball," Vic growled, but he couldn't keep the smile off his half of a face, and neither could I.

Nyx let out another happy growl and licked him again. Vic grumbled some more, but then he spotted my Grandma Frost standing behind me, and his eye widened.

"Geraldine?"

"Vic."

The sword's gaze swiveled back to me. "What's going on? Why do you both have such gloomy expressions on your faces?"

I put Nyx on the floor so she could run around and plopped down on my bed. "It's a long story."

"Well, I think it's one we'd both like to hear," Grandma Frost said, sitting in my desk chair. "Tell me everything that happened, and everything the Protectorate said to you."

"The Protectorate?" Vic said. "What are those bloody fools doing here?"

"Apparently, deciding whether I live or die," I mumbled.

I told them what had happened at the coffee shop, the amphitheater, and the academy prison. After I finished, they were both silent, although Vic's eye was narrowed in thought. His eye was a strange shade, not quite purple, but not quite gray either—more like the color of twilight, that beautiful shade that softened the sky just before nightfall. Although there was nothing soft about the sword's gaze right now. The fury in his eye made it glow as bright as a star.

"Those bloody fools," Vic growled again. "Sometimes, I don't think the members of the Protectorate can tell a hole in the ground from their—"

"Vic," Grandma said in a warning tone. "That's enough of that kind of talk."

The sword glowered at her a little, but he kept right on grumbling about the Protectorate, although he mostly did it under his breath.

"What am I going to do?" I asked her. "Do you really think they'll find me guilty? That they'll actually put me in prison . . . execute me?" I had to force myself to whisper the last few words.

Grandma shook her head. "I don't know, pumpkin. I just wonder who made these accusations against you in the first place. If we knew that, I think we'd know what was really going on."

I got to my feet and started pacing from one side of my room to the other. "It's got to be some plot by the Reapers. But why? To make everyone at Mythos hate me? To get me expelled? None of those things will keep me from fighting the Reapers and being Nike's Champion . . . will they?"

"Of course not," Vic snapped. "The goddess chose your family to give her magic to. She chose you to be her Champion, Gwen. *You*—not anyone else. There's nothing the Protectorate can do about any of that. Not one bloody thing."

I thought of the cold way Linus Quinn had looked at me. I wasn't so sure about that, but I didn't tell the sword my fears. If I did, Vic would just say something about how he could convince Logan's dad to drop the charges—while his point was pressed against Linus's heart. Vic was rather bloodthirsty that way. One of his favorite things to do was talk about all the Reapers we were going to kill.

Normally, I tried to ignore Vic's Reaper rants as best I could, but tonight I thought about the one Reaper I actually wanted to take down—Vivian Holler. Once again, I flashed back to that night in the forest when Vivian had climbed on top of her Black roc, a huge, mythological bird, and had flown away with Loki riding behind her. I wondered where Vivian was right now. According to Metis, the Pantheon hadn't heard so much as a whisper of where Vivian had gone. Something else that frustrated me. What good was it being a Champion if I couldn't even avenge my own mom's murder?

I stopped pacing, pulled back the curtain, and stared

out one of the picture windows. My eyes scanned the lawn below, and it took me several seconds to spot Inari's thin figure. He had his back against one of the trees and looked like just another dark shadow in the night. If I hadn't known he was there, I wouldn't have noticed him at all.

Grandma Frost got up and peered out the window as well. "Is that one of the Protectorate guards?"

"Yeah, his name is Inari Sato."

She nodded. "A Ninja. I've heard of him. He's supposed to be one of the Pantheon's best warriors and one of the leaders of the Protectorate."

"Yeah, him and Logan's dad apparently," I sniped and let the curtain fall back into place. "There are others who will be guarding me too. A Russian guy named Sergei Sokolov and his son, Alexei. He's a third-year student from the London academy. Logan acted like he knew him, and Daphne met him before at some archery competition."

Grandma didn't say anything, but she heard the fear and frustration in my voice. She reached over and gently took my hand in hers. As always, the warmth of her love washed over me as soon as her skin touched mine. I focused on that sensation, letting it drown out everything else, all the bad things that had happened today, and all the bad ones that might come to be tomorrow.

"Don't worry, pumpkin," she said in a distant voice. "Everything will work out in the end. You'll see."

Her eyes were empty and glassy, like she was looking at something only she could see. She was having one of her psychic visions, and I felt this force stir in the air around her—something old, patient, knowing, and watchful. I stayed where I was, still and quiet, and held her hand.

"Things will be difficult for a while, but they'll eventually get better," she murmured. "You'll see."

That force tightened around both of us for a moment, almost like arms pulling us close for a comforting hug, before it abruptly faded away altogether. Grandma blinked, her eyes cleared, and she was herself once more.

Nyx jumped up, batting at the silver coins dangling from her scarves, and Grandma laughed and stooped down to pet the wolf pup. She didn't say anything about what she'd seen, and I didn't ask. It was difficult for Grandma to have reliable visions about family or friends in the first place, since her feelings for someone could influence what she saw. So she rarely told me about the glimpses she got of my future, claiming that she didn't want me to make important decisions based on something that might or might not happen. I understood that Grandma wanted me to take my own path in life, but sometimes a little hint about all the Bad, Bad Things that were on the horizon would have been nice.

Grandma walked over to my desk and picked up a metal tin shaped like a giant chocolate chip cookie. "How about something to eat?" she asked. "I'd just finished making some oatmeal raisin cookies for you when Metis called."

Grandma Frost loved to bake, and she was always making some sweet, delicious treat for me to bring back to the academy and share with my friends.

"I also stopped and got you a sandwich," she added.

She pointed to a white paper bag on my desk, and I knew she was talking about the Pork Pit, one of my favorite restaurants. But I didn't feel like eating anything tonight, not even cookies.

Still, I made myself smile at her. "Maybe later."

Grandma stayed with me the rest of the evening, while I called Daphne and filled her in. I called Logan too, but he didn't answer his phone. He was probably still arguing with his dad, so I left him a voice mail, saying that I was going to bed and that I'd see him tomorrow morning at weapons training.

Finally, just before the ten o'clock curfew, Grandma got to her feet and said that she'd better go before the dorms locked down for the night. I was on the floor playing with Nyx, and I gathered the wolf pup up in my arms once more and got to my feet. A tear leaked out of the corner of my eye at what I had to do now.

"I think you should take Nyx home with you," I said in a sad voice. "I don't want the Protectorate to find her here and take her away."

"Yes, do please send the fuzzball away," Vic said in a snarky tone. "All that fur is terrible on my allergies. Terrible, I tell you!"

The sword sniffed as if to prove his point, but I could see the gleam of a tear in his eye. In his own way, he loved Nyx just as much as I did.

Grandma nodded. "That's probably for the best, pumpkin. There's a lot going on right now. Better not to take the chance."

I passed Nyx over to Grandma Frost. She tucked the

Fenrir wolf pup inside her coat so Nyx would stay warm on the walk across campus to her car. I petted Nyx a final time, whispering that I'd come see her just as soon as I could. I hugged Grandma tight, and they left.

My room seemed so quiet, so still, so terribly *empty*, without them, especially without Nyx bounding from corner to corner, sniffing, growling, and exploring the room like she hadn't been living here all her short life. I'd never realized how sad and suffocating the quiet could seem until now.

I wiped away a few more tears and got ready for bed. Taking a shower, putting on my pajamas, getting my books together for my morning classes. Nothing too difficult, but by the time I finished, I was exhausted.

I crawled into bed and snuggled down under my purple and gray plaid comforter. Normally, I would have left Vic on his spot on the wall, but tonight, I laid the sword and his scabbard on top of the bed, right next to me. I'd already lost Nyx—I didn't want to lose him too.

"Don't worry, Gwen," Vic said. "You'll find out who's behind all this, and when you do, I'll be right there to help you deal with the Reaper scum. Why, we'll slice them to bloody ribbons! We'll wear their guts for garters! We'll . . ."

And on and on he went, each fantasy a little bloodier and more violent than the last. Despite the situation, I couldn't help but smile. So many things had changed in my life since I'd come to Mythos, but Vic was one of the constants. I could always count on the sword to be exactly who and what he was. Something that comforted me tonight more than ever.

"Good night, Vic," I said when he finally wound down. "We'll talk more in the morning."

"Good night, Gwen."

The sword yawned, his half of a jaw popping in the darkness. His eye snapped shut, and a few minutes later he started snoring.

I reached over and rested my hand on top of the sword, and I didn't let go of him, not even when I finally drifted off to sleep.

Chapter 6

To my surprise, I fell into a dark, dreamless sleep until my alarm startled me awake the next morning.

I got ready for the day and peeked out the window at the lawn, but Inari wasn't in sight. I guess the Ninja had pulled the night shift, and now it was time for someone else to take over the horrible duty of guarding me. Well, I had things to do, and I wasn't going to wait around for the Protectorate to show up.

I didn't have to. When I opened the door to my room, I found Alexei waiting outside in the hallway. The Russian warrior was leaning against the wall, his arms crossed over his lean, muscled chest. A black backpack lay at his feet, and I could see the hilts of two swords sticking out of the top of it.

"So you get to follow me around all day. Yippee-skippee," I grumbled, looping the strap of my gray messenger bag over my head and chest.

Alexei didn't say anything, but his mouth twitched up into something that almost looked like a smile. Well, at least someone was amused by my suffering.

I locked the door behind me, brushed past Alexei, and headed down the stairs. He fell into step right behind me, as close to me as my own shadow. Once again, he didn't make any noise as he walked, not a single sound, not even when he went over the squeaky step at the bottom of the staircase. His eerie, watchful silence made me feel like there was a ghost haunting me. The only difference was that I could actually see Alexei when I turned around.

I made it to the bottom of the steps, walked down a hallway, and stared out the front door of the dorm. The morning was ice-cold, and the frosted grass glinted like thousands of tiny silver daggers, stretching out as far as the eye could see. The sun had barely come up, but the faint rays had already given the frost a bloody, crimson tint. What was the old saying? Something about a red sky in morning being a warning. Yeah, I had a feeling it was going to be that kind of day.

I reached into my coat pockets and pulled out my dark gray gloves, scarf, and toboggan, all patterned with glittery silver snowflakes. When I was all bundled up, I went outside, shoved my hands into my coat pockets, and stepped onto one of the cobblestone paths that wound up the hill to the main quad. Since it was so early, Alexei and I were the only ones outside.

We walked in silence for about two minutes before I looked over my shoulder at Alexei.

"So what's your deal?" I asked.

"My deal?"

I shrugged. "Your deal. You know, where you're

from, what kind of warrior you are, why the Protectorate would assign a kid my own age to guard me."

Alexei studied me, as if he couldn't decide whether or not this was some kind of trick to get supersecret Protectorate information out of him. Heh. If I wanted to do that, all I would have to do was touch him. Unlike me, Alexei wasn't wearing gloves. His hands hung bare by his sides, instead of being tucked into his coat pockets like they should have been on such a chilly morning. Maybe the cold didn't bother him. Some of the Mythos kids had magic that made them immune to extreme temperatures.

Even though I'd decided awhile back not to use my magic to pull secrets out of people unless it was absolutely necessary, I couldn't help eyeing his hands and wondering if I could yank off my gloves, touch him, and flash on him with my psychometry before he realized what I was up to. Probably not without an Amazon's quickness.

Still, the temptation to try was so *strong*. I wanted to know what Alexei, and more important, the Protectorate, knew about me. I especially wanted to know what they knew about my touch magic—and if they'd realized that I'd killed Preston with it.

I shivered, but it wasn't because of the chill in the air. A guy's face filled my mind. Once, it had been a handsome face, but now it was twisted with pain, and his blue eyes were cold, dead, and empty—all because of me. Metis and Grandma Frost had always told me that my magic would keep growing, that I'd be able to do other things with it besides just touch objects and see memories, but I never thought I could actually *kill* someone with it. But that's what I'd done to Preston. I'd used my psychometry to kill him so that I could live. That was bad enough, but the worst part was that I knew I could do the same thing again—to anyone, at any time. I could feel the magic, the power, the knowledge deep inside me, a dark whisper that rasped along in time to the beat of my heart. *Use me, use me, use me . . .*

"I'm from Saint Petersburg, Russia," Alexei finally said. He must have decided that my questions were harmless after all. "However, I attend the London academy since that's where my dad spends most of his time with the Protectorate these days. I'm a Bogatyr warrior, and I'm not your age. I'm eighteen, a third-year student."

I rolled my eyes. Yeah, yeah. I knew that all the academies all over the world had the same structure, with first-year students who were sixteen or so all the way up to the sixth-years, who were around twenty-one. Second-year, third-year, it wasn't that big a difference.

"I'm here to guard you because my father is a senior member of the Protectorate, and I'm training to be a member too someday. And also because I'm . . . familiar with some of your classmates."

I raised an eyebrow. "Familiar how? And what's a Bogatyr?"

"We're going to your weapons training now, yes?"

I nodded.

"You'll see."

And that was all he said. He didn't explain anything

else about himself, who he was, or why he was here. Okay, okay, so he wanted to be all dark, brooding, and mysterious, something that his cool Russian accent definitely helped him with. Whatever.

We walked the rest of the way to the gym in silence. I pushed through the double doors that led into the main space and headed for the bleachers on the far side, but Alexei stopped a moment to look around. I didn't see what was so interesting. Bright banners dangling from the ceiling, polished wooden bleachers jutting out from the walls, thick mats covering the floor. The gym looked like any other—except for the racks of weapons.

Since Mythos was a school for the descendants of ancient warriors, gym class was a little more strenuous than just running laps and shooting hoops. Here, gym was really weapons training, where Coach Ajax and the rest of his staff taught us kids how to use everything from swords to staffs to daggers to bows. All those weapons and more were lined up in neat rows, their sharp points glinting underneath the lights, just waiting for the students to come and grab them.

Of course, I hadn't had the lifelong weapons training the other kids had had, which was why I schlepped over to the gym every morning before regular classes started to put in some extra training time with Logan, Kenzie, and Oliver. Since Loki had escaped, Daphne and Carson had started coming too. We all wanted to be ready—for anything.

Everyone except Oliver was already in the gym, and Logan, Kenzie, and Carson were over at the weapons racks figuring out what we were going to practice with today. I put my messenger bag on one of the mats and plopped down on the bleachers next to Daphne. Even though we'd come here to sweat, the Valkyrie looked as pretty as ever in her pink designer yoga pants and matching cropped top. Her blond hair was pulled back into a sleek ponytail, and just the right amount of makeup brought out her dark eyes and the beautiful color of her amber skin.

"I see you brought your shadow with you," Daphne sniped, watching Alexei wander over and put his own bag down on the mat next to mine.

"Be nice," I said. "It's not his fault that he's stuck with me. At least, I don't think it is."

She snorted, but she didn't say anything else. The guys decided on staffs and passed out the weapons. Logan hesitated, then gave a staff to Alexei, who hefted it in his hands with an easy, familiar grace.

"What's a Bogatyr warrior?" I asked Logan when he handed me my own staff. "That's what Alexei said he was."

The two of us watched Alexei work with the staff. He'd gone through a short warm-up and was now twirling the weapon around and around, moving it from one hand to the other as he executed a series of complicated moves. He didn't seem to have a Viking's super-strength, but there was something about the way he moved, flowing from one attack position to the next, that told me he was as dangerous as anyone else at Mythos. The staff kept moving faster and faster in his hands, until it was nothing more than a blur swirling through the air around him. If I hadn't known better, I would have thought him some sort of dancer—he just moved that fluidly, that gracefully.

"Bogatyrs are ancient Russian warriors," Logan said. "They're similar to Romans in that they are exceptionally fast, but the way they move . . . it's like nothing I've ever seen before."

"You mean the way he looks like he's dancing instead of fighting?"

Logan nodded. "I've heard Coach Ajax say that a battle is almost like a dance to them, and the longer a fight goes, the stronger they get because they train themselves to always keep moving, to always keep attacking. They have incredible endurance. Most of them also use two weapons at once, one in either hand, like two swords or two daggers. I'm not sure what other powers they have, but Bogatyrs are some of the fiercest warriors in the Pantheon, right up there with Spartans."

In addition to their inherent warrior strengths and skills, all the kids at Mythos also had other powers, bonus magic as it were, everything from enhanced senses to the ability to heal others to being able to call up storm clouds and control the weather. At Mythos, what kind of warrior you were, what kind of weapon you used, and what kind of magic you had were all just status symbols, along with the kids' expensive cars, designer clothes, and pricey electronics.

We watched Alexei work with the staff. Carson, who also used a staff, seemed especially awestruck by him. The band geek leaned on his own weapon, his face scrunched up in concentration as he tried to follow

Alexei's quick, complicated moves. Kenzie stood beside Carson, also watching Alexei.

Beside me, Logan drew in a breath and let it out. I looked at him, wondering what was on his mind.

"I'm sorry about yesterday," he finally said. "And everything that happened. I still can't believe that my dad is doing this to you, that he thinks you somehow helped the Reapers. I tried to talk to him last night, but he just wouldn't listen to me. He *never* listens to me—about anything."

Bitterness filled Logan's voice, and his eyes were dark and angry. I reached over and threaded my fingers through his. The Spartan's emotions washed over me, the way they always did, but as I held his hand, flickers and flashes of other things began to flood my mind, things I'd never seen before—memories of his dad through the years.

Most of the images were the same—Logan slumped over at a table while his dad paced back and forth in front of him, his face stern, talking in a sharp voice. *Do this. Don't do that. Why can't you get better grades? Why is your room always such a mess? Why don't you straighten up and act like a real warrior, like a real Spartan? Your mother and sister would be so disappointed in you.*

The images and fragments of conversation flashed by one after another, faster and faster, until all I could see, feel, and hear was Linus lecturing his son over and over again, each harsh word hurting more than the last. And I experienced Logan's emotions too—all his anger, frustration, and the aching disappointment in himself that twisted my stomach into tighter and tighter knots.

"It's okay," I said, shaking my head to clear away the feelings and memories. "You don't have any control over what your dad does or what he thinks of me. This is what the Protectorate does, right? Investigate claims that folks are Reapers?"

Logan nodded. "Among other things."

"Don't worry, okay? We'll get through this, just like we always do."

He wrapped his arms around me and drew me close. I breathed in, just enjoying the heat of his touch, the warmth of his body next to mine, the steady *thump-thump-thump* of his heart under my fingers. I didn't know what was going to happen from one day to the next, from one minute to the next, actually, but we were together now, and I was determined to enjoy it while I could. If there was anything that fighting Reapers had taught me, it was to appreciate the good times that much more—because you never knew when they and the people you loved could be taken away from you.

"Anytime you two lovebirds are ready," Daphne called out, twirling her own staff, pink sparks of magic crackling in the air around her. "I don't know about everyone else, but I feel like hitting someone today— *hard*."

Carson winced. "Just don't break my glasses, okay?"

Daphne walked over and kissed him. "Would I do something like that?"

"Well, you wouldn't break *my* glasses," he said. "But you definitely would a Reaper's."

"And that's why you love me and my fierce Valkyrie self," Daphne purred.

Carson smiled and kissed her back. Kenzie laughed.

Logan and I stepped apart. A door at the far end of the gym banged open, and Oliver Hector rushed inside. The Spartan hurried across the mats and slung his bag down with everyone else's. The Spartan turned and smiled.

"Hey, guys, sorry I'm late—"

Oliver's voice cut off the second he spotted Alexei. I'd thought the Spartan would be surprised by Alexei's appearance, but it was almost like Oliver had seen a ghost. All the color drained out of his face, and his green eyes widened, as if he couldn't believe what he was seeing.

"Alexei? What are you doing here?" Oliver said.

Alexei's head snapped up at the sound of the Spartan's voice. He lost his concentration, and the staff that he'd been so gracefully twirling slipped through his fingers and rolled across the mats.

"Oliver! I didn't know if you'd be here this morning or not." Alexei walked over to where Oliver was standing with me and Logan. "I looked for you at the assembly yesterday, but I didn't spot you in the crowd. It's good to see you again."

"I didn't notice you there either." Oliver hesitated. "It's good to see you too."

And that was all they said. The four of us stood there in silence, with Daphne, Carson, and Kenzie looking on.

Finally, I cleared my throat. "Alexei has been assigned by the Protectorate to . . . watch me while they investigate the charges against me."

Oliver's face tightened, and he glared at Alexei. Instead of glaring back at him, a sad look flashed across the Bogatyr's face before he was able to hide it.

"I will go work with the Valkyrie and the Celt," Alexei said in a stiff voice. He turned and walked away.

"I'll help them get started," Logan said and headed after him.

I raised my eyebrows at Oliver, waiting for him to explain. He sighed and ran a hand through his sandy blond hair. He looked at me, as if hoping that I'd leave things alone. Please. He knew me better than that. I crossed my arms over my chest and kept staring at him.

"Spill it, Spartan," I said. "Because it's obvious that today isn't the first time you and Alexei have met."

Oliver sighed again. "Alexei is the guy I was telling you about. The one I've been texting with."

"The one you met over winter break?"

He nodded.

"Oh. *Oh*."

Oliver was gay, and for a long time, he'd had a crush on Kenzie, who was his best friend and straight. But Oliver had told me that he'd met someone over the holidays, someone he thought might have boyfriend potential. I'd just never thought that person would be Alexei.

Oliver stared at me, his eyes searching mine. "I've texted with Alexei a few times since the break, but he didn't tell me that he was coming to Mythos. He didn't tell me about any of this. If he had, I would have warned you. You know that, Gwen."

I did know that. The Spartan was one of my friends, and he'd tell me if he knew something bad was going to happen to me, just like I would tell him. Well, I guess this explained why Alexei had said he was familiar with me and my friends—Oliver had probably told him all about me, Logan, and everyone else.

Part of me couldn't help but be a little pissed about that. My magic let me know other people's secrets—I didn't like it when folks knew mine. Plus, Oliver had been my friend first, before he'd ever met Alexei. He should be taking my side in this and vowing not to have anything else to do with Alexei—ever. And I knew he would do that, if I asked him to.

But then Oliver looked at the Russian warrior, and I saw the longing in his face. It was obvious that Oliver had a crush on Alexei. I knew how hard it had been for him to watch Kenzie start dating Talia, and I didn't want Oliver to miss out on finding happiness because of me. I sighed. Sometimes, being a friend meant muzzling your inner, petty, jealous bitch, and this was one of those times.

"Well, I have to say that you have good taste," I drawled. "He's really cute, if you like dark, brooding warriors. And that Russian accent is wicked cool. Why, I'd almost think about dating him myself, if it wasn't for Logan and that whole pesky *Gwen's-on-trial* thing. And if he wasn't more interested in you than me."

Oliver rolled his eyes. "Have I ever told you that being your friend is impossible, Gypsy?"

"Only once or twice, Spartan. Now, go over there and let the Bogatyr know that the two of you are cool. As long as he's here at Mythos, you might as well get to know him better. He could still turn out to be a toad, or he might just be your Prince Charming. Only one way to find out."

Oliver flashed me a grateful smile and went over to the others. He and Alexei walked away from everyone else, and the two warriors started talking. Oliver said something, and a small smile broke out on Alexei's face. For the first time, I realized that maybe something good could come out this whole horrible situation.

At this point, that small hope was the only one I had.

Chapter 7

My friends and I sparred in the gym for the rest of training time before going back to our dorm rooms to shower and change. Thirty minutes after that, I was sitting with Logan in the dining hall. Usually, I ate with Daphne and Carson, but the two of them had to go to some meeting about the winter band concert, and since our date had gotten interrupted yesterday, Logan had suggested that we eat breakfast alone together.

Well, us and Alexei.

He'd disappeared to shower and change just like the rest of us had, but once again he'd been waiting outside my dorm room when I'd opened the door. Now, he stood a few feet away with his black bag at his feet and his back against the wall. Alexei stood next to one of the many suits of armor in the dining hall, looking just as solid, still, and imposing as the metal figure. A large oil painting of some great mythological feast hung on the wall above his head.

With its paintings, suits of armor, and tables topped with fine white linens, delicate china, and gleaming flatware, the dining hall was way, way more upscale than your typical school cafeteria. In fact, it looked more like an elegant restaurant than a place where students ate on a daily basis. Adding to the illusion was an open-air indoor garden that stood in the middle of the enormous room. Olive, orange, and almond trees rose up into the air, while grapevines snaked up, around, and over all the branches, before plunging into the black soil. Statues could also be seen in the garden, food and harvest gods mostly, like Dionysus and Demeter. The statues were hidden here and there among the trees and twisting vines, although their faces stared out at the students as they ate.

Unfortunately, the food was even fancier than the décor. Lobster, veal, and escargot were among the daily items on the lunch line, all of which the academy kids loved. Yucko. Even when it came to more normal food, like cheeseburgers, pizza, and lasagna, the Mythos chefs were always using exotic ingredients and whipping up weird sauces to serve them with, which completely ruined the dishes. At least for me.

I didn't have much of an appetite so I just picked at my ambrosia fruit salad drizzled with honey-lime dressing, moving strawberries and kiwis from one side of my bowl to the other, even though it was one of my favorite items on the breakfast menu. Meanwhile, Logan scarfed down a pile of pancetta and his second Greek omelet topped with spinach and thick crumbles of feta cheese. I sighed, put my fork down, and pushed away my bowl.

"Do you want me to get you something else, Gypsy

girl?" Logan asked. "The chefs set up a smoothie station this morning."

I didn't want a smoothie, but he was trying to make me feel better, so I forced myself to smile. "Sure, that would be great. Maybe mango, if they have it?"

Logan grinned. "I'll be back in a minute."

The Spartan grabbed his now-empty plate, probably to get another omelet while he waited for the chefs to make my smoothie. Alexei watched him go, but he didn't move from his spot beside the wall. He hadn't gotten anything for himself, not so much as a bottle of water or a granola bar. I wondered if not dining with the enemy was some kind of Protectorate protocol.

I looked at him, then gestured at the table. "You can sit down with us, you know. I'm not going to bite you."

Alexei gave me a cool stare. "Members of the Protectorate, even those who are only in training like me, take our responsibilities very seriously. We do not eat with people we are supposed to be keeping an eye on."

Apparently, I'd been right about the protocol thing. Yeah for me.

"I'm not some kind of criminal," I muttered. "I didn't do anything wrong."

"No, you just let Loki escape from his prison and doomed the entire world. Isn't that right, Gwen?"

I looked up to find Helena Paxton standing on the opposite side of the table—and she wasn't alone. Her Amazon friends stood on either side of her, along with several guys. Anger filled all their faces, and the emotion rolled off them in hot, furious waves.

I pushed my chair back and got to my feet. Helena jerked her head, and her friends formed a loose circle around me, trapping me between them and the table. The conversation around us died down, as the other kids in the dining hall stopped eating and turned to stare at us.

"Are you enjoying your breakfast, Gwen?" Helena asked in a sweet voice. "It looks like you've hardly eaten a thing. Maybe your conscience is finally bothering you. It should."

I didn't say anything. There was no point in it. Helena hated me, and she wouldn't believe a word I said anyway. But my silence only made her angrier. She stepped forward, her eyes narrowing to slits.

"I can't believe you just walked in here this morning like everything was okay, like we all don't know what you did—and what a traitorous Reaper bitch you are."

The kids circled around me murmured their agreement. My gaze went from one face to the next, but I all saw was anger—anger and no mercy. I wasn't psychic, not like Grandma Frost was, but I knew what would happen now. The other kids couldn't take their rage and frustration out on the Reapers who'd murdered their loved ones, so they were going to lash out at the next best thing—me.

"I didn't do what the Protectorate says I did," I replied. "I didn't do anything wrong."

How many times would I have to say those words before people believed me? I could scream them for hours, and it wouldn't make a difference. Not after the assembly. And especially not right now.

Helena arched an eyebrow. "Really? Because I remember seeing you at the Crius Coliseum the day the other students were murdered. My friend, Samantha Diego, was one of the girls who got killed. Tell me, Gwen, was it you who stabbed her in the back? Or one of your Reaper friends?"

More murmurs of agreement filled the air, even uglier and harsher than before, and the students around me crept forward. For the first time, I noticed that many of them had their weapons in their hands, swords and daggers mostly. That was bad enough, but what made my heart quiver with fear was the way the other kids were clenching the hilts and skimming their fingers along the sharp blades, like they were thinking about using them.

On me.

Panic pulsed through my body, but I made myself stand still. I looked past the ring of students, but I didn't see Logan. I scanned the rest of the dining hall, but I didn't spot any of my other friends either. It took me a few more seconds to realize that all the chefs had suddenly, mysteriously, vanished as well. In fact, I didn't see any adults dishing up pancakes and waffles at the food stations closest to my table, no professors eating their own breakfast, no staff members grabbing a cup of coffee before heading out to do their morning chores. Even more ominous was the fact that all the statues in the garden had dropped their heads and were staring at the grapevines twisted around their feet, as if they didn't want to see what was about to happen.

Desperate now, I looked over at Alexei. His job was

to guard me. I hoped it meant protecting me too, because this was not going to end well—for me.

Alexei pushed away from the wall. Hope sparked in my chest that he would grab his two swords out of his backpack and come to my defense, but all he did was stand there. He didn't make any move to break up the mob that had circled me. I wondered if Linus had ordered Alexei to let the other kids do whatever they wanted to me. That would be one way for me to be punished—for me to be executed.

I wondered if Alexei would stop after the kids had beaten me or if he'd actually let them murder me right here in the dining hall. An image of my dead, broken body lying on the floor popped into my mind, my blood oozing over the marble, the scarlet stream getting soaked up by the black dirt in the garden and feeding the gnarled vines there—

I shook my head, banishing the image. That wasn't going to happen. I wasn't going to let it happen. I might not be as skilled a fighter as the other students, but I'd defend myself as best I could, even if I knew I wouldn't win in the end. Not against so many other kids.

Too bad I'd put Vic and my messenger bag underneath the table when Logan and I had first sat down. I could just see the bag's strap peeking out from beneath the white tablecloth on the far side of the chair I was standing next to. My heart sank. I knew I wouldn't be able to get to the sword in time, but I still had to try. It was all I could do.

I took a step back so I could get around the chair, but

I bumped into a guy standing behind me. I whirled around, and the upperclassman brandished a sword at me and grinned. I tried to move to my left to get away from him, and one of the Amazons stopped me. I shifted back to my right, and there was Helena, holding a dagger.

"Did you really think you would get away with it?" Helena snarled. "Killing our friends at the coliseum. Letting Loki loose. All of that is your fault, Gwen— *your fault*. People are dead, our friends and family are dead because of what you've done. Well, I say that we get our revenge on *you*, right here, right now."

The ring of kids muttered their agreement and crept even closer to me. Once more, I looked at Alexei, but he stood in the same position as before, his arms still hanging by his sides, his face completely blank. No help there. Looked like it was up to me to save myself—or die trying.

Helena took another menacing step toward me, the dagger flashing in her hand, and I reached out and grabbed my fork off the table. It wasn't much of a weapon, but hopefully I could surprise her with it, shove her away, and break free of the mob before they all piled in on me—

"Leave her alone," a low voice growled.

Logan pushed his way through the kids until he was standing by my side. The Spartan was holding a plate with another omelet on it, along with a tall, frosty glass that contained my mango smoothie. The sight of the bright orange liquid made my stomach twist that much more.

"Get out of the way, Quinn," Helena snapped. "This is between us and Gwen."

Helena and the guy with the sword stepped forward again, and Logan moved to shield me from them—all of them. His blue eyes narrowed, and his hands tightened around the plate and the glass.

"I suggest you leave now," Logan said in a dangerous tone. "Before I show you just how deadly Spartans can be."

Everyone froze. All the Mythos kids knew about Spartans and their killer instinct, how they could pick up any weapon—or any *thing*—and automatically know how to kill people with it. That's why Logan rarely carried a weapon. He didn't need to, since he could grab whatever was handy and fight with it. He was only holding a plate and a glass, but he might as well have been brandishing two swords.

Helena sucked in a breath. For a moment, I thought she would lunge forward and try to stab me with the dagger, but she slowly tucked it back into the purse hanging off her arm. The guy with the sword lowered his weapon as well. Alexei also moved back, crossed his arms over his chest, and assumed his position against the wall once more.

"This isn't over, Gwen," Helena spat out. "If the Protectorate doesn't make you pay for what you've done, then we *will*. Do yourself a favor, and leave Mythos while you still can. Or do us all one and stay here so we can deal with you ourselves. Win-win for us, either way."

The Amazon smirked at me, then turned and stalked off to her table a few feet away. One by one, her friends followed her, and the other kids headed back to their seats as well. Still, only hushed whispers filled the dining hall, and everyone kept staring at me, wondering what I would do now.

"C'mon. Let's get out of here," Logan said, putting down the dishes.

I bit my lip, nodded, and got my messenger bag out from underneath the table. The Spartan grabbed my hand, and we headed for the doors. To my surprise, instead of following along behind me like he usually did, Alexei fell in step with us and flanked me on the other side.

Just before we stepped outside, something slammed into my back. I froze, wondering if someone had shot an arrow at me, but it didn't hurt enough for that. A second later, the thing on my back slid off and clattered to the floor, and I realized what had happened—someone had thrown a plate of food at me.

I looked over my shoulder at the mess. Chunks of Logan's omelet were sticking to the back of my gray hoodie, sprayed across my back like the paint on my dorm room door, while the plate had broken into a dozen pieces. I reached back and felt a few chunks of cheese sticking to my hair. Ugh.

"Bull's-eye." Helena's voice rang out loud and clear, and she started laughing.

Anger, frustration, and embarrassment made my cheeks burn, but I didn't give Helena the satisfaction of turning around and glaring at her. That would only make the Amazon laugh louder and make her that much more determined to torture me.

Instead, I straightened up and walked out of the dining hall, the cruel laughter of the other students ringing in my ears and adding to the misery already in my heart.

Chapter 8

My day didn't get any better after that.

After going back to my room to shower and change again, I went to my morning classes. I sat in my usual seats and tried to concentrate on all the lectures and homework assignments, but I was always aware of Alexei standing in the corners of the rooms, watching me.

Actually, he had to stand in the corners, since the other students pulled their desks away from mine as soon as I stepped into the classrooms. The first time it happened, I thought maybe we were breaking into study groups, so I got to my feet and started to scoot my desk around with everyone else's, until the Viking in front of me turned around and glared at me.

"You stay right where you are, Reaper," he hissed as he grabbed a desk in each hand, lifted them up, and carried them across the room.

Seconds later, I was sitting by myself in the middle of the floor with everyone lined up on the opposite side of the room. Even worse, they were all staring at me with hate-filled eyes, including Mrs. Melete, my English-lit professor.

The same thing happened in my other classes. Desks pulled away, me sitting alone, everyone glaring at me.

At lunch, I raced over to the dining hall, grabbed a soda and a hot, grilled ham-and-swiss panini off the lunch line, and ran back to my dorm room before anyone could come after me again. Alexei trailed behind me the whole while, easily keeping up with my quick strides. Once again, he didn't get anything to eat. I was starting to wonder if he just existed on air, silence, and fixed stares.

I climbed the stairs to my room and was reaching for my key to go inside when I noticed that someone had tagged my door and walls again. Grandma Frost had gotten the worst of the graffiti off last night, but someone had come along and traced over the words in Reaper-red paint again.

MURDERER. KILLER. REAPER BITCH.

My stomach clenched, and tears pricked my eyes, but I blinked them back just like I'd been doing all morning. Alexei stood beside me, staring at the door, his expression as blank as ever.

"Here," I muttered, thrusting the bag with the panini in it into his hand. "You might as well eat this. I don't want it anymore."

I went into my room and shut the door behind me, leaving Alexei out in the hallway. I stood there in the middle of the turret, just breathing—in and out, in and out, in and out. I wasn't going to cry. *I was not going to cry.* I wasn't going to give Helena, her friends, and everyone else that satisfaction, even if no one was around to see me break down.

My emotions seesawed from upset and scared to sad and melancholy to indignant and angry. Once again, I latched on to the anger, remembering every insult, every curse, every enraged glare, and imagined stacking them together like bricks around my heart to block out the pain.

It took several minutes, but I finally felt calm enough to get ready for the rest of the day. The first thing I did was swap out the books for my morning classes for the ones I'd need this afternoon. It didn't make me feel any better, but at least it kept me busy for a few minutes.

Vic's eye snapped open as I pulled him out of my messenger bag and propped him up on my desk. "Don't worry, Gwen. It'll be okay. You'll see. You're not the first student who's ever been falsely accused of being a Reaper. Once the Protectorate clears you of all the charges, things will go back to normal."

I thought of the rage and disgust that I'd seen in all my classmates' eyes today, as well as in the faces of my professors and everyone else.

I shook my head. "I don't think things will ever be the same again. The way everyone looked at me today . . . like I was a bug they wanted to crush under their shoes . . . the absolute hate in their eyes . . ."

Emotion clogged my throat and made it hard to speak, but once again I managed to hold back the tears. "And I could feel it all, you know. With my magic. I could feel exactly how much everyone despises me. It was like a sword slicing into my heart over and over again. It hurt worse than anything else I've ever felt before, even when Preston stabbed me."

I rubbed a spot right over my heart. Despite the fact that Metis had used her healing magic on me, I had a thin scar on my chest from Preston's attack. Another scar sliced across my right palm where Vivian had cut me with the Helheim Dagger. Metis said that sometimes artifacts as powerful as the dagger made wounds or left behind scars that just wouldn't heal or fade away no matter how much magic you used on them. Today, I felt like I had another scar to go along with those, only this one was on the inside where no one could see it—except me.

"Gwen?" Vic asked.

"And it only got worse as the day went on," I continued in a dull tone. "It was like the longer people looked at me, the more they hated me. So no, I don't think things will ever get back to normal. I don't even think I know what *normal* is anymore."

Vic gave me a sympathetic look, but he didn't try to soothe my worries again. He was a sword, after all, something made to do battle. Vic knew as well as I did that at the end of the day someone had to step up and fight the Reapers. And right now, that someone was me—even if this battle was only against my classmates' fear, frustration, and anger.

My gaze landed on the photos of my mom propped up on my desk. One showed my mom when she was about my age, her arms around Metis's back when they'd both been Mythos students. The other was a more recent photo, one she'd had taken shortly before her death last year. I grabbed that photo, sat down on my bed, and pulled the picture out of the frame. As I ran my hands over the slick, glossy surface, images of my mom flooded my mind, along with my love for her— and all the love she'd had for me too.

Violet eyes are smiling eyes, my mom's voice whispered in my mind. It was something she'd always jokingly said, since she had the same strangely colored eyes that Grandma and I did. I focused on her voice, replaying her words over and over again, until all I could hear was the love and laughter in her tone, until all I could see was the light in her eyes and the soft, knowing curve of her smile.

I concentrated on those images and feelings, pulling them up and letting them fill my mind, my body, my heart, letting them wash away all the anger I'd felt surging off the other students. Those images of my mom, the love she'd had for me, made me feel just a smidge better and gave me the strength to face the rest of the day.

I sat on my bed holding her picture until it was time for my next class.

I put my head down and just tried to get through the rest of the day without drawing any more attention to myself, but of course my afternoon classes passed even slower than the morning ones had. Even Professor Metis's myth-history class, which was normally one of my favorites, was torturously long.

At least in that one, I didn't have to sit by myself. Carson kept his desk right where it was in front of mine, and the band geek glared back at all the kids staring at me, almost like he was shielding me from their accusing looks. I would have leaned forward and hugged him, if that wouldn't have made the other kids angrier at him than they already were for sticking up for me.

Finally, sixth period ended, and I schlepped back to my dorm. Normally, I would have snuck off campus to go see Grandma Frost, but the Protectorate had told me to stay put. I doubted Alexei would let me get within ten feet of the academy walls anyway, since he took his guard duty so seriously. Plus, the Protectorate had probably put some magic mumbo jumbo on the sphinxes at the gates just to make doubly sure I stayed on the grounds right where they wanted me.

Besides, Grandma would take one look at me and demand to know what was wrong, and I didn't feel like talking about it. All I wanted to do was forget that today had ever happened, even though I knew I never would.

I stayed in my room for a while, reading comic books, but the bright, colorful pages failed to cheer me up like usual. I couldn't really concentrate on the stories anyway, not today, so I got my things together and headed over to the Library of Antiquities.

Once again, Alexei was waiting outside, and he snapped to attention as soon as I opened the door. He'd been quiet all day long, barely speaking to me. Daphne was right. He was like a shadow—a very dark, dangerous, brooding shadow. I wondered what he would do if I tried to make a break for it. Probably chase me down, catch me, and drag me off to the academy prison. I had no false hopes that I could outrun or outfight the Bogatyr warrior. I'd seen Alexei working out in the gym this morning, so I knew how tough and strong he was. He'd probably gone through a bunch of superspecial Protectorate training to make him even harder to beat than he naturally was.

"I'm going to the library," I told him. "I work there a couple of afternoons a week as sort of an after-school job."

Alexei shrugged, like it was of no interest to him what I did or didn't do. I rolled my eyes, locked the door, and headed down the stairs.

I walked over to the library, with Alexei trailing along behind me. It was after four now, and students were moving back and forth across campus, going from the main quad down to their dorms and back again, as they went to whatever club meetings, sports, or after-school activities they were involved in. I spotted Carson rushing toward the gym, pages and pages of sheet music clutched in his hands as he headed to band practice.

Carson was a Celt, a warrior bard, which meant that he had an innate talent for music. He could play practically any instrument he picked up, and he was one of the leaders of the band. Ever since we'd come back from the holiday break, he'd been talking almost nonstop about all the preparations the group was making for its annual winter concert, something that was taking place Saturday in the Aoide Auditorium down in Asheville.

Carson waved at me, and I waved back—and then realized that I shouldn't have. The motion only drew more attention to me from the kids milling around on the quad.

"Traitor."

"Murderer."

"Reaper bitch."

Those were some of the nicer things the other students muttered as I walked past them. If Alexei heard the Greek chorus of mean, he gave no indication. I was beginning to wonder whether he ever did anything but look blankly at other people. Other than that soft smile he'd given Oliver this morning, his expression hadn't changed all day long. Or maybe that was just because I was public enemy number one at Mythos.

As I hurried toward the library, I realized that not all of the kids were going to be content with just cursing at me. A couple of guys broke away from their group of friends and started following me across the quad.

"Where are you off to, Reaper girl?" one of them called out. "Got some more of our friends to kill? Going to run through some more kids with your sword?"

Anger surged through me at his words, and my steps slowed. For a moment, I thought about turning around and confronting the guys, but there was no point in it. They would believe what they wanted to about me, and nothing I said would change their minds. Besides, out of the corner of my eye, I saw another guy moving off to my left, flanking me. I didn't want a repeat of what had happened in the dining hall this morning—especially since Logan wasn't around to help me.

I quickened my pace, and the guys following me did as well, their hoots and hollers growing louder and louder the faster I walked. I'd just reached the library steps when the guy on my left threw his soda at me. I managed to jump back before the can hit me, but the liquid inside still splattered all over my jeans. I was so surprised that I just stood there, staring down at my soaked pants.

Of course, the guys who'd been following me thought this was the funniest thing *ever*. A second later, another can of soda came my way. I managed to avoid this one too, and it sailed through the air and hit one of the gryphon statues that were planted on either side of the library steps.

Eagle heads; lion bodies; wings tucked in against their sides; razor-sharp beaks; long, curved claws that glinted in the weak winter sun. The gryphons were some of the fiercest-looking statues at Mythos. For months, I'd found all of the statues to be sinister and creepy with their all-seeing eyes, but the gryphons had especially freaked me out since it seemed like they were *always* watching me, more so than any of the other statues, even the sphinxes. But ever since I'd learned that my mom had hidden the Helheim Dagger in a secret compartment in the base of one of the statues, I'd come to admire the gryphons and think of them as protectors of the entire academy—including me.

So while maybe I deserved to get doused with soda, the statue did not. Instead of hurrying up the steps before I got beaned in the head by another can, I walked over to the gryphon statue, grabbed a pack of tissues out of my messenger bag, and started wiping the sticky, orange-colored liquid off the dark gray stone.

"Sorry about all this," I mumbled. "It's me they're really after, not you. Because of what happened with the dagger. Because the Reaper girl used it to free Loki."

The gryphon didn't speak to me, but it almost seemed like its eyes narrowed in thought. Okay, protector or not, that was still a little creepy.

I managed to wipe off the last of the soda. I glanced over my shoulder at the guys, who were still watching me. One of them had another can, this one unopened, which he viciously shook. He smiled at his friends, then started walking toward me, the can held out in front of him. I sighed. I knew what was coming next—Gwen getting sprayed in the face.

I thought about going inside the building, but the guy would probably just follow and unleash the soda on me as soon as he got close enough. No doubt that would happen when I was in the middle of the library and among all of Nickamedes's precious books. I weighed getting a lecture from the librarian versus getting soaked out here on the steps. I decided to get soaked. Nickamedes and I were on better terms these days, but I still didn't want to give him any reason to be upset with me. Getting soda all over his books would do it, even if it wasn't my fault. Oh, I knew he wouldn't be mad at me, given the circumstances, but a ruined book was still a ruined book. My day had already sucked. There was no need to make his as bad as mine had been.

But that didn't mean I was going down without a fight.

I knew better than to draw Vic out of my bag. If I did that, the guys would pull out their own weapons, and things would be even worse than they had been in the dining hall. So instead, I reached into my messenger bag, my fingers clutching around my own soda, the one I'd grabbed during lunch and hadn't drunk yet. If I was getting soaked, then so was the guy coming at me.

The guy reached the bottom of the library steps. He grinned at his friends, then turned and headed in my direction—

A low growl ripped through the air.

The guy stopped. His head snapped left, then right, as he tried to figure out where the sound had come from. After a second, he shrugged it off as just his imagination and started up the steps again.

Once more, a low growl sounded.

The guy took a step back, suddenly uncertain. The growl kept going and going, like a rumbling train getting a little louder and a little closer with each passing second. His friends also looked around, confused by what was happening. I was the only one who noticed that the eyes of the gryphon statue had narrowed to slits and that its angry gaze was fixed on the guy in front of me.

The guy looked at me, and I casually crossed my arms across my chest and leaned against the statue. He stared at me, and I glared right back at him.

"She's not worth it," he finally muttered to his friends. "Let's get out of here. I'm freezing my ass off."

Grumbling, the guys headed the opposite direction across the quad. I stood in my tough-girl pose until they were out of sight, then I sighed and slumped against the gryphon.

"Thank you for that," I whispered.

The side of the gryphon's mouth curled up, almost like it was smiling. I patted it on the head, then turned to go inside the library.

Alexei, who'd been hanging back through all of this, finally stepped forward. He gave me a strange look, as if he couldn't believe that I was talking to a statue, but at this point, I didn't care what he thought of me.

"You can stand out here in the cold if you want, but I'm going inside the library where it's warm," I said, walking away.

I reached the doors that led inside the library and looked over my shoulder. Alexei was following me, although he was striding up the exact center of the steps, giving the gryphon statues suspicious looks and as wide a berth as he possibly could. For the first time today, a smile pulled up my lips.

Maybe there was something to be said for creepy statues after all.

Chapter 9

I went inside the building, walked down a hallway, and stepped through the open double doors into the main space of the Library of Antiquities.

With its seven stories, the library was the largest building on campus, and it simply had the biggest and best of everything—the widest balconies, the tallest towers, the most lifelike statues. And it was just as impressive inside as it was on the outside. The main room was shaped like an enormous dome that let folks on the first floor gaze up at each one of the library's many levels. Supposedly, the curved ceiling featured amazing frescoes, images of great mythological battles, embellished with layers of gold, silver, and sparkling jewels. But I'd never been up to the top level to look for myself, and all I could see from the ground floor were shadows. Maybe it was better that way, since the statues of the gods were already staring at me.

The second floor of the library featured a balcony that boasted white marble statues of all the gods and goddesses from all the cultures of the world. Egyptian deities like Ra and Anubis. Norse gods like Odin and Thor. Native American figures like the Coyote Trickster and Rabbit. The only god who wasn't featured in the circular pantheon was Loki, and there was an empty spot where his statue would have been.

After seeing the evil god in person, I was glad there wasn't a statue of him here or anywhere else on campus. He terrorized my dreams enough already, his one red eye burning into both of mine. I already had to live with the sick knowledge of how I'd failed everyone. I didn't need to look up and see Loki's twisted face grinning down at me, another reminder of the horror I'd unleashed and the death and destruction that he and his Reapers of Chaos were planning.

Instead of going down the main aisle toward the checkout counter, I headed back into the stacks. Alexei followed me, still as silent as a shadow. I kept going until I came to a familiar, remote spot, then looked up. Nike's statue stood right above me.

The Greek goddess of victory looked the same as she always did. A toga-like gown wrapping around her body, ringlets of hair falling past her slim shoulders, wings peeking up over her back, a crown of laurels resting on her head. Every time I came into the library, I took a moment to walk back here and speak to the goddess. It seemed like the polite thing to do.

"Well, here I am in trouble again," I murmured. "But I'm sure you already know all about it. You always seem to know everything. Want to give me some clue as to how I can get out of this? Without being executed?"

But of course, she didn't answer me. Like the other gods, Nike only appeared to mortals on her own terms, and I was no different, despite the fact that I was her Champion. She was rather mysterious—and annoying—that way.

Then again, the goddess was probably busy trying to fix the mess I'd made by not stopping Vivian from freeing Loki. Nike had told me that there was a war coming, one we all needed to prepare for, including the gods. But how could I help her win a war when I was in danger of losing everything?

"Anyway, I'm going to go to work now. But if you want to drop by the checkout counter later, well, I'll be there, just like always," I told the statue. "Just don't let Nickamedes see you. He'd probably tell you that togas aren't allowed in the library or something silly like that. You know how he is."

The statue's lips lifted up into a smile at my words. It was a small gesture, but it made me feel a little better, like Nike knew exactly what was going on and she hadn't forgotten about me. Like she was watching out for me. Like she knew that everything was going to be okay in the end.

Alexei gave me a wary look, obviously thinking I had a serious case of the cray-cray and was off my rocker for talking to yet another statue, but I ignored him and headed to the main part of the library. As soon as I stepped out of the stacks, all eyes turned to me, and the students sitting at the study tables put their heads together and started whispering. I squared my shoulders, lifted my chin, and pretended I didn't even see them, much less realize that they were talking and texting about me.

"I can't believe she actually showed her face here."

"What is she thinking?"

"Doesn't she know that everyone hates her?"

I snorted at that last comment. Oh yeah. I knew *exactly* how much everyone despised me, since they'd all made it so abundantly clear all day long.

I stepped behind the long checkout counter that divided the library in two and slung my messenger bag down into its usual spot. I turned to Alexei and pointed to a stool at the far end of the counter.

"You can sit over there," I said. "It'll be more comfortable than standing around while I work."

Instead of moving over to the stool, he crossed his arms over his chest and took up a spot by the door that led into the glass complex where the librarians had their offices. Definitely a silent, stubborn shadow. Ah, well. I'd tried.

I put Alexei out of my mind as I plopped down onto my own stool. A few seconds later, a door behind me squeaked open, and Nickamedes stepped out of the office complex. The librarian looked at me, then did a double take, as if he was surprised to see me.

"Gwendolyn? What are you doing here?" He looked down and checked his watch. "It's not even five o'clock. You're early. You are *never* early."

I bit my tongue to keep from sniping at him. I didn't always show up exactly on time for my library shifts. Okay, okay, so I was almost always late, but only because I snuck off campus to go see Grandma Frost. I got here eventually. But apparently, my being on time was more of a shock than I'd realized because he kept right on talking about it.

"Not once, in all the months you've been working here, have you ever been *early*. On time, occasionally. Late, excessively. But never, ever *early*." Nickamedes's eyes narrowed. "What are you up to?"

My jaw clenched. Even when I did the right thing, he *still* gave me grief over it. Sometimes, I thought the librarian and I were just destined to disagree.

"I thought you might need some extra help today," I said through gritted teeth. "But if you don't want me here, I can always leave and came back later. Much later, like I normally do. Maybe I'll be so late that I won't show up until tomorrow."

The librarian frowned. "Well, if you want to come in early today, I *suppose* it will make up for one of the times you've been late in the past. But only one. I keep a record, you know."

Of course he did. Nickamedes was just that kind of obsessive control freak. Despite the fact that there were other librarians, Nickamedes was almost always here working. I wondered if he ever took a day off. I doubted it. Someone might shelve a book in the wrong place if he wasn't here to watch over everything.

His tone was just as snarky as mine was, but after a moment his features softened a bit. "And if any of the students have any particular problems this evening, you come and get me immediately. Do you understand?"

I nodded. I knew exactly what *problems* he was talking about—the ones everybody had with me now.

"And you." He fixed Alexei with a stern stare. "Your job is to *protect* Gwendolyn, not just watch her like a hawk. I suggest you do that, rather than standing by like a rock as you've been doing. The Protectorate isn't the only one with eyes and ears around campus."

Alexei flushed a little. "I'm just doing what the Protectorate has told me to do."

Nickamedes arched a black eyebrow. "Really? Because I thought the Protectorate was in the business of protecting the students here—not letting them be hurt, abused, and bullied by their classmates."

So the librarian had heard how the other kids had been treating me. No surprise there. You'd have to be blind not to see the anger simmering in everyone's eyes whenever they looked at me. Still, Nickamedes's concern touched me. The librarian and I didn't always get along, but I knew that he cared about me in his own way.

"I'm fine," I said. "I can fight my own battles. That's what Champions do, right?"

Nickamedes stared at me. After a moment, he nodded. "That you can, Gwendolyn. But sometimes it doesn't hurt to have someone watching your back. Someone who actually *cares*."

He gave Alexei another pointed look, then went back into the office complex.

Hot tears pricked my eyes for what seemed like the hundredth time today. Now, even Nickamedes was being nice to me, which told me exactly how much trouble I was in. I wondered what would happen tomorrow during my trial and how the Protectorate would ultimately rule. Would they agree that I'd been fooled by Vivian? Or would they think that I'd helped her? That I'd freed Loki on purpose?

I didn't know the answers to my questions, and I knew that worrying would just drive me crazy. Well, crazier. So I logged on to one of the library computers, determined to get to work and not think about the Protectorate, Vivian, or Loki.

As I glanced out at the study tables in front of the checkout counter, I realized that all the students were looking at me once again. I looked from one face to another, and they all met my gaze with hard, flat stares, anger glimmering in their eyes and radiating off their bodies.

I sighed. It was going to be a long, long night.

I spent the next hour sitting at the checkout counter— alone. No one came over to find out where a book was shelved. No one asked me to track down reference material. No one needed any help at all. Instead, the other students just sat and stared at me, whispering to each other. In a way, it was worse than it had been at breakfast, since the library was one of the places where kids came to Hang Out and Be Seen.

Just as many students were here as had been in the dining hall this morning, and with me sitting behind the checkout counter, it was almost like I was on display for everyone to glare at. More than a few kids walked by the counter and muttered curses at me under their breath. Some were bolder and spoke loudly enough for everyone at the study tables to hear.

Apparently, it became some sort of game because after the kids passed by me, they went back to their seats, high-fiving and fist-bumping with their friends, before they all dissolved into fits of laughter. My cheeks burned, but I ignored them as best I could. Behind me, Alexei stood against the wall, his face as expressionless as ever. He could give Coach Ajax a run for his money in the stoic department.

Since no one was going to come over to the counter to ask me for help, I decided to shelve books. That way, I wouldn't be a sitting duck, and the other kids would actually have to get up and make an effort in order to glare at me. So I grabbed one of the metal carts and pushed it back into the stacks. The wheels *squeak-squeak-squeaked* the whole time, but I didn't care. All I wanted to do right now was get away from the other kids and their anger. At least for a few minutes.

But there was no escaping Alexei. He followed me into the stacks and stayed right behind me, just like always.

"Geez," I muttered. "Don't you ever take a break?"

Alexei arched an eyebrow, but he didn't say anything. Of course he didn't. I was a dangerous Reaper criminal. His job was to watch me, not talk to me.

I ignored Alexei as best I could as I pushed the cart through the stacks. I actually didn't mind shelving books because it gave me an opportunity to look at all the artifacts on display.

The Library of Antiquities was full of, well, antiquities. Armor, weapons, jewelry, clothes, and more that gods, goddesses, warriors, and mythological creatures had used over the centuries they'd been battling each other. Hundreds of glass cases stood inside the library, each one containing something different. Like a pair of talon-tipped gloves that had been worn by Bastet, the Egyptian cat goddess. Or a gold coin that had come from the treasure trove of Andvari, a dwarf in Norse mythology.

When I'd first come to Mythos, I thought all the artifacts and the plaques and cards that told about their histories, users, and supposed magic had been kind of lame, but now I thought they were some of the most interesting things on campus. Besides, tonight, reading about other warriors and their possessions gave me a much-needed escape from my own problems.

It only took me twenty minutes to shelve all the books, but I stayed back in the stacks for two hours, just wandering from one bookshelf, one row, one display case, to the next. Alexei trailed along behind me the whole time. The good thing about him being so quiet was that he didn't complain when I finally parked the empty cart in an aisle next to the office complex, sat down on the floor, and pulled my knees up to my chest. I stayed like that for a long time, staring off into space and worrying about the Protectorate and what the rest of the Powers That Were planned to do to me tomorrow during my trial—

A sharp *bang* snapped me out of my thoughts. A second later, a voice drifted over to me—a loud, angry voice.

"This is unacceptable, Nickamedes. Completely unacceptable."

I looked over at Alexei. He'd heard the noises too because he'd turned in the direction of the sound and was peering through a gap in the bookshelf at something. I scrambled to my feet and hurried over to stand beside him.

Nickamedes stood on the back side of the glass office complex, away from the students and study tables—along with Linus Quinn. The two men had their arms crossed over their chests, glaring at each other.

"No, Linus," Nickamedes snapped. "What is unacceptable is the way you are persecuting Gwendolyn for something she didn't do. You read my report. And Aurora's and Ajax's and even Raven's. You know what happened that night and how Loki really got free. But yet, here you are, putting an innocent girl on trial."

Alexei pointed at the far end of the bookshelf, silently telling me that we should walk away from the adults. I shook my head and stayed where I was. Yeah, maybe it was wrong, but I was totally eavesdropping on this conversation. Maybe if I knew why Linus disliked me so much, I could figure out a way to fix things—or at least get him to quit being so frigid toward me.

Linus's face hardened. "Oh yes. I've read the reports on Gwen Frost. That girl has been nothing trouble since she came to Mythos. Sneaking off campus, using her magic to extort money out of the other students, claiming that she's some sort of Champion. And now, when I actually come to the academy to conduct a proper investigation into her actions, I find her out on a date with my son. *My son*, Nickamedes. Your nephew. The one you vowed to protect. Or have you forgotten that promise?"

Nickamedes stiffened. "Logan doesn't need protecting from Gwendolyn. The two of them are . . . friends."

"Friends." Linus let out a bitter laugh. "Like you and Grace Frost were *friends*?"

A muscle twitched in the librarian's jaw, but he didn't respond. A couple of weeks ago, Nickamedes had told me that he'd known my mom back when they'd attended the academy and that the two of them had once been a couple—in love. But over the years, my mom had grown tired of being Nike's Champion so she'd left Mythos and everything it represented behind when she'd finally graduated from the academy—including Nickamedes.

"It's because she's Grace's daughter, isn't it?" Linus said. "That's the reason you're protecting the girl instead of having her expelled like you should have months ago." He shook his head. "I see she has you wrapped around her little finger just like Grace did."

Nickamedes uncrossed his arms. His hands lowered to his sides, and his fingers slowly balled into fists. "You never liked Grace because she was chosen to be a Champion, and you weren't. And not just any Champion, but *Nike's* Champion, the best of the best. You were always jealous of her for that—and because she didn't want to join the Protectorate after graduation like you did. You knew what a coup it would be to get Nike's Champion to enter the Protectorate, and you wanted to use her to further your own career. Grace was always better than you, and you resented her for it. I never understood the obsessive need you had to compete with her in the classroom, in the gym, and everywhere else."

"And I never understood why you always leaped to her defense," Linus snapped back. "We're Spartans, Nickamedes. *We're* the best of the best. And yet, someone else was chosen to be Nike's Champion instead of one of us. It doesn't make any sense. It didn't back then, and it certainly doesn't now. Logan should be a Champion, Nike's Champion, not this—this foolish *girl*. From what I see, she's even worse than her mother was, and Grace was by no means Champion material. Nike should have done us all a favor and cut ties with the Frost family years ago. I thought perhaps it had finally ended when Grace was killed by Reapers. I'd certainly hoped so anyway."

Rage erupted in my heart, blotting out everything else. That was enough. *That was enough!* It was one thing to snidely talk about and blame me for the mistakes I'd made. I deserved nothing less for my epic failure to keep Loki imprisoned. But my mom was gone.

Dead. Murdered. She couldn't defend herself, and I wasn't just going to stand around and listen to someone bad-mouth her when she'd died serving Nike, when she'd died trying to protect us all.

Hands clenched, I stalked out of the stacks. Alexei tried to grab my shoulder, but I ducked his hand and hurried forward. Nickamedes and Linus whirled around at the scuff of my sneakers on the marble floor.

I walked right up to the head of the Protectorate and put my hands on my hips. "Don't you dare talk about my mom like that. She was a good person, and she did everything she could to fight the Reapers. She's the one who hid the Helheim Dagger from them. She's the reason they didn't find it and use it to free Loki years ago. So don't you dare blame her for anything. Not one *thing.*"

"And you're the one who found the dagger your mother so carefully hid," Linus said in a soft, accusing voice. "And now, Loki is free, and the Reapers are on the verge of declaring a second Chaos War. If your mother had been smart, if she'd been a *true* Champion, she would have destroyed the dagger when she had the chance. Or at least made sure that *you* never found it."

I couldn't argue with his logic, since the same thoughts had crossed my mind more than once. But he was talking about my mom like she was some kind of villain, like *I* was some kind of villain, when Vivian was to blame for everything that had happened—including my mom's murder. Where had Linus been when Vivian had kidnapped me? Where had the Protectorate been when she'd used my blood to free Loki? When she'd killed Nott? Why hadn't they come to the rescue then? Why hadn't they stopped her?

I opened my mouth to tell him exactly what I thought about him and his stupid Protectorate when a low voice called out behind me.

"Enough, Dad. That's enough."

I turned around, and Logan stepped out of the stacks.

Chapter 10

Logan walked over and stopped beside me. Linus frowned at the sight of his son standing so close to me, as though I could infect Logan with my recklessness just by being next to him. The Spartan glared right back at his father.

"I think Logan's right," a soft, feminine voice called out. "There's been enough arguing—on everyone's part."

To my surprise, a woman appeared behind Logan— one who was beautiful enough to be a goddess. She had long, honey-colored hair, bright green eyes, and flawless bronze skin. She wore a simple black pantsuit, but somehow she made the fabric look regal, as though it were the finest silk draped around her tall, slender figure. A gold necklace glimmered around her throat. Four small, round gemstones had been set into the chain, and the faint flash of the alternating rubies and emeralds only added to the woman's elegance.

Nickamedes's face hardened at the sight of her. "Agrona."

She tipped her head to him. "Nickamedes."

I looked at Logan, my eyebrows raised, and he finally realized that I didn't know who she was.

"This is Agrona Quinn. My stepmom. Agrona, this is Gwen Frost."

My mouth opened, but no words came out. I knew that Logan's mom had been murdered by Reapers when he was five, but he'd never mentioned that his father had remarried.

I hesitated, wondering if she hated me as much as her husband did. Finally, I nodded at her. "Hello. It's nice to meet you."

Instead of glowering, she smiled back at me, her face warm and inviting. "It's nice to finally meet you, Gwen. I've heard a lot about you."

Nickamedes barked out a laugh. "I just bet you have, since you're Linus's right hand in the Protectorate and on the academy board."

I frowned. "In the Protectorate? Then that means..."

Agrona stared at me. "That I'll be among the Protectorate members hearing your case tomorrow."

Her smile turned into more of a grimace, as though she didn't like the thought of my being on trial any more than I did. Somehow, the disappointed expression only made her seem even more radiant—and made Nickemades scowl that much more.

Linus walked over to his wife and kissed her cheek. "There you are, darling. I was wondering when you were going to arrive."

Agrona smiled at her husband. "The driver dropped me off twenty minutes ago. You said you were stopping by the library, so I came straight here in hopes of catching you. I spotted Logan coming inside, and he told me that you might be back here."

Linus's whole face softened as he looked at her. It was obvious that he loved Agrona, and the expression almost made him seem human. Then, he noticed me watching them, and his lips clamped down and the brightness was snuffed out of his eyes. Almost.

He turned to Logan. "I was just talking to your uncle about you. Perhaps, you, Agrona, and I can go out for dinner tonight. We have a lot to discuss."

Logan stared at his father, then Agrona, and finally at me.

"It's okay," I said, not wanting to cause any more problems between Logan and his dad. "Go ahead."

The Spartan shook his head. "I think I'll pass. I'd rather stay here with Gwen."

His words warmed my heart, even as they caused his dad's face to ice over that much more. But Linus reined in his temper.

"Breakfast tomorrow, then," he said in a tight voice. "And that's not a request."

Logan glared at his dad, both of them bristling with anger. Agrona stepped in between them and threaded her arm through Linus's.

"Breakfast, it is then," she said in a soft voice, trying to smooth over the situation, something she probably had to do a lot between them. "It will be wonderful catching up with you, Logan."

The Spartan tried to smile, but he couldn't quite manage it. "And you too, Agrona."

Linus looked at his son another moment before turning back to Nickamedes. "Our previous conversation isn't over. Don't forget what I said in the meantime. I'd hate to have to repeat myself."

"How could I ever do that when such pearls of wisdom always seem to fall from your lips?" Nickamedes replied in a snide voice.

Anger flashed in Linus's eyes, but Agrona held on to his arm and kept him by her side.

"You might be head of the Protectorate, but I'm in charge of the library," Nickamedes said. "And I think it's time for you to leave. Gwendolyn needs to get back to work, and so do I."

Linus stiffened, then turned on his heel and stalked around the back of the office complex and toward the front of the library. Agrona gave everyone an apologetic smile. Her eyes lingered on me a moment before she turned and hurried after her husband.

"Good riddance," Nickamedes muttered.

The librarian stood there, his features pinched with anger, before he glanced at me. "I have to go out and run some errands, Gwendolyn. I'll be back in time to close the library. Do me a favor and try not to destroy anything while I'm gone, please?"

He didn't even wait for me to answer before he went into the office complex, slamming the door so hard behind him that the glass shuddered. Nickamedes grabbed some books and other items off his desk, then headed out of his office and pushed through the door that led out to the front side of the library. That left me standing with Logan, and of course Alexei, who was hovering in the background as usual.

"What was all that about?" I asked Logan.

The Spartan sighed. "It's a long story. Come on. Let's get something to drink, and I'll tell you all about it."

Logan went over to Raven's coffee cart and bought us a couple of cold sodas, while I stayed in the stacks. The Spartan came back and handed me a ginger ale. He also passed one to Alexei. To my surprise, the other guy took the soda. Then again, it was Logan who had given it to him, not me, the evil, evil Reaper girl.

Logan looked at Alexei, who'd once again stayed quiet through all the conversations and confrontations. "Alexei, can you give us a little space, please?"

Alexei looked at me, then nodded. He moved about twenty feet away, drinking his soda and pretending to be interested in two swords that were housed in one of the artifact cases. Or maybe he really was into the swords. It was hard to tell with him.

Logan and I sat down on the floor in the same spot where I'd been before. We drank our sodas, Logan gulping his down, while I only sipped mine. I had even less appetite now than ever before. A minute later, the Spartan crumpled his empty can in his fist and put it down.

"I'm sorry about my dad," he finally said. "Like I've told you before, he and Nickamedes do not get along."

"Why not?"

Logan sighed. "Because of what happened to my mom and sister. My dad was off on Protectorate business, some special meeting he was called to at the last minute. Nickamedes blames him for not being home when the Reapers attacked. He thinks if my dad had been there, then my mom and my sister might still be alive." He drew in a breath. "And my dad blames me for not protecting them from the Reapers, for not standing and fighting with them. So when we're all together, my dad and Nickamedes argue about every little thing. I get called in to referee, and they eventually make me take sides and choose between them. Then, my dad tells me how disappointed he is in me, how I'm not living up to my *full potential* as a Spartan, and I end up getting pissed at him. Soon, we're all yelling at each other. Some happy family, huh?"

"I'm sorry," I said. "So sorry that you have to go through that with your dad and Nickamedes. They shouldn't put you in the middle like that. But surely, your dad must realize that you couldn't have done anything to save your mom and sister. That they sacrificed their lives to save yours. Besides, you were only five when it happened. There was nothing you could have done to stop the Reapers."

The images flashed through my mind. Logan's mom screaming at him to run while she and his older sister stepped up to fight the Reapers. Him hiding in a closet, clutching a small sword, as screams and shouts tore through the air. And finally, Logan standing over the bloody bodies of his mom and older sister, crying because he hadn't been able to protect them, because he hadn't been able to save them. And I felt all the Spartan's emotions from that terrible day—all his fear and anger and shame and hatred of himself.

The Spartan thought he'd been a coward because he'd hidden from the Reapers like his mom had told him to. It was a secret he'd kept to himself for years, one that he'd finally shown me a few weeks ago. Logan might not like it, but I knew his actions that day made him the person he was—that they'd driven him to be the best warrior at the academy.

Logan shook his head. "According to my dad, a *real* Spartan warrior would have stood his ground and fought that day—no matter if he knew that he was going to die."

For months, Logan had told me that I wouldn't like him if I knew the truth about who he really was, and his feelings about what had happened to his family were what had kept us apart. Of course, that wasn't true. I couldn't have been prouder of him—or loved him more. But suddenly, his fears made sense. Because all these years, his dad had made him feel like he should have died that day too, instead of being grateful that his son was still alive.

"I'm so sorry," I said again. "Your dad shouldn't have said that to you. He shouldn't have made you feel like that—*ever*. He should have been happy you survived."

Logan shrugged. We sat there in silence for a few minutes.

"What about Agrona?" I asked. "What's your stepmom like?"

He brightened a little. "That's something else that's complicated. She's actually really nice, and my dad obviously loves her. She's the only one who makes him seem close to human—or happy."

"But . . ."

"But Nickamedes has never liked her, and he won't tell me why," Logan said. "I think it has something to do with the fact that Agrona and my dad got married just a year after my mom and sister were murdered. I think Nickamedes feels it was too soon for my dad to have gotten over their deaths—or at least remarried."

"Well, you can't blame Nickamedes for feeling that way, can you?" I asked. "Your mom was his sister. He lost her too that day. And his niece."

"I know, and that's what makes it all so frustrating. Nobody's completely right, and nobody's completely wrong. Everybody has their own side, and none of us are on the same one. Sometimes I wish I had a different family," he muttered.

"Just be glad you have the family you do," I said. "That they're here with you and not gone."

Logan looked at me, and I knew he could see the pain in my face. I would have traded just about anything for one more day with my mom or the chance to spend time with my dad, Tyr. He'd died when I was two, so I didn't even remember him. Grandma Frost loved me, and I loved her, but that didn't keep me from missing my mom or wishing that I'd known my dad at least a little bit.

He let out a breath. "You're right, Gypsy girl. It's just—they make me crazy, you know? Especially my dad. He always thinks he's right about *everything*."

"I know, but that's what family is for, right? To make you crazy?"

Logan laughed, and some of the tension drained out of his body. He got to his feet, then held out his hands. I grabbed them, and he pulled me up.

"Do you know what I love about you, Gypsy girl?"

My breath caught in my throat, but I made my voice light and teasing. "Hmm. That's a tough one. My daring fashion sense? My sparkling personality? My witty one-liners?"

"No," he said, staring into my eyes. "The way you can always make me laugh, no matter how bad things get."

Before I could respond, the Spartan's arms tightened around me, and he lowered his lips to mine.

For a moment, I was lost—completely, utterly *lost.* The feel of Logan's lips on mine, the strong circle of his arms around me, the way he smelled, his long, lean body pressing against my own, the warmth of his feelings for me streaming into my own body. Everything about the Spartan overloaded my senses, forming a soft, dizzying rush that made me feel like I could float away, like I could soar through the air, like I could do absolutely anything, even touch the stars—

The sharp, deliberate scuffle of shoes on the floor made me realize that we had an audience.

"Logan!" I hissed, pulling back. "Alexei is staring at us!"

The Spartan glanced over his shoulder at the other warrior, who was pretending he hadn't just seen the two of us totally make out. Logan grinned.

"Let him look," he whispered and kissed me again.

Chapter 11

Logan and I spent a few *very* enjoyable minutes in the stacks before Alexei started clearing his throat. The Spartan pulled back and dropped his arms from around my waist, although his blue eyes flashed with laughter.

"I think Alexei's getting impatient," Logan said. "That, or he's just jealous that he's not back here with someone."

I thought of how Alexei had looked at Oliver in the gym this morning. "Maybe. Either way, I have to get back to work, remember?"

"Did anyone ever tell you that playing hooky is more fun than working?"

This time, I laughed. "Never. But that's what I have you for, Spartan. To tell me these things."

I stood on my tiptoes, leaned forward, and kissed Logan on the nose. He let out a playful growl, but I slipped away before he could wrap his arms around me again.

By this point, it was after eight, and most of the kids had left the library. I guess since I hadn't been at the checkout counter for them to glare at, they'd decided to go back to their dorms for the night. Well, that was one small favor, although I knew things would be just as bad tomorrow. Maybe even worse, as more and more kids found the courage to mess with me, with Helena Paxton no doubt leading the charge. But there was nothing I could do about any of that tonight, so I tried to put it out of my mind.

I'd thought Logan would leave as well, but the Spartan wandered out of the stacks and planted himself on a stool behind the checkout counter. I gave him a questioning look.

"I'm staying here, and I'm walking you back to your dorm tonight." His face darkened. "Just in case some more jerks decide they want to take matters into their own hands where you're concerned. I called in reinforcements too. They should be here any minute."

"Reinforcements?" I asked. "What reinforcements—"

The sound of shoes smacking against the marble floor caught my attention. A second later, Daphne strode into the library, followed by Oliver. Daphne marched down the center aisle, her enormous Dooney & Bourke purse in one hand and her cell phone held up to her ear. Both the purse and the phone were pink and matched the rest of her clothes. The Valkyrie was the only person I knew who could wear one color from head to toe and totally pull it off. I would have looked like a wad of cotton candy if I'd tried to wear so much pink at once.

"Yeah . . . yeah . . . uh-huh. Glad you're having a good practice. Okay, we're at the library now, so I have to go. Talk to you later. Bye, babe." Daphne hung up and slid her phone into her purse. "Sorry about that. Carson's stuck at band practice and can't make it."

"You and Oliver are Logan's reinforcements? You guys came all the way over here just to walk me back to my dorm?" I asked. "You didn't have to do that."

Daphne gave me a sharp look. "Are you kidding? After the way Helena and her flunkies surrounded you in the dining hall this morning? One of us is going to be with you everywhere you go from now on, Gwen. I only wish I'd been there this morning to bitch-slap Helena back down to size."

I hadn't mentioned the incident at breakfast to Daphne, not wanting her to worry, but Logan must have told her, along with the rest of our friends.

"You don't have to do that," I protested, not wanting to drag her and everyone else into the middle of my problems with the other kids. "Besides, isn't that what Alexei is for? Guard duty?"

The Valkyrie crossed her arms over her chest and glared at Alexei, who was standing behind me in his usual position once more. "Apparently, he's not up to the job, since he almost let you get lynched this morning. No offense, Bogatyr."

"None taken," Alexei replied in a mild voice.

"Anyway," Daphne said. "We've all agreed, so there's no point in arguing with us, Gwen. No point at all."

The Valkryie sat down at the study table closest to the checkout counter. Pink sparks of magic hissed and cracked in the air around her, telling me just how riled up she was on my behalf. I glanced at Logan and Oliver, who had the same sort of determined looks on their faces, and I could tell that nothing I could say was going to change their minds. I loved them for their concern, but it made me feel guilty that they even had to defend me in the first place. Being my friend shouldn't be so hard—or dangerous.

"Thank you, guys," I said, blinking back tears yet again. "I appreciate your standing by me. I know that being my friend isn't always easy. Especially not right now."

Oliver shrugged. "We wouldn't really be friends if we bailed at the first sign of trouble, now, would we?"

I smiled at him and then busied myself lining up the carts behind the checkout counter so he and the others wouldn't notice me wiping the tears out of the corners of my eyes.

Logan moved over to talk to Daphne about the band concert. Carson wasn't the only one involved in the event. The Spartan, along with Oliver and Kenzie, was in an honor guard that had been assigned to watch over the band members, since the concert was taking place at the Aoide Auditorium and not here on campus. Apparently, staging the concert at the auditorium was an annual Mythos tradition, one that the Powers That Were were determined to uphold, despite the fact that Loki was free. I guess they and the Protectorate wanted to send a message to everyone—students and Reapers alike—that the Pantheon wasn't afraid and that they weren't going to hunker down and hide from the war that was coming.

Oliver drifted over to me. Alexei watched us both from his spot against the wall of the office complex.

"Logan told us what happened this morning," Oliver said in a low voice only I could hear. "I'm sorry that Alexei didn't help you. He seemed so cool when I met him over winter break. But now that I know he just stood by while you were facing down those other kids..."

Sad longing made his shoulders droop, and the same miserable expression was on Alexei's face as well. I knew that if I asked him to, Oliver would ignore Alexei and pretend they'd never met. But Oliver had been there for me when I'd needed him, and I wanted my friend to be happy, even if it was with Alexei.

"Go," I said, giving the Spartan a little push. "Go talk to him. This trouble that I'm in doesn't have anything to do with the two of you. If you like him, that's good enough for me. I just hope he's good enough for you. Because if he hurts you, Protectorate or not, I will totally kick his ass."

I paused. "Or maybe get Daphne and Logan to help me kick his ass. Not sure I could do it by myself. Either way, his ass will definitely be kicked."

Oliver flashed me a grin. "Did I ever tell you what a good friend you are?"

I grinned back at him. "Well, this good friend thing doesn't last very long. So you'd better get over there and talk to him before I change my mind."

Oliver's grin widened. He straightened his shoulders and walked over to Alexei. The two of them started talking in low voices, and it was like Alexei suddenly changed into a completely different person. He was so serious when he was watching me, so remote, so reserved, but with Oliver, warmth filled his face, his eyes crinkled at the corners as he smiled, and his whole body was totally relaxed. It made my spirits lift a little to see the two of them together.

While I'd been back in the stacks, Nickamedes had set out one more cart of books that needed to be shelved. Since everyone else was busy talking, I grabbed the cart. I'd just started to roll it around the counter when a loud yawn caught my ear. I looked down and noticed Vic staring up at me out of the top of my messenger bag.

"Finally waking up from your latest nap?" I asked.

The sword blinked. "Well, it's not like I have anything else to do, you know. Not until you find us some more Reapers to kill. I was just dreaming about Lucretia and how I plan to cleave her in two the next time we meet."

Lucretia was Vivian's sword, which talked just like Vic did. From what I'd gathered, Vic and Lucretia were old enemies, since Lucretia had been passed down through Loki's Champions over the years, just like Vic had been handed from one of my Frost ancestors to the next. The swords were just another way in which Vivian and I were eerily similar, along with the fact that we were both Gypsies gifted with magic from our respective gods. While I'd been given psychometry, or touch magic, Vivian had what she called chaos magic, although really it was more like telepathy. Either way, the Reaper girl's power let her make people see and hear things that weren't actually there. Sometimes, I thought that Vivian and I were like the opposite sides of the same coin—so alike in some ways and so very different in others.

"I don't have any idea where Vivian or Lucretia are," I told the sword. "You know if I had the slightest clue where they were hiding, I'd be out there leading the charge against them."

"I know, I know," Vic grumbled. "And more's the pity that you don't know. Because I would be happy to cut them to pieces for you."

His half of a mouth turned down into a sullen pout, as if he'd just lost out on his favorite treat. I sighed. I knew if I didn't do something to cheer him up, Vic would be in one of his *moods* for the rest of the night. And people thought teenagers were temperamental. Please. They should spend some time with Vic.

"Wanna go for a ride?" I asked.

Vic rolled his eye. "Well, it would certainly beat staring at the bottom of the bloody counter for another hour or taking yet another nap. Even I can only sleep for so long."

I grabbed the sword, pulled the blade out of his scabbard, and propped Vic up on top of the metal cart so he could see where we were going. Then, I pushed the cart back into the stacks and started shelving the rest of the books.

Vic kept up a steady stream of conversation while I worked, going on and on and *on* about all the horrible things he was going to do to Lucretia the next time the two swords met in battle. Every once in a while, I chimed in with an *uh-huh* or an *of course you will* or even a *really?* But Vic didn't need me to keep the conversation going. Sometimes, I thought the sword would have talked forever—whether or not he had an audience.

Finally, I shelved the last book, turned the cart around, and headed toward the checkout counter. The library was closing in ten minutes, and I was more than ready to grab my bag and go back to my room for the night.

I steered the cart down an aisle until I came to a crossway in the stacks. A movement caught my eye, and I turned my head just in time to see someone duck behind a bookcase several feet away.

I froze, wondering if I'd only imagined the movement, if perhaps my eyes were playing tricks on me. I squinted and looked through a gap in the bookshelves. Sure enough, a second later, I saw someone moving through the stacks up ahead and to my right. The figure had its back to me, so I couldn't make out who it might be through the shadows that cloaked this part of the library.

I sighed. One of the reasons the library was so popular was because kids loved to sneak into the stacks and hook up with their latest crush—and we weren't talking about just a little kissing, like Logan and I had done. Oh no. Lots of the Mythos students thought that going All the Way in the library was a supercool thing to do. Whatever. I always hated it whenever Nickamedes made me clean back here because I'd always find lots of disgusting things, including used condoms. Yucko.

No doubt the mystery figure was one of the warrior

whiz kids who'd just made out with his current honey. Or maybe one of my classmates just wanted to mess with me a final time tonight. Stacking up books so they'd eventually tip over and scare me when I was working late was another game some students loved to play. And given what had happened in the dining hall, I wouldn't put it past Helena or someone else to be lurking around, waiting to jump me and beat the stuffing out of me like they'd wanted to this morning—or worse.

Wary now, I pushed the cart forward, moving parallel to the shadowy figure. Apparently, for once I'd eased all the *squeak-squeak-squeaks* out of the wheels because they barely made a sound as I rolled the cart across the floor.

I'd just stepped into another crossway, trying to catch up to the figure, when the edge of a black robe whipped around a bookcase twenty feet ahead of me.

I froze again, my knuckles cracking as my hands tightened around the cart's handle. Because hookups or not, pranks or not, Mythos students did not wear black robes—Reapers of Chaos did.

Heart pounding, I grabbed Vic off the top of the cart and hurried after the figure.

"What are you doing?" the sword asked in a slightly muffled voice, since his mouth was underneath my hand. "Why are you leaving the cart behind? You've got to take it back to the counter too."

"Shut up, Vic," I murmured. "I think there's someone else in the library."

But the sword didn't listen to me. "Of course there's someone in the library. Your friends are here, remember?"

"Yeah," I replied. "But none of them is wearing a black robe."

Vic's purplish eye widened, and I felt his mouth curve into a smile beneath my palm. "Bloody Reapers," he said with obvious relish. "Let's kill them all!"

I resisted the urge to tell him to shut up again and raced forward. We were on the back side of the library, behind the glass office complex, and once again voices murmured up ahead. I eased up to the edge of one of the bookcases and peered around the corner.

Oliver and Alexei stood about thirty feet away from me, almost in the same spot where Nickamedes and Linus had argued earlier tonight. I'd thought perhaps the two of them had slipped back here to hook up, but then I noticed that they were glaring at each other. Had something gone wrong between them already?

"You should distance yourself from Gwen," Alexei said. "From what I hear, things are not going to go well for her tomorrow. At the very least, she'll be expelled from the academy. I don't have to tell you what the maximum punishment is for those convicted of being Reapers."

Oliver chewed on his lip. Apparently, he knew that the Protectorate could execute me if I was found guilty. I wondered if the others knew too. Probably. My friends had grown up in the mythological world. They knew the rules—and the consequences of breaking them—a lot better than I did.

"Please," Alexei said, holding out his hand. "Can't we just go back to the way things were over the holidays?"

For a moment, Oliver's face softened with memories. Longing filled his eyes, and he stared at Alexei's hand, obviously wanting to take it. But he slowly shook his head.

"Gwen's my friend," Oliver said. "And I'm not going to abandon her just because she's in trouble, especially since she didn't do the things the Protectorate said she did. She almost died trying to find the Helheim Dagger and keep it safe from the Reapers. You should have seen her that night we found her in the forest by that Garm gate. She was devastated by everything that had happened."

Alexei sighed and slowly dropped his hand to his side. "Maybe she was, but that won't be enough to save her. Not from the Protectorate. She'll be found guilty, and so will anyone who aligns themselves with her."

The two guys stood there, shifting on their feet and not quite looking at each other. Guilt twisted my heart. Oliver finally had a chance at happiness, and he was pushing it aside because of me. I don't know that I would have done the same, if our positions had been reversed, if Logan had been standing in front of me, pleading with me with like that. Oliver was a far better friend than I was—

Once again, I spotted a flicker of movement in the stacks. My head snapped in that direction, and I tightened my grip on Vic.

"Come on," I whispered. "Show yourself."

A second later, a Reaper stepped into view.

The Reaper wore a black robe with the hood pulled up, black leather gloves, and a garish rubber mask—one that resembled the melted half of Loki's face. The same twisted, melted, ruined face I saw whenever I closed my eyes. I shuddered. Somehow, the mask looked even more hideous on the Reaper, maybe because I knew there was a real person under there, someone who'd pledged to serve Loki, someone who happily did all the terrible things that the evil god commanded his Reapers to do. Like lying to their friends. Sacrificing people. Killing warriors. Murdering kids like me.

Still, I forced myself to look at the Reaper to see if I could get any clue as to who was really underneath that horrible rubber mask. Despite the billowing folds of the robe, the figure seemed slender, but it still could have been a man or woman, old or young. I didn't think it was Vivian Holler, though. Vivian was about my size, and this Reaper was several inches taller than I was. Besides, Vivian had no reason to hide her identity with a mask since everyone knew that she was Loki's Champion.

"Reaper," Vic snarled in a soft voice. "Let's go kill it, Gwen."

I nodded at the sword and started forward when I spotted another figure moving through the stacks. I stopped and blinked, wondering if my eyes were playing tricks on me—but they weren't.

Because this figure was wearing a black robe too—

and it wasn't alone. Two more figures crept through the stacks behind it, then several more after that, so many I lost count. My blood turned to ice at the horrible sight.

Reapers—Reapers had somehow gotten inside the Library of Antiquities.

And they were about to kill Oliver and Alexei.

Chapter 12

The first Reaper that I'd spotted held up a fist, and the others stopped. The leader made a hand signal, and the others slowly began to spread out, forming a semicircle around Oliver and Alexei. The two guys had started arguing again, so they didn't even notice the Reapers creeping up on them.

My head snapped to the left, as I looked for Logan and Daphne, but I didn't see my friends. Had the Reapers—had the Reapers gotten to them already? Killed them already? The terrible thought made me want to scream, but I forced myself to take a breath and focus on what I had to do now—save Oliver and Alexei. I turned and darted deeper into the stacks.

"Where are you going?" Vic demanded. "Why are you running away? The Reapers are back that way!"

"I know!" I hissed at the sword. "Just trust me!"

I raced back to where I'd left the metal cart, grabbed it with my free hand, turned around, and headed back in the direction that I'd come, pushing the cart in front of me. When I reached the crossway, I veered to the right, then took a left three bookcases up.

A Reaper, a man from the size of him, stood at the far end of the aisle. A curved sword glinted in his hand, and he swung it back and forth a few times as he prepared to spring out of his hiding place and attack Oliver and Alexei. I picked up my pace, forcing myself to run faster. The Reaper must have heard the sound of my footsteps smacking into the marble floor or maybe the faint *creak-creak-creak* of the cart's wheels because his head turned in my direction—but it was too late.

I rammed the cart into the Reaper as hard as I could. He cursed and stumbled back. He tried to regain his balance, but he tripped over his own feet and sprawled to a stop in the middle of the open floor—right in front of Oliver and Alexei. The guys stared at the Reaper, then at me, with shocked expressions.

"Reapers!" I screamed. "Reapers in the library!"

As if my words had magically summoned them, Reapers suddenly surrounded us, erupting out of the stacks like a swarm of killer bees. Black-robed figures darted here, there, everywhere. In front of me, the Reaper I'd hit with the cart started to get onto his feet, so I rammed the metal cart into him again. He fell back to the floor.

The cart didn't hurt the Reaper, not really—but Vic did.

I shoved the cart out of the way, stepped forward, and brought the sword up, then down into the center of the Reaper's chest. Blood sprayed everywhere, the warm, wet, metallic stench of it stinging my nose. The man screamed once, and then he was still. Maybe I should have felt bad about stabbing him when he was on the ground, but I didn't because I knew that he would have done the same thing to me if he'd had the chance.

I whirled around. Oliver and Alexei stood back to back, their fists up and ready, as the Reapers crept closer and closer to them.

"Oh, look," one of the Reapers said in a low, throaty voice. "Two little warriors without a sword between them. This is going to be *fun*."

The Reaper who'd spoken was the leader, the one I'd first noticed. A man, judging by the deep voice, although something about his tone seemed a little . . . off. Like he was pitching his voice lower than it really was for some reason.

The leader laughed, and all the others joined in, the chuckling sounds full of sly, deadly malice. My heart sank because I realized that the Reaper was right. No matter how brave or skilled they were, without weapons, Oliver and Alexei would be easy targets, since all the Reapers carried long, curved swords. Sure, Oliver was a Spartan and didn't really need a weapon to fight, but he couldn't sidestep all those Reapers and all their swords—not for long.

I looked around, wondering how I could save them, and a gleam of glass caught my attention. My gaze locked onto the artifact case that Alexei had been looking at earlier—the one with two swords in it.

A Reaper broke away from the circle around Oliver and Alexei and rushed toward me. I waited until the figure was in range, then spun around him and ran toward the artifact case.

I skidded to a halt in front of the case. Something glimmered on the black velvet next to the swords, and I realized that it was the silver foil on the card that identified the weapons. *The Swords of Ruslan.* That was all I read before I raised Vic up high, then turned my head and brought the sword down as hard as I could. The glass shattered with a roar, and I felt pieces zip through the air, stinging my hands and arms, but I didn't care. The pain was small compared to what would happen to Oliver and Alexei if I didn't help them.

The two swords were crisscrossed over each other and sheathed in a double scabbard made of gray leather, so I was able to grab everything with one hand—

Images flooded my mind as soon as I touched the scabbard.

I wasn't surprised that my psychometry kicked in, but the intensity of the memories and feelings associated with the scabbard and swords took my breath away. In an instant, the library was gone, and I was standing in the middle of a fierce blizzard, frozen to the bone, screams ringing in my ears as a fight raged all around me.

Panicked, I turned this way and that, trying to push the memories away. I didn't have time for this, not when Oliver and Alexei were in danger and a Reaper was racing after me. But the faster I turned, the more the scene sharpened, as though I was zooming in on it with a camera. My gaze snagged on a man in the heart of the battle. It took me a moment to realize that he was fighting with two swords, probably the two swords I was holding right now. But there was something familiar about him, something about the way he moved, as though he was dancing with his enemies instead of fighting them—

"Gwen!" I heard Vic say, although the sword's voice seemed distant and far away. "The Reaper's coming after you! Snap out of it! Right now!"

I shook my head, and the images and memories vanished, although my teeth still chattered from the cold and it seemed as though my breath frosted in the air. But how was that possible? It was warm in the library—

"Gwen!" Vic screamed again.

On instinct, I ducked to the right.

CLANG!

The Reaper I'd sidestepped earlier brought his sword down where I'd been standing a second before. His weapon got stuck in the wooden base of the artifact case, and he cursed, trying to pull it free. What was it with people always trying to kill me in the library? Nickamedes *so* needed to put up warning signs. *Danger: Working here could be hazardous to your health.*

Since my hands were full with Vic and the other swords, I kicked out and managed to catch the Reaper in the knee. Something popped under my sneaker, and he howled with pain as his leg buckled and he went down to the floor.

"That's my girl!" Vic yelled. "Kick him again!"

So I kicked him again, slamming my sneaker into the Reaper's rubber mask as hard as I could. He moaned and rolled away from me, trying to get under the artifact case so I couldn't kick him a third time. But I was already turning away and running toward the circle of Reapers.

The other Reapers were so focused on Oliver and Alexei that they didn't realize I'd gotten back into the fight. I put my shoulder down and barreled into the one closest to me, shoving the Reaper out of the way, and breaking through the ring.

"Oliver! Alexei! Weapons!" I yelled and shoved the scabbard into Alexei's hands.

Alexei smoothly drew one of the swords out before offering the other one to Oliver, who shook his head.

"You take the second sword. Give me the scabbard instead!" Oliver barked.

Alexei held the leather out to him. Oliver pulled the double scabbard away, leaving Alexei to wield the two swords. Oliver hefted the empty scabbard in his hand, and then he actually *smiled*. I didn't know why or what Oliver thought he could possibly do with a piece of leather—

The Spartan ducked a Reaper's blow, then spun around so that he was behind his attacker. In an instant, Oliver had wrapped the straps of the scabbard around the Reaper's throat like some sort of leather vise. Oliver twisted the pieces of leather, and the Reaper's neck snapped with an audible *crack*.

Oh. So that's what he was going to do with it. I should have known he had something in mind, that his Spartan killer instinct would prompt him to do something clever and deadly. Oliver noticed me staring at him with wide eyes. He grinned at me and stepped up to fight the next Reaper.

And just like that, the whole battle changed.

The Reapers, who'd been laughing and inching forward, stopped in their tracks, and Oliver and Alexei pressed their advantage. The two of them charged into the ring of Reapers, Alexei's twin swords flashing like silver fire underneath the library's lights, while Oliver wrapped the ends of the scabbard around another Reaper's neck. In a second, they'd killed two Reapers. In another, two more had fallen to the floor.

But there were still plenty of Reapers left. One came at me, and I tightened my hands on Vic and stepped up to meet him.

Swipe-swipe-swipe.

The Reaper swung his sword at me over and over again, but I focused on his hands and feet, and I was able to anticipate his moves and defend against them. Then, I went on the attack, slashing Vic out in vicious arcs and stabbing lines. On my fifth pass, I managed to slice the blade across the Reaper's shoulder. He screamed, and I followed that move up by running Vic through his heart. The Reaper dropped to the floor, still screaming—

Crack!

A fist slammed into my jaw, and I realized that a Reaper had crept up on my blind side. I staggered back. My sneakers slipped in a pool of blood, and I hit the marble floor hard. The Reaper laughed and brought his sword up. Dazed, I raised Vic, putting the sword between us, even though I knew I didn't have the strength to deflect the blow that was coming—

A golden arrow blossomed like a flower in the middle

of the Reaper's chest, and he toppled to the floor. I looked behind me and spotted Daphne standing on top of one of the study tables on this side of the library, her onyx bow in her hand. Sigyn's bow, the one she'd gotten from the Crius Coliseum, the one that kept reappearing in her dorm room no matter how many times she gave the weapon back to Professor Metis.

A puff of golden smoke appeared, and the Valkyrie reached around into the matching onyx quiver strapped to her back and pulled out another golden arrow to replace the one she'd just fired.

A moment later, Logan was by my side. The Spartan held out his hand and helped me to my feet. Logan was okay, Logan and Daphne were both okay. Relief roared through me.

"Gypsy girl, I leave you alone for a few minutes and what happens? Reapers invade the library," he said, his icy eyes almost glowing with anticipation.

Logan grinned at me and waded into the fight. Soon, he was beside Oliver and Alexei, the three of them moving in almost perfect step with each other as they battled the Reapers, while Daphne picked off others with her bow and arrow. In seconds, my friends had killed two more Reapers and were closing in on the rest.

I whirled around, ready to fight the next Reaper, when I noticed one of them slipping into the stacks. Not just any Reaper, but the tall, slender leader. I frowned. The fight was out here. So why would one of the Reapers be retreating? They never retreated. Their whole purpose in life was to kill warriors—not run away. My eyes narrowed. Unless maybe killing us wasn't the only reason they were in the library.

There are many artifacts here that he wants, many powerful things and people here that he needs in order to finally defeat us, Nike's voice whispered in my mind.

It made perfect sense. The artifacts in the Library of Antiquities had a lot of power, and Nike had told me that there were items here that Loki would love to get his hands on, things that could help him and the Reapers finally defeat the Pantheon. What if—what if the fight was just a distraction? A way for the Reapers to hide why they'd really come here tonight?

I was going to find out.

I tightened my grip on Vic, pushed past another dying Reaper that Daphne had just shot through the neck with an arrow, and darted into the stacks.

"Gypsy girl!" Logan called out. "Wait!"

But I didn't want to wait. I wanted to get answers, and all I had to do to get them was catch the Reaper.

Chapter 13

I raced back into the stacks, my head turning from side to side as I tried to figure out which direction the Reaper had gone or what he could possibly be after. I came to a crossway and stopped, breathing hard and trying to calm the rapid *thump-thump-thump* of my heart so I could hear where the leader had gone.

For once, Vic stayed quiet, and I forced myself to take in soft breaths of air. I cocked my head to one side, then the other, wishing I had the enhanced senses that so many of the Mythos students had. But I didn't. All I had were my instincts, so I headed right toward the front half of the library. The Reapers had come in from the back, so whatever they were really after wasn't on that side. Otherwise, they would have left with it already. That made sense, right? I didn't know how sound my reasoning was, but I decided to follow my instincts.

I moved through the stacks as quickly as I could, stopping at the end of every bookcase, every aisle, every crossway, to look and listen. But the Reaper had too much of a head start on me, and I didn't see any hints of movement anywhere. Finally, just when I was about to give up and head back to the others, I heard the distinctive *tinkle-tinkle* of glass hitting the floor. I paused. The sound came again, and I veered in that direction.

I hurried forward, still stopping to peer around every shelf. Just because I thought the Reaper was after something didn't mean this couldn't be a trap, and the leader might be hiding in a dark corner, ready to take my head off with his sword. Reapers were full of tricks like that. Vivian certainly had been. I didn't think the Reaper I was chasing was Vivian, but she'd fooled me before, and I wasn't going to let it happen again.

Finally, I spotted the Reaper through the shelves. I crept up to the bookcase that was closest to him and peered around it.

The Reaper stood before an artifact case that was in front of a shelf with a few old, tattered books on it. The Reaper had already smashed the glass on the top of the case and was using a sword to knock the last few fragments out of the way. Something white flew out of the case and fluttered to the ground, along with the glass, but the Reaper didn't seem to notice, and I couldn't tell what it was from here. Maybe an ID card of some sort.

The leader reached inside the case and drew out a beautiful, rectangular box that was resting on a wide, black velvet stand. The box was made of a smooth, milky-looking stone, and a series of gems had been set into the gleaming surface, including a topaz, an emerald, and a bloodred ruby, along with matching jeweled chips.

The Reaper tossed the stand aside, grabbed the box,

and held it up high with one hand, admiring the way the jewels caught the light and reflected it back, before slipping the box into one of the pockets of his robe. He reached into the case again and pulled out a topaz ring, an emerald bracelet, and a necklace that featured a large, heart-shaped ruby surrounded by smaller ones. Those items disappeared into his pockets as well.

I stepped forward, determined to stop the Reaper—and my sneakers squeaked on the floor. I froze, hoping the sound hadn't carried, but of course it had.

The Reaper whirled around but didn't seem all that surprised to see me standing there. Instead, I got the impression that he was smiling underneath that horrible Loki mask. A bit of red fire flashed to life in the depths of the leader's eyes—that Reaper-red color that I'd come to hate more than anything else.

"Stay where you are!" I commanded. "You're surrounded!"

It was a lie, but I raised my sword and walked toward the Reaper like the fight was already over with, and Logan and my friends were really here to help me. The Reaper snorted, not believing my lie for a second. I tightened my grip on Vic, expecting the evil warrior to charge at me, but instead the leader did something completely unexpected—he turned and ran away.

"What are you waiting for?" Vic demanded. "Catch that bloody Reaper so I can cut him to ribbons!"

I sucked in a breath and gave chase. The Reaper zoomed down the aisle we were in, then started zigzagging through the stacks. He broke right, then left through a crossway, then right, right, right, and finally left again. I fell behind with each step until I was just barely keeping the other warrior in sight.

"Faster, Gwen!" Vic shouted. "You're losing him!"

As if I couldn't see that for myself. I gulped down another breath, made myself run that much quicker, and rounded a corner—only to realize that the Reaper had vanished.

My steps slowed, then stopped, and I looked left, then right, searching for the Reaper, but all I saw were books and more books, along with a few study tables and artifact cases. Frustration filled me, but I kept scanning the area. Nothing—absolutely nothing.

I'd just started to head down another aisle when a cool breeze kissed my face.

My eyes narrowed. The library was climate-controlled to protect all the books and artifacts. There shouldn't have been any sort of breeze—unless someone had opened a door or window.

I followed the swirls of air, stepped around another bookcase, and found myself in front of one of the side entrances to the library. The door was standing wide open. So that's where he'd gone. Clutching Vic even tighter, I eased through the door and peered outside.

Night cloaked the upper quad, and shadows had stained everything an inky black. A bit of snow had fallen while I'd been inside the library, the white patches standing out like silvery ponds against the darkness. The balcony that wrapped around the building was deserted, as was what I could see of the main quad. I stepped outside and walked over to the wall that ringed the balcony. I stared out into the darkness, scanning the quad, hoping that I'd get a glimpse of the Reaper running across the snow-dusted grass, but I was too late.

The Reaper was gone—and so were the artifacts he'd stolen.

Disgusted with myself for not catching the Reaper, I hurried back inside the library, making sure to shut the side door behind me. I had no doubt that my friends had taken care of the other Reapers by now, so I retraced my steps back to the artifact case that the leader had broken into. I wanted to know exactly what had been inside it and how the items could possibly be used against the Pantheon.

The Reaper had smashed in the top of the case, and chunks of wood and glass littered the floor. Some books had fallen off the shelf above as well, adding to the mess, so it took me a few minutes to pick through everything and find the ID cards that had been inside the case.

To my surprise, there was only one card, despite all the items I'd seen the Reaper grab.

> Apate's Keepsake Box. This box and jewelry were rumored to have belonged to Apate, the Greek goddess of deception. Apate was known for her love of jewels and collected so many of them that the other gods were jealous of her finery. To keep her possessions safe, Apate put an enchantment on the box so that

if anyone opened it except her, the box would appear to be empty, instead of filled with valuables as it truly was . . .

Okay, so the box had some kind of magic mumbo jumbo attached to it, some kind of illusion that kept whatever was inside safe. I frowned. From the card, it didn't seem like the box had any great magical powers, and there was no mention of the jewelry at all. So why would the Reapers risk coming into the library to steal them? Sure, all those gems were no doubt priceless, but Loki had rewarded his followers with gold, silver, and more, just like the other gods in the Pantheon had their supporters. The Reapers had just as much money as everyone else did in the mythological world. So why go to all the trouble to swipe more gemstones? Why not go after some of the swords in the library? Or the armor? Something with more obvious magic and power?

"A box?" Vic asked, voicing my thoughts. "The Reaper took a bloody box? Why, it's not even a weapon!"

My head started aching from all the questions that crowded into my mind, but try as I might, I just couldn't figure out what was so special about the box or the jewelry. There had to be something here that I was missing because the Reapers never did anything without a purpose, without an end goal, in mind.

"Gwen!" Daphne's voice drifted across the library to me. "Where are you? Are you okay?"

"Over here!" I called out. "I'm fine! Stay put! I'm coming back to you!"

Still troubled, I took one more look at the smashed case before I returned to the others.

Logan, Daphne, Oliver, and Alexei were in the back of the library huddled in a tight knot in the middle of the dead Reapers. The Valkyrie caught sight of me first, and princess pink sparks erupted from her fingertips like fireworks, telling me just how glad she was to see me.

"There you are!" Daphne said, pulling me into a tight hug. "Why did you just run off like that? We were so worried about you!"

"I know. I'm sorry. But you guys were winning against the others, and I didn't want to let that last Reaper get away."

I told the others about seeing the Reaper slip away and how I'd chased him back into the stacks, only to find him stealing artifacts.

"What artifacts?" Oliver asked.

I shrugged. "That's the weird thing. It was just a box and some jewelry. It didn't even seem to have that much magic attached to it, according to the ID card I read. I don't know why they would go to so much trouble to break in here just to take those things. Why didn't they take some of the weapons instead? Things that are more powerful? Or at least more useful in a battle?"

"Reapers don't have to make sense," Logan said in a dark voice.

I gestured at the bodies lying on the bloody floor. My friends had pulled off the rubber masks, revealing the Reapers' dull, glazed eyes and pain-filled faces. The group was pretty evenly split between men and women, all adults.

"And what about the Reapers? Does anyone know who they are? Or how they could have gotten onto campus and into the library without raising any sort of alarm?"

Logan shook his head. "I don't recognize any of them. You, Alexei?"

He shook his head as well. "No. None of them look familiar to me."

"Maybe Gwen can find out something with her magic," Oliver said, looking at me. "You know, like you did at your grandma's house."

I grimaced. Oliver was talking about how I'd used my magic to flash on the man who'd been with Preston and Vivian when they'd attacked Grandma Frost a few weeks ago—the man my grandma had killed instead. I hadn't liked touching that dead man, and I certainly didn't want to do the same to a bunch of dead Reapers, but Oliver was right. Maybe my psychometry would give me some information about the Reapers and what they'd wanted with the artifacts.

"Gypsy girl?" Logan asked.

I sighed. "I don't like it, but I'll do it."

One by one, I went from Reaper to Reaper, pulling off their bloody gloves, touching their hands, and seeing what vibes I got off them. But all the memories and feelings attached to the men and women had already started to fade away, and the only images I saw were of the Reapers fighting my friends and then the blinding flashes of pain they felt before they died from their wounds.

I finished with the last Reaper, shook my head, and got to my feet. "Nothing there. Just a few memories of the fight. Everything else is gone already."

Oliver slung his arm around my shoulders. "Well, I'm just glad we made it through okay. Alexei and I would have been in a world of hurt, if you hadn't managed to get those swords and that scabbard to us, Gwen."

I lightly elbowed him in the ribs. "You would have done the same for me."

Oliver grinned. "Maybe."

I elbowed him a little harder. "Definitely."

We stood there, staring at the bodies.

Logan drew in a breath. "Well, I guess I'd better call my dad and tell him what's happened. Metis and Ajax too—"

"Gwendolyn?" a familiar voice called out. "Where are you? Why aren't you at the checkout counter?"

I'd forgotten all about Nickamedes leaving to run some errands, but now he was back—and the library was a disaster area once more. Books and broken glass littered the floor, not to mention the dead Reapers lying in the middle of the mess like dolls someone had forgotten to put away. I winced. This was *so* not going to be pleasant.

"Gwendolyn?" he called out again.

But there was no hiding it from him, so I yelled back. "Over here!"

A few seconds later, Nickamedes rounded the corner

of the office complex. "What are you doing back here? I'm ready to close the library for the night—"

The librarian looked up from the book he'd been reading and stopped in his tracks. His eyebrows shot up in his face, and his eyes bulged as he stared at all the blood and bodies on the floor. His mouth dropped open, and a familiar spark of anger began to burn in his blue gaze. He looked at me.

I winced again. I knew what was coming now. "I can explain—"

Nickamedes held up his hand, cutting me off. "I don't even want to hear it."

"But—"

I tried again, but Nickamedes just shook his head, his shoulders sagging.

"No, Gwendolyn," he said in a resigned tone. "It's my fault. I should have known better than to leave you alone in the library. Things always seem to get . . . broken whenever I do that."

Well, that was one way of putting it. At least he wasn't yelling at me—

Nickamedes straightened up to his full height. "I'm glad you are all okay, but Reapers or not, my library is once again in a state of total disarray . . ."

The librarian's voice got a little louder and a little sharper with every word, but I just stood there and listened to his lecture in silence. I figured I owed Nickamedes that much for wrecking the library for the second time in less than a year.

Chapter 14

Nickamedes lectured me for a good five minutes before he finally calmed down enough to call Metis, Ajax, Raven, and Linus.

I knew he had to tell Linus what had happened, but it wouldn't do anything to raise the other man's low opinion of me—especially since Logan had been involved. Linus thought I was a bad influence on the Spartan, and part of me was starting to wonder if he was right. I was a Champion, which meant I was a target for the Reapers. That was bad enough, but the fact that I was Nike's Champion pretty much made me number one on the Reapers' kill list. As long as Logan was with me, he would always be in danger—and so would my friends.

I loved Logan, and I loved my friends, but sometimes I couldn't help but wonder if they would all be better off without me. Carson had almost died at the Crius Coliseum a few weeks ago, and it was only a matter of time before someone else got hurt—or worse. But I also knew I couldn't be a Champion without them. I just couldn't. They were my rocks, my friends, my family now. Without their love and support, I would have been dead long ago. But I didn't know what I could do to protect my friends, other than kill Loki. Something I still had no clue how to do.

Those were the dark, guilty thoughts that swirled through my mind as my friends and I sat at the study tables in the back of the library. I'd already grabbed my bag from underneath the counter, wiped the blood off Vic, and put him back into his leather scabbard. I didn't know what, if anything, the Protectorate knew about the talking sword, but I had a feeling it would be better if he was out of sight. Besides, Vic was happy to take a nap now that the fight was over.

"It was a good night's work," Vic said in a satisfied voice before letting out a loud yawn. "Would have been even better if we'd gotten the last Reaper, but you're coming along nicely, Gwen. Next time, we'll get them all . . ."

His eye drifted shut, and he was snoring a minute later.

I'd just slid Vic into my messenger bag when Metis, Ajax, and Raven arrived, along with men and women wearing black coveralls and pushing metal gurneys. For the first time, I noticed that the men and women all had the same emblem stitched into their collars in white thread—the hand-and-scales symbol. It must be some sort of Protectorate mark because the same symbol was also stamped onto the black body bags the workers had brought with them.

I sat next to Logan and watched Ajax, Nickamedes, and Raven oversee the workers, who cleaned up the mess and loaded the Reapers' bodies onto the gurneys to roll over to the math-science building, where the academy morgue was. The bodies were quickly removed, but my gaze lingered on all the blood still on the floor. I shivered. Once again, I couldn't help but think that could have been our blood splattered everywhere— my friends' blood, my blood. The thought made me sick.

Professor Metis came over to the table and laid a hand on my arm. "Are you okay, Gwen?"

I nodded. "I'm fine."

And I was—physically anyway. I'd only gotten a few bumps and bruises during the fight, along with some cuts from smashing the artifact case that had held the Ruslan swords. In fact, we'd all come through the battle more or less okay. Oliver had a deep gash on his left bicep, Alexei had a nasty cut that slashed across his right cheek, and Logan had several scrapes and bruises on his hands and arms, but Metis and Daphne used their magic to heal us all.

Once that was done, Alexei grabbed a rag from one of the workers and started cleaning the blood off the swords. Oliver and Logan clustered around him, examining the weapons, with Daphne chiming in that they weren't nearly as cool as her bow was. While my friends talked, I sat still and silent and watched the bodies being loaded up, with Metis standing by my side.

"Is it wrong that I'm sort of getting used to this?" I finally asked.

She gave me a grim smile. "I don't know about wrong, but sad—definitely sad."

We watched the workers a few more minutes before Metis jerked her head. "You said that the Reaper took some artifacts. Show me where and which ones."

I led her into the stacks and showed her the smashed display case, the fallen books, and the broken glass. Logan followed us, and so did Alexei. Apparently, he was back to guarding me now that the fight was over.

Metis studied the mess for a minute before she turned to me. "Gwen?"

She was asking the same thing Oliver had—if I would use my magic to see if I could get any vibes off anything. I nodded, crouched down on my knees, and wrapped my hand around a broken piece of wood.

My psychometry kicked in, and the image of the Reaper slamming a sword into the case and splintering the wood filled my mind, along with the *crash-crash-crash* of breaking glass. I concentrated, touching other pieces of wood and glass, but all the memories were the same. After a minute, I got to my feet.

"Anything?" Metis asked.

I shook my head. "Nothing important, just like with the bodies I touched earlier. All I saw was the Reaper ripping into the case."

Metis picked up the ID card and read it, just as I had earlier. Then, she looked at the empty case. "I don't understand," she murmured. "Why would the Reapers take something like this? Why go to all the trouble when there are so many much more valuable things in here?"

"I know, right?" I said. "The box and the jewelry are

beautiful, but it doesn't seem to me that they have any real power at all."

"Or maybe this is all just a clever ruse to throw the Protectorate off your trail," a low voice cut in.

I turned to see Linus striding down the aisle, followed by Inari and Sergei. Agrona was with them as well, trailing along behind the others. The Protectorate members stopped, forming a single row across the aisle. I sighed. Here we went again.

Linus fixed me with a cold look. "Once more, it seems you're right in the middle of a Reaper attack, Miss Frost. That's a nasty habit of yours. Care to tell me what happened?"

I looked at Metis, who nodded. I drew in a breath and told him everything—seeing the Reapers sneaking up on Alexei and Oliver, warning them of the attack, the battle, then chasing after the Reaper, realizing that the evil warrior was stealing artifacts, and finally how the Reaper had escaped.

When I finished, Linus focused his frosty glare on Alexei.

"You were not supposed to let Miss Frost out of your sight," he barked at the younger man. "So why is it that she was in the stacks alone, supposedly shelving books?"

A flush spread across Alexei's cheeks, and he opened his mouth, but I cut him off.

"Because I had work to do and I was tired of him watching me like a freaking hawk, so I told him I was going to the bathroom and gave him the slip," I lied. "He was probably asking Oliver where I was when the Reapers attacked."

Alexei's brows drew together in surprise, but Linus's face got even frostier than before.

"You were chosen for this assignment because you are one of the most promising young warriors in the Pantheon," Linus snapped. "Yet you didn't even make it through the day without being outsmarted by this girl."

Maybe I'd been hanging around Vic too long, but I couldn't help but speak up. "Well, I am rather clever that way," I said in a snide voice.

A vein started to pulse in Linus's temple, and I could almost hear him grind his teeth together.

"Even the most dedicated warriors can have a momentary lapse," Inari said. "It happens to the best of us."

"Give my boy a break," Sergei chimed in, his voice much louder and more defensive than Inari's. "Everything worked out okay in the end, didn't it?"

Linus turned his glare to the other man. "If by *okay* you mean Reapers somehow breaking into the Library of Antiquities without raising any sort of alarm, attacking students, and stealing artifacts, then yes. I suppose everything worked out *okay.*"

Sergei let out a huff of air, but he didn't say anything else. Inari put a hand on his shoulder, silently signaling his friend to take it easy. Agrona stood next to them, still quiet, although her beautiful features were pinched together in thought, and she kept toying with her necklace, rubbing the gold chain between her fingers.

Linus swung his gaze back to me. "Or perhaps this was part of your plan all along to deflect suspicion from yourself, Miss Frost. Steal away from Alexei and then raise the supposed alarm about Reapers attacking.

Maybe the reason they didn't raise any alarms was because you let them into the library. Maybe the reason the last Reaper got away with the artifacts was because that was your plan all along."

"My plan?" I said, my voice as cold and angry as his. "My plan was just to stay alive and help my friends do the same. Nothing else. Despite what you think, I'm not some criminal Reaper mastermind. I'm trying to stop them."

Linus snorted. "Oh, I doubt that, given the evidence we've collected."

His words made my stomach twist with worry, but I forced myself to stay calm and not let any of my fear show. Logan stepped closer to me and took my hand in his. As soon as his fingers touched mine, his warm concern washed over me, sweeping away everything else. I flashed him a grateful smile.

Linus's gaze lingered on our linked hands a moment before he sighed. "All right. Let's round up the others and go over it all again. You too, Logan. I want to hear what you saw as well. Come with me."

Linus whirled around, his gray cloak billowing out around him as he strode down the aisle. Sergei, Alexei, and Metis followed him. Logan looked at me, a question in his eyes.

"It's okay," I said. "Go ahead."

Logan nodded and hurried after the others, leaving me standing alone with Agrona in front of the smashed case. She fiddled with her gold necklace another moment, before finally sighing and letting it slip through her fingers.

"I'm sorry about my husband," she said in a soft voice. "He's under a lot of pressure now that Loki is free. Plus, he and Logan have a . . . difficult relationship. They always have."

She smiled, and I was struck again by just how very beautiful she was. I wondered what she saw in a man like Linus, who seemed so judgmental and cold to everyone around him.

"But he really does love Logan," Agrona added. "I was resting when Linus got the call about the attack, but he dropped everything to come over here. I barely caught up with him before he left."

I nodded. Maybe Linus really did care about Logan, but I thought he had a strange way of showing it—or rather not showing it. Or maybe I just didn't like him because of all the hurtful things he'd said about my mom—and me too.

Agrona gave me another sad smile and went to join the others.

I looked at the smashed remains of the artifact case, wondering once again why the Reaper would take a keepsake box instead of something more powerful, something that could be used to hurt another person. I crouched down among the glittering glass. My gaze landed on something sticking out from under the book-shelf, and I realized it was the velvet stand that the box had been sitting on. I remembered seeing the Reaper touch the stand, although the warrior had been wearing gloves at the time. Still, maybe I could use my psychom-etry to see why the Reaper had wanted the box so badly.

I leaned forward and stretched out my hand toward the stand—

Something moved off to my left. My eyes darted that way, and I realized that Inari was watching me from the shadows farther down the aisle. I'd thought he'd left with the others but apparently not. I hadn't even heard him creep up behind me. There were a couple of Ninja students at Mythos, so I knew that stealth was one of the skills they prided themselves on—being able to slip behind enemy lines undetected and kill Reapers before they even knew what hit them. Daphne had also told me that Ninjas had some sort of power, some sort of magic mumbo jumbo, that let them get into any building, no matter how heavily it was guarded. The ability was something like invisibility, but instead of actually fading into nothingness, Ninjas somehow blended into the shadows and background so that other people just sort of looked past them without really seeing them.

Just like the attack in the library tonight.

I flashed back to the way the Reapers had moved so quietly through the stacks, especially the leader. Despite being trained warriors, neither Oliver nor Alexei had noticed the Reapers creeping closer and closer to them. Then again, the two guys had been having a pretty intense argument at the time. Still, I couldn't help but notice that Inari had the same slender build as the leader had.

I didn't believe in coincidences—not anymore. And having Reapers of Chaos attack the Library of Antiquities the day after the Protectorate showed up was just a little too convenient. Vivian Holler had seemed like the quietest, nicest, shyest girl at Mythos, but she'd turned out to be Loki's Champion. So it wouldn't be too much of a stretch to think that one of the Protectorate members was really a Reaper in disguise.

I dropped my hand to my side. If Inari was a Reaper, I didn't want to give him any clue that I suspected him— or that I thought I could get a vibe off anything here. Instead, I used a piece of wood to slide the velvet stand farther under the bookshelf. I'd come back later and touch the stand and the shelves around it and see what my psychometry revealed to me.

I also made a big show of dusting off my hands, getting to my feet, and rejoining the others. Inari kept watching me, his face expressionless, as though he was one of the statues looking down on me from the second-floor balcony. After a few seconds, he fell into step behind me and followed me out into the main part of the library.

Apparently, Linus had decided to question Logan first, because he was standing beside his son, with Agrona hovering nearby. From the tense expression on Logan's face, I knew they were talking about me. Metis was speaking with Sergei, Nickamedes, Daphne, and Oliver. She waved at Inari, and the Ninja moved over to join them. I didn't see Raven anywhere. She must have left with the workers and bodies already.

That left me alone—until Alexei came over to me. I'd thought that he would just silently watch me like he'd been doing all day, but instead, he reached out and touched my arm.

Alexei hesitated. "I wanted to thank you—for saving

my life tonight. Oliver's too. If you hadn't warned us when you did . . ."

"It was nothing."

"It wasn't nothing," he protested. "My first assignment from the Protectorate, and I let myself be . . . distracted by Oliver when I was supposed to be watching you. I failed the Protectorate, and I failed my father."

"Your dad seems okay with how you handled yourself," I said. "Besides, everyone makes mistakes. Trust me. I've made some gigantic ones recently. You know, getting tricked into finding the Helheim Dagger, being forced to free Loki, dooming the entire world."

I winced. I'd tried to make my voice light, but even I could hear the darkness in my words. They were nothing to joke about. Especially not now.

"Yes, but you jumped into the middle of the fight," Alexei said. "And you made sure that Oliver and I had the weapons we needed to defend ourselves."

"You would have done the same for me, for any warrior."

He shook his head. "I don't know about that. My orders were to watch you—nothing else."

"Is that why you didn't do anything in the dining hall this morning? And when those guys threw their sodas at me outside the library? Because Linus told you not to interfere?"

He nodded.

"And now?"

He shrugged. "Now, I don't know what to think."

Sergei gestured at his son, and Alexei walked over to him. Well, it wasn't quite an apology for standing by while I'd been threatened, but it was a start. Right now, I'd take what I could get. Because I had a feeling things were going to get a lot worse before they got better—if they ever could.

Finally, an hour later, everyone had given their statements to the Protectorate, and we were all free to leave the library.

"Go straight back to your dorm room, Miss Frost," Linus warned me. "Alexei, make sure she gets there."

Alexei nodded, relief on his face at the fact that he was being given a second chance to watch me.

"I'm going too," Logan said.

Linus opened his mouth to argue, but he saw the stubborn set of Logan's jaw. "Fine. I'll see you at breakfast in the morning, just as we planned. Don't be late."

Logan sighed, but he nodded at his father. I said my good-byes to Daphne and Oliver, then left the library with Logan and Alexei.

It had grown bitterly cold while we'd been inside, and more snow had covered the ground since I'd stepped onto the balcony looking for the Reaper. I shivered and wrapped my gray scarf a little tighter around my neck to help keep out the chill. It was almost ten o'clock, and all the other students were already safe and snug inside their dorms for the night. The three of us made it over to Styx Hall without seeing anyone else. We stopped at the bottom of the steps, and Logan turned to Alexei.

"Can you give us a few minutes alone, please?" the Spartan asked.

I thought Alexei would say no, given what Linus had

said to him in the library, but the Bogatyr nodded and drifted off to stand underneath one of the trees that ringed the dorm. Logan stared at me, his blue eyes somehow bright, despite the shadows around us.

"How are you holding up, Gypsy girl?" he asked in a soft voice.

"Oh, you know. Another day, another night, another battle to the death with Reapers in the library," I joked. "It's the Mythos Academy special."

Logan smiled a little, but we could both hear how hollow my words really were.

"Why do you think the Reaper took that box?" he asked. "I know you said you didn't get any big flashes off the case with your magic."

I shook my head. "No, nothing useful. Just the Reaper smashing the glass and taking the artifacts. I'm going to go back tomorrow and try again, just in case I missed anything."

Logan nodded, and we were quiet for a few seconds.

"I'm sorry about my dad," he said.

"It's okay. He's just doing his job. I'd rather he be here and worried about you than not around at all, wouldn't you?"

Logan shook his head. "Maybe. But I'd rather he not dis my girlfriend every chance he gets. He started in on you again tonight in the library before Agrona distracted him by changing the subject."

My breath caught in my throat at the word Logan had just said. "Girlfriend?" I whispered.

Logan gave me a crooked grin. "Well, yeah. That's what we are now, right? Together? As in a real couple?"

Despite all the horrible things that had happened over the past few days, happiness erupted in my heart like fireworks streaking up into the sky and exploding in a hundred happy colors. If I'd had a Valkyrie's magic, sparks would have been shooting out of my fingertips like lightning. For a moment, everything was bright, beautiful, and perfect—simply perfect.

Then, Logan frowned, as if another thought had just occurred to him. "Unless you sneak back into the stacks and make out with just any guy who saves your life a few times."

I rolled my eyes and lightly punched him in the shoulder. "And there you go again, ruining the moment."

The Spartan laughed and drew me into his arms. The heat of his body washed over me, driving away the cold and awakening all the feelings I had for him—feelings that made me wish Alexei wasn't standing a few feet away.

"I'm glad you're okay," I whispered, gazing up at him.

"You too."

"When I saw the Reapers in the library, I was so worried that maybe they'd already killed you and Daphne—" My throat closed up, and I couldn't get the words out to tell him how scared I'd been of losing him.

"But I made it through another battle and so did you, Gypsy girl," he said in a gentle voice. "No matter what happens, I'll always come back to you."

"Promise?" I asked in a shaky voice.

Logan's eyes burned with icy determination. "Promise." He leaned forward, resting his forehead against mine.

I stood up on my tiptoes and kissed him once, softly, before putting my head on his chest. Logan's arms tightened around my back, and he pulled me even closer. And we stayed like that, just holding each other in the cold dark for as long as we could.

Chapter 15

I hadn't thought it was possible, but the next day was even worse than the one before.

Word got out about the Reaper attack at the library, the way it always did, and it only made the other students angrier at me. Apparently, they all believed that I'd planned the whole thing, just like Linus did. Harsh mutters and snide comments followed me wherever I went.

"Where's your black robe, Reaper girl?"

"Going to bring more of your friends on campus to attack us?"

"Why don't you just get lost, you murdering bitch?"

I'd been used to being ignored by the other kids, but now I was the center of attention at Mythos. Everyone watched me all day long, and every time I reached into my messenger bag for a pen or a piece of paper, the other students and even some of my professors tensed up, as though I was going to pull Vic out of his scabbard and go all Reaper on them. Some of my classmates, like

Helena Paxton, probably wanted me to do that very thing so they could lash out at me with their own weapons.

I kept my face blank, and I didn't respond to the threats and taunts, even though the words and accusations hurt, like invisible daggers slicing off my skin one layer at a time, leaving me bloody, exposed, and aching from head to toe.

But my friends kept their promise to watch my back. Daphne and Carson walked me from class to class to class in the morning, while the three of us sat with Logan and Oliver during lunch. The other kids glared at my friends, but nobody wanted to take them all on, especially not Logan.

Alexei was there too, watching and following me all day. He didn't talk much, but every once in a while he would nod his head at me. He seemed to have thawed a little bit toward me.

But my friends couldn't be with me in my classes, and all the other students pulled their desks away from mine once again. Finally, it was time for gym. Yesterday, I'd stood by myself at the edge of the mats all period long, watching everyone else fight. Today, I was wondering if it would be even more humiliating—or dangerous. I'd thought that some of the students might decide to come after me with their weapons, but to my surprise a few folks stood up for me.

"I'll be sparring with Gwen today," Morgan McDougall announced in a loud voice before Coach Ajax could randomly assign us partners like he sometimes did. The Valkyrie twirled a staff around and around in her hands, green sparks of magic shooting out of her finger-tips.

"Me too," Talia Pizarro chimed in. The Amazon stood next to Morgan, slashing her sword through the air.

The girls were issuing a clear warning to the others, and I gave them grateful smiles. Morgan winked at me, her hazel eyes warm.

"Hey," she said. "Us school sluts have to stick to-gether, right?"

I knew that Morgan meant the word *slut* as a sort of in-joke between us, and my smile widened a little. "You'd better believe it."

Carson also stuck up for me again in myth-history, leaving his desk right in front of mine and grinning at me before burying his nose in a stack of sheet music and staying that way until Metis started class. Carson was obviously stressing about the winter concert tomorrow, so I left him alone. Besides, I had other things on my mind too—my impending trial, for one.

With the other students taunting me and the Reaper attack, I hadn't had a chance to think too much about the trial, but Linus had said that it would start after classes today. All day long, I'd kept gazing at the clocks on the walls, watching the hours and minutes tick away until I was all out of time.

The last bell of the day rang, signaling the end of myth-history. I sat in my seat and waited until all the other students had filed out before getting to my feet. Once again, I kept my face calm, but my movements were slow and stiff, and I felt like there were a pair of hands deep inside my chest, tying my insides into tighter and tighter knots. Alexei stood in the corner, watching me, just like he had all day long.

Metis tucked her papers in her briefcase and turned to face me. "It's time," she said. "Please follow me."

I nodded, not sure what else to do, not sure what else I *could* do without opening my mouth and insisting once again that the Protectorate had it all wrong, that I wasn't a Reaper.

I slung my messenger bag over my shoulder. It felt light, empty almost, without Vic in it. I'd taken the sword back to my room after gym class. I didn't want him to pipe up and say the wrong thing at my trial and risk the Protectorate taking him away from me. Naturally, Vic had grumbled about being left behind—

"Gwen?" Metis asked. "Are you okay?"

"Sure," I said. "Just terrific. Let's go get this over with."

I followed Metis out of the classroom, to the end of the hallway, and then outside. Alexei trailed along behind me, and Sergei and Inari were waiting at the bottom of the steps of the English-history building, I supposed to keep me from bolting.

The two men fell in step on either side of me, with Metis leading the way and Alexei bringing up the rear. We crossed the quad in silence, although stares and whispers sprang up in our wake.

Daphne, Carson, Logan, and Oliver were out on the quad too, right outside the math-science building. My friends stared at me, their faces tight with concern. They weren't allowed at my trial, so this was the only support they could give me. I looked at my friends and smiled, as though everything was going to be okay, but I didn't stop to talk to them. If I did that, I didn't know if I'd be able to get through this.

I trudged up the steps to the math-science building and went inside with the others. Then, down, down, down, we went, with Metis punching in codes on keypads and chanting a bit of magic mumbo jumbo when necessary.

All too soon, though, we were on the bottom level in front of the door that led into the academy prison. I eyed the sphinxes carved into the stone, but once again the creatures stared at their feet instead of me.

Metis used her skeleton key to open the door, and I felt Sergei's hand on my arm a moment, gently guiding me forward. I swallowed and stepped through the opening to the other side.

The prison looked the same as always—Raven's desk in the corner, glass cells stacked on top of each other, the hand-and-scales carving on the domed ceiling. But there were two new additions. A stone interrogation table stood in the same place as before, directly below the carving, although it was twice as big as the one where Preston had always sat. But what really caught my attention was a second table that had been erected on the far side. Together, the two tables created a loose *T* shape, with the second table forming the top part of the letter. The second table had also been set on a stone dais, raising it up several feet off the ground, and seven chairs were arranged behind it. That's where my jury would sit, I thought bitterly. Looking down on and judging me from above.

A hand touched my shoulder, and a faint, familiar *jingle-jingle-jingling* sounded. I turned, and Grandma Frost was there. She wore a black pantsuit with her usual black shoes, and she'd tied a violet scarf around her throat and another one in her hair. The silver coins on the ends glimmered in the light.

"Grandma!" I said and hugged her tight.

She smoothed down my hair. "Don't you worry, pumpkin. I'm right here with you. We'll set these yahoos straight."

"And so am I," another voice cut in.

I let go of Grandma to see Nickamedes standing behind her. "I don't understand."

The librarian straightened up to his full height. "I'm to represent you in your defense and see that your rights are not violated."

"You would do that for me? Even though I wrecked the library again last night?"

He grimaced a little, but his eyes remained kind in his face. "Even though."

"If the pleasantries are over with," Linus Quinn said, striding into the prison, along with Agrona, Ajax, and Raven, "let us begin."

The door clanged shut, sealing us all in the prison. The sound seemed to echo through the whole chamber over and over again, until the force of it rattled my teeth.

I swallowed my growing dread and followed Nickamedes over to the interrogation table. I took a seat in the middle, with the librarian on my right and Grandma Frost on my left. Grandma took my hand in hers, but the warmth of her fingers and the feel of her love wasn't enough to drive away the cold that had seeped into my bones and the fear that quickened my heart.

Alexei moved to stand behind me and off to my right. The others climbed the steps to the dais and took their seats behind the table there. Linus sat in the middle, with Agrona, Inari, Sergei, Raven, Metis, and Coach Ajax taking the other chairs. Metis gave me an encouraging smile, but I knew the odds were stacked against me. There were seven people on the jury, which meant that I needed at least four to get a majority vote. Metis and Ajax would be on my side, but I doubted any of the others would be, except maybe for Raven.

I looked at the old woman, and she stared back at me. For an instant, her features flickered, as though they weren't her true face, as though there was another person lurking underneath the wrinkles and liver spots. The same thing had happened a few weeks ago at the Crius Coliseum. I blinked, and Raven was just Raven again. Strange, but then again everything about her was strange, including the fact that she already looked bored. Well, I didn't care if she was bored or if she slept through the whole freaking trial, as long as she sided with Metis and Ajax in the end.

But even if she did, I'd still need at least one more member of the jury to vote for me, and I didn't know who it might be. Certainly not Linus, who'd made his feelings about me so clear already. I doubted Agrona would vote against her husband, so that left Inari and Sergei. I looked at them, and they both stared back at me with smooth expressions, telling me nothing of what they might be thinking or what they'd uncovered about me while they'd been on campus.

When everyone was seated, Linus picked up a small gavel and rapped it against the table. "We will now come to order."

Everyone quieted down, and I drew in a breath—my trial was about to begin.

Chapter 16

Linus shuffled some papers around on the table, while the others did the same. Everyone except for Raven, who seemed to be reading another one of her celebrity gossip magazines. At least, I thought I saw a bright, glossy cover hidden in among the stacks of papers in front of her. She noticed me watching her and gave a little shrug. Good to know she was taking this so seriously.

While the Protectorate got ready to start, I stared up at the domed ceiling. Maybe it was a trick of the lights, but the hand holding the set of scales looked particularly prominent today, almost like the hand was straining to punch through the stone above my head. As I watched, a soft *creak* filled my ears, and the scales began to tilt to one side, as if I'd already been found guilty. It fact, it seemed like the scales were dropping lower and lower, almost as if they might erupt out of the ceiling and crash down on my head, crushing me where I sat—

I blinked, and the carving was just a carving once more, and the scales were perfectly balanced. Sometimes, my Gypsy gift made me see things that weren't really there, like the pictures that always seemed to come to life in my myth-history books, but those tilting scales had been creepy, even for Mythos. I shivered and dropped my eyes from the ceiling. Or maybe I was just especially freaked out because of what was at stake right now—my life.

Finally, all the papers were shuffled, and all eyes turned to me. Grandma Frost tightened her grip on my hand, letting me know that she was there for me no matter what. I gently squeezed her fingers.

Linus banged the gavel once more. "Let us begin," he said. "Bring out the basket."

Basket? What basket?

Raven got to her feet, walked down the dais steps, and headed over to one of the cells. She punched in a code, and the glass *whooshed* back. The old woman stepped into the cell, bent down, and picked up a small wicker basket that I hadn't noticed before. She turned and carried the basket over to the stone table where I was sitting. Raven glanced over her shoulder at Linus, who nodded at her to go ahead.

The old woman took the top off the basket, stuck her hand inside, and brought out a snake.

I let out a gasp and lurched back in my chair.

"Easy, Gwendolyn," Nickamedes said in a low voice. "This is just part of the process. Don't worry. You have nothing to fear."

"Now," Linus said. "Shackle the girl to the table."

"Shackle me?" I asked. "Why?"

He ignored my question. "Ajax, if you will."

Coach Ajax grabbed something from under the table. He stood up, and I realized that he was holding a set of handcuffs attached to a long chain. Ajax came over to the interrogation table and put the cuffs and chain on top of it. The harsh *clink-clink-clank* of the metal rattling together made me wince.

"Hold out your hands, Gwen," the coach said. "Please."

I bit my lip and looked at Grandma and Nickamedes. They both nodded, indicating that I had to do this. I reluctantly held out my hands, and Ajax clinked the handcuffs around my wrists, then secured them and the chain to the stone ring in the top of the table.

I drew in a breath and waited for my psychometry to flare up and show me all the awful memories of everyone who'd worn the cuffs before me—but nothing happened. I got an idea of the cuffs being made, and Ajax handling them with a sense of regret, but that was it. No other memories, no other feelings, were associated with either them or the chains. My breath hissed out in relief.

"I made sure they were brand new," Ajax said in a low voice. "And not the ones we used on Preston."

I nodded, grateful for his thoughtfulness. I'd been in Preston's head plenty of times, but I had no desire to feel what he had when he'd been shackled to the interrogation table, to experience all his rage and hatred of me.

Linus gestured to Raven, who stepped forward with the snake. Before I could open my mouth to ask what she was doing, the old woman held the creature out, and the snake sank its fangs into my right wrist.

"Ouch!" I shrieked. "It bit me!"

I yanked my hands away from the snake as far as I could and stared down at my wrist. Two drops of blood trickled out of the puncture marks and spattered onto the table, but the stone soaked up the crimson liquid like a sponge. I expected the wounds to start throbbing, but to my surprise the bite didn't hurt all that much. Instead, it felt more . . . uncomfortable, like a couple of IV needles had been slipped into my skin. I was also aware of a cool sensation flowing through my body, like some sort of medicine had just been injected into my veins.

Raven placed the snake on the table right in front of me. For a moment, I thought it was going to bite me again, but the creature ignored me, as though its job was done. I hadn't noticed it before, but a small circle had been carved into the stone. The snake settled into the groove like the creature was familiar with it, like it belonged there. Its body curled around and around until its head finally came to rest on top of the table—an inch away from my fingers.

"That is a Maat asp," Linus said. "Named after the Egyptian goddess of truth. Over the years, the Pantheon has discovered that the asp's venom has an unusual property. It acts as a sort of truth serum and encourages people to answer honestly—or suffer the consequences."

Well, I guess that explained the cold sensation that continued to spread through my body. "Consequences?" I asked. "What consequences?"

"If you tell the truth, the venom is harmless, and your body will flush it out in a few hours," Linus said.

"And if you don't tell the truth?"

"Every time you tell a lie, the venom heats up a little more in your veins, like liquid fire, until it can feel like being burned alive from the inside out," he answered. "It's quite painful, from what I've seen."

So they were going to torture the truth out of me. Trial by fire, indeed. Great. Just great.

"The asps themselves also have an unusual ability," Linus continued. "They can sense whether or not someone is telling the truth, and they act accordingly."

"What do you mean by that?" I asked.

"When someone tells the truth, the asp will do them no harm," he said. "But when someone lies, the asp gets quite agitated. The more a person lies, the more agitated the asp becomes until it strikes out at the person who is lying. That second bite acts as an immediate trigger for the poison already in your veins. Death is often thought of as a blessing. Those lucky—or unlucky—enough to survive a second bite from a Maat asp often wish they hadn't."

"And why is that?" I couldn't help but ask the question.

"The side effects are quite brutal and include everything from permanent paralysis to rotting limbs," Linus said. "The effects vary from person to person. No one knows exactly why, except that ironically enough, the punishment usually fits the crime. For example, if a Reaper is caught stealing artifacts and lies about it, the asp's bite will usually make a finger or two rot and fall off. Sometimes, a Reaper's whole hand or arm. Like I said, most Reapers who survive that second bite wish they hadn't—or that they'd just told the truth to start with."

I eyed the snake. I'd been face-to-face with Nemean prowlers, Fenrir wolves, and even a Black roc, and the Maat asp seemed like a harmless little garden snake in comparison to the massive size of the other mythological creatures. In fact, the asp's shimmering blue and black scales made it look quite dainty and pretty, almost like a jeweled bracelet you could wear around your wrist. The creature blinked sleepily at me, its eyes the same deep, vivid blue as its scales. Its black tongue flicked out of its mouth, tasting the air. I wondered if it could sense my fear. The emotion was probably radiating off me like anger had off the other students for the past few days.

"As long as you tell the truth, you'll be fine, Miss Frost," Linus continued. "Keep in mind that you lie to us at your own peril."

Yeah, I'd gotten that message loud and clear. I swallowed and looked at Grandma Frost, who patted my shoulder.

"It's okay, pumpkin," she said. "That itty-bitty snake can't hurt you because you're innocent. Soon, these fools will realize it too."

Linus arched his eyebrows at my grandma, who gave him a serene smile in return. He shuffled a few more papers around on the table before looking at me again.

"Now," he said. "The first accusation against you is

that you murdered another student. Jasmine Ashton, a Valkyrie in your second-year class. According to the charges, Jasmine found out that you had stolen an artifact called the Bowl of Tears from the Library of Antiquities back in the fall. She was attempting to stop you from sacrificing another student, Morgan McDougall, to Loki, and you killed her for it. Is that correct?"

Is that correct... correct... correct...

His words echoed in my head over and over again. It was almost like he was speaking a foreign language because it took me several seconds to process the words. To realize what he was really saying—and what he was actually accusing me of.

I shook my head. "No—no way. I didn't do any of those things. That's not what happened—not at all. Jasmine is the one who stole the Bowl of Tears, not me. I was the one who realized that she was planning to sacrifice Morgan. I was the one who stopped her, not the other way around."

"And why would Jasmine want to kill Morgan?" This time, Inari was the one who spoke. "According to our reports, the two Valkyries were friends—best friends."

"Because Jasmine found out that Morgan was messing around with Samson Sorensen, Jasmine's boyfriend," I said. "And because Jasmine was a Reaper and that's what Reapers do. You guys should know that better than anyone."

"Keep the editorial comments to yourself, Miss Frost," Linus said. "We are not the ones on trial—you are. You would do well to keep that in mind."

I clamped my lips together to keep from telling him

what I really thought about him, the Protectorate, and this stupid trial.

"But you don't deny that you killed Jasmine by shoving a spear through her chest?" Agrona asked.

I hesitated. I wasn't the one who'd actually killed Jasmine—Logan was. The Spartan had saved me that night, first by killing the Nemean prowler, a big, black, panther-like creature, that Jasmine had sicced on me and then by killing the evil Valkyrie herself. I didn't want to get him in trouble, especially not with his dad, by telling the Protectorate what had really happened. I didn't want Logan dragged in here and facing the same sort of torture that I was—but I didn't want to die by snake bite either.

The Maat asp raised its head, and its tongue flickered out of its mouth again, almost like it was about to test the truthfulness of my words. I couldn't lie, not with the snake an inch from my hand and the cold venom running through my veins, just waiting to ignite.

Desperate, I looked around the prison, as if the empty glass cells would give me some idea how to get out of this mess, but of course they didn't. Neither did glancing at Grandma Frost, Nickamedes, or the hand-and-scales carving. Finally, my gaze dropped to the cuffs and chains, which made me think of Preston. He used to scream and struggle whenever I came down to the prison to peer into his mind with my magic. Vivian had told me what had upset Preston so much was knowing there was nothing he could do to hide the truth from me.

The asp and its venom might be deadly, but for all its

power, the snake didn't have my Gypsy gift, my psychometry magic. All it had to go on were my words— just words and not any of the memories and feelings behind them. An idea popped into my mind, a way I could get through this—and keep at least some of my secrets to myself.

"Answer the question, Miss Frost," Linus said.

No, I couldn't lie—but maybe I didn't have to.

"I fought with Jasmine," I said, choosing my words carefully and sidestepping the question. "I had to or she would have killed me instead. And Morgan too."

The asp eased its head back down, apparently satisfied with my answer. Okay, well that told me a little something about the rules of the game. Outright lying was a no-no, but omitting certain facts was just fine.

Magic. For all the ways it was supposed to be foolproof, it always seemed there was at least one loophole you could wiggle through, and I fully intended to exploit this one.

"But why did you destroy the Bowl of Tears?" Sergei asked. "It was a priceless artifact, one of the Thirteen Artifacts used during the final battle of the initial Chaos War. It was irreplaceable, yet you smashed it as if it was nothing more than a common dish."

"I smashed it because Jasmine was kicking my ass, and the bowl was somehow feeding her power," I said. "I thought if I broke it, that might stop whatever magic mumbo jumbo she'd started—and it did."

The members of the Protectorate stared at me, doubt and disbelief filling their faces. Linus, Sergei, and Inari all stared at the asp, obviously expecting it to lunge forward and sink its fangs into me again, but a minute passed, then another one, and the snake stayed still on the table.

"Let's move on," Linus finally said.

I let out a breath. Round one of the inquisition was over. Time for round two.

Chapter 17

Linus shuffled some more papers around on the table, and the others did the same.

"Let the record show that so far, Miss Frost has admitted to killing another student and destroying an important artifact," Linus said.

Agrona nodded, and I realized there was a small device sitting on the table next to her—something that looked like a digital voice recorder. So there was to be an official transcript of my trial. Wonderful.

"You're twisting everything around," I protested. "I only did those things to defend myself and my friends."

"You will not speak unless spoken to or asked to answer a question, Miss Frost," Linus said.

I opened my mouth again, but Nickamedes placed a hand on my arm and shook his head in warning. So I clamped my lips shut.

"Let's move on to the next infraction on Miss Frost's record," Linus said. "A series of events that occurred at the Powder ski resort during the annual Winter Carnival getaway. Miss Frost is accused of setting off an avalanche that threatened students, faculty, and staff members, both of the academy and the resort itself, and caused massive amounts of property damage; letting a Fenrir wolf run loose on the resort grounds; injuring two Spartan warriors, Oliver Hector and Logan Quinn; and attacking Preston Ashton, brother of Jasmine Ashton, whom she has already admitted to killing. Miss Frost, what do you have to say about these charges?"

"Not guilty," I sniped.

Apparently, my sarcasm amused Coach Ajax, who let out a faint chuckle. Linus glanced at him, but Ajax just crossed his arms over his chest and leaned back in his chair. After a moment, Linus turned his attention to me once more.

"So you deny that you caused an avalanche during the carnival?" he asked.

"Of course, I deny it because it isn't *true*," I said in an exasperated tone. "Preston's the one who caused the avalanche. He wanted revenge for Jasmine's death, and he wanted to make me pay for kill—"

The asp stirred on the table, its tongue flicking out of its mouth again, reminding me that I had to be very, very careful. I might have figured out a way around the asp's magic, but one wrong word, one slip of the tongue, and I was still dead.

I drew in a breath. "He wanted to make me pay for what happened to his sister. So, Preston pretended that he liked me in hopes of getting me alone so he could kill me. He almost succeeded too, during a party outside the Solstice coffeehouse."

"And what stopped him from killing you that night?" Linus asked.

I looked at him. "Your son. Logan came outside just as I was going to leave with Preston. Logan's the reason I didn't go with Preston that night."

Linus didn't say anything to that. He paused a second before clearing his throat and continuing.

"But you attacked Preston later," he said. "In a part of the ski resort that was under construction. The Spartans, Oliver Hector and Logan Quinn, were injured in the battle. Tell me, Miss Frost, why were you trespassing in the construction site to begin with? Why would you willingly go to such a deserted area if you thought a Reaper was trying to kill you?"

"Because I mistakenly thought Oliver was the Reaper instead of Preston," I said. "I'd run into Oliver upstairs in the hotel, and I wanted to get away from him. I was in a panic so I went down the emergency stairs and wound up in the construction site by accident."

Linus raised an eyebrow. "You mean, Oliver came across you ransacking his room, correct?"

I ground my teeth together. "Yes, I searched his room because I wanted to find out whether or not he was a Reaper. For the record, he isn't."

"Apparently, you think common rules about things like breaking and entering don't apply to you, Miss Frost. In fact, you seem to make your own judgments about all sorts of things," Linus said. "Including a Fenrir wolf at the resort. Our reports show that you let the wolf escape, first during the avalanche and then later on during the fight in the construction site, rather than alerting your professors to its presence so they could properly deal with the creature. Isn't that correct?"

"The wolf wasn't evil, not like Preston was," I said. "So yeah, I let her go. And she wasn't just some *creature*. Her name was Nott, and she was my friend."

Linus, Agrona, Inari, and Sergei made some sort of notation on the papers in front of them. Metis and Ajax just sat there, still, silent, and unmoving. Raven discreetly flipped another page in her gossip magazine.

"Now, let's go back to the fight," Linus said. "You say that Preston was the one who shot Oliver with a crossbow. Are you sure that *you* weren't the one who actually pulled the trigger, Miss Frost?"

"Yes," I snapped. "I did not shoot Oliver. I did not cause the avalanche. I didn't do anything but defend myself and my friends from Preston."

"And how exactly did you do that?" This time, Inari asked the question. "According to the information we've uncovered, your mother, Grace Frost, and your grandmother, Geraldine Frost, hid their involvement in the mythological world from you."

Beside me, Grandma Frost stiffened. I opened my mouth to respond, but she put her hand on my shoulder. "Let me, pumpkin."

Grandma Frost got to her feet and glared at Linus and the other members of the Protectorate. "We did that so our little girl wouldn't grow up always being afraid of Reapers and Nemean prowlers and the like. You raise your children the way you see fit, spoiling them with fancy clothes and cars and jewelry. Well, we wanted her to have a normal life, at least for as long as possible, so yes, we hid our *involvement*, as you call it, in the mythological world from her. I thought it was the right decision back then, and I know it is now. My Gwen is a fine girl, a strong girl, and I couldn't be prouder of her or love her more."

She squared her shoulders and lifted her chin, daring the members of the Protectorate to challenge her again, but none of them did.

"But the question remains," Inari said after my grandma finally sat back down. "You'd only been using weapons for a few months before going to the ski resort. So, how did you manage to defeat a Viking like Preston who'd been training his whole life for just such a fight?"

I sat there and thought and thought, but I couldn't figure out a way to sidestep the question. Finally, I sighed. "I used my psychometry on Logan. That's how I was able to beat Preston."

"You used your magic on another student?" Linus's voice dropped to a dangerous rasp. "On my *son*?"

"It was the only way I could defeat Preston," I said. "Logan knew that as well as I did. He let me use my magic on him, let my use my psychometry to tap in to his memories, his fighting skills. Once I did that, I was able to use his skills like they were my own. That's how I was able to beat Preston, because Logan's memories made me almost as good a fighter as he is."

"Students are not supposed to use their magic on others," Agrona said, toying with her necklace. "Not even in extreme situations like that. It denies the other student's free will, which is what we're all here working so hard to protect."

Metis and Nike had said more or less the same thing to me before, but the words seemed strange coming out of Agrona's mouth, almost like she didn't really believe them. Or perhaps that was just because her voice wasn't as loud as her husband's and she didn't seem quite as eager to convict me.

"Well, it was either that or let Preston take off my head with his sword," I said. "I happen to like my head right where it is, thank you very much."

Ajax let out another laugh. This time, Linus didn't even bother looking at him. Instead, the head of the Protectorate leaned forward and fixed me with a fierce glare.

"Take us through the fight, exactly what happened, Miss Frost. Step by step. And be sure you include everything—especially what you did to my son with your magic."

I sighed again, wondering if the questions and accusations would ever end.

And on and on it went. Somehow, the Protectorate had found out about everything I'd ever done since coming to Mythos. All the times I'd been late for my shifts at the library, all the lost and stolen items I'd found for kids using my psychometry, all the catty comments I'd ever made about other students. It seemed they went out of their way to focus on the bad things, all the rules I'd broken and all the mistakes I'd made, whether on purpose or by accident.

And they seemed to have a grand time doing it, especially Linus. If the others hadn't been around, he probably would have gleefully cackled every time I confessed to something, especially when it came to all the times I'd slipped by the sphinxes on my way to go see Grandma Frost. Apparently, I'd snuck off campus more than fifty times since I'd been at Mythos.

"By far the worst infraction of that particular rule ever recorded in the annals of academy history," Linus said almost in a cheery tone, making another mark on his papers.

I slumped over the table a little more.

"And now we come to the charges that are at the heart of these proceedings," he finally said. "Accusations that Miss Frost willfully conspired with Reapers of Chaos to murder students and staff members at the Crius Coliseum, steal artifacts from the coliseum, recover the Helheim Dagger, and use said dagger to free Loki from the prison realm the other gods placed him in."

I shook my head. "No. That's not what happened at all. None of that is true. Not one word of it."

"We'll see," Linus said.

Nickamedes got to his feet. The librarian had been quiet while I'd been questioned, although he'd been taking tons of notes. I wondered if this was the point when he finally went on the attack and actually, you know, defended me.

"So far," Nickamedes said, "you've offered a vastly

different interpretation of events than what actually transpired, given that Metis, Ajax, Raven, and I were there to witness some of the things you've accused Gwendolyn of. But you haven't offered one shred of proof that things happened the way you claim they did— not one single shred. Unless you have that proof, I see no reason for this absurd trial to continue any further."

Linus gave his former brother-in-law a thin smile. "Why, I thought you'd never ask, Nickamedes. We do, in fact, have a different perspective on the situation, especially on what transpired at the Crius Coliseum and everything after that. We have a witness who claims to have been present at all the events in question, the person who made the accusations against Miss Frost in the first place. She's been quite convincing in her testimony so far, which is why the charges were initially brought against Miss Frost."

"What witness?" Nickamedes asked in a guarded tone.

"Why don't we bring her in, and you can see for yourself?"

Linus nodded to Agrona, who got to her feet, stepped off the dais, and went over to the entry. Agrona pulled on the door, which slowly opened with another loud *screech*.

"You can come in now," Agrona called out.

Something whispered out in the hallway, and a second later, the very last person in the world that I expected to see walked into the prison—Vivian Holler.

A Gypsy, just like me. Loki's Champion. And the Reaper girl who'd killed my mom.

Chapter 18

I was just—stunned.

Absolutely stunned that Vivian was back at the academy after all the things she'd done. Tricking me into finding the Helheim Dagger, kidnapping me, slicing my palm open with the dagger, using the weapon and my blood to free Loki.

Anger exploded in me, blocking out everything else. The trial, the Protectorate, the endless questions. All I was aware of was the rage pulsing through my veins—the same red-hot rage I felt whenever I thought of Vivian and how the other girl had murdered my mom—and laughed about it.

Vivian stepped into the prison, flanked by two men and a woman wearing black coveralls. I leaped up out of my chair and started to charge at the other girl, but I'd forgotten about the handcuffs and chain. I lunged for her and almost pulled my shoulders out of their sockets when the chain stopped me short. I looked down at my shackles. This was how Preston had felt, I thought bitterly. The Reaper had wanted to kill me more than anything else, which was exactly what I wanted to do to Vivian right now.

The Reaper girl stepped closer and gave me a sly, satisfied smile, and I knew that I'd reacted exactly how she'd wanted me to.

"Temper, temper," Vivian said in a mocking tone. "See? I told you she was violent."

"When it comes to you, violent doesn't even begin to cover it," I snarled.

Everyone stared at me, and I had to struggle to get my rage under control. Here I was shackled, and Vivian had strolled right into the academy prison as if she had every right to still be at Mythos.

"Long time no see, Gwen," she said.

"Shut up, you Reaper bitch," I snarled again.

Linus pounded his gavel on the table. "Enough! That's enough, from both of you."

I looked at him. "What is she doing here? Why haven't you arrested her and put her on trial for everything that *she's* done?"

"That's the problem," he said in a thoughtful voice. "Vivian came to us a few weeks ago, right after Loki escaped, and she's been in Protectorate custody ever since. She told us a very interesting story about what happened that night, and your part in it. Quite simply, Miss Holler claims that she is really Nike's Champion—and that you are the one who serves Loki, Miss Frost."

For a moment, the world went black. Completely, utterly black. There was just—nothing. No prison, no

Protectorate, no trial. Just darkness. All the air left my lungs, my heart stopped, and all the blood froze in my body. Then, a second passed, and another one, until I finally snapped back to reality.

"She says that she's Nike Champion?" I whispered. "Why would she say that?"

Vivian smirked at me again. "Because it's *true*, Gwen. You know it's true. I'm Nike's Champion, and you're Loki's Champion, not the other way around, like you've been claiming all this time. Did you really think you would get away with it? The truth always comes out, you know. Good *always* triumphs over evil."

Once more, rage filled my body that she would come in here and say something so absurd. Was I the only one who could hear the sarcasm in her voice? The acid dripping from her words? Was I the only one who could see the calculation and lies in her eyes? Surely, the Protectorate wouldn't be dumb enough to actually *believe* her—

My gaze zoomed from one face to another, but to my surprise and horror, they all seemed to be buying her story. Agrona, Inari, Sergei, and Linus all nodded at her words, as though they made perfect sense, as though it was perfectly *logical* that she was Nike's Champion instead of me.

But there was one person who was as outraged as I was.

"She's your witness?" Nickamedes asked in a harsh voice. "You knowingly let a Reaper of Chaos, let *Loki's Champion*, back onto the academy grounds? Why would you do something so foolish? So reckless? So stupid?"

Linus looked down his nose at the librarian. "As I said before, Miss Holler tells a very convincing story. Of all of us here, only she and Miss Frost were actually at the Garm gate when Loki was freed. They are the only ones who know what really happened that night."

"Then strap her down here with the snake, and we'll see how long she lasts," I snapped. "Because every word out of her mouth is a lie."

The asp raised its head again at the sound of my voice, peering at me with its bright blue eyes. For a moment, I thought I saw a flicker of understanding in its gaze, but the snake put its head back down before I could be sure. From taking care of Nott and Nyx, I knew that mythological creatures were quite intelligent. I wondered if the asp was as well, if it would be able to see through Vivian's lies when the Protectorate seemed so determined not to.

Linus nodded. "That's precisely what we intend to do, Miss Frost."

The guards flanking Vivian ushered her forward and arranged themselves around the table, with one of them standing at each corner, and Alexei stepping up to occupy the fourth spot. Soon, she was sitting across from me, chained down just like I was, the snake bite on her wrist oozing blood. I looked at the other Gypsy. Frizzy auburn hair; golden eyes; pretty face; lean, strong body. So similar to me, and yet so very different. Since, you know, I wasn't the right-hand girl of the ultimate evil.

Vivian smirked at me again, and I saw that spark of Reaper red in the depths of her eyes. How could the others not see it? Were they blind? Or just so convinced I was guilty that they were ready to believe whatever lies Vivian had told them?

But the worst thing was that the Reaper girl had outsmarted me again, and I hadn't even seen it coming. As soon as the Protectorate had arrested me, I should have known she was involved. Now, here I was, venom in my veins and one wrong word away from being poisoned to death, while she waltzed in like she hadn't done anything wrong. Like she hadn't tricked me into finding the Helheim Dagger, used it to free Loki, and killed Nott while she was at it.

Nott. My heart quivered with pain at the thought of the Fenrir wolf and how she'd fought so fiercely to protect me at the Garm gate, how she'd tried to save me, even though she'd been slowly dying from the Reapers' poison all the while.

Vivian wasn't going to get away with it, I vowed. She wasn't going to get away with murdering Nott and my mom. Somehow, some way, I was going to make her pay for those things—more than she'd ever dreamed.

So I forced myself to put aside my anger and think. The Reaper girl had to have some sort of plan, other than getting me kicked out of the academy or executed by the Protectorate. Sure, she'd be delighted with either one of those, especially the second option, but I knew Vivian well enough to realize that she was always thinking ahead, always plotting her next move. But try as I might, I couldn't figure out what my trial would really get her—or how it tied in with the Reaper attack at the library and the artifacts that had been stolen. The two had to be connected, but I just couldn't figure out how.

Once Vivian was chained, Linus resumed the trial. At least he had the same chilly expression on his face when he looked at her that he'd always shown me.

"Now, Miss Holler, since you were so eager to come here today and tell your side of the story, why don't you have at it?"

"Of course," Vivian said in a soft voice, as though she was the victim in all of this. "It all started at the Crius Coliseum. I was there, finishing up my myth-history assignment when the Reapers attacked . . ."

I sat there and listened while Vivian told the most ridiculous story I'd ever heard. She twisted everything around, blaming me for all the things she'd done. She even claimed that Lucretia was the weapon that Nike had gifted her with and said that Vic had been given to me by Loki himself.

"I knew that Gwen was telling people she was Nike's Champion, but I just thought she was doing it because she was new at Mythos and wanted to impress the other kids," Vivian said in a soft, sweet, innocent voice that made me grind my teeth together. "I didn't realize it was all part of her plan to discredit me until she used the Helheim Dagger to free Loki."

I wanted to throw myself across the table and strangle the other girl, but I couldn't reach her because of the handcuffs and chain. So I eyed the Maat asp, waiting for it to strike out and bite the Reaper girl again and again for all the lies she was telling—but it didn't.

No matter what Vivian said, no matter how outrageous a lie she told, the venom in her veins didn't slowly heat up and roast her from the inside out like it was supposed to, and the snake didn't lash out at her. Instead, the asp slithered out of the groove on the table and twined its tail around Vivian's right wrist, and its head around mine until it was stretched between us like a jeweled rope binding us together. Creepy. I tensed, waiting for the snake's memories to flood my mind, but the only vibe I got off the creature was one of curiosity, as though it really were listening to and weighing her words.

Vivian stopped her story, and I saw the fear in her eyes that the snake would bite her a second time and trigger the poison. But she quickly masked the expression and continued talking. She wasn't just omitting facts or sidestepping questions like I had about Jasmine's death. The Reaper girl was outright *lying*, but the asp didn't seem to notice.

She must have found some way to beat the snake's magic, I realized. Some way to tell huge, whopping, horrible lies without it biting her like it was supposed to. *Another bloody loophole*, as Vic would say.

So I ignored her words and focused on Vivian herself. If I could figure out how she was fooling the snake, maybe I could stop it. I studied the other girl, but Vivian looked the same as I remembered, and there was nothing special about the black cashmere sweater and designer jeans she had on. The only jewelry she wore was a gold ring on her right hand.

I eyed the band. It was actually quite plain, compared to some of the oversized bling the other kids had. Instead of diamonds, the ring sported two small faces, one turned left and crying, the other turned right and laughing. Vivian had once told me that it was a Janus ring, in honor of the Roman god of beginnings and endings who had two faces, one looking back into the past and the other peering ahead into the future. The two faces also symbolized Vivian's secret loyalty to Loki.

The longer I looked at the ring, the more the faces seemed to move and change, until they were both turned and grinning hideously at me, the ruby chips of their eyes gleaming Reaper red—

Wait a second. Ruby chips? I didn't remember there being any gems on the ring before. I pulled up all the memories I had of the ring. Creepy faces, yes. Rubies, no. No diamonds, no emeralds, no jewels of any sort. I frowned. So why would there be gems on it now?

Maybe it was the rubies' red flash, but I thought of the box that the Reaper had stolen from the library— the one that had belonged to Apate. The Reaper had lifted the box up, and the jewels on the surface had sparkled, along with smaller bits of gemstones—just like the chips on Vivian's ring.

My eyes narrowed. So that's why the Reaper had wanted the box. Apate was the Greek goddess of deception, so it only made sense that her box and all the jewels on it would have some sort of magic, some sort of power that was letting Vivian lie to the Maat asp without being bitten.

I opened my mouth to shout out my theory when another thought occurred to me. According to what Linus had said, Vivian had been in Protectorate custody for weeks now. Even if they really believed that she was Nike's Champion, there was no way they would have let her out of their sight, not even for a minute, which meant that she couldn't have been in the library last night with the other Reapers. No, someone else must have stolen the box and given the ruby chips to Vivian, so she could pull off all her elaborate lies today. Vivian had to be working with someone, most likely a member of the Protectorate—someone who was probably in this very room.

Linus, Inari, Sergei, Agrona. My gaze went from one face to another, but they were all looking at Vivian, listening to her story, and scribbling down notes. Nothing out of the ordinary there, and none of them did anything remotely incriminating, like give the Reaper girl a sly wink. The same thing went for Alexei and the other guards. They were just doing their jobs and standing watch.

Frustration and anger surged through me once again, but there was nothing I could do but sit still and keep my mouth shut. I doubted the Protectorate would believe that one of their own was working with Vivian, and my accusation would only tip off the Reaper that I was on to him or her. So how was I going to get out of this situation? Because, Reaper or not, if enough members of the jury believed Vivian, it was going to be lights out for me—permanently.

"And I've been on the run ever since Loki was freed," Vivian said, finishing her ridiculous story. "Wrongly accused of being his Champion when I've been serving Nike this whole time. I was just lucky that I was able to get a message to the Protectorate, to all of you, so I could come here today and finally clear my name."

"You couldn't clear your name with a bucket of bleach," I snapped.

Vivian just gave me a sad, wounded look, like she couldn't believe I would say something so hurtful. Her *poor, pitiful me* act only made me that much more disgusted.

The asp tightened its grip around my wrist, almost as if it agreed with my anger. I looked at the small, jewel-toned snake. It was really the only impartial creature here. At least, it would have been if Vivian hadn't found a way to fool it. Stupid magic loopholes—

Magic loopholes . . . magic loopholes . . .

The words bounced around in my mind. Sure, Vivian had used the jewels' magic to fool the asp, but she wasn't the only one here with power. Maybe there was a way I could prove my innocence—and Vivian's guilt once and for all.

Linus stared at Vivian, then me. "You both tell a convincing story. But what I find most interesting is that the asp hasn't attacked either one of you, yet obviously one of you must be lying. At the very least, you can't *both* be Nike's Champion."

Everyone's eyes focused on the asp on the table. The creature flicked out its tongue, almost like it realized we were all staring at it, but it made no move to bite either one of us.

"You should go ahead and confess, Gwen," Vivian said. "Make things easier on yourself."

She smirked at me. I glared back at her.

"And that concludes the interrogation," Linus said. "Rest assured that we will carefully review everything you've both said today . . ."

He started talking about exactly how the Protectorate would make its decision. It was all very blah, blah, blah, so I ignored him. It was obvious that the Protectorate didn't want to believe me, but I didn't think they'd wholeheartedly swallowed Vivian's story either. I could see the doubt in even Linus's face about what she'd told them. But I was determined to show everyone just what a liar Vivian really was.

Professor Metis had once told me that there was more to my psychometry than just touching objects and seeing things. That was the mental aspect of my power, but Metis had said that there was a physical component to my magic as well. That I could touch people and actually influence them, get them to see what I wanted them to see, feel what I wanted them to feel. I'd done it once before with Nott, when I'd showed her memories of my Grandma Frost. Those memories and my love for my grandma had convinced the wolf to go protect her when Vivian and Preston had been on their way to kill her.

Now, I was wondering if I could do the same thing with the snake.

My gaze dropped to the Maat asp, which was still wound around my wrist. I wondered what the creature would do if I showed it what had really happened—if I showed it the truth about Vivian.

I had no illusions that I would be found innocent by the Protectorate. At the very least, I'd broken enough rules to get expelled from the academy. At the very worst, I'd be found guilty of conspiring with the Reapers, hauled off to prison, and eventually executed. Something that was a real possibility with one of the Protectorate members likely a Reaper in disguise. Either the snake would turn, bite me again, and trigger the poison in my veins that would kill me, or the Protectorate would find me guilty and chop my head off later. Either way, Vivian would win.

Using my magic on the asp was the only move I had left in this weird, twisted game Vivian had dragged me into, so I focused on all the memories I had of her, both as herself and when she'd been hiding behind a rubber mask as the Reaper girl. I called up all the images I had of that night at the Garm gate, when Vivian had freed Loki and then stabbed Nott. Rage pulsed through me, along with the memories, but I forced myself to be cold, calm, and keep my emotions under control. Finally, when I had all the images, all the memories, all the feelings, firmly fixed in my mind, I concentrated on the asp wrapped around my wrist, on the soft, smooth feel of its cool velvet skin against mine. Then, I pushed the memories at the creature, using my psychometry to show them to the asp—every single one.

I felt the asp tense, as the memories invaded its mind, the sights and sounds and feelings that weren't its own. It wasn't as easy as it had been with Nott, probably because the wolf had trusted me and this creature didn't. It was harder to show the images to the asp, harder than I'd thought it would be, and I was soon sweating from the effort. I could feel the asp pushing back, trying to shove me out of its mind, but I hung on until I got to the final image I had of Vivian—her riding up into the midnight sky on a Black roc with Loki strapped in a harness behind her. Me helpless to stop them, my life's blood draining from where Preston had stabbed me with the Helheim Dagger.

Come on, I thought to the snake. *I'm the one telling the truth, not her. We both know it. So do your job, and bite her . . . bite her already . . . bite her right now!*

The asp snapped at the Reaper girl.

Vivian must have sensed the change in the creature because she jerked her hand back at the last possible second, and the asp only ended up biting empty air.

Everyone froze.

But the snake wasn't done. It struck at her again and again, in a frenzy now, as though it wanted nothing more than to kill her. I knew the feeling because it was *mine*—one I'd also shown the asp. Vivian leaped to her feet and yanked on her handcuffs. They must not have been magically reinforced because she was able to use her Valkyrie strength to break the metal links, along with the chain that shackled her to the table. Vivian stumbled away from the table, making sure she was out of range of the writhing asp, before she stabbed her finger at me.

"It's Gwen! She's done something to the asp with her magic! I know she has!" Vivian shrieked.

This time, I smirked at the Reaper girl. "Why would you say that? Because the asp finally wised up and realized what a liar you are? It tried to bite you, Vivian. *You*—not me. At least someone here has finally seen through your lies."

Vivian's gaze flicked to the dais, as though she was looking to someone there for direction or possibly even help—as if someone there was a Reaper just like she was. My eyes narrowed, and I followed her gaze, but I couldn't tell exactly whom she was looking at. Sergei, Inari, Agrona, Linus. It could have been any one of them. I didn't think Logan's dad was a Reaper, but I hadn't thought that Vivian was Loki's Champion either. If there was one thing I'd learned since coming to Mythos, it was that appearances could be very, very deceiving, especially when it came time to decide who to trust—and who not to.

Apparently, the asp realized that Vivian was out of range because it stopped snapping. Instead, the snake decided to wind itself around and around my wrist before putting its head down onto the table. Its black tongue flicked against my skin, and a sense of understanding filled me. The asp knew the truth of what had happened. I just hoped this display would convince the Protectorate as well.

"Did you see that, Linus?" Nickamedes said, surging to his feet. "Clearly, the asp knows who is guilty and who is not. I demand that you release Gwendolyn and drop all the charges against her immediately."

"The trial is over, Nickamedes," Linus replied, eyeing the snake. "But we have not started our deliberations yet. The asp's actions are hardly conclusive in this case. We will decide who is telling the truth—Miss Frost or Miss Holler—and we will act accordingly."

Linus rapped his gavel a final time on the table, and everyone got to their feet. Nickamedes went over to Linus and started arguing with him, while the other members of the Protectorate looked on, along with Grandma Frost and Metis. Raven walked over, carefully uncurled the snake from my wrist, and put it back into its wicker basket, while Ajax stepped forward and un-chained me. I stood, and the two of them moved off to the cell that Raven had gotten the basket out of earlier.

That left me standing across the table from Vivian. Although I wanted nothing more than to attack her, I knew I wouldn't even get a chance to reach for her be-fore Alexei or one of the guards watching would drag me back. So I settled for glaring at her instead.

"I'm going to kill you," I said in a cold voice that only Vivian could hear. "Maybe not today, maybe not tomorrow, but someday soon. For my mom and for Nott and for everyone else you've ever hurt in your mis-erable life."

Vivian smiled, completely unconcerned by my threat, although that spark of Reaper red still flashed in her topaz eyes. "Oh, I imagine that you'll try, Gwen. But I won before at the Garm gate, and I'm going to win again this time too. You'll see. And by the time you figure out what my plan is, it will be too late for you—and everyone you love."

With those ominous words, Vivian walked out of the academy prison, flanked by her three guards, and all I could do was just stand there and watch her get away—again.

Chapter 19

After the guards whisked Vivian off to parts unknown, Grandma Frost came over and hugged me tight.

"Are you okay, pumpkin?" she whispered. "I know how awful it was, seeing her again. If I'd had any idea she was going to be here..."

Grandma's voice trailed off, and I could tell she was thinking the same dark thoughts I was—that the world would be a better place without Vivian in it.

"I'm okay," I said. "At least I got through to somebody."

While the others were still arguing, I told her about pushing my thoughts at the asp and how I'd been able to show it what Vivian was really like.

"I just wish I could do the same to Linus," I said. "I *could*, if I touched him."

Grandma shook her head. "It's not worth the risk, pumpkin. Vivian's got them so turned around, I doubt he'd believe you. He'd probably just think that you have her telepathy magic."

I wondered if that was the real distinction between

my magic and Vivian's—that she could worm her way into people's brains and make them see things that weren't really there without laying a hand on them. So far, I'd only used my power to make Nott and the asp see my memories, things that had actually happened, and I'd had to touch them to do it. Another way Vivian and I were eerily similar but still different.

I let out a frustrated sigh because I knew Grandma Frost was right. At this point, the Protectorate would think what they wanted about me, and there was nothing I could do to change their minds one way or the other.

But I could do something about Vivian. The Reaper girl had told me that she was up to something, and I was willing to bet it had a lot to do with the attack in the library last night. Whatever Vivian and the other Reapers were planning, they weren't going to get away with it. Just because I was on trial for my life didn't mean that I was going to stop fighting against them. They'd already taken away so much from me. They weren't taking anything else, and they weren't hurting anyone else that I loved.

Now, I just needed to find a way to stop Vivian and the Reapers—before it was too late.

The Protectorate was going to take the weekend to decide my fate, which meant I could stay on campus until Monday afternoon, when they made their final decision about me—and Vivian.

I wondered if they found me guilty, did that mean Vivian would be declared innocent and be allowed to come back to Mythos? Could that be what she really wanted? Was that what all the false accusations had been about?

No, I thought. It was too simple. Vivian wouldn't have risked contacting the Protectorate just so she could come back to school. She had to be up to something bigger, something that would hurt the Pantheon a lot more than just discrediting me as Nike's Champion. Sure, I imagined she'd be thrilled if the Protectorate decided to sentence me to death, but I couldn't shake this nagging feeling that there was something else going on.

"What are you thinking about, Gwendolyn?" Nickamedes asked, packing up his papers. "You've been awfully quiet."

I shrugged. "Just going over everything that's happened. Everything that Vivian said."

"Don't worry about her," Nickamedes replied. "Despite my feelings toward Linus, I cannot believe he would be foolish enough to believe her. You'll be cleared of all charges and get to stay right here at Mythos where you belong. Trust me."

I nodded, even though I didn't really believe that.

Since my trial was over, everyone except for Raven left the prison and walked up the many stairs to the ground floor of the math-science building. Agrona, Inari, and Sergei paused just inside the door that led outside and started talking among themselves, but Linus gestured at me to stop.

"Don't forget, Miss Frost," he said, giving me the same frigid stare as always. "Your trial might be over, but you are still under arrest, so the same rules apply.

You are restricted to campus for the weekend, and you will be watched at all times."

I frowned. "But the winter band concert is tomorrow. I had plans to go. One of my friends is in the band—"

"Forget it, Miss Frost," he interrupted. "You're not going to the concert. If I were you, I'd take this weekend to think about all the things you've done. Perhaps even consider confessing and throwing yourself on the mercy of the Protectorate. That sort of gesture might mitigate your punishment—somewhat."

So he'd already decided that I was guilty.

"But I didn't do anything wrong," I said once again.

Instead of answering me, Linus stared at me another second, then turned and strode over to the other members of the Protectorate.

"Don't worry, Gwen," Metis said, walking over to stand beside me. "Everything will be okay. The asp lashed out at Vivian, not you. The Protectorate has to take that into consideration."

I shook my head. "No, it won't," I said in a low voice only she could hear. "Not with Linus hating me like he does. And especially not since one of them is probably a Reaper."

Metis frowned. "What do you mean?"

I told her about seeing the ruby chips on Vivian's ring and how I thought they'd been part of Apate's box. I also told her how Vivian had looked at one of the members of the Protectorate after the asp had tried to bite her.

"One of them has to be helping her," I said. "It's the only thing that makes sense."

Metis's mouth tightened. "I'll tell Nickamedes and

Ajax. We'll quietly ask around and see who was where when the Reapers attacked. If one of them is a Reaper, we'll find out who it is—and deal with him or her. You can count on that."

I nodded, grateful that she believed me, that she didn't think I was crazy or guilty or up to no good like Linus would have.

I headed outside, along with Grandma Frost, Metis, Ajax, Nickamedes, and, of course, Alexei, who was back to shadowing me again. The trial had gone on longer than I'd thought because twilight had already fallen over the campus, giving everything a faint lavender sheen.

My friends were waiting for me on the quad— Daphne, Carson, Oliver, and Logan. They'd been huddled together on the building's steps and got to their feet when they saw me. Grandma Frost spotted them too.

"I need to speak to Metis," she said. "Are you going to be okay tonight, pumpkin?"

"I'll be fine," I said. "I want to talk to my friends about what happened, and I need to warn them about Vivian."

She nodded. "Well, you call me if you need me. Day or night. I love you, and don't you worry. Everything's going to work out the way it's supposed to. You'll see."

For a moment, that distant, glassy look filled her eyes, and that ancient, invisible force stirred around her, as though she was getting a glimpse of the future—my future. Then, her gaze cleared, and the force vanished, blown away by a cold gust of wind. Still, her words made me feel a little better.

I hugged Grandma Frost, then watched her walk across the quad with Metis, Ajax, and Nickamedes, all of them with their heads together, talking softly. Looked like I wasn't the only one trying to come up with a plan. But I was the one who was Nike's Champion. I was the one who was supposed to protect everyone from the Reapers, and I was the one who was supposed to kill Loki. I loved my grandma, and I knew the other adults were watching out for me too, but I also realized that I couldn't rely on them to get me out of this mess. No, being a Champion meant fighting your own battles, and I was determined to win this struggle against Vivian.

All of my friends came over and hugged me in turn. Oliver, Carson, Daphne, and finally Logan, who held me close and didn't let me go.

"How was it?" he asked, his blue eyes searching mine.

"Awful," I said. "But the worst part was that Vivian was there."

"What?!" Daphne said, her voice rising to almost a scream, and pink sparks exploding in the air around her. "What was she doing at your trial?"

"Blaming me for everything she's done," I said.

We weren't the only kids on the quad, and Daphne's shout made the others turn to look at us. I stared back at the other students, once again feeling their anger wash over me, but this time, I also wondered which of them might be Reapers—and plotting against us. Vivian hadn't been the only Reaper student at Mythos, and I had no idea how many other kids she had spying on me and my friends. Yeah, maybe I was being paranoid, but

I didn't want to talk about my trial out here in the open where just anyone could walk by and hear.

"Come on," I told my friends. "Let's get inside out of the cold, and I'll tell you all about it."

We ended up squeezing into my dorm room. Once again, Alexei had trailed me across campus. He stopped in the hallway outside my room and leaned against the wall as usual. His face was smooth, but his shoulders sagged just the slightest bit, and I could tell he was tired, just like I was.

I stood in the doorway. "Would you like to come inside?"

He shook his head. "I don't think that would be a good idea."

I nodded. I knew he was still smarting from the talking-to Linus had given him last night, and I couldn't blame him for not wanting to get on the Protectorate leader's bad side. Still, I felt I owed him something. The Bogatyr had fought alongside my friends in the library, and he'd helped us survive. He wasn't a bad guy, just caught in an awkward situation. If things had been different, we might have even become friends.

"Well, if you change your mind, just open the door and come on in," I said.

A smile flickered across Alexei's face, but it quickly vanished. "I will be just fine out here."

I nodded, went into my room, and closed the door behind me.

The others had already settled in. Daphne and Carson were sitting cross-legged on the floor, while Oliver slouched in my desk chair. Vic was hanging in his scabbard on the wall above Oliver's head, and the sword's eye snapped open as I walked across the room to him.

"Well, it's about time you got back," Vic said. "Do you know how bloody boring it is being stuck here wondering what's going on? Why, I didn't even have the fuzzball to keep me company this afternoon."

My gaze went to Nyx's empty basket, and a hollow ache filled my chest. "I miss her too," I told the sword. "And I missed having you with me today."

I gave Vic a pat on the head, which seemed to mollify him. Then, I went over and plopped down on the bed next to Logan.

"You know, this is the first time I've been in your room. I like it, although I didn't think we'd have an audience when we were in here," the Spartan whispered to me.

I rolled my eyes, but I couldn't help the smile that stretched across my face. Only Logan could crack a joke and make me feel better at a time like this.

"All right, Gwen," Daphne said, crossing her arms over her chest. "You've kept us waiting long enough. Spill it."

I told them everything that had happened in the academy prison, from the Protectorate's questions to the Maat asp to Vivian claiming that she was really Nike's Champion.

Oliver let out a low whistle when I was finished. "Vivian's even more diabolical than I thought."

"You're telling me," I said. "No wonder she was in the drama club. She really is a great actress. She was so convincing that even I might have believed her, if I didn't know what really happened. And I couldn't do a thing to stop her. Not then, anyway."

"Uh-oh," Daphne muttered. "I know *that* look. What are you up to, Gwen?"

"What makes you think I'm up to something?"

The Valkyrie snorted. "You're breathing, aren't you?"

I glared at my friend.

Carson pushed his glasses up his nose. "Daphne has a point, Gwen. You do tend to . . . take matters into your own hands, especially when it comes to Reapers."

I turned my glare to the band geek, who winced and ducked his head.

"Come on, Gypsy girl," Logan said. "You might as well tell us what you're thinking. We're your friends. We're here because we want to help you."

"The boy's right," Vic chimed in. "Help you, kill Reapers, it's really all the same."

I looked at them—Daphne, Carson, Oliver, Vic, and finally Logan. When I'd first started going to Mythos back in the fall, I hadn't had a single friend—not one. Now, I had them, and they'd stood by me again and again, even when all I did was put them in danger. But I could see the determination in their faces, and I knew they wouldn't leave until I told them everything. Hot tears of love and gratitude pricked my eyes, and it took me a few seconds to blink them away.

"All right," I said, letting out a breath. "So I may be thinking about finding out what Vivian and the Reapers are really up to, but there's just one problem—I don't know *how* to do it. Supposedly, the Protectorate has Vivian under guard somewhere, at least until they decide what to do with the two of us. So it's not like I can go and question her—and she wouldn't tell me the truth anyway. Even if I could find out where she is, the Reaper inside the Protectorate would stop me from getting to her."

"What?!" Daphne yelled. "What do you mean, the Reaper inside the Protectorate?"

That's when I told them my suspicions about the ruby chips on Vivian's ring and how I thought one of the Protectorate members had to be working with her.

"Who do you think it is?" Logan asked.

I shrugged. "Maybe Inari? The Reaper leader had the same sort of slender build that he does. But who knows? Vivian found a way to fool me, so this Reaper might have too. Inari, Sergei, Agrona, Linus. It could be any one of them."

He stared at me. "My dad is not a Reaper, and I don't think any of the others are either. I've known Inari and Sergei for years. They helped train me. And Agrona is my stepmom."

I hesitated. I didn't want to believe it either, but Vivian couldn't have planned all this by herself, and I'd seen her look at *someone* on the dais during the trial.

"I don't want to believe it's your dad," I finally said. "But we all know that anything's possible when it comes to Reapers."

Logan kept staring at me, his face pinched with hurt, but I didn't say anything else. Nobody spoke for a minute. Finally, Oliver cleared his throat.

"But you have something in mind," he said. "A way to find out what Vivian might really be up to."

I shrugged again. "I'm going to head back to the library tomorrow and see if I can get any more vibes off anything the Reaper might have touched when he stole Apate's box. I wanted to do it today, but I didn't get a chance because of the trial. Tomorrow will be better anyway because it's Saturday, so I don't have classes, and most of the other kids will be at the band concert. It'll probably be a waste of time, but at least it will keep me from sitting in my room all day worrying."

"They're not going to let you come to the concert?" Carson asked, his shoulders drooping.

I shook my head. "Nope, I'm still restricted to campus until the Protectorate makes its decision. I'm sorry I won't be there, but I know you guys will all do a great job. Especially you, Carson."

The band geek blushed a little, but he grinned at me.

We sat there talking for another hour, throwing out ideas about what Vivian could really be up to, but none of us had a clue as to what her plan was. I didn't say anything else about which member of the Protectorate might be helping her, and no one else brought it up either. Not after seeing Logan's reaction. Finally, the ten o'clock curfew rolled around, and my friends had to leave to go back to their own dorms for the night.

"Just be careful, okay, guys?" I said. "I wouldn't put it past the Reapers to try to wreck the concert tomorrow."

Or for Vivian to hurt one of you to get at me. That

was the darker, more ominous thought that filled my mind, but I didn't tell the others my fear.

"Don't worry, Gypsy girl," Logan said. "Oliver, Kenzie, and I are serving as the honor guard to protect everyone in the band. My dad and the other members of the Protectorate are going to be there too, along with Metis, Ajax, and Nickamedes. If any of the Reapers dare show their faces at the concert hall, we'll take care of them."

I didn't say that a Reaper would be there already, hiding among the other Protectorate members. I knew the Spartan didn't want to believe that one of the people he trusted was really a Reaper, and I didn't want to upset him any more than I already had. Besides, surely one Reaper couldn't do that much damage with everyone else on guard. That's what I told myself, even if I didn't quite believe it.

Logan kissed me good-bye and left with the others. Alexei went with them, telling me that Sergei would be standing guard outside my dorm tonight.

I went over to my window, pulled back the curtain, and watched my friends disappear into the darkness. Still, despite their assurances, I couldn't shake the feeling that something was seriously wrong—and that the Reapers were going to strike sooner rather than later.

Chapter 20

I took a shower and crawled into bed, determined to get some sleep, but the night was anything but restful. Images crowded into my dreams, everything I'd seen, heard, and felt the last few days. Thanks to my psychometry, I was almost always downloading information into my brain, even if all I did was touch a library book and flash on how bored someone was doing his homework. During the day, I was able to ignore such things, but sometimes at night all the sights, sounds, and emotions welled up inside my mind, going by one after another, faster and faster, even as my subconscious struggled to make sense of them.

Tonight was one of those nights.

The Reapers sneaking up on Oliver and Alexei in the library. The leader lifting up the Apate box, the wicked flash of the rubies on it painting everything a harsh crimson, even the library books. Vivian striding into the academy prison. The two ruby chips on her Janus ring winking at me like evil eyes. And finally, the Maat asp curled around my wrist, its scales red instead of blue.

The snake flicking its tongue against my wrist, its eyes glowing with Reaper-red fire before it surged forward and sank its fangs into me, poisoning me, killing me—

I woke up with a scream in my throat, my wrist stinging as though the asp had really bitten me. The sensation felt so vivid, so *real*, that I snapped on a light and held my arm up, but my skin was smooth and unbroken. Even the two tiny puncture marks I'd gotten earlier in the prison had vanished.

"Gwen?" Vic mumbled, letting out a loud yawn from his spot on the wall. "Is something wrong? Why did you turn on the light?"

"It's nothing, Vic," I said. "Just a bad dream. Go back to sleep."

"Okay," the sword mumbled again. "Just let me know when you need me to wake up and kill Reapers . . ."

His voice trailed off, and seconds later he was snoring again. The soft, familiar sound cut through the last of my panic and dream-filled confusion. I let out a breath, turned off the light, and lay back down on my bed.

But no matter how hard I tried, I couldn't go back to sleep.

The next day just before lunch, I stood in the parking lot behind the gym, saying good-bye to my friends. The winter concert wasn't until late that afternoon, but the band members and other folks involved were getting on a couple of buses and going to the concert hall early— along with a heavy guard.

Ever since Vivian had freed Loki, I'd thought things would change at Mythos—that there would be more rules, more guards, more security. And all of those things had been added to campus—discreetly. The Powers That Were didn't want everyone to panic. No, they wanted to make the Mythos students feel they were just as safe as they'd been before Loki escaped, even if we all knew it was just an illusion. That's why the winter band concert was still on—because the Powers That Were didn't want to be seen as giving in to the Reapers and adding to the fear of another looming Chaos War.

I understood what the Powers That Were were trying to do, and I was glad my friends would be protected, but I still couldn't help but have a bad, bad feeling about this. I couldn't see the future, not like my Grandma Frost did, but something about the situation felt wrong to me, like we were playing right into the Reapers' hands, even though the concert had been planned for months and was being held down in the city.

"Call me if you see anything suspicious," I told Daphne for the third time in as many minutes.

She'd volunteered to help set things up for the concert so she was getting on the bus with everyone else.

Daphne rolled her eyes. "Don't worry, Gwen. There are so many guards going with us that there's no way the Reapers would dare to attack, even if one of them is a member of the Protectorate."

I started to point out that no one had thought the Reapers would break in to the library either, but I kept my mouth shut. This was supposed to be a fun day, a way for everyone to forget about Reapers, at least for a few hours, and I wasn't going to ruin it with my suspicions, especially not for Carson, who was nervous enough already about performing. The band geek's face had a decidedly greenish tint to it, and I could hear his stomach gurgling.

"Knock 'em dead, Carson," I said.

He tried to smile at me but ended up clutching his stomach instead.

"Are you sure you're going to be okay here by yourself, Gypsy girl?" Logan asked.

"I'll be fine," I said. "Besides, Alexei will be here with me."

I jerked my thumb over my shoulder at the other warrior, who was talking with Oliver, Kenzie, and Talia. Alexei had been waiting outside my room just like usual this morning, and he'd come over to the gym with me, although he'd actually walked beside me this time, instead of trailing behind a few steps. Maybe I was growing on him. I snorted. Not likely.

One person I was definitely not growing on was Linus. He stood next to one of the buses, along with Agrona, Inari, and Sergei. The members of the Protectorate were going with the students to, well, protect them, along with Metis, Nickamedes, and Coach Ajax. They were all part of the guard for the concert.

I just wondered which one of them was really a Reaper.

Was it Sergei with his big smile and boisterous laugh? Quiet, soft-spoken Inari who always faded into the background? Beautiful Agrona? Or even Linus himself? My gaze went from one of their faces to another, but everyone was acting normal. When I'd first walked over here, Metis had pulled me aside and told me that she, Ajax, and Nickamedes hadn't been able to find out anything concrete about who had been where during the attack in the library. Metis had promised to keep digging for answers, but I had a feeling it was already too late.

Linus noticed me staring at him—and the fact that Logan was by my side. His mouth flattered out into a thin line.

"Ignore him," Logan said, realizing who I was looking at. "Or just be glad you don't have to spend the afternoon with him. He's probably going to be looking over my shoulder the whole time, telling me how I should do things, how a *real* Spartan would do things."

His voice was mocking, but pain shimmered in his icy eyes. Even now, after everything that had happened, it was obvious that Logan still wanted his dad's love and approval—and more important, his understanding for Logan's not fighting alongside his mom and sister when the Reapers had attacked them.

"Things aren't any better between the two of you?" I asked.

Logan shook his head. "No, but I don't want to talk about him right now. Just be careful today, okay? It would be just like the Reapers to try something on campus while we're gone—or the other kids."

"Don't worry," I said. "I can hold my own against a few Reapers or pissed-off mean girls like Helena Paxton."

He gave me a crooked grin. "That you can, Gypsy girl. That you can."

We kissed, and then everyone boarded the buses. I

stood in the parking lot and waved as the engines started up, and the drivers steered the buses through the gate on this side of the academy. Alexei came over to stand beside me, his backpack hanging off his shoulder.

"Don't worry," Alexei echoed my words to Logan when the last of the buses had disappeared. "Your friends will be okay. My father and the other members of the Protectorate will make sure of it."

I nodded, although I didn't really believe him. For all his Protectorate training, for all his skill and magic as a Bogatyr, Alexei hadn't been there the night Loki had escaped. He hadn't looked the god in the eye like I had, and he hadn't felt the evil intent rolling off Loki, the burning desire to kill every single member of the Pantheon. Alexei simply didn't realize that none of us was safe, not anymore—not even at Mythos Academy.

But there was a way I could make sure that my friends were as protected as they could be—by finding out what Vivian and the other Reapers were really up to.

"Come on," I told Alexei. "I hope you have your walking shoes on because I have things to do today."

On the weekends, the Mythos kids spent most of their time sleeping late, hanging out in their dorms, or browsing through the shops in Cypress Mountain. Today, the other students were getting ready to go to the band concert in a few hours, so the main quad was deserted as I headed toward the Library of Antiquities. To my surprise, Alexei once again walked beside me. He kept glancing at me, like something was on his mind.

"Something you want to say?" I finally asked.

He didn't answer me for several seconds. "Oliver told me what you said to him about me ... about how what was going on with you didn't have anything to do with him and the way I feel about him. I just wanted to thank you for that."

"I know what it's like to be totally into someone," I said. "I just want Oliver to be happy, and if you make him happy, then that's fine by me. Although if you end up hurting him, I will make you wish you hadn't, Protectorate or no Protectorate. Understand?"

He nodded. "I understand."

We reached the library steps, and I stopped to look at the two gryphons. Maybe it was my imagination, but the statues seemed ... troubled. Their eyes narrowed, their brows furrowed like they were worried about something. Maybe they could sense the tension in the air. It was almost like I could see the storm clouds gathering overhead. I just didn't know where the lightning would strike first—or who would get burned by it. I shivered, pulled my gaze away from the statues, and walked on.

All of the students were encouraged to attend the band concert, well, except for me. But there were a few folks who'd decided not to go, for whatever reason, which was why the library was open today. Besides, Mythos students *always* had homework to do, concert or no concert. I spotted a couple of kids sitting at the study tables near the checkout counter, including Morgan McDougall. I waved at the Valkyrie, who returned the gesture before going back to the book she'd been reading.

But instead of sitting down with her or at one of the other tables, I headed into the stacks.

"What are you doing?" Alexei asked. "Where are you going? You don't have your bag with you, so I know you don't have any books to do your homework with."

"That's because I'm not here to do homework," I said. "More like extra credit."

Alexei frowned at my cryptic words, but he fell into step beside me.

Deeper and deeper into the stacks I went until I finally reached the spot where the Reaper had broken the case holding Apate's box and jewelry. All the glass had been cleaned up, although the case was still here—at least what was left of it. The Reaper had smashed the wood on top, but the base and the legs were still intact. I guessed that Nickamedes just hadn't gotten around to getting the case fixed or replaced yet. Either way, I was glad it was still here.

I drew in a breath, pushed up the sleeves of my purple hoodie, reached out, and touched the case with both hands.

Memories and images flooded my mind. I got a sense that the case had stood in this particular spot for a long, long time, decades even, and I saw flashes of all the students who'd touched, leaned against, peered at the items inside, and even decided to make out right next to or even on top of the glass and wood. Ugh. I would have been happy not seeing those particular images.

And then, finally, there was the last memory associated with the case—the Reaper raising the hilt of his sword, smashing all the glass, reaching inside, and stealing the box and jewelry.

I focused on that last image, concentrated on it, and pulled it into sharp focus. Then, I rewound the image and played it again and again, trying to get all the information I could from it, hoping there would be something I'd missed the first time, some clue I'd overlooked. I knew that the Reapers had wanted the box and its jewels for Vivian, so she could trick the Maat asp into thinking she was telling the truth. Now, I wanted to know what else they might use the items for—and which member of the Protectorate might really be a Reaper.

Nothing—I saw and felt nothing.

Well, nothing out of the ordinary. Just the Reaper smashing the case and grabbing the items inside. Nothing that I didn't already know, and nothing that would help me figure out what Vivian's ultimate plan was.

I opened my eyes and ran my fingers back and forth across the case, touching every inch of it, but I didn't get any more flashes. No memories, no vibes, nothing.

"What are you doing?" Alexei asked.

"Using my psychometry," I said. "But it's not telling me anything new. Not yet, anyway."

I was disappointed, but I wasn't ready to admit defeat just yet. Since the case wasn't giving me any vibes, I branched out and searched the rest of the aisle. I got down on my hands and knees and ran my fingers over the marble floor around the entire area. Once again, I got the sense of all the students who had walked by this spot, their shoes slapping and scuffing against the floor, but nothing to do with the Reapers.

Getting desperate, I got down on my belly and looked underneath the bookshelf behind the case. Something long and black was lying there. I squinted, trying to make out what it was, and then I realized that it was the black velvet stand that had been in the case. The one I'd scooted underneath the shelf when I'd noticed Inari watching me.

I grabbed the stand and pulled it out from underneath the shelf. Then, I sat on the floor and ran my hands all over the soft, now dusty surface.

Nothing—once again, I saw and felt nothing important. Just the Reaper lifting up the stand and grabbing the box and jewelry. Disgusted, I put the stand inside the case, then got back down on the floor and peered under the shelf again.

But there was nothing else there, except for a couple of forgotten pens and a wad of dust bunnies that made my nose itch. I sighed, but I still wasn't ready to give up, so I slithered across the floor to the shelf on the other side of the aisle and looked under it as well. More pens and more dust bunnies, along with a shriveled up piece of gum. Yucko.

I'd just started to turn away when I noticed a small, white piece of paper lying on the floor back in the shadows.

My eyes narrowed, and I shoved my shoulder underneath the case and reached back as far as I could. It took me a few seconds, but I managed to snag the paper and pull it out into the light.

"What's that?" Alexei said. "Did you find something?"

"Maybe," I murmured, getting to my feet.

I flipped over the paper and realized that it was an ID card that had been inside the case. I'd thought I'd seen something white flutter to the floor when the Reaper had smashed the glass. The Reaper must have accidentally kicked it under the shelf or maybe I had when I'd chased after him. I waited a few seconds, but I didn't get any big vibes off the card, so I looked at the information on it.

> Apate's Keepsake Jewels. In addition to their obvious beauty, each piece in Apate's jewelry collection is rumored to be imbued with the goddess's deceptive power. In fact, each individual gemstone in the pieces supposedly has a different magical property. For example, the emeralds are believed to have a hypnotizing effect, while the topaz can cause hallucinations. However, the rubies are thought to be the most powerful and have a variety of magic attached to them, everything from letting people deceive others to even overcoming a person's mind and compelling him or her to act against his or her own free will . . .

So I'd been right about the box and how Vivian had used the ruby chips on it to fool the Maat asp. But the knowledge didn't make me feel better—if anything, it only made my worry grow. Because the only jewelry Vivian had been wearing had been her Janus ring. So what had happened to the box and the rest of the jewelry? What were the Reapers planning to use the other gems for?

"What's that?" Alexei asked again. "Have you found something?"

I hesitated. It was one thing to have the other warrior follow me around—it was another to trust him. Alexei seemed like an okay guy, and Oliver liked him. Then again, I'd liked Preston Ashton and look how well *that* had turned out.

Oh, I didn't think Alexei was a Reaper. Vivian hadn't looked to him for help during the trial, and I hadn't gotten any strange vibes off him the past few days. Plus, he hadn't acted like a Reaper would have. He hadn't tried to cozy up to me and be my friend, in anticipation of stabbing me in the back later. But I'd been fooled before, and there was still a small chance that he was one of the bad guys. One way to find out.

"Give me your hand," I said.

"What? Why?"

"If you want to know what I'm doing, give me your hand," I repeated.

Alexei looked at me, suspicion in his hazel eyes. For a moment, I thought he wasn't going to do it, that he really might be a Reaper after all, but he finally held out his hand.

I wrapped my fingers around his and closed my eyes. Images immediately filled my mind, flashing by one after another, like a home movie cranked up to high speed. I saw Alexei growing up over the years, in school, at home, even in the gym learning how to fight. I saw him battling Reapers, a sword in either hand, and I felt how smooth his movements were as he flowed from one attack position to the next. Fighting really just was a complicated dance to the Bogatyr, a series of steps to be mastered before striking that final, fatal blow. I even saw the spark at the very center of his being—a pale golden spark full of quiet pride and honor.

All the while I sorted through the memories, looking for any hint that he might be a Reaper. But I didn't sense anything like that—just Alexei's determination to become the best warrior he could be and to follow in his dad's footsteps in the Protectorate. They were the same feelings that Logan had about those things.

Finally, an image of Oliver popped into my mind, and I felt what Alexei did whenever he looked at the Spartan—that warm, soft, fizzy feeling that seemed to make everything else worthwhile. That special emotion that made the golden spark of his soul brighten . . .

I opened my eyes and dropped his hand. He wasn't a Reaper, but I had learned something new about the Russian warrior—just how much he cared about Oliver.

"What was that all about?" Alexei said, more suspicion filling his face. "Did you just use your magic on me?"

"Yes, and you passed," I said. "Now look at this."

I showed Alexei the card, then told him about the ruby chips I'd seen on Vivian's ring. He read the information and frowned.

"But Vivian has been in Protectorate custody for

weeks now," he said, echoing my suspicions. "Before any of these things were stolen. There's no way she could have been one of the Reapers who broke into the library. She's been closely watched, and as far as I know, the only people she's had any contact with are senior members of the Protectorate."

"Who?" I asked. "Who exactly has Vivian been in contact with?"

Alexei shrugged. "All the members of the Protectorate who are here for your trial. Linus, Inari, Agrona, my father. Why do you ask?"

Because that means one of them is a Reaper. The only way Vivian could have gotten her hands on the ruby chips was for the Reaper who had stolen the box to have given them to her. I could almost see the wheels turning in Alexei's mind as he thought about everything, but I didn't tell him my suspicions. I didn't know if he would believe me, especially since his dad was one of the people who'd seen Vivian—one of the people who might be a Reaper.

I slid the card into my jeans pocket. I didn't know that it was enough to prove Vivian's guilt, but it was a start.

Energized by my discovery, I continued my search. I went over the case again, but I didn't get any new vibes off it so I moved on to the bookcase, running my hands up and down the shelves and then over every single one of the books lined up on them. I didn't get any big flashes off the shelves, just the sense of students grabbing the volumes off them. The same thing went for the books. They were just reference books, after all, and no one had any big emotional attachment to them, other than needing the info inside in order to finish their homework.

I was just about to stop looking, when my fingers brushed against a book directly above the artifact case, and an image of the Reaper's gloved hand touching it filled my mind.

I froze, wondering if I'd only imagined the image, but I skimmed my fingers over the book, and the same memory popped into my head. I focused on the image, going deeper into the memory, and replaying it over and over again. There was nothing particularly sinister about the Reaper reaching for the book, but I felt there was something more to the image, something I was missing, so I stood there and kept concentrating, focusing on every little thing my magic could show me.

It took me a few seconds to realize that the Reaper had reached for the bookshelf first—before he'd even glanced at the artifact case.

I ran my fingers over the other books. The images, the memories, were the same. The Reaper standing here and going from book to book to book, the warrior's gloved fingers skimming over each volume, trying to find the one he wanted.

I frowned. Why would the Reaper rifle through the books? Why not go for the box and jewelry first? Unless the gems weren't the only things the Reaper had taken— and stealing them wasn't nearly as important as finding the right book was.

I touched all the books again, one after another, concentrating on the images that much more and going even deeper into the memories. Once again, I saw the Reaper rifling through all the volumes until the warrior found the one he was looking for. The Reaper slid the book into a pocket in his robe, hiding it from sight. It was only then that he looked at the case and started smashing the glass to get at the artifacts inside . . .

I let go of the memories, opened my eyes, and scanned the books. Now that I knew one was missing, it was easy for me to see the slight gap on the shelf. I turned my head to the side and read the titles of the other ones, hoping they would give me some clue as to what book the Reaper had taken and why.

Merging Bodies, Merging Minds. Soul Swap. Notable Transformations.

Notable Transformations . . . My gaze snagged on that title, and I found myself staring at the silver foil letters as if they meant something more. *Transformations* . . . That word kept echoing through my mind. I'd heard someone say something about a transformation not too long ago—

A memory erupted out of the dark of my mind, one from the night Loki had escaped.

Quickly . . . *Get him on the roc before they blow the horn again. He's still weak, and we can't let them capture him. Not now. Not before he's ready for the transformation.*

A Reaper had said that when Vivian and the others had been loading Loki onto the Black roc so she could escape with the evil god. I'd wondered then what the Reaper had been talking about. I still didn't know, but I was determined to find out.

Because I had a feeling that my life—and my friends' lives—depended on it.

Chapter 21

I dropped my hand from the books, then headed out of the stacks and toward the center of the library.

"Now what are you doing?" Alexei asked, an exasperated note creeping into his voice.

"Research."

I went around the checkout counter, entered my password into one of the library computers, and started searching through the catalog. Thanks to Nickamedes and his obsessive need to organize and label every single thing in the library, I was able to pull up a file of all the books that were supposed to be on the shelf above the ruined artifact case.

"No, no, no," I said, clicking the mouse and scrolling through the list. "No, no, no, there!"

Morgan McDougall and the other kids at the study tables were staring at me, since, you know, I was muttering to myself, but I didn't care because I finally saw a title that wasn't on the shelf with the others. *Great Transformations Through the Ages and How They Were Achieved.*

Okay, that was certainly a long and pretentious enough title, but it didn't really tell me anything—like what the book was actually *about*. I clicked a few more times, pulling up additional info about the book, but all that had been entered into the catalog was the call number and a few other minor details and key words.

Behind me, Alexei sighed and leaned back against the glass office complex. From the looks he was giving me, I knew he'd thought that I'd gone off the deep end, but I ignored him and continued my search. I was on to something. I could feel it in my bones.

I kept clicking, but I couldn't find any more information about the book. So I went to a different screen to see if there was another copy of it in the library. So many kids used some of the reference books that Nickamedes had multiple copies of many of the titles. But of course there wasn't another copy of *Great Transformations*, because that would have just been too freaking *easy*.

I fumed for a few seconds before pushing aside my frustration and getting back to work. I kept looking and clicking through the files. Apparently, the book was one of a kind, because not only couldn't I find another copy in the Library of Antiquities, I couldn't find another copy *anywhere*. Not in any of the libraries at the other Mythos academies in the United States and not in any of the ones located overseas either.

I'd thought there was nothing else I could do when I noticed a tab that said *Related Books*. I clicked on that. Once again, there wasn't much there to help me. Still, I clicked, scanned, and scrolled through all the pages on the off chance I'd find something.

And I finally did—*Great Transformations Through the Ages and How They Were Achieved: Volume II.*

That was the title of one of the *Related Books*, one that sounded like a newer, updated version of the book I was searching for. I clicked on that link, hoping the library might have a copy. No luck. There wasn't a copy in the Library of Antiquities, but I kept searching—and finally found one at the Crius Coliseum.

Excitement bubbled up in my chest. I logged off the computer, looked at the clock on the wall—and my heart sank. Just after one o'clock. The buses that went from Cypress Mountain down into the city only ran half a day on Saturdays in the winter, which meant I'd already missed the last bus. So how was I going to get from the academy, down the mountain, and over to the coliseum?

Well, I could walk, but it would take *forever*—and I just didn't have that kind of time. Not to stop whatever Vivian and the Reapers had already put into motion. No, I needed a car. If Oliver had been here, I would have just asked him to take me in his SUV, but he was at the concert hall with Logan and the rest of my friends. I could call my Grandma Frost to come pick me up, but she was probably busy with her fortune-telling clients. Plus, I didn't know how long it would take for her to come get me, and I needed to get to the coliseum as soon as possible.

But those were my only options. It wasn't like I could just ask some random kid in the library to drop what he was doing and give me a ride. He'd laugh in my face—or worse, pull his weapon on me. Still, I was desperate enough to consider it, and I gazed at first one student, then another, trying to find someone who might be slightly sympathetic—or at least not outright hate me.

I noticed a green spark of magic out of the corner of my eye, and I looked to the left. A few more sparks shot up into the air as Morgan McDougall turned the page in the book she was reading. Morgan wasn't my enemy, but she wasn't quite my friend either. Still, she had helped me in the past, and she'd stuck up for me in gym class yesterday.

I hopped off my stool, went around the checkout counter, and walked over to Morgan. The Valkyrie looked up from her book.

"Do you have a car?" I asked. "Please, please, *please*, tell me you have a car."

"Of course, I have a car." Morgan's hazel eyes narrowed in suspicion, but I could hear the interest in her voice. She wanted to know what I was up to. "Why do you ask?"

I grinned at her. "How would you like to go on a little field trip?"

"No," Alexei said. "Absolutely not. Are you out of your mind?"

"Were you not listening during my trial?" I said. "Because if you were, you would know that the answer to that question is almost always *yes*."

Alexei and I were standing by the main academy gate just below the two sphinxes perched on the wall. After

I'd told Morgan what I wanted and she agreed to help me, I'd raced out of the library, gone back to my room, and grabbed a few things I thought I might need—like Vic. I'd told the sword what I'd discovered in the library, and his purplish eye had brightened.

"Excellent!" Vic had said. "Now that you're on the trail of the Reaper girl, let's get on with the business of finally killing her."

"You got it."

After I'd grabbed my things, I'd jogged down to the main gate to wait for Morgan to get her car from the lot where she parked it over in Cypress Mountain.

The only problem was that Alexei had come with me.

He'd followed me from my dorm room all the way down to the gate. Now, he was standing in front of me, a grim expression on his face.

"You can't leave campus, Gwen," he said. "The Protectorate gave me strict instructions. I'm supposed to make sure that you stay at the academy—no matter what."

"You can try," I said in a quiet voice. "I don't want to fight you, Alexei, but I will if I have to."

He scoffed at that. "Do you really think you can beat me, Gwen? I've been training for years. And not just regular warrior training—Protectorate training. The most physical, intense combat training a warrior can go through. I've seen you fight in the gym. You're not bad, but you're not as good as me. We both know it."

I did know that, but that still didn't stop me from putting down my bag, drawing Vic out of his scabbard, and holding the sword up in an attack position. Alexei's gaze dropped to his backpack, which was on the ground at his feet. The hilts of two swords stuck out of the top like usual, but he didn't reach for the weapons—yet.

"I know you're better than me," I said. "Stronger, tougher, more experienced as a warrior, but I'll still try my best. Because this is about stopping Vivian, about stopping the Reapers and whatever they have planned. This is about saving people, Alexei. That's what warriors are supposed to do—that's what *we're* supposed to do."

Alexei eyed my sword, and Vic glared right back at him.

"Get out of our way, Bogatyr," Vic snapped. "Gwen is Nike's rightful Champion, and you know it. If she says this is important, then it's important. You should be helping her—not standing there like a fool worrying about the bloody *rules*."

Trust Vic to make following the rules sound like the lamest thing ever. Still, the sword had a point. Well, another one besides the actual sharp tip at the end of his blade. Sometimes at Mythos, you had to bend the rules to protect the people you cared about. I just hoped I could convince Alexei of that.

"Please, Alexei," I said. "This is important. I know it is. Vivian and the rest of the Reapers have something planned—something bad. But I can stop them. I just have to figure out what's inside that book the Reaper stole. Why the Reaper took that first, even before snatching the jewels. As soon as I know that, I'll call Metis, and you can call Sergei. I'll surrender peacefully then. After that, well, I'm sure Linus will throw me into the academy prison—probably for good—and you'll never have to see me again. At least, not until my execution."

I smiled at my bad joke, but Alexei just looked at me. He stared at me a long, long time. Finally, his gaze went back to Vic, and I tightened my fingers around the sword. If Alexei came at me, I'd only have one chance. Despite what I'd said earlier, I wasn't going to fight him. He was right. I wouldn't win. Instead, I'd shove past him and then hope I could run fast enough to get through the gate and that Morgan brought her car around before he caught up with me.

I wasn't too optimistic about my chances, though. I'd seen Alexei fight in the gym and then against the Reapers in the library, so I knew exactly how quick and deadly he was. Still, I had to try.

Just when I thought he was going to attack me after all, the Bogatyr sighed. "Very well. We'll go to the coliseum and see if we can find the book. But if we can't or it turns out to be a dead end, we are coming straight back here. Understand?"

I nodded. "Thank you, Alexei."

He grunted, but he didn't say anything else.

"Let's go," I said, sliding Vic back into his scabbard. "Because I don't think we have any time to waste."

Chapter 22

A beep sounded, and a red Aston Martin stopped on the street outside the gate. Morgan rolled down her window and waved her hand at us.

Alexei stepped over to the gate and slipped through the iron bars, but I paused and looked up at the sphinxes. They were still staring down at their feet and refusing to look at me, but the sphinxes' faces were furrowed, and I sensed the same sort of tension and wary watchfulness in them that I had the gryphons at the library. They knew something was up, just like I did. I only hoped I could figure out what was going on in time to stop it—and Vivian—for good.

"Come on, Gwen!" Morgan yelled. "This was your bright idea, so let's go!"

I slipped through a gap in the bars, jogged across the street, and slid into the passenger's seat. Alexei had already gotten into the back. As soon as I closed the door, Morgan hit the gas, zooming away from the curb much faster than was safe and throwing me back against the seat.

"This is your car?" I asked.

"What?" she said, an edge in her voice. "Girls can't have kick-ass sports cars?"

"Of course girls can have kick-ass sports cars," I said. "I just didn't think you would."

"What kind of car did you think I would have?"

"I don't know," I muttered, buckling my seat belt and gripping the door handle. "Something . . . slower."

Morgan just laughed.

Despite the Valkyrie's need for speed, we made it to the Crius Coliseum in one piece. While Morgan parked her car, Alexei and I headed inside the museum.

An enormous, circular room served as the center of the coliseum, with hallways and exhibit areas branching off the main space. Towering pillars made out of white marble gave the museum its grand, ancient, coliseum-like feel, while bits of gold, silver, and bronze glinted on the walls before spreading up to cover the ceiling. Jewelry, pottery, clothing, weapons, and armor filled the exhibit area, all protected and preserved by artifact cases similar to those in the Library of Antiquities. Visitors strolled through the coliseum, peering at the artifacts and browsing through the expensive replicas that were for sale in the gift shop, while the museum staff, all dressed in long, white togas, helped folks with whatever they needed.

Everything was perfectly normal, but the more I looked around, the more the coliseum and everything in it began to change. The faint shadows darkened, until they resembled thin, bony fingers crawling along the floor and walls. Screams echoed in my head, and the coppery stench of blood made me gag. Suddenly, Reapers swarmed over everything, their swords flashing a sinister silver as they arced up and then rammed into the backs of the panicked students who were trying to get away from them—

"Gwen? Is something wrong?" Alexei asked.

I shook my head, and the phantom sights, sounds, and smells disappeared back into the bottom of my mind with the rest of the horrible memories I'd rather forget. "Just remembering the last time I was here."

"During the Reaper attack?"

I nodded.

Alexei didn't say anything else, but he gave me a sympathetic look. He knew all the awful things that had happened here as well as I did—and all the awful things my friends and I had done just to survive that day.

"Come on," I said, my voice harsh and raw with emotion. "We need to find out where the book is."

The *Great Transformations* book wasn't listed in any of the exhibit brochures, so we asked one of the staff members, and he told us to look in the library at the very back of the coliseum. Morgan caught up with Alexei and me, and the three of us headed in that direction. Since it was Saturday, the coliseum was crowded, with people going from room to room and case to case, looking at all the treasures of the mythological world.

Everyone seemed to be completely focused on what they were doing, but a shiver swept through me all the same. I felt that if I could only turn my head quickly enough, I'd realize everyone was staring at me, even though no one paid any real attention to me. I eased my hand inside my messenger bag and curled my fingers around Vic's hilt. The feel of the smooth metal against my palm only made me that much more tense, as if I might have to draw the sword and start fighting at any second.

"What's wrong?" Morgan asked, noticing me clutching the sword.

I made myself pull my hand away from Vic. "I'm not sure. I just have a bad feeling about this. Something's not right. Let's find the book, see what it says, and get out of here."

We finally reached the library and stepped inside. It was much, much smaller than the Library of Antiquities, but it was still impressive. The library was made out of the same white marble as the rest of the coliseum, and the roof was one large skylight, making the entire room bright, sunny, and warm even in the middle of winter. Floor-to-ceiling shelves took up two of the walls, while a third was filled with old, yellowed maps that chronicled great mythological battles and campaigns throughout the centuries. Normally, I would have lingered in here, going from shelf to shelf and map to map until I'd seen everything, but there wasn't time.

I put my messenger bag down on one of the tables, then looked at the slip of paper the staff member had given me. "According to this, the book is in section G."

It took us a few minutes to find the appropriate shelf

and a few more still to find the actual book, but there it was, sitting on the shelf right where it was supposed to be: *Great Transformations Through the Ages and How They Were Achieved: Volume II.*

Instead of immediately reaching for the book, I frowned.

"What's wrong?" Alexei said in an impatient tone. He'd put his backpack down too and was leaning against the table.

"This feels way too easy," I said.

Morgan snorted. "You think all that research you did in the Library of Antiquities, sneaking off campus, and asking me to drive you down here was *easy*? I think you need a new definition of the word, Gwen."

I ignored her. Alexei, Morgan, and I were the only ones in this part of the coliseum, and the conversation and chatter from the other visitors had long since faded away. I didn't hear so much as a whisper of movement, but I still glanced back toward the door, half-expecting to see a group of Reapers rush inside, swords out, ready to skewer us.

I waited and waited—but nothing happened. Finally, I turned back to the shelf, staring at the book and the words on the spine—*Great Transformations Through the Ages and How They Were Achieved: Volume II.*

Morgan snorted again and grabbed the book off the shelf, causing green sparks of magic to shoot out of her fingertips. I sucked in a breath, but once again nothing happened.

"See?" she said. "It's just a book. You are being totally paranoid. Now, can we please get on with this?"

"I agree with the Valkyrie," Alexei said. "Everything
seems normal here. So use your magic on the book, and
let's leave."

"Fine," I muttered. "But if things go bad, and I start
screaming my head off, don't say I didn't warn you."

Alexei and Morgan glanced at each other before she
held the book out to me. I drew in a breath, took it from
her, and waited for the images and feelings to enter my
mind so I could learn all the secrets the book might contain.

The memories flooded my brain, and I got flashes of
all the people who'd looked at, touched, and read the
book over the years. Nothing unusual there. Disappointment filled me, and for a moment I thought that
those would be the only images attached to the book—
but I was wrong.

Snatches of conversations and whispered words tumbled through my mind, one after another.

"A difficult thing, transferring a soul to another
body..."

"Have to make sure the host subject is exceptionally
strong..."

"Once the soul is transferred, it will overpower the
other until there's nothing left of the original subject or
soul..."

The voices were all cold, clinical, and detached, as
though they were talking about experimenting on lab

rats instead of human beings. I shuddered at the words and their horrible implications, but I tightened my grip on the book and went even deeper into the memories, searching for anything that would tell me what was so important about this book that the Reapers would risk breaking into the Library of Antiquities to steal the original volume of it—

Vivian's face popped into my mind.

I immediately grabbed on to the image, bringing it into sharper focus and letting myself fall into the memory.

Vivian stood in the coliseum library. She looked around, her golden gaze going from one corner of the room to another, as though she was expecting trouble. The library lights were dim, and stars shimmered through the glass roof, instead of sunshine. The Reaper girl must have broken into the coliseum at night.

Finally, when she was sure no one was coming to in-vestigate, Vivian turned her head, and I realized there was someone else in the library—someone wearing a black robe. The hood was up, and the person had his back to Vivian so I couldn't see who it was. Somehow, though, I knew it was the Reaper I'd chased in the li-brary, even though all I could make out was a pair of black gloved hands clutching a book—the same *Great Transformations* book I was holding right now.

"It's no good," the Reaper said, his voice seeming higher than it had before as he snapped the book shut and held it out to Vivian. "What we need isn't in here. The Pantheon must have decided the information was too dangerous and removed it from this edition."

"Are you sure?" Vivian asked, grabbing the book and flipping through the pages. "The others were positive that this was the right book."

The Reaper shook his head. "Some of the information is in here, but not all of it. We need the list of jewels and the entire ritual from start to finish in order to transfer Loki's soul into the body we have in mind. Believe me when I tell you there is no room for error or mistakes of any kind. We only get one shot at this, and we have to make sure it goes smoothly, or our years of waiting and watching will be for nothing, and our lord will be in even worse shape than he already is. We'll have to get the original book after all."

"And where would that be?" Vivian asked.

"The Library of Antiquities," the Reaper said.

Vivian blinked, apparently surprised by the information. After a moment, she shook her head. "There's no way you'll be able to get onto the grounds, much less into the library. Not now, with all the extra security they've added to campus."

"We always knew it was a possibility that we might need the original book, and we've planned accordingly. This is where you come in," the Reaper said. "You're going back to school."

Vivian rolled her eyes. "Do I have to? I've already wasted enough time at that stupid academy."

"Oh, I think you'll like it much better there this time around, especially since it will give you a chance to make life miserable for your good friend, Gwen Frost. By the time we're through with her, the Protectorate will decide to execute her and do your job for you. All you'll have to do is sit back and watch her suffer."

A smile stretched across Vivian's face, and a bit of Reaper red flashed to life in the depths of her golden eyes. "Well, why didn't you say so in the first place?"

"Come on," the Reaper said, moving to the doorway, his back still to Vivian. "Let's get out of here before someone finds us."

The image of the library started growing dim and hazy, and I knew that this particular memory was coming to an end. Still, I held on to the book, straining to see every last thing I could—including the Reaper's real identity.

Come on, I thought. *Turn around and show yourself.*

My heart sank as the Reaper neared the entrance to the library. One more second, and the evil warrior would be gone—and so would any chance I had of discovering who the Reaper was.

Vivian put the *Great Transformations* book back on the shelf, but she was in a hurry and didn't push it back far enough. The book fell to the floor. The sound cracked like thunder in the library. Vivian winced, leaned over, and picked up the book.

The Reaper whirled around, and I realized that the person wasn't a man at all. She wasn't wearing a mask, and I finally saw her face—her beautiful, familiar face. Her green eyes narrowed, and she glared at Vivian.

"Quiet!" Agrona Quinn hissed at the girl. "Do you want the guards to hear—"

I was so surprised that the rest of the memory slipped away, even though I could still hear Agrona muttering at Vivian. After a moment, even that vanished.

I drew in a shaky breath, opened my eyes, and glanced down at the book. The leather cover seemed to burn my fingers, but I knew that was just my shock at what I'd discovered.

Logan's stepmom was really a Reaper of Chaos? I didn't want to believe it. She'd seemed so calm, so nice, so *good* to the Spartan, helping Logan and smoothing things over with Linus whenever the two of them were arguing. Logan would be so hurt when he found out that she'd been lying to him and his dad this whole time.

Then, another thought occurred to me. Maybe— maybe Vivian had tampered with the book, planted some false memories in it, just like she'd done before when she was trying to keep me from figuring out that she was Loki's Champion. Vivian's telepathy let her do that sort of thing, made people see and feel things that weren't really there—even me. For the first time, I really hoped that the Reaper girl was messing with me again.

I reached out with my psychometry, going back through all the images and memories, but I saw exactly what I had before. Vivian and Agrona talking about the book and finding a new body for Loki. The memories were all sharp and clear, and I didn't get the sense they'd been tampered with in any way. Before, when I'd touched Vivian's Janus ring, the one she'd planted the fake images on, it had felt like there was something slightly off about all the memories associated with the ring. But I didn't get that sort of vibe from the book— not at all. No, the memories attached to it were genuine.

I'd been prepared to see Inari's face, or Sergei's, or

even Linus's. After all, I'd thought the Reaper was a
man, because of the low voice I'd heard in the library,
but Agrona must have found some way to disguise her
voice. How, though? How could she do that—

And that's when I remembered her gold necklace, the
one I'd seen her fiddling with more than once—the one
that was set with two rubies and two emeralds.

> . . . the emeralds are believed to have a hyp-
> notizing effect, while the topaz can cause hal-
> lucinations. However, the rubies are thought
> to be the most powerful and have a variety of
> magic attached to them, everything from let-
> ting people deceive others to even overcoming
> a person's mind and compelling him or her to
> act against his or her own free will . . .

That's what the card had said about the Apate jewels,
and I was willing to bet that changing your voice would
be easy to do with them. I frowned. But I'd seen Agrona
wearing her necklace before the jewels had been stolen.
Were there more gems out there with magical proper-
ties? I didn't know, but it wasn't really important right
now.

Because the fact was that Agrona Quinn was a
Reaper—which meant Logan and the rest of my friends
were in big, big trouble.

"Well?" Alexei said. "What did you see?"

"Yeah, Gwen," Morgan chimed in. "Spill."

I shook my head. "Nothing good. I think—I think the

Reapers are planning some kind of ritual, some way that they can transfer Loki's soul or whatever into a new body. Is that even possible?"

Alexei's face darkened at my words. "I've heard stories of such things from my father and other members of the Protectorate, but that's all I thought they were—stories. So did my father. The fact that Loki is injured and weak from his imprisonment is all that gives us a chance of defeating him and the Reapers. If what you say is true, and this is what the Reapers are planning, if they manage to find a new body for him..." His voice trailed off. "Then Loki will be returned to his full strength—and no one will be able to stop him. Not even the gods themselves."

"In other words," Morgan said, "we'll all be royally screwed."

"You don't know the half of it," I replied.

I told them everything I'd seen and heard—including the fact that Agrona was really a Reaper.

Alexei's eyes widened at the news, but then he frowned, thinking about it. "Agrona had access to Vivian," he finally said. "In fact, she was assigned to guard Vivian most of the time. It would have been easy for her to slip Vivian some of the Apate jewels to put on her ring."

"We have to warn Metis and the others," I said. "Right now, before it's too late—"

"You aren't going to be warning anyone about anything, Gypsy," a familiar, mocking voice called out.

Alexei, Morgan, and I all froze and looked toward the doorway. A figure stood there, blocking the exit. She was wearing a black robe, although the hood was down, and her face was visible. She wasn't bothering to hide her real identity with a rubber Loki mask this time. She didn't need to, not anymore.

Vivian Holler grinned at me.

Chapter 23

The Reaper girl stepped into the library. I immediately shoved the book at Alexei, lunged forward, reached into my messenger bag, and drew Vic out of his scabbard. Vivian also held a sword in her hand, one with a woman's face inlaid in the hilt, and the bulging red eye snapped open and glared at me and Vic.

"Lucretia," Vic growled.

"So we meet again, Vic," the other sword answered in a low, feminine voice. "But you won't make it through this fight."

"I'll shut you up for good this time, you psychotic piece of steel!" Vic crowed.

Vivian clucked her tongue. "Temper, temper, little blade. Looks like your sword is just as bloodthirsty as mine is, Gwen. He'll make a fine weapon for one of my Reaper friends when I take him out of your cold, dead hands."

"Dream on," I snarled. "I know what you're up to, and I'm going to stop you, Vivian. You and Agrona and whoever else is involved."

She frowned. "How did you know about Agrona . . ." She looked at the book in Alexei's hand. "The book. I forgot to use my magic on the book and muddle the memories so you couldn't look at them with your stupid psychometry."

"Well, you have been a little busy, murdering people, framing me for your crimes, and whatnot," I said. "Hard to keep track of everything."

Vivian shrugged.

"How did you get away from the Protectorate? And why are you here now? Shouldn't you be out helping your Reaper friends with the transformation? Getting ready to put Loki's soul into one of his minions?"

"I got away from the Protectorate because I killed the three people who were guarding me," Vivian said. "They never saw it coming."

Alexei hissed in anger. Vivian smirked and gave him a saucy wink.

"Don't worry, Bogatyr," she said. "You won't have time to miss your precious Protectorate friends."

Then, she grinned at me again. "As for your other questions, yes, I will be helping with the ritual. But who says we're using a Reaper for the transformation?"

I eyed her. Somehow, I didn't think she was lying—not about this. No, her voice was way too smug. But if they weren't using a Reaper for the ritual, then who? I couldn't imagine anyone who would willingly let their soul be eaten away by Loki's.

"Apparently, you just can't stick a god's soul into just *any* old body," Vivian said. "I volunteered, but Agrona had someone else in mind already. You see, the new body has to be strong enough to make it through the ritual and contain the soul, and of course we only wanted the absolute best for Loki. Someone who was strong, smart, cunning, and one of the fiercest warriors of his generation."

She smirked at me, and I knew exactly who she was talking about.

"Logan," I whispered. "You're going to put Loki's soul into Logan's body."

Everything inside me just—froze. My blood, my breath, my heart. All cold, dull, still, and heavy, as though I'd been encased in a tomb of ice. After a few seconds, the shock faded, but the cold stayed behind, along with the fear—terrible, terrible fear for Logan.

"Correct again, Gwen," Vivian sneered. "You really aren't as dumb as you look. It's just too bad that you won't actually be there to see your boyfriend go through the transformation. I'm told that it's *extremely* painful."

"What do you mean?" I mumbled through my numb lips.

The Reaper jerked her head at the book. "You don't think we just left that behind by accident, do you? Agrona knew you'd seen her swipe the Apate jewels, and she thought you might figure out that wasn't all she'd taken from the library. So we left the book here and put a watch on it just in case you decided to come snooping around. As soon as you walked through the front door, our guy at the coliseum called me. And here you are, way back here where no one will hear you or your friends scream. You never can leave well enough alone, Gwen. Although I have to say it's rather convenient how your nosiness leads you into my traps every single time."

So my coming here had been another part of their plan, a way to lure me away from the academy so Vivian could kill me. I looked at Alexei, but the Bogatyr was staring at the Reaper girl, his eyes narrowed, his jaw clenched, his free hand balled up into a fist. No doubt he was thinking about the Protectorate guards she'd killed and how he'd like to do the same thing to her. I glanced at Morgan. The Valkyrie dipped her hand into her purse and pulled out a dagger, which she discreetly lowered to her side. Morgan nodded at me, telling me she was ready to fight.

My hand tightened around Vic's hilt. "Believe me when I tell you that this will be the last time I fall into one of your traps, because you're not getting out of here alive."

Vivian let out a happy laugh. "Oh please. As if you could ever beat me in hand-to-hand combat. Even if by some *miracle* that happened, you'd still be too late to save your precious boyfriend. I told you I was going to take away everything you love, Gwen. I think Logan will be a nice start, don't you?"

Rage erupted in my heart, exploding like a bomb, and burning away the cold fear that had paralyzed me. I let out a fierce yell and charged at Vivian. The move surprised the Reaper girl, who backed up a few steps.

"Now!" she screamed.

More Reapers streamed into the room, swords up and ready to kill. They must have been waiting outside for her signal, but I didn't care. Right now, I only had eyes for Vivian. I threw myself at the Reaper girl, raised Vic high, and brought the sword down as hard and fast as I could.

CLANG!

Red and purple sparks hissed through the air as Vivian brought Lucretia up, stopping Vic from splitting her skull in two. I pressed forward, trying to get through her defense, but I couldn't do it. Not only was Vivian a Gypsy, but she was a Valkyrie too, which meant that she was much, much stronger than I was. I remembered exactly how much stronger a second later when she snapped up her fist and punched me in the stomach.

Stars flashed in front of my eyes, or maybe that was just the red sparks of magic streaming out of Vivian's fingertips. I couldn't really tell. The force of the blow knocked me back and shoved the air out of my lungs, but I was in such a rage that I sucked down another breath and threw myself forward again.

I had never wanted to kill Vivian as much as I did in that moment. I had never *needed* to do it so badly as right now. The Reaper girl had already murdered my mom and Nott, attacked Grandma Frost, and now, she was going to help turn Logan into . . . into . . . I couldn't even begin to *imagine* what having Loki's soul in his body would do to the Spartan. How it would destroy everything that made Logan, well, Logan.

But that wasn't going to happen, I vowed. Because I was going to save Logan, and I was going to stop the Reapers—starting with chopping Vivian's head off her shoulders.

Clash-clash-clang!

Back and forth through the library we fought, turning over tables and chairs, ripping down maps, and trampling over books in our fury to kill each other. Every once in a while, I got a glimpse of Morgan and Alexei out of the corner of my eye. The Valkyrie was holding her own. She'd used the dagger in her purse to take down one Reaper already. Morgan snatched up the sword of the warrior she'd just killed and attacked the Reaper who was battling Alexei, making the evil warrior jump back.

Alexei, who had been using the *Great Transformations* book as a sort of shield against the Reaper's vicious blows, threw the book down. He grabbed the two swords out of his backpack and turned to battle another Reaper who was creeping up on his other side.

I would have liked to help them, but I had my hands full with Vivian. Despite my anger, the Valkyrie had been right when she'd said that she was the better fighter. The surprise of my initial attack had already worn off, and she went on the offensive, swinging Lucretia a little closer to my throat with every single pass she made.

"Come on, Gwen!" Vic yelled underneath my palm. "Cut her to ribbons! Hack them both to pieces!"

"I'm trying!" I yelled back.

I quickened my pace, upping the tempo of my attacks, trying to surprise Vivian again. That didn't happen, but something almost as good did—she tripped over one of the books that had fallen to the floor and stumbled back against a shelf. Alexei ran his swords through a Reaper's stomach, while Morgan pulled her dagger out of the chest of the last one. I looked at them, and they both nodded at me. Together, weapons up, the three of us advanced on Vivian.

"What are you going to do now that all your friends are dead?" I said in a mocking voice, stopping in front of her.

Vivian looked left and right, but Alexei and Morgan fanned out, cutting off her escape routes.

"And now, I think it's time for you to finally get what you deserve," I snarled. "For my mom and Nott and everyone else you've ever hurt."

"Sorry, Gwen," Vivian said, grinning once more. "Maybe someday you'll learn that you can't beat me— and that Chaos will always win."

I rushed forward, but even as I did, I knew I was going to be too late—too late *again*.

Vivian let out an ear-piercing whistle, and the glass ceiling above my head shattered.

I threw myself to one side and put my arms up over my head, trying to get out of the way and protect myself from the falling glass as best I could. Beside me, Alexei and Morgan did the same. A shadow blotted out the sun, and a Black roc crashed down, creating a massive hole in the ceiling.

The bird was enormous. Its wings were a slick, shiny black, although I could see the crimson highlights ribboning through its thick feathers, as well as that Reaper-red spark that burned deep in its inky black eyes. The Black roc pecked at me, its sharp beak snapping out like the point of a sword about to run me through. I shrieked and rolled under a table away from it. The roc's beak slammed into one of the table legs, shattering it like a matchstick and causing the wooden top to tilt to one side.

Vivian hurried over to the roc and threw herself into the leather harness on the bird's back. "Fly! Fly! Fly!" she screamed.

The roc spread its wings wide and launched itself off the ground. It hovered in the middle of the library, as though it were having trouble fully taking off, black wings flapping and ripping even more books off the shelves until the heavy volumes fluttered up and down on the air like snowflakes. I wiggled out from underneath the table, got to my feet, and rushed forward, but I was too late. The bird let out a series of harsh *caw-caw-caws*, pumped its wings again, and shot up through the smashed ceiling.

I craned my neck up, but there was nothing I could do to stop the bird. So for the second time in my life, I watched Vivian and her Black roc soar up into the sky.

I stared up at the hole in the ceiling, as if I could make Vivian and her roc come back, as if I could reach up, latch on to the bird, and drag them both back down into the library, if only I wished hard and long enough for it. But they were gone, and all the wishing in the world wouldn't bring them back. But I had a good idea where they were going—after Logan.

If Agrona hadn't gotten to him already.

I almost screamed at the thought that Logan was already gone, that the Reapers had already worked their foul magic on him, that they'd already forced Loki's soul into his body, but I pushed the horrible thoughts away and forced myself to breathe—just breathe. In and out, in and out, in and out, until I felt I was in control of myself again and wasn't going to totally lose it.

Alexei recovered quicker than I did. He got to his feet, put his swords down, pulled his cell phone out of his jeans, and called someone. So did I, dialing Logan.

No answer.

I tried the Spartan again, but the call went straight to his voice mail. And a third time, with the same result. I tried Oliver next, then Kenzie, Daphne, and Carson. Nobody answered, and I knew it was because they couldn't. The Reapers had already put their plan into motion. I wondered if my friends had been captured—or if Agrona and whoever she had working for her had killed them already.

No. I couldn't think like that. I just couldn't. There was still time. There had to be time to save them—to save Logan.

"No one's answering their phone," I told Alexei. "What about you?"

He shook his head. "No, no one. I've tried my father, Inari, and Linus, but none of them are picking up."

Morgan frowned. "You think Reapers are at the auditorium?"

"Yes," I said. "They have to be there because that's where Logan is, and they need him for the ritual. Come on. We have to get over to the auditorium."

"And do what?" Alexei said. "No one's answering because the Reapers have most likely captured everyone already. Maybe even killed them. What we need to do is call in reinforcements."

"No. That will take too long, and you know. it," I snapped at him, my voice rising higher and higher with every single word. "I don't know what we can do, but we have to try. We can't let the Reapers do this to Logan while we stand around and wait for more members of the Protectorate to arrive. We can't let them put Loki's soul in his body. We just *can't*."

By this point, I'd thrown my hands up and was waving Vic at Alexei, as though I was going to attack the Bogatyr. That's how panicked and angry I was.

"Easy, guys, easy," Morgan said, stepping in between us. "You're forgetting one thing."

"What's that?" Alexei snapped.

She held up her hand, her car keys dangling from her index finger and green sparks of magic flashing in the air around her. "That I'm the one with the car. You two go where I go."

The Valkyrie looked at me. "And I say we go over to the auditorium and kick some Reaper ass."

"Sounds like a plan to me," I said.

Morgan turned to Alexei. "So are you coming with us or are you going to let us girls have all the fun?"

After a moment, he nodded. "I'm with you—both of you."

"Good," I said. "Then let's go. We don't have a second to spare."

Chapter 24

Morgan, Alexei, and I grabbed our stuff and ran out of the library, passing the museum staff who were racing down the hallway to see why the alarms were blaring. Yeah, so I'd pretty much wrecked another library, but there wasn't time to stop and explain. Not now. Not when Logan and the rest of my friends were in so much danger.

We made it to Morgan's car. Alexei once again got into the back, while I slid into the front. Morgan cranked the engine and peeled out of the parking lot, throwing me back against the seat for the second time. I laid Vic across my lap and fished my phone out of my jeans pocket. Instead of trying my friends again, I called someone else. She answered on the second ring.

"Pumpkin?" Grandma Frost asked in a sharp voice. "Where are you? What's going on? Something's wrong. I can feel it."

I told her everything that had happened and what the Reapers' plans for Logan really were.

"I can't get anyone to answer me," I said. "Not Logan, not Daphne, no one. We're on our way over to the auditorium right now."

"I'll meet you there, pumpkin," Grandma said. "And I'll bring my sword with me."

We hung up, and I had to clutch the door to keep from tumbling over when Morgan took a curve a little too quickly for my liking. The Valkyrie saw me eyeing the speedometer.

"What?" Morgan said. "We need to hurry."

"Just don't kill us before we get to the concert hall, okay?"

"Oh yeah," she snorted. "I'd hate to rob the Reapers of their chance to run us through. I hope you have some sort of plan, Gwen."

"Working on it," I muttered. "Working hard on it."

But I didn't have a plan. I had no idea what we'd find once we made it to the auditorium or what shape my friends would be in—if they were even still alive.

No, I told myself again. *No.* My friends were alive. They had to be. I couldn't think of them being hurt. I couldn't think of them being dead, or I would lose myself in my guilt, grief, and fear.

The Aoide Auditorium was only about five minutes away from the Crius Coliseum, but it seemed to take *forever* to get there. Finally, it came into sight. The auditorium reminded me of a massive circus tent—a circular building with a roof that arced up to a point. Long, swooping lines had been carved into the pale brown stone, adding to the effect.

Morgan cruised around the auditorium, and I spotted the Mythos buses in the parking lot—along with two men standing by the main entrance. They weren't wearing black robes, but I didn't recognize them as being Mythos staff members either. Morgan's car was the only one rumbling by on the street, and the men eyed the vehicle with cold, flat stares.

"Do you want me to stop?" Morgan said.

"No," I said. "Keep going and park around the corner of the block. I don't like the look of those guys."

She did as I asked, and the three of us got out of her car and stood on the sidewalk.

"Now what?" Morgan asked. "Do you have an actual plan? Or are we just going to go storm the castle and hope for the best?"

I winced. That was exactly what I had in mind. "Does anybody have a better idea?"

Alexei and Morgan looked at each other. After a few seconds, they both shook their heads.

"All right," I said. "Storming the castle it is."

"At the very least, we need more weapons," Alexei said. "Because those Reapers aren't just going to let us walk past them."

"I know, but we don't have time to go get more weapons," I said. "We'll just have to make do with what we have."

"Maybe not," Morgan said.

She went around to the back of the car and hit a button on her key, popping the trunk. Alexei raised his eyebrows at me, but I just shrugged. I had no idea what the

Valkyrie was up to. Morgan opened the trunk, sighed, and moved over so Alexei, Vic, and I could see what was inside.

Weapons—dozens and dozens of weapons. Several swords, four axes, three shields, a bow and two quivers filled with arrows, a plastic box full of throwing stars, even a leather belt studded with daggers. All silver, shiny, and ready to be used. It was like looking into the trunk of a serial killer's car.

"*Nice*, Valkyrie," Vic said. "Very nice."

Alexei nodded in approval, but all I could do was stare at the weapons and their glittering, pointed edges.

"Why do you look so shocked? You didn't think that dagger was the only weapon I had, did you?" Morgan said. "Geez, Gwen. You really haven't learned much about Mythos kids, have you?"

"Apparently not. You actually drive around with this stuff in your trunk?" I asked. "All the time?"

A faint blush stained the Valkyrie's cheeks, and a few green sparks of magic snapped off her fingertips. Shadows darkened her hazel eyes. "Ever since Jasmine basically turned me into her zombie puppet, I've been stockpiling weapons. I have them everywhere. In my car, in my dorm room, in my purse. I even stashed a few in Metis's classroom and some of the others on campus. Having weapons around makes me . . . feel better."

I touched her arm. "I understand. About the weapons and everything else."

Morgan pulled herself together, and the three of us raided the weapons stash. Alexei took an axe and slid it through a loop on his belt. He also pulled a double scabbard out of his pack and strapped it to his back, although he carried the two swords that went in it in his hands. I wasn't sure, but the scabbard and the weapons looked like the ones I'd given him that night in the Library of Antiquities.

Morgan strapped a quiver of arrows to her back and slung the bow over her shoulder. I stuffed a couple of the daggers into my hoodie and jeans pockets, then belted Vic's scabbard around my waist since I already clutched the sword in my hand. The Valkyrie shut the trunk and locked the car. Then, we headed toward the auditorium.

A park took up most of the block across from the auditorium, and we darted from tree to tree before creeping behind some thick holly bushes. The bushes served as a sort of wall for the park, so we were able to skulk along behind them until we were directly across the street from the auditorium entrance. I peeked through a gap in the bushes. The two men I'd seen earlier were still standing guard by the doors. They both wore long black coats, although I could make out the glint of swords underneath the fabric.

"Do you know those guys?" I asked Alexei.

He shook his head. "I've never seen them before. They aren't members of the Protectorate."

"I haven't noticed them at the academy either," Morgan said.

"They're Reapers, then," I said. "Which means that they've probably taken the others hostage already. Agrona has to be inside overseeing things. Vivian might be in there by now too."

"Well, what are you waiting for?" Vic demanded, his eye already glowing in anticipation of the battle to come. "Let's march over there and kill the bloody lot of them, along with any others who are foolish enough to get in our way!"

I tightened my grip on Vic, trying to muffle the sound of his voice. The sword narrowed his eye at me, but he fell silent.

We crouched behind the bushes and stared at the two men. I wondered how we could get past them without them sounding some sort of alarm and letting the other Reapers inside know that we were here. The element of surprise was the only advantage we had, and I didn't want to lose it.

Alexei opened his mouth to say something when my cell phone started buzzing. I pulled it out of my jeans pocket and answered the call.

"Pumpkin?" Grandma Frost's voice filled my ear. "I'm at the auditorium. Where are you?"

I told her that we were in the park staking out the front of the building, and a minute later, she slipped down behind the bushes with us. She wore a long coat, but I noticed that she had her sword strapped to her waist underneath the gray fabric, just like the Reapers did.

Grandma hugged me, then cupped my cheek with her hand. The warmth of her love washed over me, along with her rock-solid support, and I knew that she would do whatever she could to help save my friends and everyone else.

"We think the Reapers are inside already, getting ready for the transformation ritual," I told her in a low voice.

"I can't believe they want to put Loki's soul into that boy's body," Grandma muttered. "That's pure evil, even for the Reapers."

"They're not going to do that because we're going to stop them." I made myself sound braver and more confident than I felt. "But first, we need to figure out how to get past the guards and get inside. Logan and the others are probably in the main concert hall."

Grandma's lips curved up into a sly smile. "You just leave that to me, pumpkin."

She got to her feet and winked at me before heading to the far end of the park.

"Grandma!" I hissed. "Grandma!"

But she didn't pay any attention to me.

Alexei put his hand on my shoulder. "Come on," he said. "She's doing her part. Let's do ours. We can come up on the Reapers' blind side while she distracts them."

Stomach churning, I nodded and followed him.

Morgan, Alexei, and I left our hiding spot. We went back through the park down to the end of the block, out of the Reapers' line of sight, then jogged over to the auditorium. A couple of cars were parked on the street, so we were able to move from vehicle to vehicle until we ended up crouching behind the car closest to where the Reapers were standing guard.

Morgan drew an arrow out from the quiver on her

back and nocked it in her bow. Alexei hefted his
swords in his hands, while I tightened my grip on Vic. I
didn't know exactly what Grandma had in mind, but
we were ready in case things didn't go according to her
plan.

Grandma appeared at the opposite end of the street
and walked toward the Reapers at a slow pace that was
not at all like her normal, brisk stride. She hunched over
and shuffled forward, as though she was older than she
really was. The sun glinted off the silver strands in her
iron-gray hair, making it look more salt than pepper. I
don't know how she managed it, but she suddenly
changed from a vibrant woman into an old, decrepit
crone. She sort of reminded me of Raven, although I
couldn't imagine Raven ever being young.

The Reapers whirled around at the sound of the coins
jingling together on the ends of Grandma's many
scarves, but they relaxed when they realized that it was
just one woman approaching them.

Grandma lifted her head as she neared the two men.
"Beautiful day, isn't it?" she called out in a cheery voice.

The Reapers nodded. Grandma kept her slow, steady
pace up until she got in between the two men, then she
pretended to stumble over a crack in the sidewalk. She
tumbled to the ground, scarves fluttering and coins jingling even louder and harsher than before.

"Oh!" she cried out, rocking back and forth on the
concrete. "Oh, my hip!"

The Reapers looked at each other, then at my
grandma, who kept right on moaning and clutching her

left hip. Finally, one of them stepped forward and put his hand on her shoulder.

"Come on, lady," he growled. "It was just a little fall. You can't possibly be hurt that bad—"

Grandma rolled over, pulled her sword out from underneath her coat, and stabbed the Reaper in the chest with it. He grunted and fell on top of her.

"Now, Morgan! Now!" I hissed.

The Valkyrie rose up from behind the car and drew back her bowstring. A moment later, the second Reaper was down, thanks to the arrow Morgan had just put into his back.

The three of us rushed over to the Reapers. Alexei helped me roll the man off Grandma and help her to her feet. Grandma Frost dusted herself off and looked down at the two dead men.

"No one ever suspects an old woman of being dangerous," she said, twirling her sword in her hand. "I'll get these two out of sight just in case there are any more of them lurking around out here. You three go on inside, and be careful. You don't know what you'll find when you get in there, pumpkin."

For a moment, a blank look filled her violet eyes, and I knew she was talking about Logan and how it might already be too late to save him. Worry knotted my stomach, but I pushed away the awful dread. Instead, I hugged Grandma Frost tight, then turned and followed Alexei and Morgan into the auditorium.

We eased inside the entrance and found ourselves in a long, wide hallway. Most of the lights were off, since the auditorium wasn't officially open for the concert yet, and shadows stretched out as far as I could see, oozing over everything. Even just standing by the entrance, I could feel that something was very, very wrong here.

The three of us stayed together in a loose formation as we hurried down the hallway. Alexei took point, with me in the middle, and Morgan bringing up the rear, all of us looking and listening for the slightest hint of trouble or danger. We went from one hallway to the next, but we didn't see any Reapers—we didn't see anyone at all. No staff members sweeping the floors, no Mythos kids getting a drink of water from one of the fountains, no members of the Protectorate patrolling the auditorium. The silence made me worry that much more.

Finally, we reached a corner and peered around it. Two more Reapers stood in front of a series of doors that led into the main concert hall. Unlike the men outside, these Reapers had black robes on and their swords in their hands. My heart sank. We wouldn't be able to take them by surprise like we had the other guards.

We pulled back and huddled in the hallway, debating what to do.

"The Reapers must already be inside the main chamber," Alexei whispered. "We're not going to be able to get past those guards without making a lot of noise. Even if Morgan picked one of them off with an arrow, the other could still shout out and let the others know we were here."

Morgan tapped her finger against her bow, making green sparks flicker in the air. "Maybe we don't have to go through them. Maybe we can go around them instead."

"What do you mean?" I asked.

"There's another entrance to the concert hall, a catwalk that looks down over the whole area."

"How do you know that?" Alexei asked.

"Because I got totally bored during last year's concert, so I decided to go exploring with Samson. We paid one of the sound guys three hundred bucks to let us go through the control room and onto the catwalk."

I rolled my eyes. "You mean the two of you snuck off so you could go make out somewhere."

Morgan gave me a rueful grin. "I've told you before, Gwen. Sometimes, being the school slut comes in handy. I just wish Samson—"

She bit her lip, but pain filled her eyes, and more sparks of magic crackled in the air around her. I knew what she wanted to say—that she wished Samson were here, that he was still alive. But Vivian had killed him at the Crius Coliseum. Despite the fact that Samson had been Jasmine's boyfriend, Morgan really had loved him. I put my hand on her arm, telling her that I understood. Her mouth tightened, and she gripped her bow a little tighter.

"Come on," she whispered. "This way."

Morgan backtracked and led us down another hallway, then another one, circling around the concert hall. A few times, we had to stop, take another route, or even crouch down in the shadows as we waited for Reapers to pass by. Two-man teams patrolled the perimeter of the concert hall, all of them armed with swords and cell phones. I would have liked nothing more than to fight them, but I knew if we did that, the alarm would be raised, and we'd lose whatever chance we had of saving my friends.

Finally, we reached a door with a sign that read CONTROL CENTER—STAFF ONLY. The door was locked, but Morgan easily used her Valkyrie strength to yank it open. I winced at the noise she made, but there was nothing I could do about it.

We slid through the opening and closed the door behind us. Several chairs flanked a large control panel, while a series of monitors were mounted on the wall above. Wires snaked every which way across the floor, and a variety of boxes and switches jutted out from the other walls. In addition to concerts, the Aoide Auditorium also hosted everything from musicals to sporting events.

"Come on," Morgan whispered. "This way."

The Valkyrie led us through the room and over to another door on the far side. This one had a sign that said CATWALK ACCESS—AUTHORIZED PERSONNEL ONLY. Morgan twisted the knob. It wasn't locked, so she opened the door, and we stepped through it.

We walked up a flight of stairs that led to a catwalk that ringed the concert hall. Lights, stage backdrops, and weighted bags were anchored to the black metal rails, along with an elaborate series of pulleys and levers. Every two hundred feet or so, more stairs led down to other areas below.

We were on the back side of the concert hall, but I

could see people on the stage below. Alexei pointed in that direction, and the three of us crept along the cat-walk over to that part of the auditorium. Finally, we stopped right above the wide stage and crouched down, peering over the side of the metal railing. The sight below made my heart clench with fear.

Because the concert hall was filled with Reapers—and my friends were trapped in the middle of them.

Chapter 25

The enormous stage took up most of this side of the concert hall. The chairs that the band members should have been sitting in had been pushed to the back, with all the Mythos students huddled together in a tight wad in the center of the glossy wooden floor. Reapers ringed them on all sides, each one brandishing a long, curved sword. The kids stared at the Reapers in fear, and I could see the silvery shimmer of the tears on their faces even from up on the catwalk.

Daphne, Carson, Oliver, and Kenzie were on the stage with the rest of the band members. Carson had his arm around Daphne, holding her close, while Oliver and Kenzie were sitting back-to-back, staring at the Reapers with watchful eyes, like they were waiting for a chance to attack. Some of the tightness in my chest eased. They were all okay—for now.

Still, as I looked down at the Reapers, something about them bothered me. Even more so than usual. Finally, I realized what it was—the fact that the Reapers weren't wearing their rubber Loki masks. The evil warriors had on their black robes like usual, but their faces were bare.

"The Reapers are going to kill them all," I whispered. "That's why they're not wearing their masks. They don't need to hide their real identities because they don't plan on leaving anyone alive."

Beside me, Alexei nodded, his face grim as he silently agreed with me.

I kept scanning the stage. The adults had been separated from the kids and moved off to the left in front of a set of stairs that led down to the auditorium floor. The adults were also sitting on the stage, their hands tied in front of them with what looked like red velvet. The curtains, I thought, noticing tattered strips of fabric dangling down on that side of the stage. The Reapers must have cut up the stage curtains to use as ropes.

My gaze went from one face to another. Metis, Nickamedes, Ajax, Inari, Sergei. They were all bound and glaring at the Reapers. Several guards surrounded them, and I noticed a pile of weapons lying off to one side. The Reapers must have disarmed them already.

Cuts, blood, and bruises marred the adults' features, especially Ajax, whose bloody, swollen face looked like it had been used for a punching bag, but they all seemed more or less in one piece.

The same couldn't be said for everyone, though. Several people, adults mostly, were on the right side of the stage, away from everyone else. They were all lying down and sprawled on top of each other at awkward angles, and it took me a few seconds to realize why—because they were all dead. Blood oozed out from underneath their bodies and dripped off that side of the stage. *Plop, plop, plop.* Despite how high I was, it seemed like I could hear every single crimson drop hitting the floor. I put my hand over my mouth and swallowed a scream.

But the thing that concerned me the most was Logan. The Spartan had been separated from the others, and he was on his knees in the middle of the stage in front of the other kids. His back was to me, and his head was bowed, so I couldn't see his face. Something gold glinted around his neck, but I couldn't tell exactly what it was from up here. But the worst part was that Logan was completely motionless, despite the fact that he wasn't tied up or being guarded like the others were. Something rectangular lay on the stage a few feet away from him. It took me a moment to realize that it was a book, most likely the original volume of *Great Transformations*—and that it was open, as though someone had been reading it.

My heart twisted in pain, fear, and dread. The Reapers had started the transformation ritual already. Otherwise, Logan would have been fighting and trying to free everyone else.

And finally, my gaze went to Linus, who'd also been pulled away from the others. He sat on the stage a few feet away from Logan, his hands bound and a horrified look on his face as he stared first at his son, then at Agrona.

The Reaper towered over her husband, a bloody sword in her hand. All the other Reapers were staring at her, and it was obvious that the evil warriors were taking their orders from her.

"You'll never get away with this," Linus's voice drifted up to the catwalk.

Agrona looked down her nose at her husband. "Oh, but I already have, *darling*. You and the members of your precious Protectorate are all nicely tied up, and I have complete control of the situation—and more important, your son."

Her words sent a shiver up my spine, but Logan stayed where he was, his head bowed, still motionless. His stiff, awkward pose reminded me of how Morgan had looked when Jasmine had used the Bowl of Tears to control her. I glanced at the Valkyrie, and the hard set of her mouth told me she was thinking the same thing.

"It won't be long now before your son is ready for the next step in the transformation," Agrona said. "Killing everyone on this stage as a blood sacrifice to Loki."

The students gasped and whimpered, and a few started crying again. Metis and the other adults were equally horrified, although they tried to keep their faces calm so they wouldn't scare the kids any more than they already were. Still, I could feel the fear blasting off the kids and adults in icy waves, even way up here in the shadows.

Agrona sliced her sword through the air, causing some of the students to scream. She laughed with delight, and I noticed a ruby ring on her right hand. The gem matched the ones she wore around her throat. I remembered thinking how pretty her necklace was the first time I'd seen it. I should have known there was more to it than met the eye, especially after the Apate jewels had been stolen from the library. But the eerie thing was that all the gems she wore, rubies and emeralds alike, seemed to be glowing—glowing with Reaper-red fire.

I thought of the ID card I'd found in the library, the one I still had in my jeans pocket that talked about the jewels. Whatever power they had, it was obvious that Agrona was tapping in to that magic. I wondered if that was how she was controlling Logan, if that was why he wasn't fighting back.

"A few more minutes, and Logan will be completely ours—just as he was intended to be all along," Agrona said in a satisfied voice.

Linus frowned. "What do you mean?"

Instead of answering him, Agrona looked over at Nickamedes. "You were right to be suspicious of me all these years. This moment has been a long time in the making. In fact, it started when Logan was just a boy—and I led a team of Reapers to capture him. Of course, things didn't quite work out as I'd planned then, but no matter. I got what I wanted in the end. I always do."

Nickamedes sucked in a breath, and so did I. I knew what Agrona was saying as well as he did—that she'd been behind the Reaper attack on Logan's family all those years ago. That she was the one who'd murdered his mom and older sister.

Linus's face paled. "You—you killed my wife and daughter? Larenta and Larissa? Why? For what purpose?"

Agrona stared at him. "Because even back then, we

knew that Loki would need a new body after being trapped in Helheim for so long. So we started searching for the perfect candidate, knowing it would take years to find just the right one. And who better than a Spartan? They're the fiercest, the bravest, the best warriors. We knew that if we combined a Spartan's natural killer instinct with Loki's soul and power, our lord would be unstoppable. But none of the Spartans were quite right—until Logan was born."

Agrona's gaze dropped to the ruby on her hand, and I realized the gem was shaped like a large heart—just like the main ruby in Apate's necklace. Agrona must have taken the ruby out of its original setting and had it fashioned into that ring. She glanced over her shoulder at Logan, but he still didn't move. She turned back to Linus.

"Our goal that day was to capture the boy and kill everyone else in the house, including you," she said. "But of course, you were called away on Protectorate business, and the boy saw us coming and warned his mother and sister. Your lovely wife screamed at the children to hide, but we'd already cut off your daughter's escape. It was too late for them and they knew it, but they fought us and held us back while they yelled at the boy to run, which he did. After we killed the women, we searched the house from top to bottom, but we couldn't find him."

All this time, Logan had felt so horribly guilty that he hadn't fought alongside his mom and sister. But if he had, he would have been captured by the Reapers. Who knows what they would have done to the Spartan—

beaten him, tortured him, maybe even brainwashed him into becoming one of them. He would have been just as lost as his mom and sister had been. The terrible thoughts made me want to vomit, but I forced myself to focus on what was happening below, even as I tried to think of a way to save everyone.

"Since we couldn't find the boy that day, we had to come up with a new plan," Agrona continued.

"So you married Linus in order to keep an eye on Logan," Nickamedes said in a disgusted voice. "I always thought that you did something to Linus to get him to marry you so quickly after my sister died, that you bewitched him in some way."

"And you were right." Agrona reached up and tapped one of the rubies on her gold necklace. "You don't need Great Artifacts like the Bowl of Tears to bend people to your will. A few pieces of power here and there are more than enough to subtly push people in the right direction, if you know what you're doing— and I certainly do when it comes to magic. Years ago, I discovered a pair of ruby-and-emerald earrings that belonged to Apate. I had the gems reset so no one would recognize them, and I used their power to infiltrate the Protectorate and then convince dear, sweet Linus that I was just what he needed after I murdered his wife."

"So our whole marriage, everything we've been through, all the battles we've fought against the Reapers . . . it was all a lie?" Linus asked.

She leaned down and stared into his eyes. "Every single *second* of it."

Linus's face was cold and calm, but rage and hurt flashed in his gaze.

She laughed at his fury. "I can't tell you how many times I've longed to see that look on your face, Linus. Why, it's even more wonderful than I'd thought it would be—"

A door banged open. All the Reapers tensed and whirled around, but they relaxed when they realized it was Vivian. The Reaper girl climbed the stairs, stepped up onto the stage, and hurried over to Agrona.

"What took you so long? Did you take care of things at the coliseum?" Agrona asked.

Vivian shook her head. "Not exactly. My roc was injured breaking through some glass, and Gwen . . . got away."

One second, Agrona was staring at Vivian. The next, she'd slapped the girl across the face as hard as she could. The *crack* of the blow echoed through the whole concert hall. I blinked. I hadn't even seen her raise her hand to Vivian. Agrona had to be an Amazon to move that fast.

"Stupid girl!" Agrona snarled. "Do I have to do everything myself?"

Vivian stumbled back, clutching her red cheek, her golden eyes bright with surprise—and fury. "It wasn't my fault. Gwen had the Bogatyr with her and a Valkyrie too. They killed the others. I barely got away on my roc."

Agrona drew her hand back for another slap, but Vivian held up Lucretia, putting the sword between the two of them.

"You might be head of the Reapers, but I'm *Loki's*

Champion," Vivian hissed. "You would be wise to remember that, unless you'd like to see exactly what I'm capable of."

Agrona stared at her. After a moment, she lowered her hand to her side. "Tell me what happened."

"Gwen found the book in the coliseum and used her psychometry to flash on it," Vivian said. "She knows that you're a Reaper and what we're planning to do to her Spartan boyfriend. Unless I miss my guess, Nike's little Champion is here right now, plotting to save him and the rest of her friends."

Agrona immediately whirled around, looking out over the empty concert hall, her gaze going from one row of seats to the next. Alexei, Morgan, and I all froze, scarcely daring to breathe for fear of revealing our position to her. After a minute, Agrona turned back to Vivian.

"Are you sure she's here?" she asked.

Vivian nodded. "Unfortunately. Gwen is annoyingly persistent that way."

Agrona paced back and forth across the stage. Thinking. Then, she stopped, and another cruel smile curved her face. "Well, if Nike's Champion is here, let's invite her to the party, shall we?"

She tightened her grip on her sword and stalked over to where the adults were seated. She looked first at Ajax, then Metis, and finally Nickamedes. She jerked her head at the librarian.

"Get him up."

Two Reapers stepped forward, grabbed Nickamedes's

arms, hauled him to his feet, and dragged him to the middle of the stage, not too far away from Logan. Nickamedes started to fight, but Agrona put her sword against his throat. Nickamedes hissed, and blood trickled down his neck.

"Gwen Frost!" Agrona called out in a booming voice. "Show yourself! Or the librarian dies!"

Chapter 26

Everyone in the concert hall froze once more. The students, the members of the Protectorate, even the Reapers.

I let out the breath I'd been holding and got to my feet. I couldn't let Agrona kill Nickamedes. I just couldn't. No matter how much the librarian and I sniped at each other, we'd become friends these past few months—sort of. Besides, my mom had once loved Nickamedes, and he'd felt the same way about her. My mom would have tried to save him, if she'd been here, and I knew I had to do the same—even though I was walking straight into a trap.

"Gwen! What are you doing?" Morgan hissed, grabbing my arm.

"I'm giving them what they want," I whispered back. "I'm going down there."

"That's crazy," she said. "How do you know they won't kill you as soon as they see you?"

"Because Reapers like to make you suffer as much as possible before they murder you," I said. "It'll be okay.

You'll see. I'll keep them busy and distracted as long as I can."

I reached into my jeans pocket and passed her my cell phone. "Call my Grandma Frost and tell her what's going on. You and Alexei need to get down from here and meet up with her. Do you think you could lead them over to that door Vivian came through? The one that's on the side of the stage where Metis and the other members of the Protectorate are?"

Morgan looked down. After a moment, she nodded. "Yeah, I know a way down there. But what good is that going to do?"

"Because all the Reapers are going to be focused on me," I said. "That just might give you, Alexei, and my grandma a chance to sneak through the doors, get on stage, and cut Metis and the others free before the Reapers realize what's going on. It's the best chance we have of saving everyone. You know it as well as I do. Besides, this is what Champions do, right? Sacrifice themselves for the greater good?"

I didn't even try to smile at my bad joke. Instead, I let out another breath. "Just be ready, okay?"

Morgan nodded. I started to leave, but Alexei stepped in front of me.

"I'm sorry I ever doubted you," he said.

"I know," I said in a soft voice.

I touched his arm, then gripped Vic a little tighter, and went down to meet the Reapers.

I went back the way we'd come, walking all the way around the catwalk, down the stairs, through the control room, and backtracking through the hallways until I reached the main entrance. The two Reapers stationed there snapped to attention as soon as they saw me, but they didn't try to stop me as I walked past them. I tensed, half-expecting them to ram their swords into my back, but they didn't.

"Here goes nothing," I muttered, pushing through one of the doors.

"Don't worry, Gwen," Vic said. "I'm right here with you. We'll get through this battle just like we have all the others. You can't lose with me by your side."

The sword's bravado helped calm my jagged nerves. I nodded at him, unable to speak.

The doors led out to the top tier of seats ringing the concert hall, and it was a long, slow, agonizing walk down to the bottom row and then across the floor. My heart picked up speed with every step, but I forced myself to keep breathing—in and out, in and out, in and out.

I stopped about fifty feet in front of the stage. My gaze locked with Metis's, and the professor shook her head.

"No, Gwen," she said. "No! Turn around and run! While you still can—"

A Reaper stepped forward and punched her in the face.

Some of the students screamed. I started forward, determined to help Metis before the Reaper could hit her again—

"Stop!" Agrona snarled.

I froze in my tracks and looked up at her. She pressed

her sword a little deeper into Nickamedes's neck, turning the trickle of blood into a steady stream. The librarian winced, but that was his only reaction.

"If you try to escape, Gypsy," Agrona said. "I'll run the librarian through and then do the same thing to Metis. Your choice."

I straightened up. "I'm not going to run."

"Good," Agrona said. "Then come up here with the rest of us."

I headed toward the left side of the stage, keeping my steps slow and steady, as though I knew I was marching to my own funeral. Really, I was, but I wanted to give Morgan and Alexei as much time as I could to find Grandma Frost and get into position.

I climbed the stairs and stepped onto the stage. Metis had pushed herself up into a sitting position. Blood trickled down the corner of her mouth from where the Reaper had hit her. The professor stared at me, her green eyes full of worry and fear, but she didn't tell me to run again. We both knew there was no point in it—not now.

So I turned away from her and headed toward the center of the stage, my sneakers squeaking against the wood. I looked over at the students huddled together. Daphne, Carson, Oliver, and Kenzie all stared back at me, as worried and upset as Metis was. Daphne kept jerking her head toward the front of the stage, like she was trying to tell me something, but I couldn't figure out what it was. And I still couldn't see Logan's face, just his bowed head. He hadn't moved a muscle this whole time.

Agrona held up her hand when I was about fifteen feet away from her. "That's close enough, Gypsy."

I stopped where I was, glaring at her. "I'm here. You got what you wanted. So let Nickamedes go. Right now."

I thought she wouldn't do it, but Agrona dropped her sword from the librarian's neck and stepped away from him. Vivian crossed her arms over her chest and smirked at me.

"You're such an idiot, Gwen," the Reaper girl said. "Because now, we're going to kill you and your friends."

"I know that," I replied. "I just thought it would be fun to watch Agrona slap you around some more from up close this time. You know, a couple of weeks ago, I thought you were the one in charge of everything. But you're just another little Reaper underling, aren't you, Viv? You don't give the orders. You take them."

Fury reddened the Reaper girl's cheeks, and her knuckles went white around Lucretia's hilt. Vivian started forward, but Agrona held out her sword, stopping Vivian.

"Let me kill her now," Vivian snarled. "So we can finally be done with this."

Agrona shook her head. "You've had your chance twice now, and you've failed miserably both times. Besides, we need a blood sacrifice for the next part of the ritual, and I think Gwen will do quite nicely. You know how much power a Champion's blood has, especially Nike's Champion. It will make transferring Loki's soul that much easier."

I tensed, ready to counter any attack she made against me. But instead of raising her sword and trying to kill me, Agrona strolled toward Logan. I still couldn't see the Spartan's face, but surely he knew that I was here—that I was trying to save him.

A flicker of movement caught my eye. I turned my head and realized that Daphne was giving off more and more pink sparks of magic. The Valkryie had a stricken look on her pretty face.

"Run!" she mouthed to me.

But I couldn't run. I had to save Logan. I had to save them all, and that meant buying Morgan, Alexei, and Grandma Frost as much time as possible. Surely, they were almost in position now. All I had to do was hold out another minute or two—

"Logan," Agrona said in a sweet voice. "Do me a favor. Take this sword, and kill Gwen with it, please."

My head snapped around at her words. Logan? Kill me? He would never, *ever* do that. I didn't care what kind of creepy ritual Agrona and the other Reapers had performed on him. I didn't care what kind of mind-controlled zombie they'd turned him into. I knew the Spartan. I loved him, and he loved me. He would never hurt me—*never*.

Logan's hand jerked forward, and he took the weapon from Agrona. Worry surged through me, but I stood my ground.

"Come on, now," Agrona cooed. "That's a good boy."

The Spartan slowly got to his feet, his back still to me. Agrona stepped away from him, and I noticed that the jewels she wore were burning even brighter now. I could feel a force emanating from the gems—the same malevolent force I'd felt when Loki had stared at me with his burning red eye. My dread increased that much more, especially when Logan started twirling the sword in his hand, getting a feel for the weapon the way I'd seen him do so many times before in gym class.

After a few seconds, he lowered the sword to his side, adjusting his grip on it.

"Go on," Agrona commanded. "She's right there behind you. Kill her. *Now*."

The Spartan paused, then slowly turned to face me. I drew in a horrified gasp.

Logan's eyes were completely, utterly Reaper red.

Chapter 27

"Logan?" I whispered. "Logan?"

Agrona let out a pleased laugh. "He can't hear you, Gypsy. He can't hear anything but what I tell him, thanks to these lovely jewels we're both wearing."

"What are you talking about—"

For the first time, I noticed that Logan was wearing a necklace, just like Agrona was. Actually, it was more like a collar. Rubies, emeralds, and topaz gleamed around a wide gold band that circled the Spartan's neck.

Once again, I thought of the ID card I'd found in the library, the one that described the magic attached to Apate's jewels. I'd wondered what the Reapers were going to do with the other gems—now, I knew. They'd needed them for the transformation ritual, along with the book.

"No," I whispered again. "No."

I looked at Logan, who stared back at me with his crimson eyes. For a moment, I flashed back to that night in the forest when Loki had been freed. It was almost like I was looking into the evil god's face again. That's how horrible it was, that's how *wrong* it was, for Logan's eyes to be Reaper red instead of their normal, icy blue. It was like I was staring into a stranger's face.

The Spartan took a step forward, then another one, and another, once again twirling the sword Agrona had given him.

"Logan, it's me," I said, pleading with him. "You don't want to hurt me. I know you don't, deep down inside. Please, *please* don't do this. You're a Spartan. You can fight anyone, you can beat anything. I know you can fight back against whatever it is they've done to you. Please, *please* try. For me. For us."

The Spartan paused. He frowned, and for a moment his eyes were clear and blue once again.

"Kill her!" Agrona ordered, the jewels she wore burning even brighter than before. "Kill the Gypsy! Now!"

The blue in Logan's eyes vanished, drowned by that Reaper red again, and I knew I'd lost him. Logan let out a roar, raised his sword over his head, and charged at me.

CLANG!

Logan tried to kill me with that first strike, and it took all the strength I had to keep him from cutting through my defense and chopping my head off my shoulders.

"Logan," I said again. "Stop! It's me! Your Gypsy girl!"

He backed away and raised his sword for another

strike. I had no choice but to defend myself, although I ended up pulling my counterattack, not wanting to hurt the Spartan.

Logan had other ideas, though. Our swords locked together, and we seesawed back and forth for a moment. Then, the Spartan smiled and punched me in the face.

Pain exploded in my jaw. I stumbled away, but Logan came after me. He slammed his sword into mine, knocking Vic out of my grasp. I elbowed the Spartan in the stomach as hard as I could, forcing him back. Then, I dove after the sword, just managing to snag Vic before he went sailing off the stage.

"Get into the fight, Gwen," Vic snapped at me as I lurched to my feet. "He's going to kill you if you don't fight back."

"No," I insisted in a stubborn tone. "It's Logan. He won't hurt me. He would *never* hurt me."

"That's not Logan right now," Vic said, sadness filling his purplish eye. "And he won't stop until one of you is dead. Do the Spartan a favor, Gwen. Put him out of his misery. You know Logan. You know he'd rather be dead than to have this happen to him, than to be twisted into some new version of Loki. Champions have to make sacrifices, Gwen. And this one is yours."

I wanted to argue with the sword some more, but I couldn't because Logan charged at me again.

I parried his attack, then lashed out with Vic, forcing the Spartan to jump back. I was at the very front of the stage, and out of the corner of my eye, I saw one of the doors on the floor level slowly open. Morgan and

Alexei eased inside, followed by Grandma Frost. They crept up behind the Reaper who was standing at the top of the steps. I knew I had to give my friends as much time as I could, so I threw myself at Logan.

Clash-clash-clang!

Our weapons crossed and crossed and crossed again, each one of us trying to get the advantage. I managed to kick out and catch Logan in the knee, and the Spartan staggered away from me. I risked another glance to the left just in time to see Grandma Frost ram her sword into the Reaper's back, and Morgan and Alexei surge past her and into the Reapers guarding the members of the Protectorate.

Surprised screams and shouts rang out. Agrona and Vivian's heads snapped around, and they realized that they were in danger of losing control of the situation.

"Kill the Gypsy, Logan!" Agrona screamed. "Kill them all!"

After that, it was just utter chaos on stage, with everyone fighting everyone else. Morgan managed to free Ajax and Metis, while Grandma Frost protected her back, and Alexei worked at cutting Sergei and Inari loose. Nickamedes rammed his shoulder into the Reaper closest to him, sending the man crashing into Vivian and Agrona. Daphne, Carson, Oliver, and Kenzie surged to their feet, lashing out at the guards who surrounded them, and Linus did the same.

But Logan didn't seem to notice the battle around us—he had his orders to kill me, and he was determined to carry them out no matter what. We'd only been fighting for two minutes before I knew that I was going to lose.

Logan Quinn was the best warrior at Mythos Academy, the best warrior of his generation. Even though the Spartan had been training me for the past few months, I was nowhere near his league, and I doubted that I ever would be. It was all I could do to keep him from chopping me into little pieces.

Desperate, I called up all the memories I had of Logan, all the memories I'd absorbed when I'd first kissed the Spartan. I focused on those feelings and images, and then I did something I'd vowed never to do— I used the Spartan's own skills, tricks, and fighting techniques against him.

It slowed him down, but it didn't stop him—and I knew nothing short of death would.

By the three-minute mark, I was almost out of breath, and my heart was beating as hard as it could and not pop out of my chest. And still, I couldn't break through Logan's defenses. But I wasn't going to give up. There had to be another way to get the Spartan to come back to himself—to come back to me.

A flash of Reaper red caught my eye, and I noticed Agrona struggling with Nickamedes. She pushed him back, and Vivian tossed a sword at her before turning to fight Sergei. Agrona caught the weapon and swung it at Nickamedes. The motion made the gems in her necklace and ring gleam with a sinister light. Suddenly, I had an idea of how I could save Logan.

The next time the Spartan came at me, I shoved him

away, then turned and ran through the fight toward Agrona. The Reaper knocked Nickamedes down and raised her sword high, ready to bring it down on his neck. I lowered my shoulder and tackled her, driving her to the ground.

I landed on top of Agrona, and her head snapped against the stage, stunning her. That gave me enough time to reach down and yank the gold chain from around her neck. The rubies and emeralds burned as bright as stars, but I tossed the necklace down onto the stage, raised up Vic, and snapped his hilt down on top of each and every one of the stones.

Crack! Crack! Crack! Crack!

The gems splintered into dozens of pieces. One down, one to go.

Agrona started to lash out at me with her sword, but Nickamedes slapped the weapon away from her.

"Hold her arm down!" I yelled at him.

The librarian nodded, realizing what I had in mind. He latched on to the Reaper, pinning her right arm to the stage.

Morgan had snapped out of her zombie-like state when I'd destroyed the Bowl of Tears, and I was hoping the same thing would happen with Logan. That's why I'd yanked off and destroyed the jewels Agrona was wearing. Now, all I had to do was get rid of the last one.

I raised Vic up again and brought the sword down as hard as I could.

CRACK!

Agrona screamed as I crushed the ring and her hand

along with it. The Apate ruby might have a lot of power, but so did Vic, since he was a Champion's weapon, *my* weapon, given to me by Nike herself.

The sword's hilt shattered the heart-shaped ruby like it was made of glass.

An angry red light filled the entire concert hall the second Vic's hilt touched the gem, searing my eyes and making several students and even some of the Reapers scream. After a few seconds, the harsh glare faded, and I looked over at Logan, expecting to see him shaking off his confusion.

Instead, the Spartan's gaze landed on me, and he headed in my direction once more—his eyes still that eerie, eerie Reaper red.

"Fool!" Agrona snarled. "He's too far gone into the ritual, and he's still wearing a collar full of Apate jewels. You won't be able to get that off him with your stupid sword. Nothing will bring him back now. *Nothing.* He'll keep coming at you until one of you is dead."

I scrambled to my feet and raised Vic just in time to keep Logan from killing me. Déjà vu. Back and forth, we fought across the stage, while I begged and pleaded with him to fight, to come back to himself, to remember who I was, how we felt about each other, and everything we'd been through.

But nothing I said worked.

I couldn't get through to the Spartan, and he just kept coming and coming and coming at me, always on the attack. My strength was almost gone, and it was all I could do to lift Vic to fight him off. In another minute,

Logan's sword would slip through my defenses, and he'd kill me. Once that happened, he'd be lost for good—if he wasn't already.

I couldn't let that happen, but I didn't know how to stop it either. Even as I battled Logan, I tried to think of a way to get through to him. But smashing the jewels hadn't worked, and I was all out of ideas.

"You're going to have to use your magic on him, Gwen!" Vic shouted above the roar of the battle. "You're going to have to use your touch magic on him. You're going to have to kill him with it the way that you did Preston!"

The thought was so horrible I froze, right there in the middle of the stage. That was all the opening Logan needed to punch me in the stomach. I staggered back, and once again the Spartan gave chase. He wouldn't stop until I was dead. His killer instinct wouldn't accept anything else.

I redoubled my efforts, fighting better than I ever had in my entire life, hoping that I could at least disarm the Spartan, but Logan matched me move for move for move. Of course he did. He was the one who'd taught me how to fight in the first place.

"Use your magic, Gwen!" Vic yelled at me again. "Now! Before it's too late!"

I didn't want to use my touch magic on Logan. I didn't want to pull the life out of his body the way I had with Preston. I'd barely been able to do it to the Reaper, and only because it had been the only way to heal the mortal wound Preston had given me.

No, I couldn't kill Logan with my magic—I wouldn't be able to live with myself if I did.

But I had to do *something*. Because once he was done with me, Logan would attack the adults and even the other kids until either everyone else was dead—or he was.

I managed to force Logan into some of the band chairs at the back of the stage. The Spartan cursed, his voice deeper and harsher than normal, and he struggled to untangle himself from the metal. But instead of going in for the kill, I stood there, my desperate gaze zooming around, trying to think of some way I could save him—and myself too.

In the chaos of the fight, the stage had been destroyed. Chairs had been overturned, instruments dropped, and other debris littered the wooden floor, but I didn't see anything useful. Nothing that gave me any idea how to get through to Logan—

Something winked on the floor a few feet away from me, and I realized it was a bracelet that one of the girls had been wearing. Maybe it was the sapphires gleaming in the design or the way the chain had curled into a perfect circle on the floor, but the bracelet reminded me of the Maat asp that had been wrapped around my wrist during my trial. Vivian had managed to fool the snake with the ruby Apate chips in her ring, but I'd used my magic to show the asp what had really happened.

My psychometry, I thought. Of course.

I couldn't get through to Logan with words, but maybe there was still a way to save the Spartan after all—

Logan finally got free of the chairs and ran at me, curses spewing out of his lips like acid. His eyes were even redder than before, and I knew I only had one chance at this—one chance to get him to remember who he really was before he was lost to me—forever.

All I had to do was touch the Spartan.

Easier said than done. I hadn't even managed to nick Logan with my sword the whole time we'd been fighting, much less get close enough to touch him with my bare hand. But that's what I needed—time to touch the Spartan, time to let my magic work, time to let my power wash over him. But Logan wasn't just going to stand still and let that happen. No, there was only one way this was going to work. I had to let the Spartan get close to me.

I had to let him hurt me.

I didn't know if my crazy plan would work, but it was the only chance Logan had left. So I drew in a breath and slowly sheathed Vic in the scabbard on my waist. Then, I held my arms out wide, an open invitation to the Spartan to do his worst. Logan stopped short, obviously thinking it was some kind of trick.

"Gwen, what are you doing?" Vic yelled. "He'll kill you where you stand!"

"I know," I said in a grim voice. "But it has to be this way, Vic. You'll see."

After a few seconds, when I made no move to attack him or defend myself, Logan let out a loud, wild, angry cry and charged at me. I waited until he was in range and then held out my right hand and jerked to the side, trying to sidestep him as much as I could, even as my fingers reached out for his. I felt his sword slice across my right palm and keep on going.

Then, with a final, fierce battle cry, Logan slammed his blade into my chest.

Chapter 28

The pain of the sword skewering me was—it was—*devastating*. Just wave after wave of red-hot agony surging through my body one right after another. For a moment, my vision went completely black. I had to struggle to focus on what I was trying to do, but I slowly reached up and wrapped my bloody fingers around Logan's hand, which was clenched around the hilt of his sword—the sword that was still in my chest.

The Spartan frowned and tried to pull his hand away, but I tightened my grip, even though it jostled the sword in my chest and made everything hurt that much more. Through my growing haze of pain, I called up all the memories I had of Logan.

All the times he'd smiled at me. All the times he'd teased me. All the times he'd looked at me, his icy eyes glowing. All the times he'd kissed me, held me close, and whispered that everything was going to be all right, even if we both knew it wasn't true.

I focused on those images and all the feelings that went with them. All the longing I'd felt for Logan when

I'd first been crushing on him, all the times he'd made me laugh, and finally that warm, soft, fizzy feeling that flooded my heart whenever he grinned at me.

Then, I showed the images to him.

It was hard—so freaking *hard*. So much harder than it had been with Nott and even the Maat asp. I didn't know if it was because Logan's mind was more complex than theirs or if it was because of the ritual Agrona had performed on him, the jeweled collar on his neck, and all the magic mumbo jumbo that was pumping through his veins right now. But I could almost *see* this wall in his mind—a Reaper-red wall that kept me from getting through to him.

But I wasn't giving up, even though I could feel the blood pouring out of the wound in my chest and my strength and magic fading with every passing second. Instead, I focused on all my memories of Logan, shaping them into a giant fist in my mind, and then I started hammering at that damn Reaper-red wall that separated us.

Let me in, let me in, let me in . . .

I started chanting the words in my mind, timing them to the blows of my fistful of memories, even as my heart slowed and sputtered.

Let me in, let me in, let me in . . .

I didn't know how long we stood there, locked together, Logan's sword in my chest, and my fingers digging into his hand, but slowly, tiny, tiny cracks started to form in the wall in his mind. My strength was almost gone, *I* was almost gone, so I pounded at the wall that much harder before it was too late—for both of us.

Let me in . . . Let Me In . . . LET ME IN . . .

More and more cracks appeared, zigzagging through the entire wall. I gathered up the remaining scraps of my strength and magic and hit the wall one final time, putting everything I had into the blow.

The wall shattered, dissolving into nothingness, and suddenly I was in Logan's head, deeper inside him than I'd ever been before, so deep that I could see that icy blue spark at the center of his being.

Remember, I whispered in my mind to him, even as I imagined cupping that beautiful blue spark in my hand. *See. Feel. Remember who you really are.*

And then I shoved my memories at him—every last one.

Logan gasped and staggered back, jostling the sword in my chest. I screamed with pain, but somehow I managed to keep my bloody fingertips on his hand. Once again, I poured all my memories of him into his mind, just the way he'd stabbed me—quickly, brutally, effectively.

Remember . . . Remember . . . REMEMBER!

I chanted the words in my head again and again, hammering them into Logan's mind the same way I'd attacked the Reaper-red wall.

Just when I thought I couldn't hang on to his fingers another *second*, I felt something crack open inside his head, like a glass that had been dropped on the floor and shattered into a hundred pieces. Everything just . . . *splintered*.

Suddenly, Logan was himself again, and I could feel his growing confusion and horror at what he'd done—to me.

The last of my strength left me, and I blinked, realizing that I'd lost my grip on Logan and that I was standing on the stage in the middle of the battle. He'd pulled the sword out of my chest, and more and more blood poured out of the wound. I looked at the Spartan, almost dreading what I'd see when I peered into his face.

"Gypsy girl?" Logan asked.

His voice was uncertain and confused, but it was *his* voice again. His face still looked vaguely blank, as if he wasn't sure where he was or what had happened, but I could tell it was Logan in there and not someone else. Just Logan—only Logan. And then, there was the most important thing—the fact that his eyes were blue once more instead of that awful Reaper red.

I smiled, thinking it was one of the most beautiful sights I'd ever seen—and that it would be the last thing I ever saw.

The pain exploded in my chest, even greater than before. I tried to open my mouth to say his name, but nothing came out, not even a whimper of hurt. My legs buckled, and I had one last thought before everything went dark.

Logan Quinn had killed me.

Chapter 29

I woke with a start. My eyes snapped open, and I found myself staring up at one of the most amazing images I'd ever seen—an elaborate fresco that gleamed with gold, silver, and sparkling jewels. It was hundreds of feet overhead, stretching all the way across the domed ceiling, but somehow I could see it as clearly as if it was right above me. It showed the image of a great mythological battle. No surprise there. This was Mythos Academy, after all. But the strange thing was that I was in the fresco—and so were all of my friends.

Logan, Daphne, Carson, Oliver, even Alexei, all holding weapons and fighting just like I was. And there were other people pictured as well, folks I didn't know, creatures I'd seen only in the pages of my myth-history book, but I got the sense that they were all somehow important. That *this* was important. My gaze zoomed right, then left, up, then down, until I'd seen the entire fresco—

I blinked, and the image was gone, cloaked by shadows once more. I sat up and realized that I was lying on

the marble floor in the middle of the Library of Antiquities, right in front of the checkout counter. I looked
down. I was wearing the same clothes I'd had on in the
auditorium, but my T-shirt and hoodie were smooth
and not torn and bloody like they should have been
since Logan had stabbed me—

"Hello, Gwendolyn," a soft, familiar voice called out.

I raised my head, and there she was—Nike, the Greek
goddess of victory.

The goddess looked as beautiful as ever. A white,
toga-like gown wrapped around her lean, strong body,
while soft, feathery wings arched up over her back. A
crown of silver laurels rested on top of her bronze hair,
but it was her eyes that always fascinated me the most—
eyes that were a swirling mix of violet and gray, silver
and lavender, and all the other soft shades of twilight.

I got to my feet, only mildly surprised when I didn't
feel any pain. I pressed my hand to my chest, but all I
felt was a thin line slashing over my heart, instead of the
deep, mortal wound Logan had given me. I looked at
the goddess and sighed.

"So am I dead this time?" I asked. "Is that why I can't
really feel the stab wound in my chest? Are you here to
take me to the Elysian Fields or Valhalla or someplace
where warriors go when they die in battle?"

Nike gave me a sad smile. "Close, but not quite. Your
friends are working very hard right now to save your
life. Focus, and you'll see."

I concentrated and felt a soothing warmth flowing
through my body. I looked down and realized that a fa-

miliar, rosy golden glow covered my chest, centered over my heart.

Come on, Gwen! I thought I heard Daphne scream, although her voice sounded faint and far away. *Suck it up! Don't you dare die on me!*

"Daphne's trying to heal me," I whispered.

Nike nodded. "And your Professor Metis too."

The goddess walked over and sat down on top of the checkout counter. No, that wasn't quite right. She didn't seem to walk or even glide as much as *float*, as if there were some force all around her propelling her movements with easy, precise grace. Still, seeing her perched on the counter and swinging her legs back and forth like a kid made me smile.

"You know, Nickamedes would have a fit you if he saw you sitting on the checkout counter. I did it once, and he yelled at me for five minutes."

Nike smiled back at me. "I won't tell him if you won't."

She patted the counter beside her, and I walked over and hopped up onto it, my movements far less graceful and effortless than hers had been. Sitting next to the goddess made me aware of the power that rolled off her in continuous waves. That cold, beautiful, terrible power that made the goddess who and what she was— victory itself.

We sat there in silence for several minutes, although I kept sneaking looks at the goddess.

"Did I—did I save Logan?" I finally asked, unable to bear the quiet any longer.

Nike nodded. "Yes, you broke the spell the Reapers had placed on the Spartan boy. He is himself once more. Physically, he should be fine in a few days."

"And otherwise?"

She shrugged. "It is a very extreme thing, forcing a soul into another body, especially one as foul and rotten as Loki's. The god himself might not have been in the auditorium, but the Spartan boy was still linked to Loki. No doubt he saw and felt things that he wished he didn't—horrible things. He will have to deal with that. Plus, the boy hurt you. He will have more guilt and pain over that than anything else."

"But Logan didn't mean to do it," I protested. "He didn't mean to hurt me. He just wasn't . . . himself."

Nike nodded. "I imagine he'll come to see that—in time."

The way she paused before she said the last two words made me shiver. In time? What did that mean? The warmth in my chest dimmed, and I hugged my arms around myself to ward off the chill I felt creeping up my spine.

"So what happens now?" I asked. "Will the Reapers try the transformation again on someone else?"

She shook her head. "The ritual can only be attempted once on a person, and Logan was the best candidate the Reapers had—the only candidate, really. The Reapers knew they only had one shot at him, which was why they had his stepmother watch over him all these years. Besides, they've used up almost all of Apate's jewels from the library, and there aren't enough left to attempt the ritual again. So you don't have to worry about that. Loki is trapped in his own ruined body—for now."

The way she said that made me shiver as well, but I focused on the other questions I wanted answers to.

"Why wasn't Loki there today? At the auditorium?"

"The Reapers didn't want to risk bringing him out of hiding if there was a chance that the ritual might fail—or that you might find a way to save your friends," Nike said. "I'm proud of you, Gwendolyn. You saved many lives today, and you kept Loki from gaining more power. You did well, my Champion."

I thought of the dead bodies that had been piled on the stage, and all the others who would have been hurt or killed during the battle. I didn't know that I deserved Nike's praise, but at least I'd saved Logan. Still, I knew the goddess wouldn't have come to me without a reason.

"So what happens next?" I asked. "What will the Reapers do now that the transformation ritual has failed?"

Nike looked out across the library, her eyes distant and far away. In that moment, she reminded me of Grandma Frost, having one of her visions of the future.

"Since Loki is still trapped in his own body, he and his Reapers will move on to the next part of his plan," she said. "They will go after objects that they think will help them win the coming war. Weapons, armor, and other artifacts with a variety of magic. Some with obvious power, and some without. We need to prevent that from happening, Gwendolyn."

The goddess turned her gaze to me once more. "You need to prevent that from happening."

I'd figured as much since stopping the Reapers from doing Bad, Bad Things was sort of becoming a regular gig of mine. I just hoped I was up to the task once again.

"Okay," I said. "So tell me what artifacts you want me to find and where they are."

She shook her head. "You know I can't tell you that. I can only guide you."

Yeah, yeah, the gods weren't supposed to meddle in mortal affairs, but that didn't stop them from getting their Champions to do it for them. I sighed again. I'd figured she'd say something like that, but hey, it didn't hurt to try.

"You know, we really need to find a way around you only being able to tell me certain things. There's a loophole for everything else when it comes to magic. Why not this? Because, honestly, I would love a map or a list or a picture or whatever you had in mind . . ."

My voice trailed off. Wait a second. I had seen a picture—the fresco on the ceiling—the one with all the people, weapons, and creatures on it. The one that was always cloaked with shadows, the one I'd never been able to see before.

I eyed the goddess, but she just smiled, her face calm and serene. Stupid magic loopholes. I was really starting to hate them. Still, I persisted.

"Okay, okay, I get it. At least, I think I do. But in case you've forgotten, I didn't do such a great job protecting the Helheim Dagger," I said. "I don't want to find the artifacts only to let the Reapers take them away from me like Vivian did with the dagger."

"That is always a risk," Nike replied. "And it is not

just a matter of finding and protecting the artifacts. It's making sure they get into the right hands as well. In a way, that's more important than whether or not the Reapers find the artifacts first. Weapons and armor may have power, may have magic, but in the end, that is all they are—weapons and armor. It is the people and creatures who wield them and their intentions that really matter. It is their free will that makes the ultimate difference."

I sighed. There she went speaking in riddles about *free will* again, something Metis always talked about in myth-history class. I had free will, and I made my own choices, which was what the Reapers wanted to take away from me by enslaving us all. I got it. Really, I did. Lesson learned.

Still, all the talk about artifacts and people made me think about my friends and the items they'd picked up in the Crius Coliseum a few weeks ago.

"Is that why Daphne has Sigyn's bow?" I asked. "And why Carson has the Horn of Roland? They tried to give the artifacts back to Metis, but they just keep reappearing in their dorm rooms. The bow seems pretty straightforward, but Carson doesn't have a clue what the horn does. He's played it and played it, and nothing much has happened, except for him giving Loki a headache that night at the Garm gate."

"The Celt will know what to do with the horn when the time comes, and so will the Valkyrie with the bow," Nike said. "Just as you will know what to do with the artifacts you find, who to give them to and when."

"And what about Loki?" I asked. "I'm assuming I'm

still supposed to find some way to kill him. Is there an artifact for that too?"

I'd meant my words as a joke, but Nike just stared at me, her twilight gaze steady and serious.

"There *is*," I whispered. "There's an artifact that can actually kill Loki. What? What is it? Where is it? How can I use it to kill him? *Please*, you have to tell me—"

Nike arched her eyebrows and tipped up her head. I followed her gaze and realized that I could see the fresco again. A shimmer of silver caught my eye, centered on the image of, well, me. With one hand, I was holding Vic, but there was something in my other hand, something silver, something that looked like an arrow, or maybe a small spear—

I blinked, and shadows covered the ceiling once more. "But what is it? You have to tell me what that is—"

Nike held up her hand, cutting me off, and cocked her head to one side, as if she was listening to something. I didn't hear anything, but the goddess slid off the counter and turned so that she was standing in front of me.

"And now, it's time for me to go," she said. "And for you to return to your friends. Can't you feel it? They've done an excellent job of healing you."

I pressed my hand to my chest. That thin line still slashed over my heart, but I realized I no longer felt cold. I looked down and realized my whole body was glowing the same warm, rosy color as Daphne's magic, mixed with the golden tinge of Metis's healing power.

"So I'm going to make it after all?"

Nike smiled. "There was never any doubt of that, Gwendolyn. Self-sacrifice is a very powerful thing, especially if you do it of your own free will. Remember that."

The goddess leaned over and kissed me on the cheek, as was her custom whenever she said good-bye to me. As always, a wave of her power blasted over me, even stronger than before, one so cold and fierce it made my breath frost in the air between us.

"Good-bye, Gwendolyn," Nike said, stepping back, her body melting into this bright, silvery light. "Be well and brave until we meet again."

I held up my hand, trying to keep her in sight, but the light was too intense, and I had to turn away from the glare.

When I looked up, the silvery glow was gone—and so was the goddess.

Chapter 30

My eyes snapped open once again.

For a moment, I thought I was still dreaming, still in that weird not-quite-a-world with Nike. But the ceiling here wasn't domed, and I wasn't looking at the mysterious fresco inside the Library of Antiquities. No, the ceiling here was covered with plain old white paint, and I realized I was in my bedroom at my Grandma Frost's house.

Something tickled my nose, and I sneezed. A second later, a warm, wet tongue licked my cheek. I opened my eyes to see Nyx standing beside me on my bed. The wolf pup let out a happy yip and licked my cheek again, her tail thumping against my ribs.

And Nyx wasn't the only one here. A shower of pink sparks dripped onto me, and a familiar face loomed into view over mine.

"Gwen!" Daphne shrieked. "You're awake!"

The Valkyrie leaned down, pulled me up, and hugged me tight, cracking my back like she always did. Nyx growled and tried to wiggle in between us.

"It's about bloody time," another voice chimed in.

I looked over at Vic, who was propped up on my nightstand. His voice might have been harsh, but his eye was bright, and he was smiling.

"What do you mean by that?" I mumbled, my mouth as dry as paper.

Daphne drew back and loosened her grip. "He means that you've been unconscious for more than a day now."

"I told you she'd wake up this afternoon, didn't I?" Grandma Frost breezed into the room, the coins on her scarves jingling together in a sweet, soft symphony.

She sat on the other side of the bed and smoothed down my frizzy hair. "How are you feeling, pumpkin?"

"Fine," I said. "A little thirsty and wondering what happened, but other than that, fine."

She nodded. "Good. I'll bring you some water and tell the others you're awake."

Nyx settled herself in my lap so I could pet her. Carson came up to my bedroom next, along with Oliver and Coach Ajax. Metis and Nickamedes squeezed into the room as well. One after another, they all told me how glad they were that I was okay, but something seemed . . . off. None of them would look me in the eye for more than a second, and I wondered why.

"What happened after I . . . did what I did?" I asked when I had gulped down the water Grandma brought me.

Daphne snorted. "You mean after you let Logan stab you in the chest like a complete idiot?"

Carson winced. "Daphne . . ."

"What?" she snapped, sparks of magic crackling in

the air around her. "We were all there. We all saw her do it, and we all saw Logan run her through with that sword like she was just another enemy he needed to kill."

Metis put a hand on the volatile Valkyrie's shoulder. After a moment, Daphne sighed.

"Fine," the Valkyrie muttered. "You tell her the rest of it."

Metis nodded. "Thanks to Morgan, Alexei, and Geraldine, Ajax and I got free, along with Sergei and Inari. While we battled the Reapers, Daphne and Carson got the students off the stage, while Oliver and Kenzie protected them. Eventually, the members of the Protectorate took control of the fight. We killed several Reapers and managed to capture several more."

I could hear the disappointed tone in her voice, and I was pretty sure I knew what she was going to say next.

"Unfortunately, we were not able to capture Agrona and Vivian," Metis said, confirming my suspicions.

I sighed. "What happened?"

"We chased them outside, but the two of them got on to Vivian's roc. Even though the creature was injured, it still managed to fly away with them," Metis said. "We don't know where they are now, but the members of the Pantheon are out looking for them."

"And we will find them," Ajax said. "Sooner or later, we'll find them, and they'll pay for what they've done."

Everyone nodded in grim agreement.

After that, the mood lightened a little, and the others took turns telling me everything that had been going on while I'd been unconscious. How Metis and Daphne had used their magic to heal me on the stage, rounding up the Reapers, taking the students back to the academy, announcing what had happened at the auditorium.

"I'm sorry I ruined the concert," I told Carson.

He shrugged. "It's okay, Gwen. It wasn't your fault. None of this was your fault."

His voice was kind, but once again, he wouldn't quite look at me, and I couldn't figure out why.

My friends came and went in and out of my bedroom, but there was no sign of the person I wanted to see the most—Logan. I assumed he was back at the academy or maybe on his way over here, now that I was awake. But the weird thing was that no one said anything about the Spartan—not a single word—even though they must have known I was dying to see him and make sure he was okay.

"Where's Logan?" I finally asked when I realized that no one was going to mention him unless I did.

Nyx had gone to sleep on the bed beside me, and Vic was snoring as well on the nightstand. Only Metis and Nickamedes were in my room at that point. The two of them exchanged a sharp look.

"Logan is gone, Gwen," Metis said in a low voice. "I'm sorry."

A cold fist of fear squeezed my heart tight. "Gone? What do you mean *gone*? He's not . . . dead? Is he?"

My voice dropped to a raspy whisper, and I could barely get out the horrible words.

Nickamedes shook his head. "No, physically, he's just fine. He became himself again when you used your touch magic on him, and he didn't seem to suffer any lasting effects from the ritual. And of course, he didn't even get a scratch during the fight itself."

"Then why isn't he here?" I asked. "What's wrong? What aren't you telling me?"

Metis and Nickamedes exchanged another look, and my worry and dread increased.

"You have to understand that what Logan went through was very, very traumatic," Metis said, her soft green eyes finally meeting mine. "We were helping the band members set up when Agrona asked Logan to follow her over to one side of the stage. She used her Amazon speed to snap that gold collar around his neck before any of us realized what was happening. Logan immediately . . . changed. Even as we tried to help him, more and more Reapers streamed into the concert hall, and we'd lost the fight before it had even really started."

Metis paused a moment. "But it wasn't just what the Reapers did to Logan that hurt him, but what he did to you."

"But he didn't mean to hurt me," I said. "Not really. He just did what he did because Agrona was controlling him with the Apate jewels. She's the one who made him go all Reaper and try to kill me. You know that, right? He's not in the academy prison, is he? Because he doesn't belong there."

"No, Logan is not in the academy prison," Metis said. "Everything you said is true. We all know it, and Logan does too, but that still doesn't make it any easier on him."

"What are you saying?" I asked. "What aren't you telling me?"

Metis and Nickamedes looked at each other a third time, before the librarian turned his sad gaze to my frantic one.

"We're saying that Logan is gone, Gwendolyn," Nickamedes said in a gentle voice. "He's left Mythos Academy—for good."

I was just—numb. Not angry, not upset, just—numb.

Of all the things that could have happened, of all the reasons why Logan wasn't here, I never expected this. He'd left? Why? Why would he do that? I just didn't understand *why*.

My mouth fell open, but no words came out. I tried and tried, but I just couldn't get the words out. Nickamedes pulled a small white envelope out of his pants pocket. I could see the pain and pity in his eyes—his icy eyes that were so much like Logan's.

"Here," he said in that same gentle voice. "Maybe this will help explain things. I'm sorry, Gwendolyn. Truly, I am."

Nickamedes put the letter on the edge of the bed and left my room. Metis squeezed my shoulder before she followed him and closed the door behind her. I sat there for a long, long time, still and frozen, just staring at the envelope as though it were a Maat asp, ready to bite me if I moved an inch. Nyx slept on the bed beside me, her paws twitching in her sleep, but for once the wolf pup's presence didn't comfort me. Neither did Vic's dreamy mumbles about killing Reapers.

Logan had left? What did that mean? Had his dad made him go somewhere for some reason? And why wouldn't the Spartan tell me himself what was going on? Why wouldn't he at least come and say good-bye?

Finally, with cold, trembling hands, I grabbed the envelope and pulled out the letter inside. I drew in a breath, opened up the sheet of paper, and started to read.

> *Dear Gypsy girl,*
>
> *I'm so, so sorry for what happened—for what I did to you. I never wanted to hurt you, and I never thought in a million years that I would. Now, I understand how you felt when you killed Preston with your magic, how shocked and horrified you were by that. How afraid you were that you would do it again to one of us—to me.*
>
> *You did what you had to do in order to survive—but I don't have that excuse.*
>
> *I stabbed you because I was under a Reaper spell, but I still can't believe I did that to you. And the worst part was that I knew it was you. I could see you clearly the whole time. I could hear you pleading with me, begging me to stop. And I wanted to—I wanted to stop so much. I tried to fight against the horrible thing inside me, against the magic they'd infected me with, but I wasn't strong enough.*
>
> *Before, I wasn't strong enough to save my mom and sister. This time, I wasn't strong enough to stop myself from hurting you.*

That's why I have to go. Metis and Nick-
amedes say that I'm fine, that Loki and the
Reapers don't have a hold on me anymore,
but I can't risk it.
I can't risk hurting you again.
So I'm leaving Mythos and going some-
where far, far away. I hope you can forgive me
someday. Please don't try to find me.

Love,
Logan

The words hurt, but they weren't the worst part. Because as soon as I touched the letter, my psychometry
kicked in, and I felt everything that Logan had when
he'd written it—all his fear and anger and shame and
hatred of himself.

With every word he wrote, the Spartan kept replaying
the fight over and over again in his mind. Everything I'd
said to him, all the times he'd attacked me, and finally,
him stabbing me. Again and again, he remembered
shoving that sword into my chest, and I felt everything
that he had during the battle.

How he'd wanted to stop fighting me. How hard he'd
tried and tried to drop his sword or even turn it on himself—even though the thing inside him had hurt him because of it.

Loki.

Through Logan's memories, I saw what the Spartan
had—this pair of eyes, one a beautiful blue and the
other an ugly, Reaper red. Those eyes had peered into

every corner of him, slowly invading his body, his mind, his heart.

Somehow, through their connection, the evil god had hurt Logan, tortured him from the inside out. The pain had been more than Logan could bear—more than anyone could bear. Just the memory of it made me want to weep. Loki had taken control, and Logan hadn't been able to keep himself from stabbing me, even though he'd been silently screaming at himself and the evil god to stop the whole time.

But most of all, I felt Logan's deepest, darkest fear— that he might still be connected to Loki. That the evil god might reach out and take control of him at any moment.

That Loki might make him hurt me again.

"Oh Spartan," I whispered in the dark. "Don't you know that I already forgave you—for everything?"

But my whispered words didn't bring Logan back to me—and I didn't know if anything ever would.

I curled into a ball on the bed right next to the still-sleeping Nyx, tears streaming down my face and spattering onto Logan's letter, slowly smearing the words. I clutched the paper to my chest like a shield, as if it would somehow protect me, even though my heart was shattering into smaller and smaller pieces all the while.

Chapter 31

A broken heart wasn't a mortal wound, at least not in the eyes of the Powers That Were, and the next afternoon, I was back at Mythos Academy.

And once again, I was standing in the amphitheater in front of all the other students, professors, and staff members. Only this time, they were hearing the truth about me, Vivian, and everything else.

". . . and so the Protectorate has dropped all charges against Miss Frost," Linus said. "We want to offer our deepest apologies to her and commend her on her bravery during the incident at Aoide Auditorium. Miss Frost, along with Mister Sokolov and Miss McDougall, saved not only their fellow students, but staff members and professors, as well as myself and several other members of the Protectorate . . ."

I looked to my right at Morgan and Alexei, who were also standing on the amphitheater stage. Morgan winked at me, while Alexei just nodded.

". . . and so we all owe them a debt of gratitude," Linus finally finished.

For a moment, everyone was silent. A few of the students started clapping politely, but Daphne decided to take matters into her own hands. The Valkyrie got to her feet, put her fingers in her mouth, and let out a sharp whistle.

"Yeah, Gwen!" the Valkyrie whooped. "Whoo!"

After that, the applause got a little louder and more enthusiastic, mainly because Daphne turned around and glared at all the kids around her. Still, more than a few folks didn't bother to clap, like Helena Paxton. She was about halfway up the amphitheater steps, but I could still see her rolling her eyes and whispering to her mean-girl friends. No doubt the Amazon was upset that she wasn't going to get another chance to kick my ass like she'd wanted to in the dining hall.

Linus stepped away from the podium and turned to me. "Is there anything you'd like to say, Miss Frost?"

I hesitated. I didn't know what to say. I barely knew what to *think* right now. Forty-eight hours ago, I had been fighting for my life on the auditorium stage. Now, here I was, back at the academy again, like it was just another Monday.

But most of all, I was still trying to come to terms with the fact that Logan was gone, that he'd left the academy, that he'd left *me*. I knew the Spartan had his reasons—I'd seen and felt them for myself—but I wished he had at least said good-bye in person. Then, I could have told him that it was okay, that I didn't blame him for what happened, that I'd seen how hard and bravely he'd battled Loki. That no one could have resisted the evil god—not even a Spartan.

"Miss Frost?" Linus asked again.

Just the thought of Logan made my heart quiver with hurt and longing, but I drew in a breath and pushed those feelings aside. The Spartan wasn't here, but everyone else was.

"Yeah," I replied. "There is something I want to say."

I stepped up to the microphone. By this point, the applause had died down, despite Daphne's enthusiasm, and the crowd was quiet once more. My gaze went from one face to another, but this time, the other students' eyes didn't glimmer with anger at me. At least, not as much. Instead, they looked curious, wary, and afraid, but determined too. I knew those feelings because they mirrored my own.

"I know you've all lost someone to the Reapers," I said. "And so have I. They murdered my mom. They've murdered your moms and dads and brothers and sisters. They've killed your aunts and uncles and cousins and friends. They've taken so many people away from us—so many people that we love."

I thought of Logan, and I had to clear my throat before I could continue. "Now that Loki is free, we all know there's another Chaos War coming. But we're going to keep fighting. We're going to keep going after the Reapers. It's what we're all here at Mythos training for. So we can learn how to protect the people we love. As long as we do that, as long as we train and fight and believe in each other, then you know what? We can win. We're *going* to win. Because there simply is no other option."

I stepped back. Daphne whooped and got to her feet

again, along with Carson, Oliver, Kenzie, and Talia. Even Savannah Warren, Logan's ex-girlfriend, joined in with my friends. But to my surprise, they weren't the only people who did so. One by one, the other kids stood up and started clapping—for real this time. And I felt one emotion pouring off all of them, all the kids, all the professors, all the staff members—hope.

Hope that things would eventually get better. Hope that we could defeat the Reapers. Hope that we could finally triumph over Loki.

I stood there and let that soaring, uplifting emotion wash over me. I reached out and wrapped it around myself like a suit of armor, letting it pour into all the dark places inside me and make them just a little bit lighter, just a little bit brighter—at least for this moment.

It didn't make up for Logan leaving, but it helped—it helped a lot.

The members of the Protectorate escorted me off stage, and we wound up at the checkout counter in the Library of Antiquities. It was time for me to work my shift like usual, despite everything that had happened—death, destruction, heartache. Yep, just another Monday at Mythos Academy.

Inari and Sergei said their good-byes to me and wished me well, and I did the same to them. Yeah, they'd arrested me and put me on trial, but they'd just been doing their jobs. I was glad that they knew I was on their side now—that we were all on the same side.

"We'll wait in the car for you, Linus," Sergei said as he and Inari left the library.

Linus nodded. The leader of the Protectorate turned and stared at me, but for once, his face was neutral.

"Thank you for saving my son," he finally said. "I gravely misjudged you, Miss Frost. And a great many other people."

Sadness and heartache similar to my own shimmered in his eyes, and I knew he was thinking about Agrona and how she'd fooled him. For the first time, I felt sorry for Linus. Sure, Logan might have left, but at least I knew he cared about me. Linus didn't even have that small comfort.

I nodded, accepting his apology. "How...how is Logan? Is he okay? Where is he? Is he ever coming back to the academy?" The questions tumbled out of my lips.

Metis had told me that Linus and Logan had had a long, long talk after the battle at the auditorium. Metis hadn't known all of the details, but she said that father and son had worked through some of their issues, trying to start undoing all the damage Agrona had wreaked on them—and what they'd done to themselves too.

"Don't worry. Logan is safe and...as well as can be expected right now. He's...troubled by what happened, as I'm sure you realize," Linus said. "Logan asked me for some time away from the academy. Some time for the two of us to really get to know each other after all these years. I'm on my way to meet him right now. I'm handing over some of my Protectorate duties to Sergei and Inari until Logan is...well again. But don't worry. However long it takes, I'll be by my son's side, taking care of him."

I nodded. I was glad that Logan and his dad were

going to spend some time together. I just wished I could have been a part of the Spartan's plans.

Linus hesitated. "Logan asked me not to tell you where he is. He also wanted me to ask you not to use your psychometry on me or anyone else to try to find him."

My gaze fell to the checkout counter. I was standing on one side, and Linus on the other, but his hand was only a few inches away from mine on top of the smooth wood. I wanted to reach out, grab Linus's hand, and find out exactly where Logan was. It would be easy—so freaking *easy*—and the temptation to do it was so *strong*.

But I'd promised myself I wouldn't use my Gypsy gift like that—that I wouldn't pull secrets out of people just because I could. If I did that, I'd be no better than Vivian, who used her telepathy magic to trick people, to dig around in their heads and mess with their emotions just because it amused her. No, the last thing I wanted was to be like the Reaper girl, even if it meant not knowing where Logan was.

Still, I curled my hands into fists and stepped back from the counter, just so I wouldn't be tempted.

"He needs some space right now, Miss Frost, and I hope you'll give it to him," Linus said, noticing my movements. "He cares about you very much, though. Never doubt that."

I nodded again, blinking back the tears in my eyes. Everything Linus had said was true—Logan needed some time and space to himself. It was selfish of me to

want him here with me when he was the one who was
hurting so much right now, but still, I wanted to see the
Spartan. I wanted to hold him close and tell him that
everything was going to be all right. I wanted to comfort him the way he'd comforted me so many times before. The temptation to use my magic to track down the
Spartan rose up in me, and my gaze went to Linus's
hand again.

After a moment, I forced myself to take another step
back, putting even more space between us.

Linus straightened up to his full height. "And we
have one more piece of business to attend to before I
leave, Miss Frost. Given what happened at the auditorium, I and the other members of the Protectorate have
agreed that you are indeed a target for Vivian, Agrona,
and the other Reapers. We've decided to assign you a
personal guard to help you deal with any . . . threats that
might come your way here at the academy."

"I don't need a guard," I said in a dull voice. "The
Reapers weren't even after me this time. Not really.
They wanted Logan. I was just collateral damage."

"Well, think of me as a friend then," a soft voice
called out.

My head snapped around, and Alexei was there, his
backpack at his feet, leaning against the wall of the glass
office complex like usual. Once again, I hadn't heard
him come up behind me.

Linus cleared his throat. "If it's all right with you,
Miss Frost, Alexei has decided to stay at Mythos Academy. Along with attending his third-year classes, he'll

also be watching over and helping you in any way you need, whenever and however you need it. With the full authority of the Protectorate behind him."

The Bogatyr gave me a shy smile, which I returned. I hadn't seen much of him since the fight in the auditorium, but I was glad he was staying at the academy. Alexei was right. I had come to think of him as a friend, Morgan too, and I knew I was going to need all the friends and allies I could get in the coming days.

"Good-bye, Miss Frost," Linus said, staring at me. "Until we meet again."

I nodded. "Actually, before you go, could I ask you to do something for me?"

"And what would what be?"

I reached into my jeans pocket and pulled out a small purple envelope. "This is for Logan. It's a letter telling him that I understand . . . and that I forgive him—for everything."

Last night, after I'd finished crying in my bedroom, I'd grabbed a pen and a piece of paper, and I'd written down everything I was feeling. I'd poured my heart out in the letter, asking Logan to come back to the academy—to come back to *me*. I didn't know if reading it would make a difference to the Spartan, but I wanted him to have it all the same.

Linus took the envelope, careful not to let his fingers brush mine. "I'll make sure that he gets it."

"Thank you," I whispered.

He nodded at me and left the library. Once he was gone, I turned to Alexei.

"So you're my bodyguard now, huh?" I asked.

He nodded. "I am. From what I've seen these past few days, I have my work cut out for me. Are things always this dangerous around you?"

I arched an eyebrow. "Why, Alexei, if I didn't know better, I'd think you were actually making a joke."

His smile widened. "Just a little one."

Alexei bent over and rummaged through his backpack. "Besides, I need to give these back to Nickamedes. I've been meaning to return them ever since the Reaper attack in the library."

He straightened up, and I realized he was holding weapons—two swords sheathed together in one scabbard. The swords were fairly plain, with a slight curve to the blades, but a symbol had been etched into each one of the blades—a man holding two swords that were crossed over his chest. I hadn't paid much attention to the weapons Alexei had been using the last few days, but I recognized them now.

"The Swords of Ruslan," I whispered.

Alexei gave me a strange look. "How do you know that?"

"There was an ID card in the artifact case the swords were in," I said. "I saw it the night I grabbed them."

I didn't tell him about the memories I'd seen when I'd touched the swords and scabbard. The blizzard, the battle, and the man who moved the same graceful way Alexei did.

"Ruslan was a great Russian warrior," Alexei said, admiring the swords. "A Bogatyr, like me. It has been an honor to carry his weapons."

An odd suspicion filled my mind, and my gaze zoomed

up to the top of the dome. For a moment, the shadows that cloaked the fresco lightened, and I saw two gleams of silver forming an X shape—like two swords crossed over each other.

And it is not just a matter of finding and protecting the artifacts. It's making sure they get into the right hands as well. Nike's words echoed in my mind.

"I think you should keep the swords," I said.

Alexei shook his head. "No, I couldn't do that. They are important artifacts, pieces of history. They should be put back on display here for everyone to see."

I arched an eyebrow at him. "In case you haven't noticed, the whole library is full of artifacts. I don't think anyone will mind if you use the swords for your own. I'll talk to Nickamedes. He'll understand. Besides, that will be one less case for me to dust."

Alexei hesitated and looked at the weapons again. "If you really think Nickamedes would let me use the weapons..."

"Don't worry. He will."

At least he would after I talked to him. I hadn't told the librarian about the new mission I'd gotten from Nike, but I would. He'd understand that the swords belonged with Alexei, and so would Metis and the others.

Alexei admired the weapons a moment longer before he tucked them and the scabbard back into his gym bag. He straightened up, and I smiled at him.

"I'm glad you're staying," I said. "For my sake—and Oliver's too."

A blush flooded Alexei's cheeks, but he just leaned

back against the wall and crossed his arms over his chest. And he stayed there, right by my side, until closing time.

Late that night in my dorm room, I read Logan's letter again, smoothing it out on top of my bed. Some of the words were smeared, thanks to my tears, and the page was wrinkled where I'd read it so much.

"How many times are you going to go over that bloody thing?" Vic said. "The words aren't going to change just because you read them a dozen times. And can you please get the fuzzball off of me? Her slobber keeps dripping on me."

Since I'd been cleared of all charges, Nyx had come back to the academy with me this morning, with the Protectorate's blessing. Since Linus had given me a full pardon, I figured it wouldn't hurt to get Nyx included in the deal as well. Linus had muttered quite a few words about *rules* and *procedures* and *This girl will be the death of me*, but in the end, he'd agreed to let Nyx stay with me.

I'd propped Vic up on my bed, and Nyx had decided that the sword made an excellent chew toy. The wolf pup had been gnawing on Vic's hilt, well, his head actually, for the last ten minutes. Still, despite the sword's cross words, I knew he enjoyed the drool-filled attention, especially when Nyx curled her tail around him and decided to go to sleep on my bed a minute later.

"I don't know," I said, finally answering his question. "I guess I keep reading it hoping that it will make sense.

That I'll understand why Logan felt he had to leave. I mean, I know *why*—because of what Loki did to him and what Logan did to me. But that doesn't make it any easier."

"He didn't want to hurt you," Vic said. "It'll take the boy some time before he trusts himself again, not just with you, but with everyone else he cares about. It's not necessarily a bad thing that he's gone for a while. Rituals are nasty business, and the transformation process is one of the most brutal things anyone can experience."

There was an odd note in Vic's voice, and I looked over at the sword. "You sound like you have some sort of personal experience with transformations."

To my surprise, the sword actually blushed. At least, I thought he did. His cheek seemed to burn bright silver for a moment before he dropped his gaze from mine.

"Well, I have seen a lot of things over the years, Gwen," the sword mumbled. He paused a moment before clearing his throat. "But back to my original point. Logan needs some time to recover from what the Reapers did to him."

"I know, but it hurts all the same."

Vic kept talking, trying to cheer me up by telling me how well I'd fought in the auditorium and how we were going to find Vivian, Lucretia, and Agrona and slice them to ribbons as soon as possible. I let his violent, cheerful words wash over me and made the appropriate noises when necessary, but my heart wasn't in it.

When he finally wound down, I took a shower and put on my pajamas. By the time I finished, Vic and Nyx were both asleep, curled up in the middle of my bed.

In between snores, the sword mumbled about killing Reapers, while Nyx let out contented little sighs, as though she was sharing his dreams.

I stood in front of the mirror, brushing out my wet hair. The motion made my pajama top slip to one side, revealing a thin white line on my chest underneath the edge of my camisole.

I had another scar now, one that slashed over my heart and the scar I had from where Preston Ashton had stabbed me. Metis and Daphne had healed the wound with their magic, but it had still left a mark, probably because Logan had been connected to Loki at the time. I also had another thin line on my right palm.

I touched the scar on my chest, and I thought of Logan. I wondered where he was and what he was doing right now. How he was feeling. I hoped he was okay, that he was getting better, that he was already thinking about returning to the academy—to me.

I finished with my hair, so I put the brush down on my desk, right next to my snowflake necklace. My fingers touched the silver strands, and my memories of the fight in the auditorium filled my mind. I'd had on the necklace during the battle, and once again, it had soaked up all of my emotions—all of my pain.

It seemed that was all I had left now that Logan gone, that pain was all I felt. But I'd meant what I'd said at the amphitheater today—about moving on and fighting until the end.

That's why I'd started the map.

I thought of it as a sort of treasure map—although the Xs marked artifacts instead of pirate booty. I sat down in my chair and looked at several pieces of paper I'd taped together and spread out across my desk. Despite my love of comic books and graphic novels, I had zero talent when it came to art. Couldn't paint, couldn't sketch, couldn't sculpt. Still, I'd grabbed a pencil out of one of my desk drawers, and I'd started drawing the fresco on the ceiling of the Library of Antiquities—the one that featured me, my friends, and the artifacts I was supposed to find.

Logan might be gone, but there were still Reapers to fight. I was a Champion, and Nike had given me a mission, one that I was determined to complete, no matter how long it took or how dangerous it turned out to be. Besides, I had to do *something* besides sit in my room and brood.

The only problem was that it wasn't much of a map. Oh, I could see the fresco clearly in my mind, thanks to my psychometry. I just didn't have the skills to draw it all that well. Still, I did my best, and the map was slowly coming along. Maybe I'd get Oliver to help me with it. He had some mad art mojo.

I looked at the small replica statue of Nike on my desk. "I hope you're not grading me on my drawing skills, because I would definitely flunk."

The statue didn't do anything, but I hadn't really expected it to.

My gaze went back to the drawing. I'd just started it tonight, so I'd only filled in the center of the fresco so far. Okay, okay, so I'd only sketched one person— Logan. I'd been thinking so much about the Spartan that it had only seemed natural to start with him.

My drawing was little better than a stick figure, but I'd tried to capture Logan's ferocity, his bravery. Not too hard to do, when he was in the middle of the fight. I wished he was here so I could show him the drawing. I could just picture him looking at it and saying something like, *Gypsy girl, don't you know I'm so much more handsome than that?*

Then, he'd grin at me, his icy eyes glittering in his face, and we'd both laugh.

But Logan wasn't here, and it didn't look like he was coming back anytime soon. I sighed. Not only did I miss the Spartan terribly, but the fact was that I could have used his help with this. Maybe he would have recognized the items he was holding. Maybe he would have known which ones the others were holding were artifacts and which were just regular weapons. Maybe he would have been able to tell me about the object I had in the drawing—that slender silver arrow, or spear, or whatever it was—the one that just might be able to kill Loki.

"How am I supposed to give these things to Logan or the rest of my friends when I don't even know where the artifacts or he is?" I muttered and looked at Nike.

This time, the statue's eyes snapped open.

I froze, and my breath caught in my throat. I'd said the words out of hurt and frustration, never thinking she would respond, but the goddess peered at me, then at the drawing, with her twilight-colored eyes. She dipped her head once before her eyes slid shut, and the statue was just a statue once more.

I let out a breath and sat back in my chair. I looked at

the statue for a few minutes, but Nike didn't reappear. Still, the goddess's nod of approval made me feel better, like I was at least on the right track. Nike had told me to find the artifacts and give them to the right people— including Logan. That meant I'd see the Spartan again. And when I saw him, I wouldn't let him go. I'd make him come back to the academy with me, no matter what it took.

The more I looked at the drawing, the more certain I felt about things. Somehow, I knew that when I found these mysterious artifacts, I'd find Logan too. After that, well, I didn't know what would happen, only that I wanted to see him again as soon as possible.

"Get ready, Spartan," I whispered. "Because I'll be seeing you soon."

I picked up my pencil and started drawing again.

BEYOND
THE
STORY

Gwen's letter to Logan

Dear Spartan,

You have nothing to apologize for—nothing at all.

It wasn't your fault that the Reapers performed all that evil magic mumbo jumbo on you. That they'd secretly been targeting you for years. And most of all, it wasn't your fault that the Reapers killed your mom and sister to try and get to you.

I know you, Spartan. I know you think that if only you'd been braver or stronger or smarter, none of this would have happened. That your mom and sister would still be alive. That things wouldn't have been so bad with your dad all these years.

That you wouldn't have hurt me.

But don't you dare blame yourself for any of it—<u>not one thing</u>.

What the Reapers did to you was horrible—so horrible it makes my heart hurt just to think about it. I saw it all as soon as I touched the letter you sent me. I know how you fought against the magic. How you fought against Loki. How you even tried to turn your sword on yourself to keep from hurting me.

No one could have been braver or stronger or fought harder than you did—<u>no one</u>.

I understand why you left, but it hurts all the same. I miss you, Spartan. I miss your laugh, your smile, even you teasing me. But most of all, I miss how you give me hope that we'll actually win this terrible war after all.

I was afraid of what I could do to you with my touch magic. Now, you're afraid of what you could do to me with your fighting skills— especially if you're still somehow connected to Loki.

Well, I say it's time that we both quit being afraid.

The Reapers are always going to be plotting against us. They're always going to try to hurt us, kill us. But as long as we stick together, we can handle anything they throw at us. But if we let them keep us apart now, then they've already won half the battle.

You are Logan freaking Quinn.

The best fighter at Mythos Academy.

The guy who can take my breath away just by smiling.

So quit feeling sorry for yourself and get back in the fight. Spartans never give up. I learned that from the best of them because I learned that from <u>you.</u>

You promised me that you would always be there for me. I'm going to hold you to that,

Spartan. Come back to Mythos. Come back to me.

Please—because I can't do this without you.

Love,
Gwen

Mythos Academy Warriors
and Their Magic

The students at Mythos Academy are the descendants of ancient warriors, and they are at the academy to learn how to fight and use weapons, along with whatever magic or other skills that they might have. Here's a little more about the warrior whiz kids, as Gwen calls them:

Amazons and Valkyries: Most of the girls at Mythos are either Amazons or Valkyries. Amazons are gifted with supernatural quickness. In gym class during mock fights, they look like blurs more than anything else. Valkyries are incredibly strong. Also, bright, colorful sparks of magic can often be seen shooting out of Valkyries' fingertips.

Romans and Vikings: Most of the guys at Mythos Academy are either Romans or Vikings. Romans are super-quick, just like Amazons, while Vikings are superstrong, just like Valkyries.

Siblings: Brothers and sisters born to the same parents will have similar abilities and magic, but they're sometimes classified as different types of warriors. For example, if the girls in a family are Amazons, then the boys will be Romans. If the girls in a family are Valkyries, then the boys will be Vikings.

However, in other families, brothers and sisters are considered to be the same kind of warriors, like those born to Spartan, Samurai, or Ninja parents. The boys and girls are both called Spartans, Samurais, or Ninjas.

More Magic: As if being superstrong or superquick wasn't good enough, the students at Mythos Academy also have other types of magic. They can do everything from heal injuries to control the weather to form fireballs with their bare hands. Many of the students have enhanced senses as well. The powers vary from student to student, but as a general rule, everyone is dangerous and deadly in their own special way.

Spartans: Spartans are among the rarest of the warrior whiz kids, and there are only a few at Mythos Academy. But Spartans are the most dangerous and deadliest of all the warriors because they have the ability to pick up any weapon—or any *thing*—and automatically know how to use and even kill someone with it. Even Reapers of Chaos are afraid to battle Spartans in a fair fight. But then again, Reapers rarely fight fair. . . .

Gypsies: Gypsies are just as rare as Spartans. Gypsies are those who have been gifted with magic by the gods. But not all Gypsies are good. Some are just as evil as the gods they serve. Gwen is a Gypsy who is gifted with psychometry magic, or the ability to know, see, and feel an object's history just by touching it. Gwen's magic comes from Nike, the Greek goddess of victory.

Bogatyrs: Bogatyrs are Russian warriors. They are exceptionally fast, and most of them use two weapons at once, one in either hand. Bogatyrs train themselves to always keep moving, to always keep fighting, which gives them great endurance. The longer a fight goes, the more likely they are to win, because they will still be going strong as their enemies slowly weaken.

**Want to know more about Mythos Academy?
Read on and take a tour of the campus.**

The heart of Mythos Academy is made up of five buildings that are clustered together like the loose points of a star on the upper quad. They are the Library of Antiquities, the gym, the dining hall, the English-history building, and the math-science building.

The Library of Antiquities: The library is the largest building on campus. In addition to books, the library also houses artifacts—weapons, jewelry, clothes, armor, and more—that were once used by ancient warriors, gods, goddesses, and mythological creatures. Some of the artifacts have a lot of power, and the Reapers of Chaos would love to get their hands on this stuff to use it for Bad, Bad Things.

The Gym: The gym is the second largest building at Mythos. In addition to a pool, basketball court, and training areas, the gym also features racks of weapons, including swords, staffs, and more, that the students use during mock fights. At Mythos, gym class is really weapons training, and students are graded on how well they can fight—something that Gwen thinks she's not very good at.

The Dining Hall: The dining hall is the third largest building at Mythos. With its white linens, fancy china, and open-air indoor garden, the dining hall looks more like a five-star restaurant than a student cafeteria. The dining hall is famous for all the fancy, froufrou foods that it serves on a daily basis, like liver, veal, and escargot. Yucko, as Gwen would say.

The English-History Building: Students attend English, myth-history, geography, art, and other classes in this building. Professor Metis's office is also in this building.

The Math-Science Building: Students attend math, science, and other classes in this building. But there are more than just classrooms here. This building also features a morgue and a prison deep underground. Creepy, huh?

The Student Dorms: The student dorms are located down the hill from the upper quad, along with several other smaller outbuildings. Guys and girls live in separate dorms, although that doesn't keep them from hooking up on a regular basis.

The Statues: Statues of mythological creatures—like gryphons and gargoyles—can be found on all the academy buildings, although the library has the most statues. Gwen thinks that the statues are all super creepy, especially since they always seem to be watching her. . . .

Who's Who at Mythos Academy— The Students

Gwen (Gwendolyn) Frost: Gwen is a Gypsy girl with the gift of psychometry magic, or the ability to know an object's history just by touching it. Gwen's a little dark and twisted in that she likes her magic and the fact that it lets her know other people's secrets—no matter how hard they try to hide them. She also has a major sweet tooth, loves to read comic books, and wears jeans, T-shirts, hoodies, and sneakers almost everywhere she goes.

Daphne Cruz: Daphne is a Valkyrie and a renowned archer. She also has some wicked computer skills and loves designer clothes and expensive purses. Daphne is rather obsessed with the color pink. She wears it more often than not, and her entire dorm room is done in various shades of pink.

Logan Quinn: This seriously cute and seriously deadly Spartan is the best fighter at Mythos Academy—and someone who Gwen just can't stop thinking about. But Logan has a secret that he doesn't want anyone to know—especially not Gwen.

Carson Callahan: Carson is the head of the Mythos Academy Marching Band. He's a Celt and rumored to have come from a long line of warrior bards. He's quiet, shy, and one of the nicest guys you'll ever meet, but Carson can be as tough as nails when he needs to be.

Oliver Hector: Oliver is a Spartan who is friends with Logan and Kenzie and helps with Gwen's weapons training. He's also one of Gwen's friends now too, because of what happened during the Winter Carnival.

Kenzie Tanaka: Kenzie is a Spartan who is friends with Logan and Oliver. He also helps with Gwen's weapons training and is currently dating Talia.

Savannah Warren: Savannah is an Amazon who was dating Logan—at least before the Winter Carnival. Now, the two of them have broken up, something Savannah isn't very happy about—and something that she blames Gwen for.

Talia Pizarro: Talia is an Amazon and one of Savannah's best friends. Talia has gym class with Gwen, and the two of them often spar during the mock fights. She is currently dating Kenzie.

Helena Paxton: Helena is an Amazon who seems to be positioning herself as the new mean girl queen of the academy, or at least of Gwen's second-year class.

Morgan McDougall: Morgan is a Valkyrie. She used to be one of the most popular girls at the academy—before her best friend, Jasmine Ashton, tried to sacrifice her to Loki one night in the Library of Antiquities. These days, though, Morgan tends to keep to herself, although it seems she's becoming friends with Savannah and Talia.

Jasmine Ashton: Jasmine was a Valkyrie and the most popular girl in the second-year class at Mythos Academy—until she tried to sacrifice Morgan to Loki. Gwen battled Jasmine in the Library of Antiquities and managed to keep her from sacrificing Morgan, although Logan was the one who actually killed Jasmine. But before she died, Jasmine told Gwen that her whole family are Reapers—and that there are many Reapers at Mythos Academy. . . .

Preston Ashton: Preston is Jasmine's older brother, who blamed Gwen for his sister's death. Preston tried to kill Gwen during the Winter Carnival weekend at the Powder ski resort, although Gwen, Logan, and Vic eventually got the best of the Reaper. After that, Preston was locked up in the academy's prison.

Alexei Sokolov: Alexei is a third-year Russian student who most recently attended the London branch of Mythos Academy. He's a Bogatyr warrior who is training to become a member of the Protectorate. Alexei has met some of Gwen's friends before, including Daphne, Logan, and Oliver.

Who's Who at Mythos Academy and Beyond— The Adults

Coach Ajax: Ajax is the head of the athletic department at the academy and is responsible for training all the kids at Mythos and turning them into fighters. Logan Quinn and his Spartan friends are among Ajax's prize students.

Geraldine (Grandma) Frost: Geraldine is Gwen's grandma and a Gypsy with the power to see the future. Grandma Frost makes her living as a fortune-teller in a town not too far away from Cypress Mountain. A couple of times a week, Gwen sneaks off the Mythos Academy campus to see her grandma and enjoy the sweet treats that Grandma Frost is always baking.

Grace Frost: Grace was Gwen's mom and a Gypsy who had the power to know if people were telling the truth or not just by listening to their words. At first, Gwen thought her mom had been killed in a car accident by a drunk driver. But thanks to Preston Ashton, Gwen knows that Grace was actually murdered by the Reaper girl who is Loki's Champion. Gwen's determined to find the Reaper girl and get her revenge—no matter what.

Nickamedes: Nickamedes is the head librarian at the Library of Antiquities. Nickamedes loves the books and the artifacts in the library more than anything else, and he doesn't seem to like Gwen at all. In fact, he often goes out of his way to make more work for her whenever Gwen is working after school in the library. Nickamedes is also Logan's uncle, although the uptight librarian is nothing like his easygoing nephew. At least, Gwen doesn't think so.

Professor Aurora Metis: Metis is a myth-history professor who teaches students all about the Reapers of Chaos, Loki, and the ancient Chaos War. She was also best friends with Gwen's mom, Grace, back when the two of them went to Mythos. Metis is the Champion of Athena, the Greek goddess of wisdom, and she's become Gwen's mentor at the academy.

Raven: Raven is the old woman who mans the coffee cart in the Library of Antiquities. Gwen has also seen her in the academy prison, which seems to be another one of Raven's odd jobs around campus. There's definitely more to Raven than meets the eye. . . .

The Powers That Were: A board made up of various members of the Pantheon who oversee all aspects of Mythos Academy, from approving the dining hall menus to disciplining students. Gwen's never met any of the board members that she's aware of, and she doesn't know exactly who they are, but that could change— sooner than she thinks.

Vic: Vic is the talking sword that Nike gave to Gwen to use as her personal weapon. Instead of a regular hilt, a man's face is inlaid into Vic's hilt. Gwen doesn't know too much about Vic, except that he's really, really bloodthirsty and wants to kill Reapers more than anything else.

Linus Quinn: Linus is Logan's dad and the head of the Protectorate. He is also a Spartan and has always pushed Logan to be the best warrior he can be. However, Linus and Logan's relationship is often strained, due in part to the murder of Logan's mom and sister. Linus feels that Logan should have done more to protect his mom and sister that terrible day, which adds to Logan's guilt that he survived the Reapers' attack.

Agrona Quinn: Agrona is Logan's stepmom and a member of the Protectorate. She is also an Amazon.

Sergei Sokolov: Sergei is Alexei's dad and a member of the Protectorate. He is also a Bogatyr.

Inari Sato: Inari is member of the Protectorate. He is also a Ninja.

Who's Who at Mythos Academy—
The Gods, Monsters, and More

Artifacts: Artifacts are weapons, jewelry, clothing, and armor that were worn or used by various warriors, gods, goddesses, and mythological creatures over the years. There are Thirteen Artifacts that are rumored to be the most powerful, although people disagree about which artifacts they are and how they were used during the Chaos War. The members of the Pantheon protect the various artifacts from the Reapers, who want to use the artifacts and their power to free Loki from his prison. Many of the artifacts are housed in the Library of Antiquities.

Black rocs: These creatures look like ravens—only much, much bigger. They have shiny black feathers shot through with glossy streaks of red, long, sharp, curved talons, and black eyes with a red spark burning deep down inside them. Rocs are capable of picking up people and carrying them off—before they rip them to shreds.

Champions: Every god and goddess has a Champion, someone that they choose to work on their behalf in the mortal realm. Champions have various powers and weapons and can be good or bad, depending on the god they serve. Gwen is Nike's Champion, just like her mom and grandma were before her.

The Chaos War: Long ago, Loki and his followers tried to enslave everyone and everything, and the whole world was plunged into the Chaos War. It was a dark, bloody time that almost resulted in the end of the world. The Reapers want to free Loki, so the god can lead them in another Chaos War. You can see why that would be a Bad, Bad Thing.

Fenrir wolves: These creatures look like wolves—only much, much bigger. They have ash gray fur, razor-sharp talons, and burning red eyes. Reapers use them to watch, hunt, and kill members of the Pantheon. Think of Fenrir wolves as puppy-dog assassins.

Loki: Loki is the Norse god of chaos. Once upon a time, Loki caused the death of another god and was imprisoned for it. But Loki eventually escaped from his prison and started recruiting other gods, goddesses, humans, and creatures to join forces with him. He called his followers the Reapers of Chaos, and they tried to take over the world. However, Loki and his followers were eventually defeated, and Loki was imprisoned for a second time. To this day, Loki seeks to escape from his prison and plunge the world into a second Chaos War. He's the ultimate bad guy.

Mythos Academy: The academy is located in Cypress Mountain, North Carolina, which is a ritzy suburb high in the mountains above the city of Asheville. The academy is a boarding school/college for warrior whiz kids—the descendants of ancient warriors, like Spartans, Valkyries,

Amazons, and more. The kids at Mythos range in age from first-year students (age sixteen) to sixth-year students (age twenty-one). The kids go to Mythos to learn how to use whatever magic and skills they possess to fight against Loki and his Reapers. There are other branches of the academy located throughout the world.

Nemean prowlers: These creatures look like panthers— only much, much bigger. They have black fur tinged with red, razor-sharp claws, and burning red eyes. Reapers use them to watch, hunt, and kill members of the Pantheon. Think of Nemean prowlers as kitty-cat assassins.

Nike: Nike is the Greek goddess of victory. The goddess was the one who defeated Loki in one-on-one combat during the final battle of the Chaos War. Ever since then, Nike and her Champions have fought the Reapers of Chaos, trying to keep them from freeing Loki from his prison. She's the ultimate good guy.

The Pantheon: The Pantheon is made up of gods, goddesses, humans, and creatures who have banded together to fight Loki and his Reapers of Chaos. The members of the Pantheon are the good guys.

Reapers of Chaos: A Reaper is any god, goddess, human, or creature who serves Loki and wants to free the evil god from his prison. Reapers are known to sacrifice people to Loki in hopes of weakening his prison, so he can one day break free and return to the mortal realm.

The scary thing is that Reapers can be anyone at Mythos Academy and beyond—parents, teachers, even fellow students. Reapers are the bad guys.

Sigyn: Sigyn is the Norse goddess of devotion. She is also Loki's wife. The first time Loki was imprisoned, he was chained up underneath a giant snake that dripped venom onto his once-handsome face. Sigyn spent many years holding an artifact called the Bowl of Tears up over Loki's head to catch as much of the venom as possible. But when the bowl was full, Sigyn would have to empty it, which let venom drop freely onto Loki's face, causing him great pain. Eventually, Loki tricked Sigyn into releasing him, and before long, the evil god plunged the world into the long, bloody Chaos War. No one knows what happened to Sigyn after that. . . .

Maat asp: A Maat asp is a small snake with shimmering blue and black scales. It is named after Maat, the Egyptian goddess of truth. The Protectorate uses the asp to question Reapers, since the snake can tell whether or not people are telling the truth. The asp's venom can be poisonous—even deadly—to those who lie.

The Protectorate: The Protectorate is basically the police force of the mythological world. Among other duties, members of the Protectorate track down Reapers, put them on trial for their crimes, and make sure that the Reapers end up in prison where they belong.

What's the next Bad, Bad Thing
Gwen and her friends at Mythos
will have to face?

Turn the page for a sneak peek at

MIDNIGHT FROST,

available in August.

Chapter 1

"Do you really think the artifact is here?"

I shrugged. "I don't know."

Daphne Cruz, my best friend, stopped in the middle of the room, put her hands on her hips, and glared at me. Princess pink sparks of magic streamed out of the Valkyrie's fingertips, telling me that she wasn't exactly happy with me right now. Daphne always gave off more magic when she was angry or upset—or aggravated, in this case.

"Well, if you don't know, then what are we doing here?" she asked.

Here was the Crius Coliseum, a museum on the outskirts of Asheville, North Carolina. The coliseum was devoted to all things mythological and featured exhibits of armor, weapons, jewelry, and clothing that the gods, goddesses, and the creatures and warriors who served them had worn and used over the centuries. Most folks who visited the coliseum thought it was an interesting look back at ancient mythology, with its rooms illustrating Greek, Norse, Russian, Roman, Japanese, and all the other cultures of the world.

What they didn't realize was that it was all *real*.

That those in the mythological world were locked in a struggle that had carried over into modern times—and that it was up to warrior whiz kids like me and Daphne to make sure the good guys of the Pantheon won.

That's right. Me. Gwen Frost, the Gypsy girl who touched stuff and saw things, was officially responsible for saving the world. Something I wasn't doing too well at so far, since I'd gotten my ass kicked more times than I cared to remember by the Reapers of Chaos. But no matter how terrible things got, I kept on fighting. It was the only thing I could do.

Today, I'd come to the coliseum in search of a net that had supposedly belonged to Ran, the Norse goddess of storms. Finding powerful mythological artifacts and keeping them safe from Reapers was the latest mission that Nike, the Greek goddess of victory, had given me.

I looked at the brochure I'd grabbed from a metal rack by the front door. "Come on. According to this, the net is in one of the rooms in the back."

"Of course it's in the back," Daphne muttered, but she fell into step beside me.

It was a Sunday afternoon in late January, just before closing time. Because of the bitter winter chill and steady snow showers outside, we were the only ones in the coliseum, besides a few staff members wearing long white togas who were taking inventory in the gift shop.

None of the staff gave us a second glance, despite the sparks of magic that Daphne was still giving off. Stu-

dents like us from Mythos Academy came into the coliseum all the time to look at the exhibits and gather information for reports, essays, and other homework
assignments. Most of the staff members were former
Mythos students themselves, so they knew all about the
mythological world and the Valkyries, Spartans, Amazons, and other warriors who inhabited it.

We walked through the main room of the coliseum,
which was filled with glass artifact cases. The metal of
the swords and spears glinted with a dull, bloody light,
while the jewels in the rings and necklaces winked like
evil eyes opening and closing and following my every
move. The gauzy silks hovered in midair like ghosts, as
if they were about to break free of the wires holding
them up, burst through the glass, and attack. But the
weirdest thing was that the walls, ceiling, and even the
white marble columns seemed to creep closer the farther
I went into the coliseum, like they were all slowly moving in on me, getting ready to surge forward and crush
me in their cold stone embrace.

I shivered and quickened my steps. Winking eyes.
Ghostly garments. Sliding walls. My Gypsy gift was acting up again.

Most of the time, I had to touch something before my
psychometry magic kicked in and let me know, see, and
feel an object's history. But sometimes, I didn't have to
touch an object to get a vibe, especially if there were a
lot of emotions already attached to it. There were a lot
of artifacts here with a lot of good, bad, and bloody
memories radiating from them, so it was no wonder I
was seeing things that weren't really there. Or maybe

my unease was because I'd been to the coliseum twice before—and both visits had ended with me fighting for my life against Reapers.

"Geez, Gwen," Daphne muttered again. "Slow down. It's not a race."

I bit my lip and forced myself to walk at a more normal pace. We left the main room behind and stepped into a hallway.

"It's all the way in the back," I said, pointing up ahead. "In a room next to the library."

Daphne sighed, and another shower of pink sparks streaked out of her fingertips.

"Look," I said. "I know you're getting tired of chasing after artifacts, but the net I saw on the coliseum's Web site looked like the one in my drawing. So I figured we might as well come and check it out. Besides, it's not like we were doing anything else important."

"Oh no," she sniped. "It's not like I wanted to spend the afternoon with my boyfriend or anything."

"I asked Carson to come too," I said, referring to her boyfriend, Carson Callahan, "but he had that band meeting about rescheduling the winter concert that the Reapers ruined."

Daphne snorted. "*Ruined* is a bit of an understatement, don't you think?"

I grimaced. She was right. *Ruined* didn't even come close to describing the horror show the concert had turned into. Reapers had planned to murder everyone at the Aoide Auditorium as a blood sacrifice to their leader, the Norse god Loki. I'd stopped their evil plan, but it had cost me—more than I cared to remember.

"Well, at least Gwen decided to look for this artifact during the day," a voice with a cool Russian accent chimed in. "Instead of dragging me over to the Library of Antiquities in the middle of the night like she did last week."

I looked over to my left at Alexei Sokolov, the Bogatyr warrior who now served as my bodyguard.

"You're just grumpy that Oliver couldn't come with us today," I said.

Alexei smiled, and his hazel eyes softened at the thought of Oliver Hector, the Spartan he was involved with. "Maybe."

"And you're just grumpy that Logan's not here," Daphne sniped again.

Her words surprised me, and I stumbled over my own feet, even as my heart twisted in my chest.

Daphne caught my arm and pulled me upright with her great Valkyrie strength. She winced at the miserable expression on my face.

"I'm sorry, Gwen. I didn't mean that—"

I held up my hand, cutting her off. "No, it's fine. I am grumpy about Logan."

Another understatement. Logan Quinn was the guy I loved—the one whose absence seemed to hurt me more every day.

"Gwen?" Alexei asked.

I snapped out of my dark thoughts. "I'm fine. Let's see if the net is here. This place is starting to give me the creeps."

"Just starting to?" Daphne muttered.

We hurried to the end of the hallway and the last exhibit room in this part of the coliseum. According to a sign on the wall, this area was devoted to gods and goddesses of the sea, the sky, and all the storms that raged between them. I went from one case to the next, looking at the artifacts, which included everything from splintered planks of the doomed boat the Greek warrior Odysseus had sailed home on to a couple of tridents that had supposedly belonged to Poseidon, the Greek god of the sea.

Finally, I spotted a bronze plaque that read RAN'S FISHING NET, and I stepped over to that case.

A net made out of something that looked like light gray seaweed lay underneath the glass. Truth be told, it wasn't all that impressive. The seaweed was gnarled and knotted and looked so thin, threadbare, and brittle in places that it would probably crumble to dust if you so much as breathed on it. But I'd learned the hard way that looks were often deceiving, especially in the mythological world, so I scanned the rest of the information on the plaque.

> This net is thought to have belonged to Ran, the Norse goddess of storms, and was rumored to be among her favorite fishing gear. Despite its fragile appearance, the net is quite strong and can hold much more than it should be able to, given its relatively small size. The braided seaweed itself is thought to have the unusual property of making whatever is inside it seem much lighter than its actual weight . . .

The plaque went on to talk about some of the mythological creatures that Ran had supposedly caught and tamed with the net, but I skimmed over the rest of the words. Instead, I leaned even closer to the glass, studying the net.

Thanks to my psychometry, I never forgot anything I saw, so I was able to pull up my memories of the drawing I'd done a few weeks ago—the one that featured all the artifacts I was supposed to find for Nike. I compared the net before me to the one in the drawing. It was a perfect match.

"Here it is!" I called out.

Daphne and Alexei moved over to stand beside me. They both looked down at the net.

"What do you think it does?" Daphne asked, her black eyes narrowed in thought.

I shrugged. "I have no idea, other than what the plaque says about it being stronger than it looks. But Nike showed it to me, so it must be important."

"Now what?" Alexei asked.

I shrugged again. "The usual. I'll call Metis, and she and Nickamedes can come and get the net—"

A flash of silver caught my eye, and I instinctively jumped back.

A Reaper's sword missed my head by an inch.

One second, Alexei, Daphne, and I were alone in the exhibit room. The next, six Reapers had appeared, all wearing black robes and twisted rubber Loki masks and all carrying curved swords.

"Reapers!" I screamed, even though my friends had already spotted them.

The Reaper next to me raised his sword again, and I pivoted and lashed out with my foot, kicking him in the stomach. The Reaper stumbled back, giving me the chance to grab my own weapon—the sword in the black leather scabbard that was belted around my waist.

I raised the blade into an attack position, and a purplish eye on the hilt snapped open. Instead of being plain metal, half a man's face was inlaid into the hilt of my sword, complete with a nose, an ear, and a mouth that I could feel curving into a smile under my palm at the prospect of the battle to come.

"Reapers!" Vic, my talking sword, said with dark relish. "Let's kill them all!"

Beside me, Daphne slung an onyx bow off her shoulder and quickly notched a golden arrow in the thin strings, while Alexei pulled two matching swords out of the gray leather scabbard strapped to his back. Like all the Mythos kids, we took our weapons almost everywhere we went, especially now that Loki was on the loose.

I tightened my grip on Vic and charged into battle.

Clash-clash-clang!

I swung my sword at the Reaper over and over again, mercilessly hacking and slashing my way through his defenses until I was able to bury my weapon in his chest.

"That's my girl!" Vic crowed as I pulled him free of the Reaper's crumpled body. "On to the next one!"

I turned to face the next Reaper coming at me—

Thwack!

A golden arrow zoomed past me and buried itself in the Reaper's chest, and he too fell to the marble floor. My head snapped around.

"You're welcome!" Daphne shouted.

I raised Vic and saluted her with the sword. The Valkyrie grinned before bringing up her bow and using it as a sort of shield to fend off another Reaper. Daphne stepped forward and punched the Reaper in the face, her Valkyrie strength throwing him all the way back against the wall. I knew she'd be okay so I charged over to where Alexei was fighting two Reapers. The Bogatyr's swords flashed through the air like streaks of silver fire as he danced back and forth, attacking first one Reaper, then the other.

"Get the net!" one of the Reapers screamed.

The last Reaper smashed his sword into the case, reached through the broken glass, and grabbed the gray net. He threw the seaweed over his shoulder and raced toward the open doorway.

"Go!" Alexei said, slicing his sword across first one Reaper's chest, then the other's, making them both scream with pain. "I can handle these two!"

I hurried after the last Reaper. He turned to see how close I was to him and slammed into another artifact case. The Reaper tripped and hit the floor hard, sliding to a stop just inside the doorway.

"Get him, Gwen!" Vic shouted.

I leaped over the smashed case and brought the sword up, ready to bring it down on the Reaper.

And that's when he threw the net at me.